THE
PRESIDENT
IS
COMING
TO
LUNCH

THE PRESIDENT IS COMING TO LUNCH

Nan and Ivan Lyons

Doubleday

NEW YORK

1988

This book is a novel and the story and events that appear herein are entirely fictional. Any resemblance of the fictional characters to a real person is unintentional and coincidental. Certain real persons are mentioned in the book for the purposes of enhancing and adding reality to the story, but obviously the fictionalized events involving either fictional characters or real persons did not occur.

DESIGNED BY PETER R. KRUZAN

Library of Congress Cataloging-in-Publication Data
Lyons, Nan.
        The president is coming to lunch / by Nan and Ivan Lyons.
            p.   cm.
I. Lyons, Ivan.   II. Title.
PS3562.Y449P7   1988
813'.54—dc19   87-30121
                                                                    CIP

ISBN 0-385-19916-3

TO BARBARA AND RALPH
—*with love and appreciation*

THE
PRESIDENT
IS
COMING
TO
LUNCH

MONDAY

LIBBY HATED THE SIGHT OF AN EMPTY TABLE. AN empty table was as threatening as a Greek chorus. If you could still get in, Libby's wasn't the place to be.

"Table 51?" Steven checked the reservations book. "Somebody Birnbaum. A deuce. Twelve-fifteen."

"It's twelve-thirty. Get rid of it."

Libby sized up the room the way she used to scout an audience from the wings. Emerald eyes ablaze with anticipation. Large crimson mouth open. Expectant. Her gamin face, framed by the red parentheses of her hair, tilted to the side. Still the dancer. One shoulder pushed forward waiting to catch the beat.

"It's too slow out there," she said, snapping her fingers.

"Seems fine to me."

"Tell them to pick it up in the kitchen."

Steven spoke in a monotone. "You're the boss."

"Tell them this isn't Lutèce!" Libby arched her feet inside the new pink suede shoes that matched her new pink suede suit.

"Is that all?"

"No." Never taking her eyes from the crowded room, her face broke into a smile. "Tell me I'm gorgeous." Without waiting for a reply, Libby stepped down into the dining room. She moved with the long-legged assurance of a Ziegfeld girl descending a staircase.

The kingdom of glitz known as Libby's had black lacquer walls. Glowing panels of frosted glass were etched with the Manhattan skyline. Deeply tufted apricot leather banquettes bordered the rectangular room. Shiny brass tubs filled with tall green palms stood like palace guards on the black tile floor. They created an illusion of privacy for people who were desperate to be seen. Like the Cantina in *Star Wars*, the room buzzed with the lingua franca of creatures from another world. Option. Layout. Pay or play. Reprint. Margin. Final cut. Points. Showcase.

"Ta-da!" Arms outstretched, Libby stood in front of Sinatra's table. "Tell me I'm gorgeous!"

He smiled, then glanced at Norman Lear. "Norman, do you think she's gorgeous?"

"You want something to eat? Tell her she's gorgeous."

Sinatra leaned over to kiss her cheek. "Baby, you're gorgeous."

She patted his hand and winked. "Who's going to argue with a big star?"

Maxie the waiter was about to hand out menus. But Libby stopped him. "Forget the classifieds. I put something very special aside for you guys." She turned to Maxie and whispered. "Mayday. Tell the kitchen I need two VIP's." She slapped him on the behind. "Very VIP!"

It was the dress at Table 21 that caught Libby's eye. It would have been an Audrey Hepburn dress even if Audrey Hepburn weren't in it. Talking intently to Mikhail Baryshnikov, she smiled as Libby approached. The two women held hands and kissed the air on either side of their cheeks as though kisses cost millions.

"Just look at you," Libby said. "You ought to be illegal." She turned her cheek for Baryshnikov to kiss. "You, too, twinkle toes."

"Would you believe it?" he laughed. "I am turning into a lunchnik."

"I saw Cal a few weeks ago," Audrey said, pressing Libby's hand. "He was looking very Hollywood."

Libby took a deep breath. "He'd better be looking very New York."

"So that's it!"

"What's it?" Libby asked.

Audrey smiled. "That glow. Cal's in town."

"Cal who?" She looked down at the table. Two Perriers. "Listen, in case you forgot, there's a kitchen attached to this saloon." She tapped her fingers on the menu. "The least you can do is eat while you have lunch."

Libby grabbed a waiter as though she had something to tell him. She didn't. It was a bluff. She needed to make an easy exit. She didn't want to talk about Cal. Instead, she focused on the plates Norm carried. Grilled goat cheese on radicchio. Smoked fresh tuna with candied ginger. She could always match the food to the face. Table 14. A pair of independent producers.

"Ta-da! Tell me I'm gorgeous."

The female indieprod, who was wearing a tie, grabbed Libby's hand. "You're gorgeous! The tuna is gorgeous! The waiter is gorgeous!"

Libby shook her head. "Is she back on Vitamin Q?"

The male, who wore a diamond earring, rolled his eyes. "Who cares! We've finally gotten through to Meryl's people!"

"Meryl's people!" Libby leaned over and kissed him. "Can Sydney Pollack be far behind?"

"Of course, we've only been talking on the phone."

Libby waved her hand, brushing aside all doubts. "Today the phone. Tomorrow the lunch!"

The indieprods looked at each other as Libby walked away. "It better not be tomorrow," he whispered. "I'm broke."

The female tugged at her tie. "Don't be stupid. We'll open a house account."

"With what as collateral? My herpes?"

"Well, I can't have you flash your MasterCard in front of Meryl. I would die of embarrassment. This is our one shot at the big time."

"Not according to MasterCard. They've reduced me to a $100 limit."

"You're such a wus! We're about to have our first power lunch and you run out of batteries!"

Moina Hayle, even in her mid-sixties, made heads turn. As editor of *Avanti,* the slickest fashion magazine on the stands, Moina held the copyright on style. All of Seventh Avenue peered into the same looking glass. "Moina, Moina, on the wall . . ." In New York, Paris, and Kyoto, she epitomized chic. But, put her on Main Street USA, and she'd be stared at as nothing more than a garishly painted old lady.

"Ta-da!" Libby posed in her new pink suit. "How do I look?"

Moina took her plate of steamed vegetables and stood up. "You look like an eraser." She crossed the aisle, waving her fork hello at Barbara Walters.

Libby grabbed hold of Steven as he passed. "Do you think I look like an eraser?"

"Yes." He smiled meanly and whispered, "Ta-da!"

Libby held tight to him. "I want to know the minute Cal gets here."

"How about a drum roll?"

"How about a punch in the mouth?"

Table 73. A young agent in the talent department at William Morris. He was short, showed lots of cuff but little promise. Turning to the Nordic blonde seated next to him, he snapped, "No soup! Nothing that can spill. The first rule of lunch is eat neat." He stood up quickly. "Libby!"

"Look who's here!" she said. "McDonald's burn down?"

"I want you to meet Wanda Fogelman. She was one of the hostages. You remember. The TWA thing."

"Oh, my God." Libby took Wanda's hand.

"She just signed with us."

Libby smiled. "So now you're a professional hostage!"

He raised his glass. "I've already spoken to Stallone's people."

Wanda followed the conversation as though watching a tennis match. The Wanda Fogelman Open.

"Lib, I'd like to get a line on Wanda in Fay Fox's column."

Libby shook her head. "Better than that. I'll introduce her

to Senior for you. Then Fay will really have something to write about."

He was ecstatic. "I knew I could count on you. Wanda sure needs some help!"

Libby smiled. "Well, that's what I'm here for." She pointed to Wanda's open menu. "Try the catfish bisque. Stallone loves it."

Doris Abrams had just taken a bite of her pheasant on rye with cranberry mayonnaise and green tomato slices when the phone rang. Swallowing quickly, she picked up the receiver. "Dr. Sawyer's table." Doris raised her eyebrows as Libby stopped in front of her. "Hi, Mrs. Sawyer. Fine. Oh, I'm sorry, but he's at a patient's table right now." Doris looked at Libby, stifling a laugh. "No, I don't think she's anyone famous. You bet! I'll have him call just as soon as he gets back. You, too." Doris hung up and groaned. "These nooners of his are going to drive me nuts." She glanced at her watch. "Speedy Gonzales must be through by now." She started eating quickly. "I wish he were a little more romantic. I can never finish before he gets back."

Libby patted her on the shoulder. "Yours is not to reason why. Yours is just to lunch and lie."

Phyllis and Donald Elgin were Libby's oldest friends. They were regulars. Phyllis, the producer of Broadway's latest smash hit, exhaled an angry stream of smoke as Libby approached. "Why can't I get anything to eat in this rat trap?"

Donald stubbed out her cigarette. "Phyllis, stop thinking about food. We came here for lunch."

Libby looked at Donald. "What happened? She only eats when she's manic."

"Jeremy turned down the London company."

Libby shrugged. "If he had any brains, would he be an actor?"

Phyllis lit another cigarette. "I've got a theater waiting in London, and no one to put in the star dressing room." She looked to Libby for comfort. "You don't know what hell it is to cast a play. You turn down a picture because of money or because of your astrologer. But everyone thinks there's only one reason to turn down a play."

Donald gloated. "Because it's a lousy play!"

"It's a hit!" Phyllis snarled.

Libby took her hand. "Let me speak to Chris Reeve. He's coming in tonight."

"My darling. I knew I could count on you. The Mother Teresa of lunch. Now, swear to me, not a word about Jeremy to that bitch Fay."

Libby put a hand to her heart. "On von Bülow's life." She watched Phyllis reach for the phone. "Who are you calling?"

"Caravelle. Maybe they deliver."

Libby slammed the receiver down as Steven came over and whispered, "He's here."

Her face lit up. "Cal?"

"Birnbaum," Steven said impatiently.

"Who the hell is Birnbaum?"

"The no-show. Table 51?"

Libby rolled her eyes. "Please, Steven. Not now."

Donald smiled. "What time is Cal coming?"

Phyllis lowered her voice. "From the gleam in her eyes, very shortly after he arrives."

"She's just jealous," Donald said.

Libby crossed her fingers. "Twenty-two years next month. If I don't screw it up."

As unusual as it was, in that room, to remain married to the same man for twenty-two years, it was even more astonishing to remain divorced. But Libby had never found anyone she loved more than Cal Dennis. And although they were no longer husband and wife, she wasn't about to give up being divorced from him. She cherished her "favored nation" status with Cal as though they had taken vows on it.

Jessica Stanford, wife of network kingpin Chaz Stanford, was known simply as J. That made it so much easier when signing checks, which was what J did most of the time. She was lunching with Mrs. Sakhrani, who wore a red dot in the middle of her forehead.

"Darling!" J extended a hand toward Libby. "You must meet my Mrs. Sakhrani. She's related to the Naipauls."

"The Mehtas," Mrs. Sakhrani corrected with a smile.

J shrugged and took a bite of her chicken livers in raspberry vinegar. "Who can keep track these days? I remember when New York used to be the Cohens and the Kellys."

Libby shook Mrs. Sakhrani's hand. "You must be working on the fund-raiser with J."

Mrs. Sakhrani nodded, picking up a slice of toast on which she spread a thick layer of California golden caviar. "We already have a million six for famine relief."

"That's wonderful." Libby caught sight of Moina. She was heading for the table, steady on the mark, like a torpedo in slow motion. In one hand, a glass of wine acquired en route. In the other, her vegetable platter. "Oh oh," Libby said. "Here comes Deep Couture."

J gasped. "How do I look?" Quickly, she brushed a crumb from her dress. "Did she get you yet?"

"Did Javert get Valjean?"

Moina stood in front of J and shook her head. "What an appalling dress. You must be raising money for the tasteless."

Libby jumped in. "Moina, darling, meet Mrs. Sakhrani. She's related to the Gandhis."

Fay Fox grew up in South Carolina. She had deaf parents and learned to read lips at an early age. As a campaign worker for Stevenson, she proved her loyalty by reporting the off-mike comments of the opposition. But instead of politics, Fay became hooked on gossip. Before she knew it, she was reading the hottest lips in town. As the "ghost" for an ailing show-biz columnist, she inherited his space but not his reputation. Fay always checked sources. "Why didn't you tell me Cal was due in?"

Libby batted her eyes. "Cal who?"

"His Agent of Agents called three times to make sure I leak it in tomorrow's column. You know, sometimes I feel like I work for the Daily Bladder."

"Cal told me he was sneaking into town."

"Honey, for Cal that is sneakin'."

"If you tell this to anyone, I'll kill you." Libby took hold of Fay's hand. "I'm going to die if he doesn't get here soon."

"That's your big exclusive? Sweetie, it's a good thing you're not in the news business or we'd still be reading about Noah on page one." Fay's phone began to blink. She picked it up, announcing, "It's me!" She rolled her eyes. "Warren, darlin', thanks much for callin' back."

Libby winked at Fay and moved on to Senior's table. Edgar F. Singer was the last of Hollywood's "golden age" moguls. Unlike his contemporaries, Senior hadn't faded out gracefully via the grave. Instead, he had been ousted from the studio after a bitter fight for control with his son. Senior and Junior had not spoken in years. Unable to accept his fate as an anachronism, Senior became one of the busiest people in Hollywood. He worked around the clock. Seven days a week. But he never closed a deal. He was in a perpetual state of negotiation. On seeing Libby, he threw her a kiss and said, "I'm deciding between the liver and the chicken."

Another meaningless negotiation. Senior always ordered the liver. He ordered the liver because he hated the liver. He let it sit there uneaten as a power play.

Senior was "negotiating" with one of his ex-wives, an over-the-hill musical comedy star who had just played an over-the-hill musical comedy star on television. Francine wanted the lead in a movie Senior had been planning for ten years. A sequel to *The Wizard of Oz* entitled, *Dorothy—The Woman.*

Libby bent over and kissed her. "The word around town is you were dynamite."

"Too bad you didn't write the review on Sunday."

"Forget the Sunday critics," Libby said. "They're like part-time whores. They really enjoy fucking you."

Moina, who had been Senior's second wife, walked over holding the Sunday review in one hand, her vegetable plate in the other. "If you ask me, I think you got off easy. You're too old to play anyone your age. As a matter of fact, you're too old to play anyone female. You should start playing old men." She dropped the review onto the table.

Libby changed the subject. She leaned close to Senior. "I want you to think about that blonde across the aisle."

"At my age, all I can do is think. Why is she sitting with that pisher from William Morris?"

Libby whispered, "They've been talking to Stallone's people."

Senior was impressed. "Stallone's people?"

"She was a hostage," Libby explained.

"In what picture?"

Moina rolled her eyes. "So much for lunch with the dead."

Libby patted Francine's hand. "How about something terrific to eat?"

Francine glared angrily at Moina and gritted her teeth. "I'll have the tartare."

"Tartare?" Libby groaned. "You could order that from a butcher!"

In truth, although the kitchen was superb, no one came to Libby's for food. They came for lunch. To *do* lunch. Lunch was the most important event of their day. They spent all morning preparing for it, all afternoon recovering from it, and they lay in bed all night thinking about it. Lunch had nothing to do with eating. Libby wasn't in the food business. She was in real estate. She rented table space.

The most popular landlord in New York scanned the table tops as a proofreader looks for misspelled words. An empty water glass on 63 needed a refill. Where was the busboy? The three-top at 80 was waiting too long between courses. Where was their coffee? There could be a hundred reasons why the pace was off. It happened all the time. Why hadn't Steven checked on it? Everything seemed to be taking forever. Most of all, it was taking forever for Cal to arrive.

Libby bent down to pick up a napkin in the aisle. She was unable to take her eyes off the fat man at 81. "Andre? Is that you?"

Andre Riley had gained nearly a hundred pounds. He rose clumsily, unable to control his new girth. "I'm in here somewhere," he said, leaning over to kiss the air in front of her lips. Breathless, he sat down. "Don't say anything."

"I wouldn't know what to say."

"And don't call the police, either." He reached into his jacket pocket and took out a check. "I added on interest."

The check was for $14,400. It covered Andre's 1987 lunches after he had been fired as story editor at Warner's. She folded the check and smiled. "You bastard. One postcard from Sicily?"

"They only had one postcard in Sicily!" He became serious. "Lib, you haven't changed at all. You still look the same."

"I could always count on you to say the wrong thing."

"Not anymore. Watch my lips." He leaned forward and whispered, "Grandma Moses!"

"What?"

Andre's eyes flashed with excitement. "I have the merchandising rights to Grandma Moses."

"You mean like T-shirts?"

Andre inhaled the Haut-Brion '70 in his glass. "I mean like a six-part series. Major funding. An Emmy," he said, catching his breath. "I mean like you should have seen them at PBS. Wall-to-wall hard-ons!"

"You really think they bought it?"

"I *know* they bought it! Listen, by now Alistair must have hemorrhoids from sitting in that farcockta chair. How much Brit shit can you take? Who needs another episode of 'Barbara Pym Gets Her Period'?"

"Andre, do you have a deal or not?"

He tapped the table with his fat forefinger. "I have every penny in this project."

Libby waved the check in his face. "Every penny?"

Andre shrugged. "I meant well. I wanted to show good faith."

Libby smiled as she tore up the check. "Well, you know what I always say. The laughs are on the house."

Andre reached for her hand. "How come I never got you into my famous Biedermeier bed? God knows, I tried. Even before I was broke."

"That was the best insurance policy you ever took out."

"Libby darling," he said, sipping the Haut-Brion. "I still can't pay for lunch."

She took his hand. It was cold. Sweaty. "What's one lunch between friends?"

Andre spoke softly. "I need five lunches."

Libby shrugged. "Did I say I was counting?"

He squeezed her hand. "There's something else."

"Oh, Andre!"

He looked deep into her eyes. "Libby," he whispered desperately, "I've just got to have a better table!"

Steven tapped Libby on the arm. He was angry. Although only twenty-three, Steven had a lifetime of injustice stored in his dark eyes. As he led her down the aisle, she stopped just long enough to change Barbara Walters's order from smoked trout to duck.

"But I hate duck!"

"Not *my* duck!"

Once at the service area, Libby leaned over and took off one of her new shoes. "They must figure if you can afford two hundred bucks, you aren't going to do much walking."

"Why didn't you tell me about Dustin?"

Libby groaned. "Dustin! Mea culpa!"

"I know it's your culpa. It's always your culpa. You never put names in the book."

"Right." She looked anxiously into the room. "There's no table for Dustin." Libby put a hand to her stomach. "I wish to hell Cal would get here." She smiled nervously. "You know, I could really use a hug."

"Dustin?" he said coldly.

Libby pushed her foot back into the shoe. "You can be a real son of a bitch, Steven."

"Shall I quote my mother or my boss?"

"Both." A deep breath. "Dustin." Suddenly, she was angry with Steven. "You'd think it was the end of the world! Who's sitting at 13?"

"The Knopf mafia."

"22?"

"The Trumps."

"Where've you got Samantha Kelly?"

"At 73."

"Not near Gloria?"

"Not near Gloria."

"What about 101?"

"Kissinger."

"Bingo!"

"Are you crazy?" Steven whispered ferociously. "You can't put Dustin at 101!"

"Grow up, kiddo. All you have to do is move Phyllis and Donald to 101. No matter how they scream. Give Dustin their table. Put Samantha Kelly between Dustin and Woody and that'll keep everyone happy. But first, call Sirio. Tell him I had to bump Kissinger and I'm calling in my chips. I need Nancy's usual table. Tell him to open a bottle of Dom Pérignon and to bill me. Then, call Kissinger. Tell him we had a bomb scare. Tell him I changed his reservation to Le Cirque. Tell him it's too dangerous for him to be here. Blah blah blah. Tell him it'll do him good to see how the poor people eat." She grabbed Steven by the lapels, pulled him close and planted a kiss on his cheek. "Now what's the big fucking deal?"

All the world was in love with Cal Dennis. He was the captain of the football team, the idealistic doctor, the square-jawed astronaut. He had a fresh-from-the-shower, blond, blue-eyed, all-American appeal that made his face equally at home on the covers of *M* and *W*. He was born to be a movie star.

Libby rushed toward Cal, eager to reach him before he stepped into the room and became public domain. She blurted out the one thing she most wanted to hear him say. "Hey, babe, you look gorgeous!"

Cal put his arms around her. "Did you know man is the only animal that can have sex three hundred and sixty-five days a year?"

"Now you tell me!"

He leaned over to kiss her. She was staring up at him. "You still keep your eyes open?"

"Only with you."

He took her hand and led her toward the checkroom. Cal motioned for the coat-check girl to leave. Once the door was shut, he took a deep breath. Cal looked away before speaking, just as he did on screen. Then a flash of blue from his neon eyes. "It's been a long time."

Libby shrugged. "A hundred years. Give or take a couple of seconds."

"Last time, I was on my way to Spain."

"To be married."

He smiled. "Yeah."

"How was it?" she asked.

"Expensive."

There was a knock at the door. Tessa's hand appeared, holding two coats. Libby took them, stuffed a claim check into her palm and closed the door. "What are you going to do now?"

Cal smiled. He took one of the coats and hid the lower half of his face. "A remake of *The Desert Song*."

Libby started to laugh. "You can't sing!"

"Maybe not. But I can make love on the desert sands." He swung the coat over his head and with a great flourish spread it on the floor. "Atop a bed of flying carpets."

"You really want to do it?"

"*The Desert Song*? No. Make love? Yes!" He reached for the other coat and threw it to the floor.

"Cal!" She started to pick them up. He grabbed hold of her.

"I want to make love on the desert sands." They kissed, eyes wide open, holding tight to one another as he slid his tongue between her lips.

Another knock at the door. Tessa's hand waved a mink-lined Burberry. Libby took it, gave her a check and then locked the door.

"On a bed of flying carpets," he whispered, tossing more coats to the floor.

Libby mumbled a half-hearted, "Don't." She threw her arms around him. "They're expensive."

Cal bit her chin. He kissed her neck. "Just think what they're going to be worth afterward." He smiled as Libby reached for the last coat. "Not that one."

Libby rubbed her hand over the fur. "I'm worth sable!"

"Says who?"

As Cal held the coat open for Libby, she saw her name embroidered on the satin lining. She looked up at Cal and gasped. "Says you!"

Cal put his arms around her, pressing into the fur to feel the outline of her body. Very quietly, very off key, he began to sing, *"One alone, to be my own."*

Libby smiled as he lowered her gently onto the pile of coats. *"I alone,"* she whispered, *"to know your caresses."* He kissed her again. She couldn't remember the rest of the lyrics. She didn't need the rest of the lyrics. Cal was on top of her. He was all around her. Then, he was inside her.

They barely moved. No sweaty, breathless passion to distract from the symmetry. It was the fit that counted. They were fully clothed but she could feel his skin on hers. "Cal," she cautioned, "we have to be careful."

"Sure."

"Any dummy can have a good marriage, but you really have to work at a good divorce."

"I know that. What the hell do you take me for?"

She held him tight and smiled. "I want to take you for all you've got."

Cal and Libby had met in the chorus of a flop musical. His name was Roger and all he talked about was going to California to become a movie star. Although they were married for less than a year, she offered Cal joint custody of Steven. Instead, Libby and Steven wound up with joint custody of Cal. No matter how many marriages or front-page affairs, he always came back to them. The other women in Cal's life were merely wives or lovers. Libby and Steven were family.

There was a knock at the door. Libby gasped, suddenly remembering where they were. "Why is it we never have time for foreplay?"

"Later," he said hoarsely. "We'll have afterplay."

More knocking. Libby began to laugh. "We can't do this now." She kissed him. "Cal! Not during lunch."

"Why not? Everyone out there is doing what we're doing. Except we're enjoying it."

The knocking continued. "Cal, I want silk sheets and champagne. I want you to undress me. I want us to take a hot shower and get steamy and soapy. I want us to wash each other in all those secret places. Smooth on warm oil while we whisper unspeakably dirty things."

Cal was frozen in place. He cleared his throat. "Why don't we just do it twice?"

Libby pushed against him. "Please."

"Don't move! For God's sake, hold still!" He took a deep breath.

She kissed him. "Can't you just put it in reverse and pull out fast?"

"Are you crazy? You want to have to pay for all these coats?"

Libby began to giggle. "Well, then what are you going to do?"

"I don't know. You're the one who's been reading *The Zen Joy of Sex!*"

"You have to take your mind off it," she said. "Think of something depressing. Something frightening. A word that conjures up nothing but horror."

"Like what?"

Libby leaned over and whispered into his ear. "Agent!"

While making his way through the crowd around the checkroom, Cal caught sight of Steven. "Hey, kiddo!"

Steven felt Cal's voice cover him like a blanket on a cold night. He was a little boy again, remembering how he used to throw himself into Cal's arms and cry. "Let me stay with you, Daddy. I'll be good." But somehow Steven was never good enough. He was always shipped back to New York. Back to Libby.

"You look terrific!" Cal started to laugh and put his arms around Steven. "Anyone asks, you're my brother."

But Steven looked no more like Cal's brother than like his son. Libby had cheated him of that as well. However much he hated her for not keeping his father at home, he hated Libby even more for her dominant genes. The short, dark-haired maître d' wanted desperately to look like the lanky, corn-blond movie star.

"So how are you?" Cal asked.

"Well, I don't have AIDS yet."

"You know, kiddo, I worry about you."

"That makes two of us."

"What's wrong?"

Steven shrugged, unable to stop the tears from welling up in his eyes. "Same old shit."

Cal hugged Steven. He held tight, patting him gently, rubbing his shoulder. Steven leaned back enjoying the masculine warmth of Cal's grip. So unlike the embraces of his anonymous boys. He wanted to hug Cal back. But that was too risky. He was afraid of not being manly enough.

"I have somebody I want you to meet," Cal said. "An art director at Paramount. I told him to give you a call."

"You promised to stop matchmaking."

"You're going to like him. He's got some sense of humor."

"We all have senses of humor. We're all artistic. We love to cook. We dress well . . ."

Cal put his hands on either side of Steven's face. "Will you shut up? I just want you to be happy." Cal stared at his son and asked, "You sure you don't have anything?" Steven shook his head no. Cal smiled and then hugged him again. They both began to laugh.

Harold "Hots" Goldberg motioned Libby over to his table. Hots made his mark during the Watergate hearings as one of the young attorneys who believed Martha Mitchell. Amid a political climate of defensiveness, the defenders reigned supreme. What once happened only to movie stars and pop singers happened to Harold. He became *hot*. His personal celebrity attached importance to cases that were unimportant. His reputation tipped the scales of justice in favor of his clients. Hots emerged as a one-man legal system.

He was still on the phone as Libby slid in next to him. "Darling," he said into the receiver, "let me be the judge." He reached for Libby's hand and squeezed it. "Absolutely not," he said into the phone. "You should get all the horses. Let him keep the house in the Algarve. What do you need to be cocking around with property in Portugal?" Hots hung up quickly. "So how much did this one cost Cal?"

"It doesn't matter."

"She got that much?"

"Hots . . ."

"You can tell me. Client to lawyer."

"You're the only one I know who can keep a secret."

"So tell me!"

"I think Cal came back to ask me to marry him."

"Then what are you worried about? Isn't that what you want?"

"Hots, are you crazy? If I married Cal, I could lose him for forever."

The moment Fay saw Cal she recognized all the signs. The nervous half-smile. The banker's tie. The squint because he wouldn't wear glasses. Cal needed money. But for what? His name was always linked with the underdog, the endangered species, the lost cause. He marched on Washington. He spoke on street corners and at congressional hearings. He never missed an election or an opportunity to campaign against the Administration. As he sat down, Fay asked, "What is it this time, darlin'? Save the seals or save the Indians?"

He leaned over to kiss her. "This time it's save me."

"I figured the señorita had you by the pesetas. But you've been divorced often enough to know what to expect."

"Murphy was an optimist." Cal laughed as he started riffling through Fay's notes.

She slapped her hand down over his. "At least you finished the picture."

He shrugged. "Vice versa. The studio took it away from me."

"Oh, darlin'. I didn't know . . ."

"Nobody does. Not even Libby. I had everything in that picture. There was nothing left for Manuela to get."

Fay ignored the blinking lights on her phone. "Don't worry about it. The studio is bluffing."

Cal smiled. "Yeah. But this time, they're *really* bluffing."

"What are you going to do, sweetie?"

"Turn a deal. Fast. Why else do you think I came back?" He looked around the room, squinting to see who was at what table. "Libby still runs the best employment agency in town."

Marsha Mason was sitting with Phyllis and Donald. Cal had left Fay's table to squeeze in next to Audrey. Moina stood in the aisle, listening to Hots tell Paloma a dirty joke.

Libby went back to working the room. She took a deep breath, inhaling the aroma of imported perfumes and impossible dreams. Table after table of herbed and spiced bodies creating appetites no kitchen could satisfy. At lunch, everyone was on the menu. A deuce of East Coast production people who wished they were West Coast production people. Goulash and pasta. She told them the latest Columbia joke and left before they stopped laughing. Ashtrays full on 41. A four top: the ambitious Lieutenant Governor and his three aggressive aides. Thin smiles. Swordfish all around. A quick handshake and a warning that she'd heard some blue suits from "Sixty Minutes" were planning to do a hatchet job on the lottery. Two women with hats at 61. Out-of-towners. They always ate the bread. She stopped Maxie as he hurried down the aisle. "What did you give Sinatra?"

He shrugged. "Who knows? Call the Bronx Zoo and find out what's missing."

Libby glanced down at the plates he was carrying. Goddamn it! They weren't putting enough dill sauce on the gravlax. What the hell was she going to do about the dill sauce on the gravlax? What the hell was she going to do if Cal asked her to marry him?

The single at Table 51 appeared to be in his late thirties, early forties. Built like a football player. Dressed like an IBM salesman. Nice face. Curly dark hair and, as he looked up at Libby, piercing black eyes. It was the no-show, "Somebody" Birnbaum.

"Hi," he said with his mouth full. "You give out recipes?"

Libby looked at his plate. "What is that?"

"This," he said solemnly, "is a very important hamburger."

"I don't serve hamburgers."

"I know. But I once read an article that said you could go into any good restaurant and order whatever you wanted. Within reason."

Libby looked at the shriveled burger. "That came out of my kitchen?"

"Reluctantly. I had to send it back twice before they got it right. Not that I'm complaining. It's the same story everywhere. Even on the Upper West Side. There's almost no one left who remembers well-done burgers or chicken chow mein."

All she could do was smile. "Looks like you've been stood up."

"No, I haven't. You just arrived." He pointed to the empty chair.

Libby shook her head. "Okay. What are you selling? Wine? Linens?"

He took out his ID. There was a badge on the outside, a plastic laminated card with his photo inside. "Special Agent Birnbaum. United States Secret Service."

"Am I under arrest?"

Birnbaum smiled. "Only if you won't sit down."

Libby's stomach started doing tricks. She looked around the room for support systems. Cal was talking to Mike Nichols. Hots was having an intense conversation with Phyllis. "Sure. My feet are killing me anyway."

As soon as she was seated, Birnbaum leaned over and spoke softly. "Mrs. Dennis, the President is going to be in New York on Thursday and would like to have lunch here."

"The president of what?"

"The President of the United States."

Without taking her eyes from him, Libby reached for Birnbaum's glass of milk and drank it all. "Why?"

"I don't know why. I'm here to tell you that he would like to have lunch on Thursday and to find out whether it's all right."

"This just isn't funny." Libby stood up. "Listen, I'm sorry. I have to go. I haven't said two words to Gloria yet."

"Mrs. Dennis . . ."

She hesitated and then sat down again. "Everyone calls me Libby."

"Libby. If for any reason you'd rather not have the President to lunch on Thursday, it's perfectly all right. You're under no obligation. There won't be any questions asked. You don't even have to give us an explanation."

She spoke softly. Without conviction. "Why wouldn't I want the President here?"

"For one thing, it will require a great deal of preparation."

"He'll eat whatever we have."

Birnbaum started to laugh. "Mrs. . . ."

"Libby."

"Libby. What I meant was, we have to coordinate with the FBI, the Police Department, the Fire Department, the Health

Department, and the Department of Hospitals. We're going to have to bring in our own phone lines, emergency power lines, medical staff, and the White House people. We have to search and secure the premises and, of course, run security checks."

There was a long silence. "Who's going to pay for this circus?"

"The White House."

Libby reached for his plate as though grabbing the trapeze in mid-air. "Don't eat that. We've got a terrific special. Lamb chops in a basil cream sauce . . ."

"I'm not much of a gourmet."

"You don't have to be. Nobody is. Raw meat. Raw fish. That's all they eat here. Shark food." Reluctantly, she put his plate down.

"Mrs. Dennis . . ."

"Libby."

"Libby. I have to be honest. A presidential visit can be upsetting."

"Listen, Birnbaum. You think you're dealing with an amateur? I'm the one who had Elizabeth Taylor and Debbie Reynolds here on the same night. What's a little President after that?"

Birnbaum started to laugh. "Have you ever met the President?"

"No."

They stared at one another, smiles fading as her answer reverberated in the sudden silence between them.

"What happens now?" she asked.

"I'd like you to keep this confidential. Don't tell your staff about it yet."

"But they're going to see . . ."

"I'd prefer they didn't know anything until our security checks have been completed."

"But *I* know."

He smiled. "I can't imagine we'll come up with anything on you, Mrs. Dennis."

The man on the flying trapeze had just let go. Libby was plummeting to earth.

As soon as Birnbaum left, Libby headed for the phone room in the vestibule. She closed the door and dialed Hots at Table 104. The minute he picked up, she said, "Don't let anyone know this is me."

"Who is me?"

"Me! Libby!"

"I remember you."

"Hold the phone close to your ear."

"You going to talk dirty?"

"Hots, I'm in trouble."

"Let me be the judge."

"There was a Secret Service agent here. He asked me if I had ever met the President. I said no."

"You're right. You're in trouble."

"Can they lock me up for lying to the Secret Service?"

"Listen, sweetheart, I have an even better question. Where are you calling from?"

"The phone room. Why?"

"Don't say another word. Just hang up. Ten to one they have the lines tapped."

Libby gasped. Narrowing her eyes, she shouted into the phone, "Birnbaum, you son of a bitch! I'll get you for this!"

o

The President of the United States sat alone in the Oval Office. He turned pages in a looseleaf notebook, comparing his intelligence files with a report from the Secretary of State. Unlike the photographs that always showed his desk clean, it was littered with papers.

On hearing the helicopter, he took off his steel-frame aviator glasses. He rose quickly and pushed aside the curtains. The helicopter had landed on the South Lawn. His aides, hands over their ears, waited for the motor to stop. Amid the protective surround of the Secret Service, he could not catch sight of the passenger they hurried down the steps and in through the South Portico. Finally, there was a knock on the door and it opened.

"Mr. President," said the agent.

"Thank you."

Libby entered the Oval Office. The door closed behind her. They were alone. "Why?" she asked.

"I couldn't wait until Thursday."

She spoke softly. "I thought you had forgotten about me."

The President of the United States walked slowly toward her. "I can order armies into battle, send men to their deaths, destroy entire nations, but I can't forget about you." Barely touching her lips, he said, "I am the most powerful man in the world." He kissed her. "I am the weakest man in the world."

Libby felt his breath on her face. She closed her eyes. His fingers traced the outline of her mouth so delicately she dared not breathe. He put his arms around her. His body pressed close. He began to undress her.

She wanted to say no, to pull away from him, but she felt submerged, as though her clothes had been swept away amid a wave of rapture. His hands fondled her breasts, then slid to the soft swell beneath her stomach. She gasped as he picked her up in his arms.

"Where are you taking me?"

As lithe and sinewy as the ancient kings who fought naked on smoldering battlefields, the President of the United States carried Libby to the altar of his power. The Oval Office desk was covered with papers awaiting his signature. He swept aside the budget proposal to Congress, the trade agreement with Honduras, the satellite memo from the Kremlin. Libby felt her senses erupt. She was on fire.

"You're on fire!" Cal whispered, thrusting deep. "Tiger, tiger, burning bright." As he raised his head from her breast, the words caught in his throat. "Hey, tiger! Open your eyes!"

Libby sighed. "Don't stop," she said to the President.

"Uh uh," Cal replied. "I never shoot until I see the whites of their eyes."

Libby stared at him. "Cal!" Then she added quickly, "Darling."

Before she could stop him, Cal withdrew. He sat on the edge of the bed. "I saw that look on your face. You were somewhere else." He lowered himself to the floor. "Goddamn it, Libby. You're the only woman who ever rejected me, and you're still doing it."

Libby slid off the bed. She put her arms around him, her mind racing for an explanation. "Babe, I was thinking about the first time you made love to me."

"That was almost twenty-five years ago. Damn it, Libby. The only man I can't compete with is myself. You're not thinking about me. You're thinking about a young Cal Dennis. You know the joke. Who is Cal Dennis? Get me Cal Dennis. Get me a young Cal Dennis. You're doing the same thing the studio is."

Libby reached for a glass of champagne and poured it over Cal's head. He didn't move. Massaging it into his golden hair, she whispered, "Hey, movie star. You want to know what I'm really thinking?" As the champagne dripped onto his shoulders, she rubbed it across his chest. "I'm really thinking that your tiny little titties drive me crazy."

Cal pulled her onto his lap. He took his glass and emptied it over her breasts. He licked off the champagne, pausing to suck gently on her nipples. "There isn't a woman I haven't compared to you."

Libby leaned over and bit his shoulder. "Bullshit."

"Say that again."

Nose to nose, pressing her lips against his, she said, "Bull-shit."

"That's what I thought you said." Cal reached for the bottle. Then he cupped his hand between her legs, pouring champagne as his fingers pushed inside to create a path for the wine.

Libby gasped as she realized what he was doing. She pulled him on top of her. "Are you crazy?" she asked, holding tight as he eased inside her. "It's supposed to be red wine with meat."

"Fuck you," he whispered, biting her ear.

"Fuck you." She bit his chin.

"Say that again."

Libby grabbed hold of his face with both her hands. She stared lovingly into his eyes. "Fuck you."

He wrapped his arms around her as he pushed forward. "That's what I thought you said."

○

Libby lay back on the pillow. Silk sheets and champagne. Cal sprawled across a pink satin quilt. Everything just the way she said she wanted it. Except for one thing. Birnbaum. Table 51. "Somebody" Birnbaum had changed everything.

Her open palm moved gently across Cal's chest. Even that had changed. "I liked you better with hair."

"I had no choice. They decided to shave everything from my sideburns down to my pubes. Even the hair on my ass." Cal started to laugh. "Would you believe the insurance company brought their own barber?"

"I don't know why you did a scene like that."

"I had to. If I said no, they'd have thought I couldn't. That I had turned to flab. Or was too old. But it's okay. I didn't embarrass the family. It's not a cock shot."

Libby kissed him. "It should have been." She pushed Cal onto his stomach and stared at his behind. "All those nice little hairs are gone."

"They'll grow back."

Libby rubbed her hand over his buttocks. "You should have asked me first."

"Oh, sure. I have half the world staring up my kazoo and I'm supposed to say, 'Excuse me, but I have to call my ex-wife to get her permission.' "

"Your what?"

"Your permission."

"No. What did you call me?"

"Oh, babe. Come on."

She slapped his behind as hard as she could. "Your ex-wife? Which ex-wife?"

Cal turned around. He smiled and took her in his arms. "Ex marks the spot."

Libby leaned her head against his shoulder. She felt the tears well up in her eyes. "I want to do it over, Cal. I need another take. All we have to reshoot is twenty-five years."

He kissed her gently. "You know what happens. You shoot it over and over. But in the end, you always stay with the first take."

"That's exactly what I want to do. I want to stay with the first take."

"What is it, babe?" He slid his hand to her breast. "We've never kept secrets from one another."

Libby was afraid he could feel her heart pounding. "I'm not supposed to tell anyone."

He pulled back. "What have you heard?"

"Actors!" Libby smiled. "Stop worrying. It has nothing to do with you." She touched his face. "What the hell! All they can do is shoot me." A deep sigh. "It seems the President wants to have lunch here on Thursday."

"Why?"

"I don't know why." She resented his question. "Why the hell not?"

"Well, let's face it, babe. The son of a bitch must be coming here for more than a meal."

"All right. You dragged it out of me. He's holding a summit conference. Disarmament. World peace. The whole thing. He wanted to use Mamma Leone's but they were closed."

Cal was upset. "When did all this happen?"

"Today. While you were playing lunchus interruptus. A guy came from the Secret Service."

"Why didn't you tell me?"

"I am telling you. Please, Cal, spare me your political paranoia. Libby's is famous. Everybody comes to Libby's. Why shouldn't the President?"

"No reason. Except he never came before. Why now? He's not up for reelection. Uh uh. He's got something on his mind. This guy's a user. He wants to use you. His coming here is no accident."

"Cal . . ."

"Guatemala was no accident. The Confidentiality Act was no accident. What did you say?"

"What do you think I said?" Libby began to laugh. "Oh, now I get it. I was supposed to ask you first. I was supposed to say, 'Excuse me, but I have to ask my ex-husband . . .' "

"You know what you're letting yourself in for? You know what those guys are going to do?" He took her by the shoulders. "I hope you've paid all your parking tickets, kiddo. There's nothing those bastards can't find out."

Libby held tight to Cal. "Don't be silly. I don't even have a car."

Cal picked her up in his arms. As lithe and sinewy as the

ancient kings who fought on smoldering battlefields, he carried her to the bed.

○

At five o'clock, Libby stood on the corner of Fifty-seventh and Sixth. She put a quarter into the phone and dialed Hots. "It's me again."

"Where are you calling from this time?"

"A street phone."

"Don't say a word. I'm going to turn on the scrambler." There were two beeps. "Okay, sweetheart."

"Hots, my whole world is collapsing. I don't know how to hold on anymore."

"Did you call just to schmooze or do you really have a problem?"

"I don't know what to do!"

"Buy a big roll of adhesive tape. Start at the left corner of your mouth . . ."

"Hots!"

"I told you what to do. Do nothing. Most of all, say nothing. Not to Cal. Not to anyone. If that schlimazel from the Secret Service comes back, tell him you're busy. Tell him you'll speak to him tomorrow. It is vital you do not say anything more to him. Not one word. Promise?"

"I promise."

○

There were over one hundred and fifty Birnbaums in the Manhattan phone book. But since he had mentioned the Upper West Side, that narrowed the list considerably. Libby sat at the bar, dialing two telephones simultaneously while the bartenders exchanged puzzled glances.

"Hello, Mr. Birnbaum?" she said. "Hold on. Hello, Mr. Birnbaum? This is Libby Dennis. Do you know me? Oh, yeah? Same to you! Mr. Birnbaum? This is Libby Dennis."

"Libby?"

"Is this you?" she gasped.

"Is this you?"

"Never mind if it's me. Is this or is this not Birnbaum of the Secret Service?"

"It's you, all right," he said.

"You live at 609 West End Avenue?"

"Is this an obscene phone call?"

"Birnbaum," she whispered excitedly.

"Yes?"

"Don't move a muscle!"

○

Libby wore a man-tailored gray flannel suit, white shirt, and a bright pink tie. As she stepped off the elevator, Birnbaum was waiting in the doorway to his apartment. Over his shirt and jeans, he wore a black-and-white polka-dot apron. Without saying a word, she edged past him and walked inside.

It was a typically large prewar West Side apartment. The décor, however, was in the midst of battle. Half the walls had been broken through prior to being removed. Chunks of ceiling were gone, exposing overhead wires and wooden lathe. There were piles of molding and chipped plaster. Portions of the floor had been ripped up. A path of newspapers led the way from room to room.

"Who's your decorator?"

"What's the matter?" he asked. "You don't like Early Stalingrad?"

Libby followed the line of papers and headed toward the bedroom. It, too, was filled with rubble and dust. The king-size bed was unmade. There was only one pillow on it. "You're not married?"

"Separated."

"What happened?"

"My wife was seeing someone else."

"You caught her?"

"No. She told me."

"She want to marry the guy?"

"No. She only wanted to sleep with him."

Libby opened the closet door. It was filled with Birnbaum's clothes. She reached in for a suit and checked the label. "Sears?"

"What can I do? I'm fashion's plaything."

Libby tossed the suit to Birnbaum. "You have kids?"

"No."

She walked into the bathroom. "Why not?"

Birnbaum smiled. "Listen, Libby . . ."

She opened the medicine chest. "Mrs. Dennis."

He stopped smiling. "Mrs. Dennis."

"You ever cheat on your wife?"

Birnbaum stood in the doorway. He was angry. "I don't like playing Trivial Pursuit."

Libby pushed back her bangs. "There's nothing trivial about me, Birnbaum." She tapped him gently, waiting for him to step aside. "You know, two can play this game."

Birnbaum was a pro. He could recognize danger. And, for him, danger was always accompanied by the scent of sex. At that moment, Libby Dennis smelled better than the entire South of France. She dazzled him. Not with her bravado. With her vulnerability. For all the armor Libby thought she was wearing, Birnbaum saw her stark naked. Stark naked in his bed. "Why don't we go somewhere and have a drink?"

Somewhere was a corner of the living room floor. Two Barcelona chairs on a carpet of newspapers. The drink was milk.

"Tell me about your wife."

"My wife orders English muffins from a bakery in Missouri. She likes witty furniture. Insolent wines. She likes to read reviews of new buildings. We were in the middle of renovating. She decided that walls were a medieval concept. When she left, she wrote me a farewell memo with her Mont Blanc pen."

"Definitely not a contender for well-done burgers," Libby said.

"Definitely not. Now suppose you tell me something."

"Sure."

"What the hell are you so worried about?"

"Nothing special. The same things everyone is worried about. Killer bees. The Shroud of Turin. Going metric. You know."

They stared at one another, sipping their milk. "You want some cookies?" he asked. "I have Oreos and Fig Newtons. After my wife left, I went back to shopping at Grand Union."

Libby looked unsmiling into his eyes. "You know what I used to like? Those marshmallow things covered in chocolate."

"Mallomars!"

"Yes," she said softly. "Mallomars."

"No cookies, Mrs. Dennis?"

Libby shook her head. "No cookies, Birnbaum."

"More milk?"

"I hate milk." She gave him her glass. Their hands touched.

"You drank milk at lunch."

"Not me. I never drink milk."

"You did. You drank all my milk."

"Impossible. Even as a kid, I lied my way out of my milk."

"Well," he said, holding up her half-empty glass, "you can't lie your way out of this milk."

"Don't bet on it, Birnbaum."

"Funny the things we did when we were kids." He leaned forward in his chair. "You know, I used to steal comic books."

Libby smiled. He had handed her a loaded gun. He was playing Russian Roulette using truth instead of bullets. "I used to sneak into Radio City Music Hall," she said. "I'd go right up to the usher and say I had to find my mother because someone had died. The idea was to storm the place as though you owned it. That way they'd never suspect you."

"I'll have to remember that."

Libby sat back in her chair. "It works every time."

"You know what else I used to do?" he said. "I used to take ice cream from the freezer case and hide it behind the canned goods."

"Did you get caught?"

"No."

Libby leaned forward. "I stole lipsticks from Woolworths."

"Did you get caught?" he asked.

"No."

"I once cheated on a chemistry exam."

"I cut school all the time," she said.

"I stood Florence Zitomer up at the Senior Prom."

"I slept with the President."

Birnbaum smiled. "I know. Page twenty-three. Paragraph two."

And that was it. I know. Page twenty-three. Paragraph two. Over and out. Libby took a deep breath. "He was only a senator at the time. How was I supposed to know he'd become President?"

Birnbaum shook his head. "God knows what happened to Florence Zitomer."

After a long pause, Libby asked, "What do you mean, page twenty-three, paragraph two?"

"Mrs. Dennis, your senator was being groomed."

"You mean followed."

"Whatever."

"How long have I been page twenty-three, paragraph two?"

"Since you spent the night together."

"Are you serious? You mean my name has been floating around Washington for over twenty years?"

"Not floating, Mrs. Dennis. Your name has been in a top secret file, not on a bathroom wall."

"Let me tell you something, Birnbaum. It would have been seen by a better class of people." Libby took a deep breath. "You asked me this afternoon whether I'd met the President. But you already knew the answer."

"Yes."

"Then why did you ask me?"

"You think the only reason people ask questions is because they don't know the answers?"

"I lied to you."

"Everybody lies. You weren't under oath."

"It's just that I didn't want Cal to find out. It would ruin everything."

"Ruin what? You're not married to him anymore."

"That's the whole point! Birnbaum, I have too good a divorce to louse it up now."

"Mrs. Dennis . . ."

"Libby."

"Why did you come here?"

"Birnbaum, I never saw him again after that night. It must be in your report." She waited for him to respond.

"Why did you come here?" he repeated.

"I want to see the report."

"The report is classified."

"How do I know what else you have in there?"

"You don't."

Libby cleared her throat. "I want to see it. I have rights under the Freedom of Information Act."

Birnbaum smiled. "All such requests must be made in writing. However, I can tell you in advance that Secret Service files on the President are exempt from any and all provisions of the Freedom of Information Act."

Libby reached across and put her hand on his. She spoke intently. "Birnbaum, what do I have to do?"

He took hold of her arm. "Let's get one thing straight. I don't take bribes and I don't fuck for favors."

Libby got up and began edging toward the door. "You son of a bitch! That's not what I meant! You could really mess things up for me right now. How do I know I can trust you?"

"Trust *me?* I'm the one who's supposed to be worried about trusting *you!*"

"Well, then, we have no problem, do we? I mean, I never could keep anything hidden. What you see is what you get." Libby gasped, realizing her back was up against the door.

Birnbaum was close enough to kiss her. "I'm sorry I shot my mouth off before. I was cooking dinner and I was edgy. I hate to eat alone. You shouldn't take what I say too seriously."

"I won't."

He smiled. "Especially the part about not fucking for favors."

Libby reached for the door knob. "I promise not to tell anyone the President is coming to lunch."

He leaned close. "Do I have your word?"

"Birnbaum! Would I lie to the Secret Service?"

○

By two o'clock in the morning, the white roses had been refrigerated. Vases and ashtrays and salt cellars were lined up on the service counters. Chairs were stacked on top of tables. The linen had been carefully counted and bundled.

Libby and Steven sat alone in the empty dining room. He was rescheduling staff while she pretended to be checking the day's receipts. Their cups of coffee had long since gone cold. Steven picked at a slice of caramel pie.

"Talk about the shoemaker's children," Libby said.

Steven looked up at her. Expressionless. "What?"

"That's no dinner for you to be eating."

"It's my just desserts."

Libby took hold of his arm. "I have an idea. Let's go on a real splashy vacation. Just the two of us. My treat. Anywhere in the world."

"Whose world?"

She let go of him. "You still seeing that architect?"

"No."

"I thought you liked him."

Steven looked down at his papers. "You ever think about minding your own business?"

"I'm sorry. I didn't realize you liked him that much."

"You want a list of all the things you didn't realize?" Steven sighed. "As it happens, I can provide you with such information in a variety of formats. By subject or chronologically. In twenty-three annual volumes."

Libby knew all twenty-three volumes. Chapter and verse. Steven blamed her for everything. Most of all, for losing Cal when he was a child. She thought he'd grow out of it once he was old enough to understand. Then, once he was through adolescence. Then, once he found himself. Or once he found someone else. "If you're not seeing anyone, what's to stop us from sneaking away?"

"The tables may be empty, but the management still reserves the right to refuse admittance."

Loving Steven was like putting letters into a mailbox that no one ever opened. Dialing a disconnected number. Taking pictures without film. Whatever she tried, there was no way to get through. "Steven, I'm worried about you."

"Me too."

She leaned forward. "What's wrong?"

Steven pushed aside his papers. "You really want to know?"

"Of course I do."

He took a deep breath. "Well, Mom, it's just no fun being a homo these days. You're not supposed to suck cock. You're not supposed to get it up the ass. You're not supposed to give it up the ass. Everybody's supposed to find fulfillment making love to a condom. Now, I ask you?"

Libby grabbed hold of Steven with both hands. "Goddamn it, I didn't deserve that." She spoke very softly. "I know I've always said that I didn't care whether you preferred men or women. Well, that's a lie. I do care. But I care much more about your being happy."

"Whatever happened to happy?"

"Steven, why can't you find someone to love?"

He looked at her coldly. "Because I hate all fags." He shuffled his papers and spoke in a thin, emotionless voice. "I'm moving Dan over to Marty's station until he's back. Everyone can take an extra table until I break Chickie in. He's smart. He looks good. He'll work out."

"The hell he will. It's one thing when you trash all over me because I'm your mother. But the same rules do not apply during business hours. I want you to get rid of Chickie first thing tomorrow. I know all about the two of you. Dan stays where he is."

Steven stared at her. "Thus spake The Great Libby."

"Steven. I love you."

"Why don't you just fuck off?"

Thus spake The President's Son.

TUESDAY

IT WAS THE MOUSE THAT AWAKENED ALFERO THE dishwasher.

The mouse was standing on his chest, staring into his face. Alfero looked over at Dolores. She was asleep. *¡Mira!* The mouse had the cheese from the trap. He was eating it as he stood on top of the man who had tried to kill him. The dishwasher smiled. Truly, a New York mouse.

Alfero glanced at the ticking alarm clock. Five forty-five. He still had fifteen minutes. He nudged Dolores. She moaned. The mouse looked up and stopped eating. Alfero nudged Dolores again. She turned away, pleading, *"Por favor."*

"Tonight," he whispered to the mouse. And to Dolores.

Alfero threw back the Eastern Airlines blanket, stood up, and stepped over Tía Rosa. She was snoring. Tío was sprawled on the floor, having slipped off his mattress again. Alfero glanced enviously at Carlos and his girlfriend asleep in each other's arms. They never slipped off their mattress, what was left of it. The niños, Humberto and Felix, were in a large sleeping bag littered with potato chips. Alfero leaned over to touch them gently on the head, then went into the bathroom and closed the door.

Damp underwear and socks hung from a criss-cross of rope over the bathtub. He reached for a pair of Carlos's red briefs, pleased that at thirty-six he was still as trim as his nephew. Then, brushing aside a roach, he turned on the cold water.

Dolores was already in the kitchen. She opened the refrigerator. "What do you want?" she asked. Alfero smiled and slid his hand between her legs. *"Por favor!"* she snapped, moving away. "What do you want to eat?" She held up a plate. "You want lobster?"

"No."

"Gravlax?"

"No."

"Foie gras?"

"No."

Dolores slammed the refrigerator door shut. "You want something else, you bring it home."

"I bring home a woman."

"Querido," she said softly. "The doctor said we must wait."

Alfero put his arms around her. "I am tired of waiting. My whole life I wait. When I was a boy, I wait to be a man."

"You are a man."

"Then I wait to come to America."

"You are in America."

"What good is it to be in America if I have no green card? What good is it to be a man if I have no woman? I am illegal. Illegal alien." Bitterly, he snapped the elastic on his borrowed underwear. "Illegal man."

Dolores put a hand to his face. *"Querido.* God has many children left. When it is time, he will give us another."

Alfero pushed himself tight against her. "You do not get things in this world by waiting for God. If we want another child, we will have to fuck for it." He pushed his pelvis back and forth against her. "That is the American way. Whatever you want, you must fuck for it!"

Alfero walked along Tremont Avenue toward the subway. It was still dark. The streets of the South Bronx were nearly deserted, silent except for the rustling of old newspapers in a chill October wind. As Alfero waited on the corner for the light to change, he picked up the handful of papers that circled his feet. I will not wait for God to make me a busboy, he thought. Then he bent down again, clearing the garbage from the sidewalk as though clearing the best table in the house. I will ask Libby! Defiantly, he waved the papers over his head for God to see.

But someone else was watching. Special Agent Tom Meehan of the United States Secret Service ducked into a doorway and took a regulation Motorola two-way walkie-talkie from his pocket. "Meehan to Control. Is everybody crazy in New York?"

It was seven o'clock by the time Alfero surfaced from the subway on West Fifty-seventh Street. He stopped into a coffee shop for *"uno bagel con schmeer"* before turning off Sixth Avenue onto Fifty-fifth Street. The first thing Alfero saw was the black-and-white striped awning half a block away toward Fifth. It was the first thing everyone saw. There was no name on the awning. Not even a number. A frosted glass insert over the doorway had "Libby's" etched discreetly in order to keep the wrong people out.

Alfero stuck a finger through the metal gate that protected the entrance. He rang the bell for the night porter, never noticing Special Agents Harmon and Davis watching from a gray Plymouth station wagon across the street. Special Agent Meehan, who had followed Alfero from the Bronx, took out his two-way. "Meehan to Control. He's all yours."

Sonny was busy checking pages on his clipboard while carrots, then potatoes, were loaded onto the receiving scale. Every item had to be weighed and inspected before it went into storage. As back-of-the-house manager, Sonny did the ordering and kept all inventories. He let Alfero work an extra shift as porter.

"Onions!" Sonny shouted. To look at him, no one would have guessed Sonny had started out as a chorus boy. He was bald, fat, and fifty. His face frozen with disdain. Years ago, when Libby still filed a short form, he had done her taxes. To repay the favor, Libby brought him clients from the restaurants she worked in between chorus jobs. Then he repaid the favor. He came to work for her.

"Onions!" Alfero confirmed. "Fifty pound." He lifted the sack off the scale. "I speak to Libby today."

"Times two?"

Alfero weighed the second sack. *"Sí."*

"About what?"

"I want to be a busboy."

Sonny shook his head. "You *españols* don't know when you're well off. They're not going to let you have two shifts in the front of the house."

"I want to get tips."

Sonny motioned for Alfero to slit the sacks, and then he looked inside and sniffed. He picked up one, two, three onions, checking for firmness. Dry skins. No sprouts. Even sizes. "You want to be a busboy, talk to Steven."

"I talk to Miss Libby."

"You *habla inglés?* I told you, talk to Steven."

"But she is a nice lady."

"I don't want you bothering Libby. You talk to Steven. He's a nice lady, too."

Louie, the Vietnamese sous-chef, stood near the dry storage room. Cartons of tomatoes were piled in front of the door. "Where mushroom?" shouted Louie.

Sonny ignored him. "Broccoli? Ten two-pound cases?"

"Sí."

"You no got mushroom?" Louie yelled.

"I got mushroom! I got mushroom!" Sonny flipped the pages of his inventory. "Where the fuck are the mushrooms?"

"Six three-pound baskets," Alfero said triumphantly, putting them on the scale.

As Louie reached for the top basket, Sonny pushed his hand away. "You know, it would be a helluva lot easier if you let me get through checking in."

Louie narrowed his eyes. "My job not to make life easy for you. My job to get food ready."

"Your job to be pain in the ass!" Sonny handed Louie a basket.

"More!" Louie grabbed two more baskets.

Sonny shook his head at Louie. "Fungus!"

Louie giggled. "Fungus you, too."

A delivery man wheeled in six large boxes. "Flowers!"

"You I want to see!" Sonny said, pointing an angry finger at the man. He held the door open to the walk-in refrigerator. As the man followed him, Sonny shouted, "What the hell kind of shit did you send me on Friday?" He closed the door behind them.

The man smiled. "You shoulda been an actor."

"You shoulda been here earlier," he said softly. "There are too many people around."

The man shrugged. "I don't see nobody." He tossed Sonny a small plastic bag. "Nobody here but us and a couple of steaks that ain't gonna be missed. If you catch my drift."

Sonny opened the bag and sniffed the white powder. He took some between his thumb and forefinger and rubbed it gently. Then he brought it to his nose, inhaled deeply and fought to keep from sneezing. "What the hell is in this?"

"Everybody's a gourmet. You want it or you don't want it?"

Sonny reached into his pocket for some neatly folded bills. "It's lousy."

"The whole world is lousy." The man took the money without counting it.

Sonny opened the meat locker. He wrapped two large steaks and put them into an empty flower box.

"You got some sweet racket," the man said taking the box. "Steaks. Lamb chops. Everything!" He hesitated. "Ain't you afraid you'll get caught?"

Sonny shrugged. "Don't worry. I blame it on the dishwasher."

o

Tessa, the checkroom girl, nuzzled against Mohammed Eli's dark brown chest. She brushed a wisp of long blond hair from her face while staring at the printing press on the kitchen table. "Oh, Eli!" she exclaimed. "You misspelled apartheid again."

"Let me see."

"You illiterate nigger," she said, pinching his behind. "You don't deserve to be oppressed."

Eli shoved her away as he leaned over the table. His blood-shot eyes nearly matched the red ink on the leaflets. "A . . . p . . . a . . ."

"Don't worry. I can still take them to school. No one at Columbia can spell either."

"No," he said. "I shall do them over. I shall do them all over. They must be correct."

Tessa groaned loudly. Eli was so much like her father. She knew Daddy would love Eli once he got to know him. But there was no common meeting ground between the Brooklyn head-quarters of the Black Liberty Congress and the house on Azalea Drive where she had grown up.

". . . r . . . t . . . h . . ."

"To tell the truth, Eli darling, I don't feel like going to school today." Mohammed Eli struck her hard across the face. Tessa took hold of his hand, kissed it, and whispered, "Think of it, tar baby. If I stayed home, you could beat me all day." She smiled. "If I didn't go to work, you could beat me all night."

He grabbed her wrist. "Did you get fired?"

Tessa screamed in pain. "There are other things I can do. I can march in the rally. I can pick pockets in the crowd. We'll get along somehow. Oh, Eli, if I have to I can dig for turnips on Ocean Parkway!"

He tightened his grip. "Did you get fired?"

"No," she sobbed. Eli let go and she slid to the floor, hug-ging his legs. "It's so demeaning to leave the honesty and pur-pose of this house and enter a shrine to decadence where socially unconscious sybarites drink carbonated grape juice and laugh as they eat unborn fish eggs. I mean it, Eli. It makes Pompeii look like Philadelphia. For God's sake, don't send me back to all that luxury and happiness."

Eli opened the refrigerator and took out a ream of paper. "You make more money than any of my wives."

"But at what price to my soul?" Tessa stood up and brushed away the tears. "Eli, look at me. I am a Romanov begging to be shot. An entire Gang of One just waiting to be executed. The Little Match Girl praying for snow. But all you want, you Mali chauvinist pig, is someone who does windows!" She took a deep breath and cleared her throat. Her tone became sharp. "Let's face it, Eli. You don't have to be Wayne Dyer to know this relationship isn't doing too much for my ego. I want to speak at the rally."

"Your presence would offend my wives."

"I'm tired of being the white sheep in your family!"

Eli smiled. He reached out to touch her golden hair. "You should not play with someone else's toys."

She pushed his hand away. "Neither should you, minstrel man."

Tessa hurried toward the subway, knowing it was too late for her "Revolutionary Ideologies" class. But she might have time to stop at the library for some advice from Schneidermann the Marxist.

As she ran down the subway steps, Tessa threw Eli's leaflets into the waste basket. Special Agent Hal Gorden reached in and pulled them out.

○

Louie sat cross-legged on the chef's table. As he sucked in the sweet smoke from his homemade cigarette, he pointed at the two prep men and snarled, "Mushroom!"

It was the prep men's job to "turn" the vegetables, to cut them into equally sized and shaped pieces. They washed, peeled, shredded, diced, chopped and sliced while chattering in rapid-fire Vietnamese to keep up with the rat-a-tat-tat of their knives.

Until the chef arrived, Louie was head man in the kitchen. And that, as far as Louie was concerned, meant that until the chef arrived, he did nothing. But, like a true boss, he did it loudly. "Mushroom! Mushroom!" Louie shouted, waving his arm like an Arctic explorer leading a dog team.

Sonny waved his clipboard as he came into the kitchen. "Jesus! This place smells like the Palladium! You're not supposed to smoke in here."

Louie opened his eyes wide. "Oh, I no supposed to smoke?" he asked, exhaling in Sonny's face. "Why? I no get ashes in pot."

Sonny grabbed the cigarette and put it out. "That's not why the Health Department gives fines. You touch your lips. You get saliva on your fingers. Then you touch the food. That's as bad as spitting into the soup."

"But no as much fun," Louie giggled.

Sonny flipped through his pages, reading off items that wouldn't keep for another day but which were good enough for the staff lunch. "I have three cod, two swordfish, four or five red peppers, and I can throw in a couple of zucchini."

"Excellent," Louie said as though suddenly inventing the word. "I sauté peppers and zucchini. Chop tomato. Add tomato paste. Maybe vermouth. Cook fish very little bit . . ."

"Why don't you cook fish more than very little bit? Yesterday you cook chicken very little bit and there was still blood on the bones."

"You eat bones?"

"No."

"You eat bones, I cook bones. You eat chicken, I cook chicken. No same thing."

"Fuck you," Sonny said.

"Fuck you."

"Where the hell is Bud?"

"Chef very busy. What you want?"

"None of your business. Where the hell is he?"

"None of *your* business."

"Fuck you."

"Fuck you."

o

Bud, Libby's thirty-five-year-old chef, lay back on the bed. He stared up at the morning sun coming through the skylight in his SoHo loft while Libby's best friend, Phyllis Elgin, buried her face between his legs.

"I'm going to bite it off," she growled. "I am. I am. I am. First, I'm going to eat this part, then . . ."

"Phyllis, it's bad manners to talk with your mouth full." If only she would shut the hell up. Sex, like a single grain of caviar, was too fragile for words. It was a taste to be savored in its purest form. No onions. No lemon. No emotion.

Ever since he crossed the Canadian border to avoid being sent to Vietnam, Bud had little use for emotion. As though to justify running away to save his hide, he determined to have the best hide possible. While working "off the books" in dozens of kitchens, doing everything from pot washer to prep man, he worked off years of Kansas corn-fed flab. As he peeled and chopped and shaped the vegetables, he began to reshape himself. By the time Bud was promoted to grill man, he was as obsessive about his own flesh as he was about the meat he cooked. He demanded no less perfection from his body than from his butcher. Suddenly, he felt secure. He discovered a new set of standards by which to live. He returned home during the period of amnesty and embraced the new American cuisine, if not the flag.

Phyllis had begun making sloppy sounds to let him know she was having a wonderful time. Bud folded his hands behind his head. He tensed his buttocks to cue her and stared directly into the blinding sunlight. It hurt. He smiled and closed his eyes. Then, according to the recipe, the man known in the kitchen as Primary Sauté began to simmer in his own pan gravy.

By the time Phyllis climbed up alongside him, she was breathing heavily. "My compliments to the chef."

Bud smelled himself on her lips. He pulled her close, kissing her, his tongue searching deep inside her mouth until he could taste himself fully. Phyllis began to moan, mistaking Bud's passion for himself as passion for her.

"What's the matter?" she asked, watching as he got up and walked to the open shower in his open bathroom. He turned on the hot water. "Are you upset?" He turned on the Jacuzzi. "Is it me? Did I do something wrong?" Phyllis wrapped the sheet around herself and followed him. "Tell me what you're thinking."

He stared at her for a moment. "I'm thinking chickens."

"What?"

Bud stepped into the shower. "Chickens. You know. Here, chick-chick."

"Oh." Phyllis stepped back as water sprayed onto her. She brightened. "Shall I come under with you?"

"No."

"No," she repeated softly. "I thought that was all the rage. Boys and girls taking showers together."

"I hate it," he said, rubbing himself vigorously with soap.

"Me, too. I like my privacy."

"If you want to brush your teeth, there's an extra brush."

"Oh, good." She lit a cigarette. "I certainly wouldn't want your toothbrush in my mouth." She inhaled deeply and blew the smoke toward him. "Did you say chickens?"

"Libby wants a new chicken dish. I can't come up with one. I'm stuck."

"So that's it. You've got chicken block. Poor darling. Don't worry. You'll think of something."

But Bud didn't just want something. He wanted something to blow the roof off Libby's. He was tired of reading about who ate there. He wanted to read about *what* they ate.

Phyllis watched as he rinsed off the soap. The last of her went down the drain. "Shall I get a towel and dry you off?"

"What?"

"Oh, fuck you!" she muttered.

Bud stepped out of the shower and into the Jacuzzi. He sat down, leaned his head back and closed his eyes. "I wasn't thinking chickens the whole time."

Phyllis sat on the edge of the tub staring at him. His eyes were tight shut. She flicked her ashes into the water. "Why don't you bring back chicken pot pie?"

"No."

She leaned over and whispered into his ear. "Would you like Phyllis to slip into the tubby with you?"

"No."

Phyllis stood up. She threw her cigarette into the water. She screamed at the top of her voice, "What the hell have you got against good old chicken pot pie?"

Phyllis and Bud left the building like two strangers, each going in the opposite direction. A third stranger was Special Agent Chuck Logan. He radioed for someone to pick up his car. He followed on foot as Bud walked the two and one half miles uptown.

o

Steven sat on the edge of the bed in his Lincoln Center apartment. He was breathing heavily as he stared into a glass of orange juice. His knee shook nervously. Without looking up, he
hurled the glass across the room. It shattered against the wall, an
arc of juice trickling down to the floor.

Donald Elgin lay naked on the bed. "Tacky. Tacky. Tacky."
For years, Donald had been one of New York's most eligible
bachelors. Heir to the Elgin banking fortune, he coasted on the
vanity of women who swore they had been to bed with him. But,
by the time he was forty-five, rumors had begun to circulate.
Enter Phyllis. Since his family's only concern was that Donald's
wife be of a different gender, they welcomed Phyllis with open
arms. Her dowry of two sex-scandal divorces was the perfect
squelch.

"I've told her, hundreds of times, to put names in the
book," Steven said flatly. "But she won't do it. The same thing
happens over and over again."

"That's the way Libby is. She doesn't mean any harm."

"Yes, she does!" Steven banged his fist against the satin
goose-down comforter. "It happened again last night. I had the
Newmans driving down from Connecticut expecting their usual
table. All of a sudden Sam appears. He gives me a big hello and
expects *his* usual table. Then in waltzes Morty Janklow and guess
what?"

Donald sighed. He ran his index finger down Steven's bare
back. "Spare me," he said with mock horror.

Steven turned angrily. "What the hell am I supposed to do?
Wave my magic wand and make everyone disappear?"

"You don't have a magic wand, Steven. Only good fairies
have magic wands and you are a very naughty fairy. Pick the
glass up from the floor."

Steven put his head on Donald's chest, his chin quivering as
he spoke softly. "Bacall was in the other night. Libby sees that
I'm taking the order myself. I mean, it's Bacall! I go into the
kitchen. I couldn't have been gone three minutes. But as soon as
I turn my back, enter Libby. Hello Betty, kissy kissy, and before
you know it the whole fucking order is changed. Even the wine.
How do you think that makes me feel?"

"What was Bacall wearing?"

Steven swept his arm across the night table, hurling the lamp, books, glasses and radio to the floor. "Don't do this to me, Donald. You said you'd get me out of there!"

"You and I both know how many restaurants open and close every year."

"You promised me!"

"This is not the time to discuss money."

"Stop talking like a fortune cookie!" Steven shouted. "I don't have any other time. I can't hold on much longer."

Donald stared into Steven's eyes, wondering whether it was all worth it. Steven was handsome enough. Not the way Cal was handsome, but then Donald was never one for manly men. He liked them young, imperfect, envious of his wealth, desperate. The ones he could play with and throw away.

Steven whispered, "Donny darling, help me."

Donald closed his eyes. "Oh, how I hate that tone in your voice. It is so faggy. It really turns me off."

Steven took hold of Donald's hands. "I know the business inside out. I've got Bud ready to leave with me. But he won't wait forever. He'll go off on his own if I don't make a move soon. Donald, I can walk out of there with half the place in my pocket."

"But you've already got half the place in your pocket. The woman is your mother." Donald pulled his hands away. "I have to be honest with you, Steven. I've always been very fond of Libby."

"You don't know what she's really like."

"I hate going behind Libby's back."

"Jesus. That takes the cake. What about going behind Phyllis's back?"

Donald got out of bed. "It's getting late. You'd better get dressed. Put on the blue suit I bought you."

"I was saving it for my funeral."

Donald laughed. "There you are. Back to your old cheery self. And wear one of those new shirts I sent you from Turnbull's." He leaned over and kissed Steven.

"You really think you can buy whatever you want."

"Of course I do. What's the point of wanting something you can't buy? You might not get it."

Steven pulled away. His eyes were ablaze with anger. "But then again, you might, Donald. You just might."

o

Special Agent Scotty Livingstone tailed the limousine. Donald dropped Steven off two blocks from the restaurant. "Livingstone to Control. Pick up my car. Am following subject on foot."

o

Libby couldn't sleep. Not with Cal next to her. Ever since their divorce, whenever they spent the night together, Libby stayed awake. She never told Cal. She knew he'd never understand why his being next to her was even more exciting than his making love to her.

She had been staring at him for hours. First, trying to find a pattern in the stubble on his chin. Then inhaling his scent. Listening to him breathe. Very gently putting her hand over his heart. The king of the jungle was on his back. Belly up. Exposed. Trusting. During those precious hours that other people squandered on sleep, Cal was hers alone.

But not tonight. The bed was crowded with guilt, regret, and fear. A law firm that specialized in losers. She could hear them shouting at her to get the hell up. Something was wrong somewhere. She had better find out before somebody else did. Before "Somebody" Birnbaum did.

Suddenly, Libby was convinced the whole place was falling apart. She had to get downstairs and fast. Capital F Fast. Instead, she stood frozen in front of the full-length mirror in her bedroom. Capital N Naked.

Libby stared into the mirror. She was afraid that even with clothes on she'd still be naked. She had been through her closet twice, three times, trying to find something to wear. But there was nothing in the kingdom to cover her up. It was as though Birnbaum had changed all the labels to read "The Emperor's New Clothes—New York/Washington/Los Angeles."

She knew she couldn't stand there staring at herself forever. Not the way she had when she was pregnant. She had watched her stomach for hours on end. Wondering whose child she was carrying.

Libby put on a pink sweatsuit, pink socks, pink sneakers. She took a deep breath and looked at herself in the mirror. Now, she thought sadly, I am in the pink.

o

As Libby rushed into the kitchen, the entire Vietnamese population stopped talking. Beer cans disappeared. Everyone was suddenly very busy and very quiet. Louie bowed. *"Chào cô!"*

Following strict protocol, she said good morning first to Louie. *"Chào cô."*

He bowed again. *"Chào cô.* You eat today with cooks, lady? I make excellent meal with Sonny garbage."

Libby took the clipboard out of Louie's hands. "What are the specials? I'm worried about the specials." She glanced down the list. Grilled duck thighs. Coconut chili. Red snapper.

"Lady, I help you?"

She ignored Louie and walked around the chef's table. Ho, the grill man, slammed down his cleaver, separating the second joint from the duck's carcass. "How you do, boss?"

"Tôi manh." She reached quickly for the carcass, checking that the skin was thick and white. Even-colored. Free of dry patches. "I'm fine."

"I fine," he repeated. Ho earned nearly as much as Louie. The grill was the most dangerous station in the kitchen and the goods he handled were the most expensive.

"You explain, lady," Louie asked, "why Long Island duckling come from Wisconsin?"

"They're the best. Everything has to be the best. Everything has to be perfect."

"Everything perfect, lady. You bet!" Louie looked at Ho and shrugged his shoulders.

Cham, who was responsible for coordinating vegetables with main dishes, had taken a handful of green beans and was blanching them in boiling water. *"Chào cô."*

"Chào cô." Libby stared at the beans. "We don't want them overdone."

Louie pushed Cham aside. "You get complaint, lady? He no do beans good?"

Libby pointed to the pot of boiling water. "Shouldn't he take them out?"

"You want out or you want blanch?"

Libby picked up a fresh bean. She stared into her palm, gasping as she read her own future. The bean hadn't been trimmed properly. Libby's heart began to pound. "Look."

"Lady, you want I kill him?"

Libby grabbed Louie's sleeve. "You always steam the ducks, don't you?"

"We steam duck, get fat out, stuff duck, then grill. Is very perfect, lady."

"But do you have enough mustard fruits? And Louie, they've got to be careful with the rice!"

He shook his head and waved his hand. "They always careful with rice! Yellow people no overcook rice. Italian, German, Spanish cook rice to death. You get complaint from customer?"

"By the time you get a complaint, Louie, it's too late. It's all over by then. The minute you think something is wrong, something *is* wrong."

Louie nodded. "Very interesting. What you think is wrong?"

Libby hurried over to Liang and Gan. *"Chào cô!"*

"Chào cô. Chào cô." The cold station men were paid nearly twice as much as the prep men. Instead of merely "turning" vegetables, cold table chefs turned vegetables into elegant garnishes. They were responsible for plating cold appetizers and entrées, composing salads, and making desserts.

Libby stuck a finger into the jalapeño cream being whipped for the coconut chili. "Louie! It needs salt!" she said, anxiously. Liang handed her the salt. Libby sprinkled some in her hand and tossed it into the bowl.

"Delicious," Liang nodded, as he mixed it in.

Louie shook a fist in Liang's face. "You make perfect or you get fire!"

Alfero should have been checking the temperature on the dishwasher. But he couldn't take his eyes from Libby. The way the pink sweatsuit clung to her body. He wondered what it would be like to put his arms around her. He had wondered the same thing about Mary Tyler Moore. He knew just what he would do. First, he would take a very clean towel and dry his fingers. Gently, he would put one hand to her face and feel her silken skin. Then with his other hand, he would slowly reach around and grab a fistful of ass.

"Alfero." Libby leaned close, shocking him out of his reverie. "I want to see the fish."

"Señora! Fish?"

She heard Sonny's voice from the basement. He was arguing with the laundry man. Something must be wrong with the linen. Thank God she had come downstairs when she did.

Alfero opened the door to the walk-in refrigerator. Once inside, Libby pushed away the seaweed covering the live lobsters, checking that they had both claws. She pulled back the paper on top of the sole and looked at the eyes to be certain they weren't cloudy or sunken. She sniffed the trout as suspiciously as a sommelier sniffs a cork.

The moment Libby saw the red snapper she knew there was trouble. It had no sheen. She lifted the gills. They were pink instead of bright red. "Did Sonny check this in?"

Sonny stood watching. "Why don't you ask him?"

Libby picked up a snapper. It was limp, not firm as though just taken from the water. "Something's fishy," she said, tossing the snapper to him.

"Says who?" he asked.

"Says the fish."

Sonny threw the snapper back in the box. "Who you going to believe? Me or some dead guppy?" He motioned for Alfero to leave them alone.

"Maybe you need glasses," Libby said. "What is it? You never used to check in crap. They wouldn't serve that fish at the A.S.P.C.A.!"

"Used to be, if the fish was no good, the chef would thicken the sauce. That's all. Simple. But not anymore. Today, everybody's a prima donna," Sonny shouted. "What the hell do you need a chef for if the fish is good?"

"What the hell do I need *you* for if the fish is bad?"

Sonny was furious. "You couldn't run this goddamn place without me!"

"Then don't let me forget it!" she shouted back. "Not for one minute. You understand?"

"No, I don't understand. What the hell are you doing down here?"

"Nobody uses thick sauces anymore!" Libby shouted. She held up her hands and then spoke softly. "It's getting harder to cover things up. Sonny, don't give me a hard time."

"What's going on?"

Libby took a deep breath. "We have a big booking on Thursday. Lots of snoopy people are going to be around for the next couple of days."

"What kind of snoopy people?" he asked flatly.

"Top of the line. They're running checks on everyone. The whole staff. I'm not supposed to tell you."

"Then why are you telling me?"

"Sonny, I don't want them to find anything wrong."

"Like what?"

"How should I know? They're coming through here with a fine-tooth comb. It's like an audit from God!"

"So? What have you got to hide?"

Libby put a hand to her forehead. She smiled and shrugged her shoulders. "That's what I'm trying to find out."

Louie stood wide-eyed at Sonny's desk. "What you mean? I have to have red snapper!" He waved a menu detail card in Sonny's face. "I need for lunch special. See? Red snapper."

"You speakee English? There is no red snapper."

"I speakee English good. Why they no had red snapper?"

"They had red snapper. But I sent it back."

"You send it back?"

"Yes!"

"What we do now?" Louie shouted.

"You change the special. That's what we do now."

Louie shook his head. "Oh, no. Chef no like that."

"Fuck the chef."

"Fuck the chef? Fuck you!"

"Fuck you!"

As Libby reached for the spigot on the coffee urn, Alfero said, "You sit in dining room. I bring coffee."

"Don't be silly. I'm right here."

"Por favor."

She knew that look. She had been in the restaurant business long enough to recognize all forms of hunger. Alfero wanted something.

Libby walked into the dining room. The overhead cleaning lights were on. She saw patches in the carpet. There were stains on the apricot leather banquettes. Scratches on the chrome. All the things you saw when looking at something in a different light.

She sat down at Phyllis and Donald's table. The best table in the house. But at nine-thirty in the morning, the best table in the house was a piece of laminated composition board on a scuffed chrome base. Darlings, she imagined herself saying at the trial. What's the big deal? It's not as though I slept with Nixon.

At first, Libby didn't recognize Alfero. He had brushed back his hair and put on a busboy's white jacket and tie. So that was what he wanted.

Alfero walked briskly to the service area for a black under-cloth, a white top and four napkins. He spread a crisp black cloth on her table and smoothed it out. He unfolded the white linen and draped it carefully on top, remembering to point the corners. He put the napkins one-quarter in from the left on each side of the table.

His hands were sweating as he positioned the black service plates, careful to lift them between parallel open palms to avoid fingerprints. Each piece of silverware was picked up between thumb and forefinger, making certain that when he put them down, the handles were on a horizontal line. He held the large crystal goblets by their stems and placed them at the two o'clock position. Butter plates at ten o'clock. Butter knives horizontally from ten to two. In the center of the table, a cut glass vase with a fresh white rose. An oblong frosted glass ashtray. Two cut crystal cellars filled with freshly ground salt and pepper. Alfero stepped back and stared at the table. He adjusted a glass, then looked up at Libby.

She was smiling. Libby had found her replacement for Chickie. "Hey, busboy!"

"Yes, ma'am?"

"Didn't you say something about a cup of coffee?"

Like an animal just released from his cage, Alfero strutted back and forth in front of the table. Once. Twice. Three times. Then, turning quickly, he tangoed down the aisle to the coffee machine. He held the cup and saucer above his head as though offering the bull's ear to a cheering crowd.

o

The kitchen was beginning to heat up. Cauldrons of whole chickens boiling on the stove. Veal bones browning in the oven. Onions simmering in large pots. The staccato of chopping and mincing had segued into the sizzle and hiss of sauté pans, the whirring of food processors, the splashing of water.

Cham was stuffing lobster hash into shells brushed with Pernod. One prep man wrapped slices of sugar-cured bacon around oysters, while another pre-portioned sausage and lentils for salad. Liang sculpted the salmon tartare with his hands. Gan added saffron to the Georgia peach chutney. Ho kept one eye on a smoking bed of charcoal while he pounded chicken breasts for the paillard.

The moment Bud walked into the kitchen, Louie shouted, "Sonny send back red snapper! Only one fish special. What we do?"

Bud looked over at Sonny. He spoke in Louie's dialect. "We put Sonny balls on menu!"

Louie stared at him blankly, then doubled over with laughter. "No enough for one portion." He immediately translated for the others.

Sonny handed the inventory to Bud. "You better find yourself another special."

Bud scanned the pages. "Why the hell does this keep happening?"

"It's called quality control."

Bud looked up. "It's called having lousy suppliers."

"Listen, chef," Sonny said, pronouncing 'chef' as though it were a dirty word. "The food may taste like shit by the time you get through with it, but either it comes in right or it doesn't come in." Both men stared at one another. "That's the way I run this restaurant."

"Fuck you," Bud said.

"Fuck you."

Bud flipped the pages on the clipboard. He hated to improvise. Professional chefing was, for him, the art of re-creation. He liked to cook because there were rules to follow. The routine itself was satisfying. Very much like sex. Sauces thickened and egg whites peaked as predictably as his own orgasms.

Finally, Bud saw just what he wanted. The most expensive item on the inventory. Truffles.

○

Special Agent Harmon sat in the gray Plymouth across from Libby's. He was thinking how much he missed San Antonio. Davis, his partner, had gone for coffee. Like the other rookies on surveillance, it was Harmon's first time away from home. After three years in a Secret Service field office investigating counterfeiters and government check forgers, he was reassigned to the New York Protective Detail, a/k/a Birnbaum University. He hated New York. He had never seen such a filthy place. Or so many crazy people. Maybe it was Fun City for the gorillas in the FBI, but not for Special Agent Craig Harmon.

Even though Harmon had majored in art history, he was as representative of the Service as were men recruited from other law enforcement agencies. They were all college graduates. They were well-spoken and well-mannered enough to exchange pleasantries with political leaders throughout the world. They had the rugged good looks that could appear as readily on a campaign poster as on a running board. An unstated prerequisite for the job. You couldn't have the President of the United States surrounded by a crew of mean-looking thugs with cauliflower ears.

It was the company they kept that most clearly distinguished the men in the Service. There were lots of educated cops and sophisticated FBI agents, but they worked in worlds populated by criminals. They had access to graft at every turn. Compromise was a private decision. It could be hidden. They could get away with it. Not so with Special Agents on protective duty. There were no gains to be pocketed. Most importantly, there were no small losses. Everything made headlines.

Harmon saw Libby come out the front door and run up the block. "Harmon to Leader. Harmon to Leader. Subject is leaving premises. Should I pursue? Repeat. Should I pursue?"

"Good morning, Harmon. This is God."

"I can't maintain surveillance. She's getting away!"

"Calm down, Harmon," Birnbaum said. "The subject is obviously a jogger. No one gets away in a shocking pink sweatsuit."

"How do you know what she's wearing?"

"You question the word of Yahweh? Harmon, you schmuck, I'm on the roof across the street. There she goes. Just as I thought. She's heading along Sixth to the park."

Harmon's voice grew impatient. "Should I follow in the car?"

"Are you crazy?" Birnbaum asked. "And give up a parking space?"

o

The kitchen was hot. All the ovens were going. Bourbon baked beans with sun-dried tomatoes. Chunks of beef braised with red onion rings and papaya. Pork chops basted with beer. Breasts of pheasant coated with fresh cranberries. Wild turkey goulash bubbling furiously next to the sedate simmer of a catfish bisque. And then there were the puff pastry cases for Bud's new special— Truffle Pot Pie.

Oblivious to it all, Bud leaned over the counter and stared at a truffle. He looked deep into it, as a gypsy would into a crystal ball. "Louie, what do you think?"

Louie shook his head. "I think I never hear of Truffle Pot Pie, boss."

Bud smiled. "This is going to make me, Louie."

"Yes, boss. Make you what?"

"All you need is one dish. And this is it. It's what they call high concept. This little sucker is going to be my Pêche Melba."

"Yes, boss." Louie looked up at the clock. "You got recipe yet?"

"No."

Louie shook his head and giggled. "I like you, boss."

Bud picked up the truffle and sniffed it. He imagined the scent of damp, cold earth in his nostrils before inhaling the pungent aroma. Like overdressed women, truffles often had more aroma than taste.

"I have excellent idea, boss. Nice cream chicken sauce. Many different veggies. Strips of ham."

"No." Bud shook his head. "Too many colors."

"Okay. You right. We use potato, onion, white turnip . . ."

"Louie, check the dumplings."

"Excellent idea."

Bud cut a slice from the center of the truffle. Dark brown, nearly black, marbled with thin white strands. A polished sliver from a culinary geode. Very slowly, he bit into it. Poised for that first instant of taste, Bud anticipated a moment of inspiration. But just then the waiters came in.

"What is he eating?" Maxie asked. "A prune?"

"You never heard of the Galloping Gourmet? Why do you think he was galloping?" Norm looked at Maxie. Maxie wasn't smiling. "What's the matter? You don't think that's funny?"

"I don't like prune jokes."

"You said prune. I didn't say prune."

"I said prune because it looked like a prune."

"You should have said cherry. If you don't like prunes, you should have said, 'What is he eating? A cherry?' "

"But cherries are red!" Maxie shouted.

"No, putz! Roses are red! Roses are red, violets are blue, I hope it's a prune and he shits on you."

"Fuck you," Maxie said.

"Fuck you," said Norm.

George, who waited Station One, sat at the bar. "Bunions. Bunions are the worst." He was talking to the bartender but his eyes were on Chickie. "Jesus H. Christ! Did you see where he put the butter plates?"

"You want some ginger ale?"

George shook his head. Chickie, the preppy Puerto Rican busboy, was driving him crazy. "You know what he listens to on his Walkman? Mantovani! He told me he has every Mantovani tape ever made. Now maybe Henry Mancini has every

Mantovani tape ever made, but a P.R.?'' Even while sipping his drink, George watched Chickie. "You see that? Do you see where he put the pepper?"

"You're a real Type A, George. You gotta learn to be more laid back."

"Let me tell you something," George said as his face grew red. "Good waiters aren't laid back. They don't come from California. They're not tan and skinny. They're like me. They got foot problems. Lousy landlords. Ugly wives. You heard of *Hollywood Wives?* Well, if Jackie Schmackie was gonna write a book about waiters, she would call it *Ugly Wives.* Oh, no! What is that sonofabitch doing now?'' George rushed toward Table 12. "Yoo hoo, Señor Ebb Tide!"

Steven was at a table in the back. He had two telephones. A folder of notes. Seating charts. The reservations book. A memory for names and faces. A head filled with gossip. A total lack of perspective that made every detail as vital as every breath. The tools of his trade.

Steven tapped his pencil on the open pages of the leather-bound book. He fingered the seating chart, as complex a piece of navigation as any planned by NASA. Libby's was not a restaurant in which customers were seated here or there in order to balance the waiters' stations. Steven "blocked the room" as though he were hanging pictures in a gallery. The prettiest ones always went up front. Two landscapes were never hung next to one another. Colors that clashed had to be kept at a safe distance. No matter that the front tables were too drafty or too close to the bar. That's where everyone wanted to be. Amateurs to the rear. Next to each name, with great relish, he wrote either WD for "window dressing" or BD for "bury the dead." For most of Libby's clientele, being buried was far worse than being dead.

The names entered first on the chart were the regulars. They were the people who regarded Libby's as a club. They called in only when they wouldn't be using their tables.

Next came the celebs. They were given maximum visibility —not merely because they wanted it, but to reassure the regulars they had rented space in the right neighborhood. Then, the worker bees were scribbled in, the people in the business of show business. Agents, editors, managers, producers, lawyers. Soldiers of fortune. Mercenaries who traded flags as easily as business cards. Recognized only by one another, they traveled in closed caravans to and from readings, rehearsals, screenings, openings, closings, and memorials. Last, and definitely least, were the great unwashed—those who came to Libby's for no reason other than to eat. With nothing but food on their minds, they were the Third World of the restaurant scene. People who lunched on the left side of the brain.

○

The waiters were never late for the eleven o'clock meeting. Not because they were prompt or cooperative, but because they had no place else to go. Hanging around the kitchen was strictly forbidden.

Maxie the waiter had a cold. It was a Health Department violation for an employee to report to work with a cold. But Maxie, who knew to the penny how much in tips were at stake, used his wife's makeup to camouflage the reddened corners of his nose. Norm leaned over to him. "Listen, if you have to sneeze, I know a way to stop it."

"You do?"

Norm whispered into Maxie's good ear. "If you think you're going to sneeze, put a finger up each nostril, stick your thumb in your mouth, and fart."

"I hate fart jokes."

"You don't like fart jokes and you don't like prune jokes! So what do you like?"

The busboys, whispering softly, entered the room in single file. As always, Victor and Paul, the bartenders, sat by themselves. Bud, in his kitchen whites, leaned against the wall.

Steven looked up, avoiding Chickie, and opened his folder. "Good morning."

Ursula, the expediter, rushed from the kitchen holding a container of yogurt. During service, waiters gave her their orders and she gave them to the cooks. It was her job to see that the waiters got their orders without having any contact with the cook staff. A woman of Wagnerian proportions, Ursula was the ultimate buffer zone. "Sorry," she said, with her mouth full. "I didn't have any breakfast."

Simon, a waiter, looked up from his racing form. "They must have run out of Elephant McMuffins."

"All right," Steven said. "Let's get going." He picked up the first sheet. "We're eighty-sixing the smoked salmon soup and the curried mussels. Instead, we have catfish bisque again and grilled oysters wrapped in bacon. Same price. I'm out of the '80 Chianti. Until the wine list is reprinted, give them the '78 at the same price. It's a better wine anyway. But don't forget the Côte du Rhône. It's not moving. Let's give it a little nudge, shall we?" He sighed and picked up the next sheet. "The specials for today are . . ." He paused while the waiters got out their pads. "Grilled duck thighs stuffed with mustard fruits . . ."

"Jesus."

"Sounds sexy."

"What the hell is a mustard fruit?"

"A guy who's queer for Gulden's."

"I didn't know ducks had thighs."

"Of course they got thighs. How else do they keep up their stockings?"

Steven turned to Bud. "Chef?"

Bud hated the waiters. They were the enemy. Trained seals who performed just to be thrown tips. "We use pickled melon rind, small seedless grapes, candied cherries, and lemon peel in a mustard caramel sauce."

"Oy vay."

"You think it's right to stuff that into the thigh of some poor dead duck?"

"How much?"

"Sixteen-fifty." Steven continued. "The next special is coconut chili. Same price. We all know what that is."

"We sure do."

"I'll have the duck thighs."

"You already have duck thighs."

"And the third special," Steven said, "is red snapper."

Bud raised his hand. "We had to send the fish back."

"Again?" Steven asked. "That's been happening a hell of a lot lately."

"Speak to Sonny."

Steven raised his eyebrows. "Do we have a third special?"

Bud nodded. "Yes. I fill a puff pastry case with sautéed mushrooms, a slice of fresh foie gras, and diced sweetbreads in a champagne cream sauce. On top of that, I put one whole black truffle that has been wrapped in prosciutto and baked. And then I cover it with a pastry lid."

There was a long silence. One of the waiters asked, "No four and twenty blackbirds?"

Steven smiled. "What is this epic called?"

Bud cleared his throat. "It is called Truffle Pot Pie."

Simon threw down his racing form. "Goddamn it! How do you expect us to sell that?"

"Listen, I didn't say a word about the stupid duck thighs," Stu shouted. "But Truffle Pot Pie? Come on! Gimme a break! Do you call that food?"

"We don't sell food here!" Libby was back from running. Her cheeks were still flushed as she came into the dining room. "This is a restaurant! We sell lunch and we sell dinner. We sell dreams. You wake them up, Simon, they leave. They find another opium den down the block. You want to sell food, get a job at the A&P."

Simon raised his hands. "I thought I was a waiter. I didn't know I was supposed to be the Sandman."

"Like I said, maybe you're in the wrong business."

"You don't have to take it so personal," Simon offered.

"I take everything personally. The name of this pit stop is Libby's. Anything you don't like about Libby's, you don't like about me."

Simon became nervous. "I just asked a question. Whatever happened to the free speech?"

"The same thing that happened to the free the lunch. Priced out of sight." She glanced at Steven. "It costs too damn much to tell the truth these days."

o

It was High Noon. It was time to turn up the air conditioning and lower the lights. The waiters, in short black jackets with black ties and white trousers, stopped talking and took their stations. The busboys, in white vests and white trousers, put away their decks of cards.

As usual, Janos Vatsl was first through the front door. Janos left Prague in 1958, deserting his grandparents, his parents, his brothers and sisters, his wife, and his sons. Twenty-five years later he was a billionaire. At sixty, he had tightly curled white hair, a white moustache, a trim physique, and a new young wife who he made certain appeared nude in as many magazines as possible.

"Handsome boychik, these are for you." Janos handed Steven a box of ties from Missoni. "Rome was so cheap. You could buy the whole city for nothing." Janos groaned and put a hand to his stomach. "Oh, do I gotta go!" He walked quickly toward the men's room.

"*Ciao, caro.*" Rikki Lee, the twenty-two-year-old Mrs. Vatsl, wore tight denim jeans, a tight white silk T-shirt and a tight denim jacket studded with rhinestones. Her long blond hair was hidden under a matching ten-gallon hat.

Steven kissed the air near her cheek. "Thanks for the ties."

"Forget it, sweetie. They were practically giving Rome away."

Steven led her down the aisle to Table 43. The worst table in the house. Next to the men's room. At the entrance to the kitchen. But Janos had a twenty-four-carat behind that left its own stamp of approval. The game of life, for Janos, was using his power and money to make the worst table into the best.

"Bring me a Coke, sweetie," Rikki said. "There wasn't a goddamn thing to drink in the limo."

Fay Fox was next. Without waiting to be escorted, she went to her table. Fay waved hello to Rikki, pointed to her cowboy hat, and then rolled her eyes at Steven. "Where were they? Graceland?"

"Rome."

Fay nodded and made a note of it. She picked up her phone and dialed. "Who's on the menu today, darlin'?"

"Jim Garner, Marlo Thomas, John Irving, Adolph Green . . ."

Fay winked and spoke into the receiver. "This is Dr. Keith's nurse," she said. "He wants a report on the condition of one of his patients. Moina Hayle. Sure will." She pointed a finger at Steven and smiled. "If you tell Hots I know about Moina, I'll scream cockroach during lunch. Hello?" Fay stopped smiling. "Well, of course, he knows about the biopsy." She was barely able to control her shock. "But he is still waiting for a prognosis." Fay sat back in her seat listening without saying a word. She hung up. "That no-good skunk," she said, staring at Moina's empty table. "I thought she went in for a face job."

Even though Phyllis and Donald ate lunch at Libby's every day, and even though Phyllis had known Steven since he was a little boy, and even though Donald was Steven's lover, Mr. and Mrs. Elgin waited for the maître d' to seat them.

"When you're haute, you're haute," Steven said, complimenting Phyllis on her dress.

"You don't think it's too Art Drecko?"

"Not at all. It's very Spider Woman."

Phyllis put a hand on his shoulder. "Thank God Libby taught you to be a good liar. It is so important in life."

Donald winked at him. "Forget plastics."

Steven led them down the aisle. "Well, here's the story so far. Rikki and Janos were in Rome. Everything was very cheap." Steven angled the table so that Phyllis could slide in. "It seems," he whispered, "that all is not well in Moinaland. But you didn't hear it from me."

As Steven seated him, Donald said, "That suit looks good on you."

"This old thing?"

Donald gave him a dirty look. "We'll have the usual." He waited until he was alone with Phyllis. "Darling, we've always been honest with one another."

"Lincoln could take lessons."

"I must talk to you," he said.

"Uh oh. I feel a wrong coming on."

"It's not you, my love. God knows we have a perfect marriage."

She leaned close. "Is it Steven?"

Donald nodded. "Yes." He spoke softly. "I hate saying this

about your best friend's son, but he's become such a tiresome little shit."

"Dear God." She put her hand on his. "You don't think he said anything to Libby?"

"No. Not as long as he wants money from me."

"We really must find you someone else, Donald." She kissed his cheek. "You still expect all your young men to love you. If only you weren't such a hopeless romantic."

Donald held her hand gently. He smiled. "It's your fault, darling. You've spoiled me."

○

The phone began ringing at Table 104 the moment Hots walked through the door. "They must smell me coming!" He rushed past Steven to answer it. "Hello?" He looked over at the waiter and motioned for something to drink.

It was Fay calling from across the room. "Would you mind telling me just what's goin' on with Moina?"

Hots looked over at her. "Jesus."

"How did she get in and out of Sloan-Kettering so fast?"

"Who the hell told you?"

"Stop stalling, Hots. I've hated Moina's guts for years. She is very important to me." She was six-figures important. Fay had just sold her unauthorized biography of Moina to Doubleday.

Janos came out of the men's room clutching a fistful of toilet paper. He was furious. Rikki narrowed her eyes. "Johnny, don't start."

"How many times have I told them about this lousy toilet paper?"

Rikki put her hands over her ears. "Johnny, please. I don't want to hear about your craps."

Janos shook his head as he picked up the phone and dialed. "You'd think with an ass like yours you'd understand." He raised his eyebrows and announced himself into the receiver. "Vatsl."

Rikki took her hands from her head. "Be nice, Johnny."

"I sign the checks. I don't have to be nice." He spoke into the receiver. "Barry? Here is the deal on the picture. My money. My director. My costar. You understand, Barry? You're going to distribute *The Last Cowboy* my way. It's going to play the houses for more than three days. I don't want her laughed at anymore. Rikki is going to be a star. I'm through flushing my wife down the toilet."

Andre smiled and raised a glass of Bernkasteler Schlossberg Spätlese '83. "Well, then, Junior, I'd say we have a deal."

Junior was Mac Singer, the "No-Good Son" of movie mogul Edgar F. Singer. In the three years since he had unseated Senior as head of the studio, Junior had been unseated as well. He was out in the cold as an independent producer and he was desperate to make a deal.

Andre had been working Junior since the night before, massaging his five-hundred-G-spot for start-up money. Stunned by the PBS decision to pass on Grandma Moses, Andre immediately called the Pritikin Center to tell them he'd be a day late. Then he found out where the A-Group was gathering. Within half an hour, he had been invited to Gloria's party and met Junior. It was going to be his fastest turnaround ever.

Andre made a toast. "To Anna Mary Robertson Moses!"

Junior glanced across the room to check that Senior was watching before he raised his glass. "To hell with her!"

Andre's stomach turned over.

"This toast is for Sissy or Goldie," Junior said.

Andre sighed with relief. "Take no prisoners!"

"I want a young Grandma Moses. At the height of her sexuality. Nobody needs a movie about some old bag with a paintbrush."

Andre smiled and shook a finger at Junior. "You know, you son of a bitch, you just may be redefining 'auteur' as the producer rather than the director."

Junior nodded. It sounded like a compliment. But with Andre who could tell? The real question was what to do next. There was still plenty of time to pull out of the deal. He kept wondering what Senior would do.

o

The New York field office of the United States Secret Service was located at 6 World Trade Center. And, as far as Birnbaum was concerned, it was the only secure place in the city. Not merely physically secure. It was emotionally secure. It was a club. It was the most private club in the world because the membership fee was private parts. You didn't get in without balls. You didn't stay in without balls. And balls, unlike happiness, were things money couldn't buy. They came as standard equipment or they didn't come at all.

The Secret Service was an elite corps. Gladiators. That was the image Birnbaum liked best. But who the hell ever heard of a Jewish gladiator?

Anders Kane, head of the White House Presidential Protective Detail, sat down next to Birnbaum and said, "I've had complaints."

"You've had complaints?"

"Yes." Anders slapped the file angrily on the desk. "These are the complaints."

Birnbaum opened the file and glanced quickly at the pages. Meehan, Gordon, Conaway, and Harmon had all made formal statements. He couldn't resist. He looked up at Anders and slowly, with as much amazement as he could squeeze into his voice, he asked, "These . . . are . . . the . . . complaints?"

"Since I do not speak Yiddish," Anders said, "would you be kind enough to translate your response?"

Birnbaum didn't like Anders but he understood him. Premenopausal Hitler Youth. Brainwashed by mayonnaise. "I was not speaking Yiddish. I was speaking New York. If I had hit myself in the head while I was saying it, I would have been speaking Yiddish."

"What the fuck did you send these guys up to the Bronx for? To Brooklyn? For what?"

Birnbaum smiled. "That's right! You got it. Now all you have to do is hit yourself in the head and call me a schmuck. I guarantee you'll have a reformed congregation in Westchester by the end of the week." Birnbaum stopped smiling. "You send me four kids trained to catch old ladies who forge Medicaid checks. You expect them to be responsible for the life of the President of the United States? The most danger they've ever been in is coming late for the movies. You bet your ass I'm going to subject them to 'excessive hardship without sufficient cause.' What the hell do they think this job is?"

Had anyone else said that, Anders would have agreed. But Birnbaum couldn't be trusted. Birnbaum had never requested a transfer to Washington. That's what Anders didn't trust. If you were in the movie business, you wanted to be in LA, publishing meant New York, the Secret Service was the White House. That's where the power was in his business. The Vice President might be only a heartbeat from the presidency, but Anders Kane was even closer. He was a heartbeat from the President. He respected power and was suspicious of men who didn't.

"I don't see any reason to have authorized all-night surveillance. I'm not worried about any of these people."

"It's *our* people I was worried about."

Anders looked through the file. "Dishwasher, coat check, chef, maître d'. Why those four?"

"I had the IRS in Albany pull the file on the restaurant and give me the names of all employees. I ran the list through the FBI, INS, and National Crime Index. I got four hits. The dishwasher is an illegal alien. The coat check girl was arrested three times for disorderly conduct at anti-Administration protests. The chef was a draft dodger readmitted during amnesty. And the maître d' was picked up twice for homosexual solicitation."

"Doesn't sound to me like any of them are up for the Hinckley Award."

"I told you, I wasn't worried about those four," Birnbaum said. "I was worried about our four."

"And so now, after one night in the Bronx, Meehan's ready for a seat in the point car?"

Birnbaum nodded slowly. He shook a finger at Anders. "You know, you're getting there. You're going to make one helluva rabbi."

Anders smiled grudgingly. "I suppose it was better than paying for them to jerk off in their hotel rooms. Get rid of the dishwasher and the girl. I don't want them near the place on Thursday. I don't see any problem with the chef or the maître d'."

"Unless he makes a pass at the President."

o

The key to people-watching in a restaurant was to keep an eye on the maître d'. But no one needed an advance man to spot Ashanti Kama. She was her own brass band. Ashanti's appearance in a cosmetics ad or fashion layout netted her an outrageous $5,000 a day, $10,000 minimum. Six feet tall, with skin the color of a Stradivarius, she was the most ravishing woman to leave Africa since Cleopatra. At thirty-eight, Ashanti still refused to wear makeup or underwear.

On seeing Junior, she stopped dead in the aisle. "Steven," she gasped. "I thought it was illegal to expose a prick in public."

Junior stood up. "I've been thinking about you."

"You'll get hair on your palms." She glanced at Andre. "What happened? You look pregnant!"

"Junior and I have just made a deal."

Ashanti rolled her eyes. "Well, I may not know nothin' 'bout birthin' babies, but I sure do know you been fucked."

Junior leaned close to her. "When can we get together?"

She whispered, "When I run out of bananas." Ashanti loped over to Hots's table.

"So how was the shoot?" he asked. "Tell me what happened."

"What could happen?" She shrugged, sitting down. "Everyone in LA is bisexual. They like men and they like boys."

Hots smiled. "Not Junior."

"I was never alone with the guy long enough to find out. In New York, two people can still go to a restaurant or to the movies. Out there, you play fill-the-limo. Hotsy, I've got to be by myself for a while. Totally alone. That's why I've decided to marry Bill Perry."

"But he's already married."

"I didn't say the wedding was tomorrow."

"The divorce can't even be tomorrow," Hots said.

Ashanti leaned toward Hots. "Old models never die, they just get poor. I need someone to take care of me. Especially now. I've been calling Moina all morning. They said she checked out."

The phone rang. Hots picked it up. "Yeah?"

It was Fay calling again from across the room. "Let me speak to Ashanti. She must know all about Moina."

Hots hung up.

"Your table is ready, Miss Borden." Steven led the slender woman down the aisle.

"Is Mr. Sessions here?" she asked.

"No."

"Where's Libby?"

Steven shrugged. "Missing in action."

Mary Borden, at forty-five, was the most powerful agent in publishing. When she left messages, she was called back immediately. When she sent a manuscript, it was moved to the top of the pile. When she asked for best offers, she got them. Mary was one of the few people in the industry who were above reproach. Not because she refused to peddle garbage. She refused to mislabel it. Mary was compulsively, transparently honest. She found passion in pragmatism, strength in truth.

Mary stopped at Junior's table. "I've got a book for you. *Before Dawn.* World War II. Behind enemy lines. Good Germans versus Bad Germans. Right up your alley."

"I'd love to see it," Junior said.

Andre began to cough. The last thing he needed was some other project to blow his deal. It had taken all night to get Junior on the launching pad and then Typhoid Mary had to show up.

Janos waved Fay over. He nudged Rikki. "You let me do the talking." Rikki folded her arms and stared angrily at the ceiling.

Fay smiled the moment she saw Rikki's expression. "Darlin', you look like you're goin' to cry."

Rikki stared into space. "Rikki Lee is not here. She is gone. I have no idea when she will return."

Janos patted the empty seat next to him. "Fay darling, tell me something." As she sat down, he asked, "Who needs money?"

Fay began to laugh. "Who doesn't?"

"I want a big star. She can't carry this picture herself."

Fay nodded. As though Rikki could carry any picture aside from an eight-by-ten glossy. "Let me chew on it, sweetie."

"Oh, Johnny," Rikki squealed. "There he is! There's our last cowboy!"

Everyone turned. It was Cal.

Mary leaned over and kissed Edgar F. Singer on the cheek. "I've got something for you, Senior. Right up your alley."

He motioned toward Junior's table. "The last thing that was up my alley is sitting over there. Have you met Wanda?"

Mary extended her hand but Wanda was busy with her soup spoon.

"She was one of the hostages," Senior said. "I'm thinking of using her in *Dorothy—The Woman.*" He smiled at her. "It's a pleasure to see a broad eat these days."

"I've got a book for you," Mary said. "World War II. Behind enemy lines. Good Germans versus Bad Germans."

"The only good German is a poor German. Besides, I've had enough war movies. *Mrs. Miniver. The White Cliffs of Dover. To Each His Own.* How much can the public take?"

Mary patted his hand. "You can't blame me for trying."

"You're not the only one. Some computer nudnik is ready to bankroll a picture called *December Seventh.* He figures it's the only way to stop people from buying Japanese." He turned to Wanda. "Don't worry, darling. Libby will know how to get the soup off your blouse."

Janos had sent Rikki on an errand. Ordinarily, she would have protested, but she wanted him to make a deal with Cal.

"You know how much money I have?" Janos asked.

"No," Cal said.

"So guess."

"I can't guess."

Janos smiled. "I have six billion dollars." Janos didn't like to ask for anything. And so before he asked, he had to establish that asking was a mere formality.

Cal looked Janos straight in the eye. "You know how big my cock is?"

"No."

"So guess!"

Janos laughed. He brought out his copy of *High Life*. "You see the new pictures?"

Cal lied. "No."

Janos opened to a nude photo of Rikki with a chinchilla coat draped over her shoulders. "Did you ever see tits like that?" Janos licked his finger quickly and turned the page. "Look at that ass and tell me you don't believe in God." He closed the magazine and flung it on the table in front of Cal. "I'll tell you something only a few people know. Rikki is a very rich woman. I made investments for her. She has five million of her own. So, Mr. Big Cock, she doesn't stay with me for my money."

Cal picked up the magazine. He was hardly in a bargaining position. They had taken the picture away from him. And all his agent could come up with was *The Desert Song*. Not that he couldn't have found a better picture. But it wasn't enough anymore to get a better picture. You had to get the right picture at the right price. For the moment, there were no right pictures. The only solution was the wrong picture at an extraordinary price. From what Fay had told him, Janos was willing to pay. The smart thing would be to take the money and run. But as desperate as Cal was, he had to run before he took the money. He threw the magazine across the table. "Why the hell do you make Rikki do this kind of crap?"

"I know you're angry with me for being late." John Sessions sat down opposite Mary. She said nothing and handed him a menu. "I couldn't help it. I couldn't get it together this morning. After you left, I watched Donahue. I was really enjoying myself, too, until I got depressed because I was watching Donahue and really enjoying myself. You think I'm a wimp for taping Donahue, don't you? Never mind. You don't have to answer. I can hear you. I heard you while I was watching. I heard you louder than the caller from Detroit. Either watch Donahue and enjoy it or turn it off! Then that despairing half laugh of yours. It's so simple for you. Black. White. Right. Wrong. I lunch, therefore, I am. Not so with writers, Madame de la Ten Percent. With writers it is, I lunch, but why? Why the fuck don't you say something and shut me up?"

Mary stared at the menu thinking how much it reminded her of John. There was nothing on it she wanted.

"What excites you?" he asked.

"Nothing."

"No," he said, pretending she had misunderstood him. "I mean on the menu."

"John . . ."

"But as long as you brought it up, what is it about me that excites you? Just what is it that's kept us together from one Joyce Carol Oates book to the next? Admittedly, not a long time. But long enough. Surely not the doggie position alone?"

"John, I invited you to lunch to talk business."

Al, the waiter, smiled at Mary. "Would you like something to drink, Miss Borden?"

Mary answered before John could say anything. "Two Perriers, please."

"And I'll have two scotches." He smiled. "Chivas. Neat." After the waiter left, John said, "Something must have happened to make me deductible."

"Abner likes *Before Dawn*."

John sat back. "You didn't tell me you sent it to Abner. He really liked it?" Then sharply, "Answer me!"

Mary stared at John. She nodded. With success came the end of the rhetorical question. John had crossed the threshold. She was about to close the deal on his first novel, thereby shutting the door on their personal relationship. There was no one she hated more than a successful author. Aspiring, struggling, frustrated, wretched—that's when writers were wonderful. It was the only time they were powerless.

"When are you going to speak to him again?"

"Tomorrow. At lunch."

"He really liked the book?"

"He loved the book."

"How much?"

"I think I can get him up to forty thousand."

"Forty thousand?"

"With a guaranteed ad campaign." She smiled. "And an author tour."

"I'm going to go on tour?"

"Yes."

John was ecstatic. "My God! You know what this means?"

"Yes." Mary leaned forward. "I want you out of my apartment by the end of the week."

Hots never looked at a menu. He had the same thing for lunch every day. A small can of Bumble Bee tuna fish. A dollop of mayonnaise. Some iceberg lettuce. A single thick center slice of tomato. A cup of Lipton tea. Just like his mother used to make.

". . . and the truffle," recited Norm, "is wrapped in prosciutto . . ."

"Oh, my God," Ashanti moaned. "To die!"

". . . and cooked in a champagne cream sauce."

She slapped Hots. "Are you listening? I want you to take all this down. This is exactly how I want to be buried." She turned to the waiter. "Be sure to tell them it's for me. But first I want some jalapeño pasta. Tell them to make it spicy. Tell them I want my insides to sizzle. Oh, where is Libby? She knows how I like it. But before you bring the pasta, be a good boy and get me a nice glass of champagne."

"Yes, Miss Kama."

"And maybe some shrimp while I'm waiting." Ashanti put a hand to her stomach. "Hurry up! Haven't you heard about the starving Africans?"

Fay sat down next to Hots. "Okay. Now listen up. I'm not leavin' here till you tell me about Moina."

"Off the record?" Hots asked.

"No deals." Fay was serious. She was three-quarters finished with Moina's book. "I want to know what she was doin' at the hospital."

Ashanti rolled her eyes. "How did Bertha Bigmouth find out?"

"So you know about it," Fay said.

"Of course I know about it," Ashanti answered. "Who the hell do you think found the lump?"

o

Birnbaum and Anders had moved into the conference room. Now that "the White House" had arrived, Birnbaum was no longer in charge. It was time for the official transfer of power. It was Anders's show and he wasn't going to play it in Birnbaum's office.

Anders sat at the head of the table as though the chair had his name on it. He opened his file and took out a copy of the memo on New York Comet. Comet was the Service's code name for the President. "We discussed all the points you raised," Anders said, "but I want him to land at Newark. Not Kennedy. I don't like anything with the name Kennedy."

Birnbaum smiled. "That's the reason for Newark?" He knew there was nothing more to be said on the matter. But at least he had ended with a question.

"The President will congratulate the customs inspectors vis-à-vis the recent drug arrests. I want him on his merry way before the FBI has time to get insulted because they weren't invited."

Birnbaum shook his head. "You've got him greeted by the Governor of New Jersey, then going to Customs, then a press conference . . ."

"We've already staffed it out. I'm here to liaise, not network. You can't handle it, I'll call in the Girl Scouts."

"You think I can't handle it?" Birnbaum asked with a smile, quickly opening his folder. He relished the look of disgust on Anders's face before clearing his throat and getting down to business. "I spoke to the Commissioner, then to Captain Metzenberg of Midtown. We'll get a tactical plan in the morning. He's requisitioning men from adjacent precincts. I estimate he'll need a couple of thousand to cover the route from the heliport to the UN and up to Fifty-fifth."

"Let Metzenberg do the estimating," Anders said. "The streets will be closed fifteen minutes prior?"

Birnbaum shrugged. "I asked for fifteen. Metzenberg said five. We compromised on ten."

"No compromises," Anders said. "Nothing is negotiable."

"Listen, you close a street in New York for fifteen minutes and you'll have every son of a bitch out there trying to kill the President. And I don't think you'd find a judge downtown who would even ask bail."

"I want the streets closed for a full fifteen minutes," Anders said. "I want to drive the route five or six times myself. I want minesweepers and mounties. I want choppers following me. I want videocams in the choppers feeding into the Command Van. I want open communication with all mobile units. I am personally going to work the man from the fucking UN to that fucking restaurant and I need fifteen minutes' advance to do it in."

"You got it."

Anders looked at the next item on his checklist. "Fire."

"Agnello will have trucks on either side of the restaurant. Men will be on adjoining roofs all hosed up."

"Inspection of the premises?"

"Tomorrow morning. I'll be there."

"Health?"

"Same time."

"Hospitals?"

"Beekman Downtown for the heliport area. University for the UN and along First Avenue. Roosevelt while he's at the restaurant. I've spoken to all three administrators. We have chiefs of staff, heads of surgery, live donors, plasma, suites, and situation rooms at each location. They've all been given work-ups on the President."

"You've gone through the nut box?"

"Protective Intelligence interviewed all the lookouts even if they haven't made any threats against the President this year. We locked up four of them. The others were too incoherent to swat a fly."

Anders nodded. "White House Communications is arranging for phone lines. I need a radio setup and a holding room for staff. I want the explosives unit and the bomb dogs in as soon as possible. What about the site?"

"Surrounding area shouldn't be difficult to control," Birnbaum said. "I've checked out each roof myself. Fifty men should secure the block."

"I need portable generators for emergency lighting."

"Con Ed will send some tomorrow."

Anders sat back. "You call the FDA?"

"They're coming, but they said they don't provide tasters."

Anders shook his head. "You met this Libby?"

"Yes."

"She worth it?"

"Worth what?"

"Dying for." Anders leaned across the desk toward Birnbaum and smiled. "That's the business we're in."

o

Phyllis poked disconsolately at her Southern fried chicken salad. "Chickens," she muttered. "Here, chick-chick."

Donald looked up from his Truffle Pot Pie. "What did you say?"

Phyllis put down her fork. She sat back. "Donald, I'm out of my mind with anxiety. I've never made as much money. I've got more clothes than Princess Di. Not to mention the most wonderful husband in the entire world."

"But?"

She smiled. "I don't think this Bud's for me."

"You'll pardon *moi,* but I never understood your infatuation with someone who cooks the dead."

"I feel like such a failure."

Donald took her hand. "I don't want to hear that kind of talk, Phyllis. Not from a ballbuster like you. Goddamn it, I thought he'd at least give you a decent fuck."

"So did I. But, Donald, he's become the Evelyn Wood of sex!"

"Darling, you mustn't get upset."

"Perhaps it's my fault. I can't seem to do anything right."

"Don't be ridiculous. There's nothing you can't do. Surely you haven't forgotten the night on Rainier's yacht. For God's sake, Phyllis, you nearly gave me an erection!"

"Oh, Donald, is it any wonder I love you?"

He took a glass of Latour '66 and brought it to Phyllis's lips. She sighed and took a sip. He lit a cigarette and handed it to her. "Now tell Donald everything that happened. And don't leave out a single gory detail."

Rikki Lee walked into the room strutting her stuff as though stuff were going out of style. As immune to fashion and good taste as she was to talent, Rikki was a genetic triumph in the field of lust. She was the nectarine of sex. Perpetually ripe. The kindest thing to be said for Rikki, as she swung a shopping bag filled with six rolls of toilet paper from the Hotel Pierre, was that she just couldn't help it.

Cal's heart sank at the sight of her. Never had a woman been so totally unappealing. There were dozens of reasons why she offended his sensibilities, but most important was the fact that he needed her.

"Is he going to do it, Johnny?" She stared at Cal while handing Janos the shopping bag.

"What the hell took so long?" Janos opened the bag eagerly. "They didn't charge you, did they?"

"No, Johnny," she crooned, unable to take her eyes from Cal. "It's a present for your asshole." She smiled at Cal. "Do we have a deal?"

"You know when you have a deal?" Janos answered. "Not when you make a deal. You know you have a deal when he tries to get out of it and can't. That's when you know." Janos took out a roll of toilet paper and a copy of the New York *Times.* "Where the hell is Libby? I have to talk to her about the toilet paper."

Rikki winced and rolled her eyes. "Oh, Johnny. You're so disgusting. I don't want to have another discussion about your taking a crap."

Janos put a hand to his stomach. "You'll talk about whatever I want to talk about."

"Rikki Lee is not here," she said, staring ahead. "I'll give her your message when she comes back. Thank you for calling."

Janos slid out of his seat. "Listen, my darling girl, I am one of the world's richest men. I drink only the finest wines and eat only the finest food. If what goes in is the best there is, then so is what comes out!" Janos grimaced. "Oh, Jesus!" He ran toward the men's room.

Rikki sat down. Very slowly, she began peeling off her jacket. It wouldn't have mattered if the temperature had been below zero, she was determined to take off that jacket. As determined as Cal was not to be caught staring at her tight white T-shirt.

"Johnny knows there's no one who can compete with him. He knows I'd never leave him. But he likes to play little games with himself."

Cal smiled. She was a lot smarter than he thought. "Such as?"

"Such as making me do outrageous things that no other husband would stand for."

A hell of a lot smarter.

"You see my pictures in *High Life?*"

"No."

Rikki had her own copy. She opened to the centerfold, never taking her eyes from Cal. "You didn't?"

It took all his control not to look down at her T-shirt. Instead, he stared at the not nearly as satisfying nude photo. Rikki turned the pages slowly showing him other poses. Cal put his hand over the magazine.

Rikki was confused. "Don't you like these pictures?"

"No."

"Did you see me in *The Purple Woman?*"

"No."

"Sister and Brother?"

"No."

She shook the magazine angrily in front of his face. "And you don't like these pictures?"

"I'm sorry."

"Well, why the hell do you want to do a movie with me?"

Rikki probably would have accepted any answer Cal chose to give her, including the truth. But Cal knew there was one thing she wasn't prepared to hear. With a big smile on his face, he said, "Because I think you could be a very fine actress."

Dr. Loren Sawyer was a nose man. *The* nose man. Women throughout the city wore their Sawyer noses as proudly as their Hermès scarves and Vuitton satchels. Tuesday was his day to lunch with Gabriella. The king of the nooners was having a consultation with his wife. Loren's secretary was back in the office, and Room 703 at the Plaza was empty.

He ordered two kir royales, then waited for Stu to leave. "What kind of idiot do you think I am?"

Gabriella looked around the room. "Shh. I'm counting noses."

"Shh, nothing! You have a pimple!"

"I don't have a pimple."

"You've been eating chocolates again."

"You're crazy."

"I'm not crazy. I'm a doctor. I know a skin eruption when I see one."

"Loren, I cannot live like this. I cannot be victimized by your insane accusations."

"Insane, my ass. You've been eating chocolates behind my back. You little fool, don't you think I can smell them on your breath? Are you trying to ruin my career showing up here with a pimple?"

"Dear God, Loren, I'd sooner die than hurt you. Help me, darling," she whispered. "I don't know what to do anymore. This morning I waited on Fifth Avenue for Godiva to open, like an alcoholic in front of a Bowery bar. Then I went to Elizabeth Arden where I locked myself in the ladies' room and ate half a pound of walnut creams."

He shook his head and sighed. He took her hand and held it gently. Gabriella meant everything to him. "Darling," he said lovingly, "perhaps you should go back on cocaine."

"The only problem with focusing on her youth," Andre said with a mouthful of Truffle Pot Pie, "is that she didn't begin to paint until she was sixty-seven. As much as I applaud your wanting to avoid the obvious, we just *might* be missing something in a movie about Grandma Moses if she's not a grandmother and hasn't begun to paint."

Junior stabbed at his smoked trout. He couldn't get Mary's words out of his head. "I've got a book for you. World War II. Right up your alley." His father had taught him to go by the gut. Junior turned around quickly. Senior was staring at him.

"You know," Andre said, dabbing the champagne sauce from his chin, "she started everything late. She didn't even get married until she was twenty-seven which, in those days . . ."

But Junior wasn't listening to him. He was listening to his gut and his gut was screaming World War II. It was time to dump Andre.

o

The indieprods were very serious. He, despite a new diamond-drop earring, wore a pair of thick horn-rimmed glasses. She wore a dark suit and clenched an unlit cigarillo between her teeth. "It has to be *that* table," she said, pointing across the room.

The male nodded, then shrugged helplessly while staring at Carol Channing and James Clavell. "They'd never give that table to us."

"Not to us, nitwit," she said. "To Meryl. The only problem is I can't figure out who should sit where."

"Boy, girl, boy, girl."

"Listen, Sparky, even if you and I could figure out which we were, that's not the way to do it. Don't you know anything about power lunches?"

"What do I know about power, period?" he asked. "In my little life, power is not letting anyone get ahead of me on the lox line at Zabar's."

"Leapin' lizards," she gasped. "I have gone into the movie business with Ashley Wilkes! Do you want to be at the end of the lox line all your life?"

"I didn't say I couldn't learn."

"All right! Lesson Number One. What rhymes with power?"

He took off his glasses and put a hand over his eyes. Then his face brightened. "Cower!"

The female reached over and held his arm as though her fingers were taking his blood pressure. "Limo. Messenger. Opening. Extra. Immediate. Rich. Big. New."

"Producer dearest, it is no secret that the sperm bank has not been running my machine ragged with messages. I am, in the immortal words of Jerry Herman, what I am. And even though you have a mother with an American Express card and I have a mother with nothing but hot flashes, we are down for the count together."

She spit a piece of tobacco from her cigarillo onto the table. "Movies make strange bedfellows."

He looked down at the tablecloth. "I want to sit next to Meryl."

"Do you want to look at her out of the corner of your eye, or do you want to stare at her head on like a man?"

"Don't be stupid. I can't do anything like a man."

"Here's the problem, Alfalfa. The lunchor should sit in the aisle in order to control the flow of service. But with a blue-plate special like Meryl, do we want the lunchee facing into the room being distracted by admiring glances?"

"No."

"Aha! But how can you possibly seat someone in the aisle who once portrayed Nora Ephron?"

"You're right. You can't."

"But then again," she said with a smile, "whose lunch is it anyway?"

Loren, kir royale in hand, was making the kind of rounds they hadn't taught in medical school. Prior to perfecting the art of making new noses from old, Loren was a major supplier of cocaine to a clientele he euphemistically called his patients. As yet another example of the adaptability of the law of supply and demand, as well as the unlimited opportunities for members of the AMA, the more sniffs he supplied, the more demand for new noses.

He went over to Junior and put a hand on his shoulder. "Why didn't you tell me you were going to be here?" Loren asked. "I could have saved you an office visit."

Junior stood up to shake hands and whispered to Loren. "I think I have a kidney stone."

"Yuch! I'll send you to someone."

"I don't want to go to someone. I want you to check me out."

"Take my advice. Go to someone else."

"I don't want a stranger feeling me up."

"Go to someone else, Junior. Trust me. The moment you take down your pants you'll ruin our whole doctor-patient relationship." Suddenly, Loren recognized the man with whom Junior was having lunch. "Is that you?"

Andre rolled his eyes. "How the mighty have swollen."

"My God. Let me send you to a doctor."

Junior excused himself, saying he had to go to the men's room.

Andre swallowed a large piece of truffle. He forced a smile.

The lump in his throat hurt almost as much as the sudden cramp in his stomach. He knew Junior wasn't going to the men's room.

On his way across the aisle, Junior passed Senior's table. Father and son looked at one another without saying a word. Mary Borden was on her way back from Fay's table. Junior stopped her. "I've been thinking about that book. And I am interested."

"I knew you would be. I'll have a copy messengered over this afternoon. No one's seen it yet."

Junior nodded. "What can you tell me about it?"

That wasn't the way Mary operated. She had already told him the book was right up his alley. That should have been enough. It would have been enough for any self-respecting editor. But as far as Mary was concerned, self-respecting wasn't an adjective that had yet reached Hollywood. "I can tell you who I would cast as your German general." She glanced across the room at Cal.

"Thanks." As Junior approached the indieprods, he stopped and smiled. "Look who's here. Children of an even lesser God."

The male got up and whispered, "Whilst we speak, Meryl is reading the script."

"Forgive me if I don't call Liz Smith yet." Junior crossed the aisle to Cal. "I was looking for you at Gloria's party," he lied.

"I got in too late," Cal lied back. "Seems everyone was there but the Lindbergh baby."

"Listen," Junior said, still ignoring Rikki, "I have something that's right up your alley. Can we do lunch?"

"Sure."

"Tomorrow?"

"I don't know."

"You might want to bring Smitty," Junior said. Nice touch, he thought, seeing the sudden glint in Cal's eyes.

"Sure. I can make it tomorrow. But Smitty's on the coast."

Junior forced a laugh. "Good. I hate making deals with agents." Perfect, he thought. Just perfect. Junior smiled and put his hand under Rikki's chin. "Nice pictures, sweetheart."

Once in the men's room, Junior picked up the phone. He used his credit card to call his lawyer in Los Angeles. "Parker? I need to know how much Cal Dennis got for his last picture. Also, what directors he likes to work with."

"How about what he wants for Christmas?"

"You still have that lady friend at Mary's agency?"

"Don't make it sound like a covert operation. It's all on the up and up. I pay her and she steals for me."

"Make sure she doesn't send anyone *Before Dawn* for forty-eight hours. I can feel it in my gut, Parker. I've got Cal Dennis just where I want him. This is going to be my deal!"

Janos sat back in the closed stall. He shook his head. "You should live so long!" he muttered under his breath.

And inside the other stall, Andre covered his face with his hands. Jesus Christ. He was going to have to cancel Pritikin again.

o

Cal slid onto the banquette next to Phyllis. He needed time between rounds with Janos. He sat next to Phyllis not because he liked her better than Donald but because male movie stars always sat next to women. "Where the hell is Libby?"

Phyllis smiled. "I assumed she was simply too exhausted after what must have gone on last night."

"What was last night?" Cal asked.

"Darling, I thought *you* were."

Donald wondered what Cal would say about his sleeping with Steven. Suddenly, he felt a kick from Phyllis. He had been wondering too long.

"Some wine?" Phyllis pushed her glass in front of Cal. "I barely touched it." She watched closely as he brought her glass to his lips. She envied the glass. Then she felt a kick from Donald. "Tell me what you know about Chris Reeve."

"He's a good actor."

"What she really wants to know," Donald said with relish, "is why he turned down her new play."

"I'm desperate to find the right leading man," Phyllis said, imagining Cal in the part.

Donald was imagining Cal in his bed. Not that Cal was his type. But wouldn't it just kill Steven?

"What about Bill Hurt?" Cal asked.

Phyllis took hold of Cal's middle finger and squeezed hard. "I need someone . . . . the part needs someone . . . . ripe."

Cal began to laugh. "How ripe? You talking Don Johnson or Van Johnson?"

"I'm talking Cal Dennis."

Cal stared at Phyllis. Broadway. That would take the heat off. Especially if he could turn it into a picture deal with some up-front money. "No," he said. No was always the first step in negotiating.

"Just think about it," Donald offered. "Let's meet at the club and talk. We can take a swim. You know, if you were on the boards, you'd be close to Libby."

Phyllis stepped as hard as she could on Donald's toe. Foxy Donald. But not foxy enough. She smiled and pulled the fourth ace. "Oh, yes! And you'd be able to keep an eye on Steven!"

○

Was Libby Dennis worth dying for?

The question reverberated in Birnbaum's head even after he left Anders. He didn't like to think of himself as being in the "dying" business. Birnbaum thought he was in the business of keeping people alive. Just like the two Alka Seltzers in his paper cup. He watched the bubbles. Jewish champagne. He held the cup to his nose and sniffed. It wasn't such a hot year.

For one thing, Birnbaum hadn't been to bed with a woman in over four months. He winced as he emptied the cup in a single gulp. Actually, it was six months. But "over four months" sounded better. In all that time he'd thought of no one but his wife, not for any longer than it took to turn a page or cross the street, but now he couldn't stop thinking about Libby. Not because he considered her a potential threat to the security of the President. She was a threat to him. It worried Birnbaum to be thinking about Libby as much as he was. It worried him that he might be adjusting to his separation. As unprepared as he had been for his wife's departure, he was equally unwilling to come to terms with it. But there he was, chug-a-lugging Alka Seltzers because he wanted Libby Dennis to fall into his arms.

Harmon opened the door. "You busy?"

"Yes. I was about to read your complaint again."

Harmon turned red. "I didn't complain about you. I objected to pulling an all-night detail without sufficient cause."

"What the hell does sufficient cause have to do with it? The law of cause and effect is strictly for cops. In the protection racket there is no such thing. Your job is to say gesundheit *before* I sneeze. Nobody gets a medal for catching the guy after he kills the President."

The younger man didn't know what to say. He looked at Birnbaum and shrugged. "Gesundheit."

"There may be hope for you yet." Birnbaum tore up the complaint.

"I came for your okay on the shower curtain." Harmon showed him a layout board with photographs of the front entrance to Libby's. Long shots. Medium shots. Close-ups. An artist had drawn the entrance to scale marking the facade for screwpoints. The idea was to enclose the entrance with what looked like a U-shaped shower curtain. The presidential limo would drive up onto the sidewalk and into the curtained area. Spectators would not be able to see the President get out of the car. Or see how many bodies were shielding him.

Birnbaum looked up at Harmon. "I don't like using this goddamn thing."

"Well, the engineer says . . ."

"I don't care what the engineer says. Harmon, I would like to point out, even though I don't have a degree in engineering, that this contraption has no top. Even with a top, it has no lining. Everybody stands out like silhouettes in a shooting gallery. We might as well send invitations to every nut in the city."

"Then why did you use it last time?"

"It was situation-expedient. He was staying overnight at the Plaza. We had all of Fifty-eighth Street covered. We needed to secure Limo One. Besides, they had a canopy for a top." Birnbaum leaned close. He spoke as though they were old friends. "What the hell, Harmon. Just between the two of us, can we get away without a top? I mean, there's no chance this rig could fall and crush the President to death?"

Harmon laughed. "Of course not. That can't happen."

Before Harmon could take another breath, Birnbaum grabbed him by the wrist and held tight. "Of course it could happen! Things happen. And they happen. And they happen. They happen because someone said they couldn't happen." He let go of Harmon. "I don't trust the curtain and I don't trust you. You're off the detail. Get the hell back to Tucson."

"But I just started . . ."

"Wrong. You just finished," Birnbaum shouted. "I don't give second chances."

He waited for Harmon to leave and then took a deep breath. He felt sorry for the kid but there was nothing to do about it. The Secret Service couldn't stay in business giving second chances. Except to Libby Dennis. He was going to give her a second chance to get into bed with him. Birnbaum asked himself again, Was she worth dying for? He sure as hell was going to find out.

○

"So?" Janos asked, pointing to the screenplay. "You like what you've read so far?"

"I haven't read it," Cal said, sitting down.

"I thought we were going to make a deal."

"We are."

"Without reading it?"

"You never said reading it was part of the deal."

Janos tapped his finger on the script. "If you had read *The Last Cowboy,* big shot, you'd know it isn't as bad as they say." Cal began to laugh. Janos shook his head. "All right. You made your point. You're only doing it for the money."

"Why does that make you angry?"

"Because you don't know anything about money. If you knew enough you'd have enough. It's no fun making a deal with someone who needs money. It's like a dying man who tries to bargain with death."

"I'm not trying to bargain. The deal is five."

"Five?" Janos roared.

"Five."

"Listen, movie star, I understand you need money. But nobody needs five million dollars."

"I need five."

Janos laughed. "Forgive me, my friend. If you need five, you don't need money. You need five. Why five?"

"I want five."

"All right. All right!" Janos rubbed his hands together. "So, thank God, we're not talking need anymore. We're talking want. Now we're talking a deal."

"We're still talking five."

"Darling boy, just for the record. *You* are talking five."

"I won't do it for less."

"Less? Who said less? Did I say less? You think I want people to say I put my wife in a picture with a nobody? You think I don't know what your price is? No, my friend, as far as I am concerned, there are forty producers out there who would do anything to get you in a picture. The only reason you have decided to make my picture instead of theirs is that you are hot for my wife!"

Cal started to laugh. "I never came on to Rikki. What the hell are you talking about?"

"I am talking about the deal."

"The deal is five," Cal said.

Janos sighed deeply and sat back. "I am the deal maker and the deal is what I say the deal is. The deal is not five, dear friend. We're going to tell everyone the deal is five because I don't want people to think you did it for the money. But the deal is six. You will make this picture with Rikki for six. You will also make love to Rikki. Included in the price. You will fuck her deaf, dumb, and blind at no extra charge except what it will cost me to make certain everyone knows you are screwing my wife."

Cal stared, unblinking, at Janos. Surely it was a joke. He was convinced it was a joke until he heard the punch line.

"And then after the entire world knows that Mr. Hollywood Handsome has stamped U.S. Grade A on her ass, then, Mr. Great Lover," Janos said, savoring each word, "she will leave you and come back to me. And *that* is the deal!"

The moment J sat down, Maxie brought her a margarita. Diane Betwee, J's junior lunchette, wore her Southern Connecticut heritage with no less bravado than Jezebel wore her red dress. A young woman of impeccable pastels, Diane was true WASP trash:

boarding school, beer, L. L. Bean, Boehm birds, and just enough ants in her pants for a few meaningless affairs with worthwhile people.

J sat back and sighed, having emptied her glass in a single swallow. "Do you drink, dear?"

Diane smiled. *"Mais oui."*

J raised her hand, summoning Maxie. "We may."

"I am *so* glad I ran into you last week. At the Morgan Library, of all places. I always buy my Christmas cards there."

"In October?"

Diane leaned forward. "I am a Christmas junkie. I do nothing but buy Christmas ornaments all year long. I know, I know. I'm crazy. But *c'est moi."*

Maxie came to the table, his pencil poised to take the young woman's drink order. J's drink was already on the first line of his pad, the rule being that when two women lunched, the older woman's order came first. Two women of the same age: the first line was for the woman closest to the door. Two women of the same age sitting equidistant from the door: the sexier woman or the one at the waiter's right went on top.

"Oh, I just don't know what to have!" Diane said, shrugging her shoulders.

J stepped on Maxie's foot. It was her signal to keep the margaritas coming. She smiled at Diane. "Why not have a boilermaker?"

"I've never heard of that."

"It was all the rage at the Vineyard. We were working on some benefit last summer. I don't remember what it was. Either Lou Gehrig's disease or Joe Heller's disease. You know how depressing those things can get."

"I'll have a white wine spritzer, please. With *two* cherries?"

"Thank you."

As soon as Maxie left, Diane leaned toward J and spoke *sotto voce.* "I know just what you mean. There are diseases and there are diseases. I had to say no to MS, Down's syndrome, epilepsy, and cystic whatever before I decided to play it safe with cancer."

Ashanti put a hand to her forehead as though the first taste of Truffle Pot Pie caused excruciating pain. She pointed her fork repeatedly at the plate while fluttering her eyes. "My culinarius has been raped! Sue the kitchen! Oh, God, where is Libby? This is delicious!"

But Hots wasn't listening. His eyes were riveted across the room. Moina, looking every bit as chic as she had the day before, posed atop the steps. "Jesus!" Hots muttered. "Welcome to the Meshuggener Brothers Circus."

Moina crossed the room, walking on conversation. Heads parted. People stopped talking. The rumor, which had spread through the room even faster than Truffle Pot Pie, was that she had traded it all in for a Bill Blass shroud.

Steven angled the table and Moina slid in gracefully next to Hots. She stared at Steven. "Why don't you get yourself a decent haircut?" Then she reached for Ashanti's hand. She held on tight.

Hots waited for Steven to leave before asking, "How the hell did you get out?"

Moina never took her eyes from Ashanti. "Isn't everything negotiable?"

Ashanti stretched across the table and kissed her on both cheeks. Then, on the lips. "Pussy, you shouldn't be here."

Moina smiled. *"Au contraire. I wouldn't have missed it."* She turned to Hots. "The pain is killing me. You'll have to get me out of here in half an hour and take me home."

"Home?" Hots whispered. "You're supposed to be in the hospital!"

Moina looked across the room and waved. She didn't know at whom but she wanted to be seen waving. "I suppose Fay has been circling my table." She sat back slowly and narrowed her eyes at Hots. "Don't look at me that way. Did you really think I'd let them chop off my tit?"

"It's better than dying."

"Says who?" Forcing a smile, she stared into the room as she gave Hots instructions. "I'll need a car every day. Promptly at twelve-fifteen. Make arrangements for a plainclothes nurse to wait in the limo. For as long as I can walk, I'll show up for lunch as though nothing has happened."

He ignored the blinking lights on his phone. "I can't let you do this."

Moina took a deep breath. "It's not up to you."

"Uh oh," Hots said. "Red alert. It's Fay." Hots and Ashanti exchanged worried glances knowing how fiercely the two women hated each other.

Fay had been reading lips from across the room. She squeezed onto the banquette next to Moina, glaring at her. Then with tears in her eyes, Fay put her arms around Moina and whispered, "You goddamn stupid vain bitch!"

Pink silk tunic. Pink wool skirt. Gold mesh belt. In uniform and reporting for active duty, Libby stood behind Steven at the reservations desk. Lunch was in full swing. All the tables were filled. She didn't have to look at the room, she could hear it playing. Instead, she watched Steven's head turn slightly in disacknowledgment of her presence.

Libby noticed how neatly he combed his hair. Not at all the way he had as a little boy. She bit her lip, wishing desperately there was something she could say to let Steven know how much she loved him. She glanced down at the seating chart. "Now that's really stupid, putting Av and Rosina in the back."

Without turning around, Steven shook his head. "The voice of the turtle."

"And why the hell would you bury Janet and John at 82? Have you lost your mind?"

"Funny. I was about to ask you the same thing. Have you been betting on the ponies or something? There are two guys sitting at the bar waiting for you. Very film noir."

Libby turned quickly. The two men at the bar nodded and got off their stools. "I don't know who they are. They could be killers."

"No. I don't have that kind of luck. You probably called them stupid and they've come to rough you up a little."

Libby turned toward the bar. "If I'm not back . . ."

"Be still my heart."

"Gentlemen?" she said, with a smile.

"Mrs. Dennis."

"Yes?"

Meehan took out his ID. "Secret Service."

"Not again!" Libby tried waving him aside. "Don't worry. I'll give the boss a good table!"

"I'm sorry, Mrs. Dennis. We have orders to take you with us."

The gray Plymouth station wagon headed downtown along Seventh Avenue, past Times Square, and into the garment center. The streets were clogged with accountants and receptionists and brothers-in-law. Flocks of overweight salesmen, like penguins on an ice floe, lined up at hot-dog stands. They shifted from foot to foot to catch the sun.

Libby stared out the window, one thought repeating itself over and over again. They had found out about Steven. After all the years and all the lies, they had uncovered the truth.

As the car slowed down, Libby's heartbeat accelerated. Meehan stepped out and held the door open. For an instant she thought of running—until she realized where she was. She was in front of Macy's.

"Mrs. Dennis?" Meehan helped her from the car. He led the way into the store. He might as well have sprouted wings and flown her to the top of the Empire State Building. It couldn't have been more surrealistic. They stepped onto the escalator, rising on the diagonal to the second floor. Lingerie. Was that where the United States Secret Service had its office?

By the time they reached China and Glassware on the eighth floor, Libby's heart had stopped pounding. She wasn't frightened anymore. She was furious. She followed Meehan through Cut Crystal and into Imported Dinnerware.

There was Birnbaum. A dinner plate in each hand. He looked at one plate, then at the other. He turned quickly, sensing someone was watching. Seeing Libby, he smiled and held out the plates. "So what do you think?"

Libby took them from him. She looked at one plate. She looked at the other plate. Then she looked at Birnbaum. Never taking her eyes from him, she smashed both plates against the counter.

Everyone within earshot turned around. Birnbaum nodded slowly. "I didn't like them either." He motioned for Meehan to take care of the stunned saleswoman. Very gently, Birnbaum took Libby by the arm and led her out of the store.

"I am going to sue you for kidnaping," she said, getting

back into the Plymouth. "And then I'm going to sue you for violating my civil rights."

"How about false arrest?" he suggested.

"That too." Libby looked out the window. They were driving uptown. "Where is your office?"

"Downtown."

"Are you taking me back to the restaurant?"

"No."

Although they were sitting right next to each other, Libby shouted at the top of her voice. "I want to call my lawyer!"

The driver was startled. He stepped on the brakes, hurling Libby forward. Birnbaum grabbed hold of her then let go quickly. He put his palms up to show he wasn't armed. Then Birnbaum opened a side panel and held out the phone. "Here," he said to her. "Five five six, five six nine nine."

Libby froze. That was Hots' number. She withdrew her hand. "You know who my lawyer is?"

"Yes."

After a moment, "Is there anything about me you don't know?"

He smiled. "All I know, Mrs. Dennis, is what I read. Most people don't realize that the Secret Service operates out of the Treasury Department." He shrugged. "So does the IRS. It's amazing how much you can find out from a tax return."

Libby stared out the window. They were heading north through Central Park.

"The other thing most people don't realize," he said, as though conducting a tour, "is that the Secret Service, when protecting the life of the President, is the only branch of government not bound by the Constitution."

"You make your own rules?"

"We can't afford to lose."

"You can do anything you want?"

"No questions asked."

"How about one question, Birnbaum? For old times?"

"For old times."

"Where the hell are you taking me?"

"Where do you think? To lunch!"

o

The Lotus Inn on 125th Street and Broadway was Birnbaum's favorite Chinese restaurant. To Libby's practiced eye, The Lotus Inn probably did a terrific business on Thanksgiving. Most of the tables were occupied by singles. Almost everyone was reading.

The waiter shouted to Birnbaum, "I save your booth for you."

Instinctively, Birnbaum positioned himself against the wall so that he faced the front door. He waited for Libby to take her seat.

She hesitated. "What the hell has this got to do with protecting the life of the President?"

"I'll figure out something."

Libby looked at the soiled vinyl booth and chipped formica table. "I don't want to eat here."

"Everybody says that the first time."

"Birnbaum, I don't like chow mein."

"You never tasted their chow mein."

The waiter brought a steaming pot of tea and two cups. He took silverware from his pocket and tossed it on the table. "You want the usual?"

"Two number one combination plates," Birnbaum said. "But with special fried rice."

"Not so fast." Libby turned to the waiter. "How do you make the special fried rice?"

"We make it in the kitchen."

"It's delicious," Birnbaum said. "And two cans of cherry soda." He smiled at her. "What the hell."

Libby took the lid off the teapot and dropped in the silverware. She pulled napkins from the dispenser and cleaned the forks and spoons. "I gather your wife took all the dishes with her."

"She commissioned some lesbian potter in Vermont to create a series of 'food environments,' as she called them. There wasn't one piece that was level. Every time you cut something, the plate rocked back and forth. She took them all, thank God. But she did leave me a set of depression glass. I couldn't tell whether it was a gift or a comment."

Libby poured tea onto the table. She rubbed at the food stains. "You come here often?"

"Not often enough."

Libby nodded. "I guess it's hard to find people to kidnap."

"You don't know the half of it."

"Birnbaum, what is the half of it? Why did you bring me here?"

He leaned toward her. "I have to ask you some questions."

"What kind of questions?"

"Personal questions." He stared at her long enough to feel guilty. She was scaring the hell out of him. He'd never been able to talk about his wife before. "I don't mean that I'm making a move on you, Mrs. Dennis."

She smiled. "Why not?"

The waiter brought two steaming plates. "Two number one combination with special fried rice."

Even before the plates were on the table, Birnbaum picked up his fork. He pointed to the chow mein. "You see all those onions? Did I tell you it was great?" Birnbaum poured on mustard and plum sauce. "Go ahead. It's like biting into a time machine. You can taste the world the way it used to be. Oh God," he groaned, inhaling deeply. "You can actually smell the MSG."

"Birnbaum . . ."

"Don't tell me you hate it," he said with his mouth full. "Not until you try it."

"What kind of questions?"

He nodded. "Right. Good idea. Let's talk business until your taste buds get acclimated. Tell me about your affair with the President."

Libby froze. "Why?"

"Why?" He put straws into the cans of cherry soda. "Why do you think? My job is to protect the President. Put yourself in my shoes. You meet someone who may or may not have a grudge against him. How are you going to find out? You ask questions. You listen to the answers. You look for clues. You have to find out if a person is dangerous. You have to understand why people do what they do." He stared at her, wondering why she did what she did to him. "You're not eating your chow mein."

Libby brought a forkful to her mouth. The onions were so

overcooked they greeted her palate with an aftertaste. But Birnbaum was right about one thing. It did bring back the past. The Lotus Inn had cornered the market on Cantonese Pentothal. "What do you want to know?"

"Just start from the beginning."

Libby put down her fork. "I can't talk and eat at the same time."

He shook his head. "You are some tough cookie, Mrs. Dennis."

"Libby."

"Libby."

"I was in a show. Out of town. Washington, D.C. It was opening night and we bombed. One of the producers had a house in Georgetown. He gave us a party but I wasn't in much of a party mood. Cal and I had separated and reconciled and then separated again just as my big chance for Broadway fizzled out. I went upstairs to one of the bedrooms. I didn't want to see anyone. I slid down into a chair. Someone came in to use the phone. It was him. His wife had just left him. He called her twice but each time she hung up. I didn't know what to do. Then I heard him start to cry."

"You're kidding." Birnbaum stopped eating. "He cried? My God! What if the Russians found out?"

"It was all right. He wasn't President yet."

"I can't imagine him crying. I just can't."

"Why not? I'll bet you cried when your wife left."

Birnbaum poured soy sauce on his rice. "Well, I'm a real sucker. I'll cry at anything." He looked up at her. "Then what?"

"He started dialing again. I didn't know who he was calling but I had heard enough."

"So what did you do?"

"I told him I'd fallen asleep in the chair."

"Did he believe you?"

"I couldn't tell. He was wearing his glasses."

Birnbaum smiled. "The tinted aviators? My God! He wore them even then? What did he say?"

"Nothing."

"Nothing? What did you say?"

"Nothing."

"Nothing?"

"He walked to the door and locked it. Then he turned off the lights."

Birnbaum put down his fork. "And that was it?"

Libby shrugged. "Sorry."

He sat back, staring at her. "Well. That doesn't give me very much to go on."

"Good. Then we're even."

"Even?"

Libby stared at him. "I'm trying to figure out how dangerous you are."

"Me? The biggest pushover since Humpty Dumpty?"

"I don't understand you, Birnbaum. I've met a lot of cops in my business . . ."

"Cops? What the hell makes you think I'm a cop? I don't go on drug busts or break into whorehouses. I never even wanted to be a fireman. I was going to be a doctor."

"What happened?"

"One day I turned on the television set and saw someone kill the President of the United States." He paused and stared at Libby. "It was the worst thing I had ever seen. I couldn't understand why anyone would want to kill the President of the United States." He took a sip of soda. "I sat in front of the television set for days, crying my first grown-up tears. I was sixteen, and still a virgin, but I lost my innocence in front of that set. It was a Zenith. Black and white."

"And that's when you decided?"

"No. It was the day of the funeral. I sat inches away from the screen, watching a team of horses pull his coffin through the streets. No V-8 engines. Just horses. It was so simple. It was so quiet. I had to check that the sound was on. But what really got me was the horse that followed right behind the coffin. In the stirrups, there were a pair of empty boots. Upside down. The symbol of a fallen leader. Now I was pretty sure he had never ridden that horse. But it didn't matter. It didn't even matter that those probably weren't his boots. It was the symbol, not the truth, that connected me to him. And by being connected to him, I felt connected to the whole human race, to thousands of years of mankind, to everyone who had ever cried for a fallen hero. I was sixteen years old and I didn't even know what the hell a President did, but I knew I couldn't live without him."

Libby suddenly realized just how dangerous Birnbaum was. "Listen to me," she said softly. "I want you to ask for the check." She pushed her plate away. "I'm not eating any more chow mein. I'm not answering any more questions." She stood up. "I want you to get me out of here, Birnbaum. I want to get away from you!"

o

Lunch was over. Everyone had left except Cal. He sat nursing a brandy and soda, trying to convince himself that he was feeling normal post-deal depression. But there was nothing normal about the deal he had just made. It was as insane as his sitting there wondering what would happen if he couldn't get it up.

Cal waved his copy of the screenplay at Steven. "What have you heard about this?"

Steven looked at the title page. *"The Last Cowboy?"* Ugh! You're kidding!" He saw the expression on Cal's face. "You're not kidding. Why aren't you kidding?"

Cal was impatient, suddenly upset by Steven's reaction. "What's it about?"

"It's about three years old. Barlow's pitched it at every table in the joint. Even the waiters know it by heart."

That was the last thing Cal wanted to hear. He grew increasingly angry as Steven continued.

"It's *The Electric Horseman* without batteries. Spoiled heiress is kidnaped, escapes and finds a home where the buffalo roam."

"What else have you heard?"

"I've heard that the only person who can save it is you and that even you can't save it."

"Who's read it?"

"All the people who've dropped their options. Barlow has collected more money than if they actually shot the picture. Everybody options it. Then they read it. Then they drop it. You know. The usual."

"I think I'm going to do it," Cal said defiantly.

"Did you read it?"

"I don't want to."

"Why not?"

Cal smiled. "It might influence my decision." Not reading it was the only way to maintain a shred of self-respect.

Steven tossed the screenplay onto the table. "If there's that much money in it, who can blame you? Everybody knew why Brando did *Superman.*"

"Except Brando."

"Pop, when the hell are you going to grow up? You really think you're Cal Dennis."

"I *know* I'm Cal Dennis. You have any problem with that?"

Steven shrugged. "I'm not the one with problems. I'm not the one doing *The Last Cowboy.*"

Cal was furious. There wasn't a producer in Hollywood he'd let speak to him that way. But then again, there wasn't a producer for whom he had ever wanted to be a hero. Cal saw himself tarnishing rapidly. Steven was right. The real Cal Dennis wouldn't look twice at that script. He had no right to be angry with Steven. It wasn't his fault that Cal was scared. "I'm doing this picture for one reason only. I need to fill the coffers before I pop the question to Libby. Steven, I want us to be a family."

"Great idea! Let's be the Bates family. I'll be Norman and you . . ."

Cal punched him gently. "A real family with a poppa bear and a momma bear."

Steven stared at Cal. He nodded. "All right. But this is my final offer. If you don't want to be the Bates family, you can be Mildred Pierce and I'll be Veda."

"Goddamn you, Steven! Be a fag on your own time!" The moment Cal heard what he had said, he put a hand to his forehead and muttered, "Oh, shit."

Cal and Steven did not reach out to comfort each other. Neither did they walk away from each other. They simply sat there. Watching each other fade out.

During the break between lunch and dinner, Tessa prepared a tally of how many of each dish was sold. Her figures gave Sonny something to check against his inventory. It also gave her a chance to tease Bud as she sat on the other side of the chef's table. She looked up and saw him crack an egg, cupping the yolk in his palm. The white separated between his fingers. "Yuck!" she groaned. "That is disgusting!"

"You don't like eggs?"

"I don't like fingers. At least, not in my food."

Bud smiled. "Where do you like fingers?"

"On triggers. Pulling pins from hand grenades. Clenched tight at the end of a dagger."

"But not in your food," he said, squeezing the egg yolk into a mixture of flaked crab, cream, and puréed ginger. Bud licked his finger.

"Is it good?" she asked.

Bud dipped his finger back into the mix and held out a taste. Tessa sucked off the crab meat.

"Is it good?" he asked.

"Fair enough as fingers go."

Bud added bread crumbs and shaped the crab into a patty. He dipped it in buttermilk and then pressed on an even coating of corn meal. Two pans with clarified butter were already on the stove. He put the crabcake in one, and some crushed green peppercorns with cream into the other.

"But not as good as Eli's fingers," she said, jealous of the attention he lavished on the two pans.

"Eli?"

"My darky Spartacus. The nigger of my narcissism."

Bud stuck a finger into the peppercorn cream. He licked it loudly, sliding the pan off the stovetop. He flipped the crabcake over and then tasted the sauce again. He shook his head. "I'm missing something."

"You need purpose. Meaning. A cause to célèbre."

"I need something for color," he said.

"What color?" she asked.

"What color?" Bud was too absorbed to realize she had just asked the same question a moment before.

Tessa caught the spark of his intensity. It didn't matter what problem he wanted to solve. The only important thing was the passion with which he sought a solution. For Eli, it was black and white. For Bud, it was a different color. For Tessa, passion was passion. "Well, darling, we don't want to be mundane and shred radicchio or sprinkle chives."

Bud slid the golden brown patty onto a plate. Very precisely, he spooned the peppercorn cream over half the cake. "To show the crust," he explained glancing up at her. He smiled. "Something red!"

Tessa opened her mouth. Bud pinched off a piece of the crabcake and fed it to her. "Mmm. It definitely needs something red." She took a fingerful of the moist white crab mixture and smeared it on Bud's lips. She leaned close and licked it off. "Red. And hot."

"How hot?"

Tessa shrugged. "I don't know. I can't figure out yet how hot you are."

Bud wasn't sure what to make of Tessa. She was working him like a piece of puff pastry. Before he realized it, her lips were on his. And then, just as suddenly, she pulled away.

"Raspberries!" she shouted.

"What?"

"Raspberries! Something red?"

"Raspberries!" Never taking his eyes from her, Bud rushed over to the refrigerator and reached in for a bowl. He smiled as Tessa opened her mouth. He fed her one perfect raspberry. And then one for himself. He leaned toward her. Their lips met, tongues exchanging berries, lips crushing them, the juice running from his mouth into hers.

Tessa licked the juice from Bud's lips as she lifted her skirt. "And now for the cream."

Steven pushed open the kitchen door, shouting angrily, "Where the hell is Chickie?" He stopped as he saw Bud let go of Tessa. "Jesus! What do you think we're running here? This isn't a singles bar."

"I was just leaving," Tessa said nervously. "Did you say you wanted Chickie?"

"Where is he?" Steven asked.

"The españols are in the back," she said, winking at Bud. "Shall I get him for you?"

"Yes."

Bud waited until Tessa left. "Cut the singles bar crap."

"I don't want you fucking around with the staff."

Bud shrugged. "I thought we were partners. I left you all the boys."

"We're not going to be partners if you spill your guts and tell her the whole deal."

"What deal?" Bud shouted. "I don't see a deal. Do you see a deal? Did you get money yet? Do we have a lease? When do we open?"

"I'm working on it," Steven said.

"You better work harder or I'll get the money from Phyllis and do it on my own. I told you, I'm tired of cooking in someone else's kitchen."

Steven narrowed his eyes, tight with anger. "What the hell do you think I've been doing all my life?"

Chickie rushed in from the back. "You want me?"

"Yes," Steven said. "Let's go." He walked toward the men's room. He held the door open for Chickie and then leaned back against it.

The boy smiled nervously and came close. He slid his hand between Steven's legs, pressing gently. "You want me to do it now?"

Steven closed his eyes, leaning his head back against the door. He felt Chickie's fingers reach for his zipper. Steven took a deep breath. He grabbed Chickie by the collar. His anger unleashed, Steven became uncontrollable. He hit Chickie as hard as he could.

The boy slid to the floor, curled up, hands over his head. "What did I do?" he cried.

Steven stood over him, breathless as he stared at his own image in the mirror. "Be a fag on your own time."

Alfero walked into the dining room, brushing his hair back and pushing his shirt into his trousers. Not that it would do him any good. Steven hated Latinos. That was why he had fired Chickie.

Steven was behind the bar, pouring juice. "You want some?"

"*Sí*. Thank you. Yes."

"What did Chickie tell you?"

"He say you fire him because you hate Latinos."

"He was wrong." Steven reached for Alfero's shoulder, running his hand along the dishwasher's firmly muscled bicep. Steven knew he was manly enough for Alfero because he had power over him. "I understand we've got a new busboy."

"*¡Dios!*" Alfero began speaking rapidly in Spanish, unable to stop the tears from welling up in his eyes. He was not being fired. Alfero blew his nose. "It is a great country, America."

Steven watched closely. Now there was a man who knew how to cry. "It depends."

"You can be whatever you want. I want to be a busboy. I am a busboy."

"You'll get scale plus fifteen percent of the waiter's tips. You might not earn as much as working two shifts in the kitchen."

"I don't care."

"You understand what I'm saying? You might get less money."

"But I will be a busboy! I will be in the front of the house. It is better to be a busboy than a dishwasher."

"Except for the money."

"Mr. Steven, you think I do this for just money?" Alfero was grinning from ear to ear. "No one in my family was ever a busboy. My father, before I leave home, say the best business is the tips business. Anybody gets a job, my father ask 'You get tips?' You say no, he shrugs. You say yes, he smiles."

Steven turned away. He had had enough of Alfero. "Good. Now your father can be proud of you."

○

It was four o'clock in the afternoon and Libby and Cal had been lying naked in one another's arms for nearly an hour. Libby held tight to Cal, seeking warmth rather than heat. She had always loved lying in his arms until that afternoon when, like an optical illusion, the phrase "lying in his arms" reversed its meaning from location to deception.

"I'm scared," she whispered.

"Me, too. What are you scared about?"

"Us," she said.

"You don't think it's love, do you?"

"I'm afraid so."

Cal smiled. "Just my luck. I've never been any good at love."

"I know."

He groaned. "Not fair."

"Listen, you want fair or you want truth?"

"What else you got?"

Libby shrugged. "Only thing left is love."

"Bite your tongue," Cal said. "Love got us into a lot of trouble." He brought his lips close and pushed gently. "On second thought, let *me* bite your tongue."

She smiled. "I have déjà vu."

"I was cured of that years ago. If I think something's happened to me, it's because it has. Although just when I'm convinced that everything has happened before, something happens for the first time."

"I know just what you mean."

"I thought this déjà vu telethon was for me."

Libby pushed him away. "Why the hell do men think they've cornered the market on anxiety?"

Cal sat up on his knees. He reached between his legs. He was erect. "This is why. This, kiddo, is why fortunes are made and empires fall. The market is up. The market is down. Euphemisms. It all starts here! It all ends here!" He pressed against her thighs, pushing her legs apart. "I am the Ganges," he whispered. "You are the Nile. As long as we're together, there is no beginning. There is no end."

Libby stared at Cal. "So what is there?"

He began to laugh. "How about sex and money?"

She put her arms around him. "Thank God for the eighties."

"Babe, what do you think our mistake was? Getting married or getting divorced?" But just as Libby was about to speak, Cal put his fingers to her lips. "No, you don't! I'm tired of hearing about what a wonderful divorce we have. For Christ's sake, happiness isn't everything." He kissed her very gently. "Libby, will you marry me?"

It was the question she most wanted him to ask. "Ask me again."

"Will you marry me?"

"Again."

"Will you marry me?"

"One more time!"

"Libby!"

She kissed him. It was the question she was most afraid he would ask. "Seems to me I did marry you. Didn't I?"

Cal shook his head. "No. I don't think so. I'd have remembered. You married some nerd named Roger."

"I loved Roger."

"As much as you love me?"

"That's not fair. Did you love Manuela as much as you loved me? Or Jane? Or Nicole?"

"At least I married them. Not like you and that anchorman. And that editor. And that waiter . . ."

"He wasn't a waiter! He owned the restaurant!"

Cal put his arms around her. "Hey, babe. I hear tell Roger needs you real bad."

Libby's eyes filled with tears. She could divorce Cal with a lie but she couldn't marry him with one. "Send him my regrets. I'm having a smashing affair with a very famous movie star." She bit his lobe and whispered confidentially, "He's absolutely crazy about me." She kissed his ear. "He even bought me a sable coat." She bit his chin. "You know what sable costs?"

Cal kissed her. "A lot less than a marriage license."

"I know why I can't marry you," she said. "I haven't a thing to wear."

"Wear your sable."

She fell back onto the bed. "You don't understand. I have nothing to wear under my sable."

Cal scooped her up in his arms. He kissed her breasts. "You don't have to wear anything but your nipples."

Libby laughed. "Don't be silly. I can't get married in my nipples."

Cal dropped her onto the pillows. "You're saying no!" He got off the bed. "I can't believe it. It must be catching. I've got déjà vu!" Cal turned away. "You're saying no."

Libby went to him. She reached out and put her hands on either side of Cal's face. "I'm going to tell you a secret," she whispered. "I have always been married to you."

"Then all we have to do is make it legal."

"Do you really love me, Roger-Cal?"

"I do."

"So," Libby asked, very softly, "how about letting me be the Ganges once in a while?"

Cal took her by the shoulders. "Listen, you want this relationship to work or not?"

"You bet your ass I want it to work."

"Those are pretty high stakes," he said.

Libby stretched her hands down his back as far as she could. She smiled, feeling the stubble where the studio had shaved him for the nude scene. "Only since you put your ass on the market."

Cal pulled back quickly. "What?"

"What?" she repeated.

"Who told you?" he asked angrily.

"Who told me?"

"Yes. Who told you?" He sat on the bed. "Who was it? Janos? One of the waiters? I should have known it was one of the waiters. Goddamn! I didn't want you to hear it from someone else." He was suddenly apologetic. "You've got to believe me, Lib. I was going to tell you. I just didn't know how." He took a deep breath. "The best I could get for *The Desert Song* was two million. I mean, who the hell is going to see *The Desert Song?* But then Janos comes along with some turkey called *The Last Cowboy.* He really wanted me and I figured I could get him up to five."

Libby sat next to him. "What happened?"

Cal shook his head. "The son of a bitch offered six!"

She began to laugh. "Six? That's wonderful!" She hugged Cal. "No one told me that. I didn't know anything about it."

"Oh, shit."

Libby cupped her hand under Cal's chin. "Why isn't this man smiling?"

"Janos wants me to sleep with Rikki."

"What?" She took her hand from his face.

"He wants the world to know that Rikki had an affair with The Great Lover and still went back to him."

Libby didn't know whether to laugh or cry. "Cal, that's the sickest thing I've ever heard."

"Actually, for Janos, it's pretty wholesome."

"I'm not talking about Janos! I'm talking about you. And me."

"This has nothing to do with you and me. It's a deal. That's all it is."

"I'm sorry, but that's a little too eighties."

"I can do *The Desert Song* for two. Or I can do Rikki for six."

"Are you asking or telling?"

"Babe, it doesn't mean anything. We're talking in and out." He turned away and spoke softly. "I need the six."

Libby stared at him. "One small fuck for man, one giant fuck for Cal Dennis."

"I need the six."

Libby rushed to the closet for her sable. "Are you in some kind of trouble?" She put the coat on and held it tight.

Cal nodded yes. "I don't know what happened. Or even when. All I know is it wasn't anything big. Nothing dramatic. It never is. Maybe the limo was late or I didn't get called back right away. It could have been as simple as someone else ordering lunch before I did. I don't know. But the minute you think it's happening, it's too late. It's already happened. You've lost the game. You begin playing another game. Same teams, but different rules. This time you start out as the loser. You bluff. You try to keep them from finding out what you did wrong. But the catch is, you don't know what you did wrong."

"Which brings us back to Rikki," Libby said. "You're not just talking money."

"No. I'm talking six million. I'm talking my price. I'm talking what's going to appear in the columns."

Libby nodded her head. She put a hand to his cheek and smiled. "But the money wouldn't hurt."

"Would it hurt you?" he asked.

She took a deep breath. "Would it hurt me?" she said slowly. She opened her mouth, then hesitated. "You want the truth?"

"I don't think so."

"Good." Libby opened her coat. Cal rolled on top of her. "I don't give a damn about Rikki. I just wish you hadn't told me."

"Babe, it's going to be all over the papers. If I know Janos, he's thinking about taking ads. I couldn't keep it a secret from you if I tried."

Slowly, she moved away from Cal. "But what if you could?"

"But I can't!"

Libby spoke urgently, looking into his eyes as though he were the Oracle of Delphi. "What if you could?"

"The last thing I want to do is hurt you. Lib, it's just that there are some things it's better not to know."

"What if you could?"

"If I could, I would lie to you. I would do everything in my power to make certain you never found out."

Even though Libby tried to smile, she felt large tears begin to fall. "I want you to remember you said that."

WEDNESDAY

THE YELLOW CHEVY WITH ONE BLUE DOOR EDGED its way down Fifth Avenue amid the morning rush-hour traffic. Alfero was driving, one hand on the wheel and the other motioning a silver Mercedes to get the hell out of his way.

Dolores sat next to Tía Rosa, whose right arm was the car's right directional signal. Neither of the automatic signals worked. Nor did the horn. And Tía Rosa worked only if you shouted.

"¡Derecho!" Alfero shouted.

Dolores turned down the quadraphonic Sony CD sound system that had been blaring *pasodobles* since they left the Bronx. *"¡Derecho!"* she screamed at her aunt.

Tía nodded. She stuck her arm out the window and spit. *"¡Maricón!"* she yelled at a chauffeur in the right lane.

Alfero whooped, pressing as hard as he could on the silent horn. "Busboy! Busboy! Busboy!" he chanted, giving the finger to all of Fifth Avenue.

Carlos and the niños joined from the back seat. "Busboy! Busboy! Busboy!"

The car came to a screeching halt in front of Libby's. Dolores reached over to turn off the music. Everyone stopped talking. Even the boys quieted down as they looked out at the black lacquered panels beneath the black-and-white-striped awning.

"Ay, ay, ay," Carlos groaned appreciatively.

"Libby's," Dolores whispered as though she had arrived at Shangri-La.

Alfero was bursting with pride. He rushed from the car and stood at the entrance, arms outstretched, his feet stamping the ground.

Across the street, in the gray Plymouth station wagon, Special Agents Logan and Meehan shook their heads.

Dolores had to be coaxed from the car, while the boys scrambled out eager to touch the ornate brass hinges and see their reflections in the shiny black panels. Carlos positioned Tía in front of the door. He took out his Nikon F3 and shouted for the boys to stop fighting.

Alfero posed with his arms around Dolores. With his arms around the boys. With one hand on the door and the other signaling thumbs-up.

Meehan asked Logan, "He's the one?"

Logan nodded.

Alfero was pleading with Dolores as he rang the bell. *"Por favor."* He wanted her to come inside with him. She pulled back as Kenneth, the night porter, opened the door.

"Holy shit!" Kenneth said. "Sorry, ma'am," he added quickly as he saw Dolores.

Alfero shrugged. "We take pictures."

"Forget the pictures." The black man raised his eyebrows. "There's something very funny going on." Kenneth nodded toward the inside. "I think she found out about the lamb chops!"

But Libby was not thinking about lamb chops as she sat at the bar. Ignoring the menus, work schedules, and seating charts spread out in front of her, she made note after note concerning the dozens of details any self-respecting hostess would be frantic over if the President of the United States were coming to lunch.

She still hadn't decided which china to use. Would brand new linen be too stiff? What about bottled water? Could she possibly call in a decorator and redesign the entire restaurant by Thursday? She put a hand to her forehead and gasped. "Place cards!" She took a clean sheet of paper to start on the wording for the cards. But she couldn't concentrate. What the hell was she going to do about flowers?

Libby reached for the phone, catching a glimpse of herself in the mirror. She was relieved at what she saw. She saw assurance. Control. Professionalism. A gray pinstripe jumpsuit with a pink silk scarf. There was even a pencil clenched between her teeth. Very Kate Hepburn, she thought. But then again, Hepburn would have had the guts to tell Cal the truth. Hepburn would have risked it. She would never have accepted love without trust. Libby sighed. It was hopeless. She was nothing like Hepburn. She was pure Lana Turner. One of those women who never meant what they said. Madame X going through life on the subtext.

She had pretended to be upset about Cal's deal with Janos. She played on his guilt to get through the night and it had worked. Cal hadn't asked her to marry him again. Now all she had to get through was lunch and dinner and lunch again without Birnbaum uncovering the truth. A piece of cake. That was what she did best. She was Queen of the Star-Struck Ballroom where no one ever wanted to hear the truth.

Libby dialed the florist, daring herself to ask whether the calla lilies were in bloom. "Sophie? Libby. *Comment ça va? Oui, oui,* it has been a *chien's* age. Listen, *chérie,* I'm up to my asparagus in problems. I need a truly exquisite arrangement with tomorrow's delivery. What do you mean *what* delivery? The *flower* delivery! Sophie, this is Libby Dennis! *Oui.* What? Since when?" Libby put a hand to her forehead and then buzzed for Sonny. "No, I didn't know. *Chérie,* let me call you back." Libby hung up. She turned quickly from the mirror, avoiding her own reflection.

Victor, the bartender, was slicing lemons at the end of the bar. Libby turned to him as though they had been in the midst of an argument. "Do you know why people come to this restaurant?"

"For the drinks," he said. "What else?"

"They come here because they know what to expect. There are no surprises. It's like *Rocky IV.* They know what they're going to get before they go in." She tapped her finger on the bar for emphasis. "And that goes for the flowers, too."

Sonny sat down next to her. "What's up?"

"Your number. Unless you've got a damn good reason for eighty-sixing Sophie."

"You unhappy with the flowers lately?"

"No."

Sonny shrugged. "So can I get back to work?"

"I want to know what happened to Sophie!"

"Same thing that happens to a lot of people. She got greedy. She kept raising her prices."

Victor shook his head. "Must be a real epidemic."

Sonny turned angrily. "The only epidemic is people with big mouths."

"What's on your mind, Victor?"

"Mixers," he said. "Used to be, Warshefsky delivered Monday and Thursday like clockwork. Now we got some bozo who delivers once a week. Once a week maybe."

"What do you mean maybe?" Sonny yelled.

"I mean like when you had to send the porter to Gristede's for tonic."

"If you weren't such a Nervous Nellie I wouldn't have sent him. You didn't run out." Sonny turned to Libby. "Prices go up. I try to keep things level. So we get a delivery once a week instead of twice."

Victor leaned across the bar. "A customer comes in here, he wants a drink. He don't want maybe."

The front bell rang. Libby jumped off the stool. She pushed aside the curtain on the door. It was Birnbaum. Libby stood in front of Door Number One. Birnbaum waved at her through the glass. She looked around. There was no Door Number Two. Her choice was the tiger or the tiger.

"Birnbaum!" she said, unlocking the door, "Thank God you've come. I'm in desperate need of your help. I simply can't make up my mind about place cards."

"Good morning."

"I don't know whether it should say Mr. President or The President or President Sweetie."

"No place cards."

"No place cards? Birnbaum, this isn't Russia!"

"No place cards. We don't use place cards for the same reason we don't paint a bull's-eye on the President before he sits down."

Libby pointed into the dining room. "You think you can hide him at the front table?"

"The front table? What makes you think I want the President there?"

"I don't care where *you* want the President. That's my best table."

He looked at his seating chart. "The President will be at 43."

"Are you nuts? At the entrance to the kitchen? Right next to the men's room? The only person who likes that table is Janos. I'm not seating the President of the United States in Siberia."

Birnbaum stared at her. No expression. "I need six tables for the immediate circle. Then another one, two, three, four, five, six around them. Twelve all together."

"Twelve?" She pointed to the reservations book. "You told me he wanted to have lunch here, not rent the place for a bar mitzvah!"

Birnbaum cleared his throat. "The President sits in the corner," he said calmly. "At Table 43. There is a circle of tables around him. And then there is another circle of tables. Concentric circles."

"Impossible. You'd have to put tables in the aisle."

"That's what we're planning to do."

"You are nuts. You can't put tables in the aisle. How will the waiters get out of the kitchen?"

"They'll use the other aisle." He shrugged and smiled for the first time. "Concentric circles. That's the secret of my success."

"Well, it's not the secret of mine!" She took a deep breath and smiled at him. "Birnbaum, darling," she began casually, "what *is* the secret of mine? Why does the President want to have lunch here?"

"I don't know."

She grabbed his arm tightly. "You must know."

"Listen, all I'm supposed to do is die for him. He doesn't have to tell me why he wants to have lunch here. As a matter of fact, I asked our people to intervene with the White House."

Libby was furious. "You what? You tried to cancel me out?"

"I thought he should have a bagel and lox in the limo and get the hell out of the city. But he didn't want to."

"You mean it was the President's idea? He thought of it all by himself?"

Birnbaum shrugged. "Well, you don't get to be President these days for nothing."

Libby leaned forward. "What did he say, Birnbaum? What were his exact words?"

Birnbaum paused. He put a hand to his forehead, then looked up as though suddenly remembering. "I think he said, 'Give me Libby or give me death!'"

"You son of a bitch."

"Or, it might have been, 'I regret that I have but one lunch to give for my country.'"

"Birnbaum, you're not funny!"

He stared at her and shook his head. He spoke softly. "I don't want you to take this the wrong way, but you're not as much fun as you used to be, either."

Libby sat back. No matter how she tried to anticipate Birnbaum's responses, there was no way to predict the pattern of his nerve endings.

He smiled. "I sure do miss the good old days."

Libby's face grew tense. "It was a million laughs."

He smiled. "I thought I was going to have a heart attack when you showed up at my apartment." He shook his head. "I'm a real sucker for tough women."

"I need your help, Birnbaum."

"All right! All right! Use the goddamn place cards!"

She put a hand on his arm. "I don't want Cal to find out."

"Well, I'm sure as hell not going to tell him."

"Birnbaum, it happened so many years ago."

"My mother used to say, 'You lie down with senators, you wake up with presidents.'"

Libby put a hand to her forehead and pushed aside her bangs. "It was all so meaningless."

Birnbaum took a pad from his jacket and a pencil from his shirt pocket. He wanted to get down to business. He started to say something but then hesitated. He looked up at her. "You know, whatever it is you're hiding, it must be dynamite."

o

Tessa lied to Mohammed Eli about having an early class. What she had was the key to Bud's loft and a vow never to set foot in Brooklyn again. She stuffed all her books into a duffel and put on five layers of clothing beneath the double-breasted camel's hair coat Daddy had given her to break up with some dumb football player whose name she couldn't even remember now. Goddamn! Eli ought to be worth an entire Porsche.

As Tessa opened the door to the loft, she was momentarily blinded by the sunlight, but she caught a glimpse of Bud naked on the bed, his hand moving up and down rapidly between his legs. As her eyes became accustomed to the glare, there was no doubt about it. Bud was masturbating. He waved hello with his other hand.

Tessa waved back. She wondered what Miss Manners would say about a host who greets you while masturbating. At first she felt put off. Insulted. But as she walked toward the bed, Bud's smile told her that she hadn't caught him with his pants down. He was doing it to please her.

Tessa watched politely for a moment and then let her books drop to the floor. "Careful. You'll burn it off."

"I never burn anything. I'm too good a chef."

Tessa walked to the closet and threw her coat on the floor. She couldn't help smiling at his expression when he realized how many layers of clothing she had on. "It's all the rage in Alaska." She began unbuttoning the first of her skirts. "Actually, it's quite common in the coat check community to wear everything you own so that you never have to hang anything up." Tessa had expected him to laugh. She shrugged and asked, "You have some music?"

"No."

She looked around the enormous open space where not

even the toilet was enclosed. "You don't have a tape deck or a radio?"

He watched as she took off a sweatshirt and then a blouse. "When I want to hear music," he said, "I go to a concert."

Tessa rolled down the legs on her second pair of jeans. "Where do you go when you want to watch TV?"

Bud smiled as she pulled off the last of her clothes. "Would you like to take a shower?"

Tessa shook her head. "Are you kidding? I'm all nice and sweaty."

Bud stopped masturbating and got up. He went to the kitchen sink and took a fresh bar of soap. He pointed toward the shower. Tessa crossed the floor stark naked, parading along an imaginary runway.

He stood her directly under the spray, grabbing a fistful of hair to keep her in place as she complained that the water was too hot. He began soaping her up, scrubbing vigorously as she squirmed. His hands were everywhere, feeling for irregularities, looking for skin blemishes, pinching and slapping as though he were examining a rump roast. When she finally passed inspection, Bud turned off the water and plunged her into a cold Jacuzzi. She screamed and huddled close to him as he took the clippers and cut her toenails. Then he carried her out of the tub and wrapped her in a large towel. His hands pressed against Tessa's body to ensure she was completely dry.

"What comes next?" she asked. "The interview or the written test?"

But instead of answering her question, he said, "I hate using condoms."

"Aren't they ever a bore?"

"I'll send you to my doctor. It'll only take a few days for the tests to come back."

"Do you think they'll have to put a clip on my ear or can we get away with merely branding my ass?"

Bud carried Tessa to the bed. "Welcome to the eighties."

She flopped back onto the pillows. "At least if I could watch television."

He lay down next to her and began to masturbate again. "You can watch me."

Tessa pushed his hand away and took hold of his penis. "What the hell. I was never one for spectator sports."

Bud lay back. "Slower. Lift it higher. Don't hold it so tight." The phone rang. Bud put a finger to Tessa's lips as he switched on the speakerphone. "Yup?"

Phyllis's voice filled the loft like the whine of a raga. "Darling, did I wake you?"

"Yes." He smiled at Tessa, motioning for her to continue.

"Oh, good. Then you haven't seen Fay's column?"

Bud rolled his eyes. "What did she say about you this time?"

"Darling, it's what she said about *you.*"

"Me?" Bud turned toward the speaker. Tessa kept going like an appliance.

"Listen to this," Phyllis gushed. " 'Not since Lindy's launched its cheesecake has this town been stood on its palate by anything as decadently delicious as Truffle Pot Pie.' "

Tessa opened her mouth in surprise. She applauded silently, then sprawled across Bud's chest as Phyllis continued to read.

" 'Bud Willis, that hunk of a super chef at Libby's,' " Phyllis paused and repeated slowly, " 'that . . . hunk . . . has come up with a dish rich enough to have its own Swiss bank account. Take it from an old Twinkie freak, this is cuisine with a capital Q!' Well, darling, how's that for a wake-up call?"

Bud was about to answer when he realized that he was wet. He had come all over himself.

○

Libby was afraid to breathe. It occurred to her, as the blood rushed to her stomach, that she might possibly be brain-dead. But no. A quick check revealed that only her heart had suffered irreversible damage. She sat back, surprised at how little immediate pain there was. No gasping for breath. Her life hadn't even flashed in front of her eyes. Yet she was having an out-of-body experience. She floated upward and, from a safe distance, watched the frozen expression on the face that was once hers.

"I'm not hiding anything," she said. "What are you talking about?"

Birnbaum stared at her. "You want me to be honest?"

"Only as a last resort."

"I don't buy what you've been telling me. I think there's more to it."

"You bet your ass there's more to it!" Libby got off the bar stool, hoping she'd think of something to say while on her feet. She began to pace. "There's a whole lot more to it!" So much for the cue. Where was the song? "Oh, Birnbaum, I had such a wonderful divorce. It was every woman's dream. And now it's gone." She sighed. "Cal asked me to marry him."

"And what did you say?"

"You know, you've got some nerve. What the hell makes you think you can waltz in here and ask me a question like that?"

"If all you did was sleep with the President once, why are you so worried about what's in the file? What are you afraid we might find out? That you saw him again? That you've been see-ing him through the years? Is that what you're afraid will ruin your wonderful divorce?"

Libby smiled. Sherlock Holmes he wasn't. As soon as lunch and dinner and lunch were over, she'd definitely have to con-sider another shot at Broadway. She stared at him and patted his hand. The bastard wanted an encore. "Oh, Birnbaum, I never figured you for an incurable romantic. Poor darling. I bet you still wait up for Santa Claus."

"Almost every night."

"That's some life you have."

He smiled. "I know. But if there really is a Santa Claus, I'm going to be the guy who finds out."

Libby suddenly felt close to him. "What price Santa?"

He began shuffling his papers. "I think we better get back to work."

"Don't be a sore loser! Just because I found out more about you than you found out about me."

"Don't count on it. I happen to be a professional in the security business."

"Well, I happen to be a professional in the *in*security busi-ness which, as anyone can tell you, is a much bigger field."

"Once the President enters the restaurant," Birnbaum said matter-of-factly, "no one will be allowed in or out."

"Don't be ridiculous. What if someone wants to leave?"

"Once the premises are secure and the President is in place, we require maximum access and egress."

"I'm tired of hearing about what you require! What about me?" Libby hadn't expected to sound as desperate. She frightened herself. "Birnbaum," she said softly.

"Yes?"

"There's something I need to know."

"What?"

Libby took a deep breath. "Meat or fish?"

"Jesus!"

"It's a perfectly reasonable question."

"Judging from my reports, there's no telling what he likes."

"Birnbaum, I don't need snide comments."

"What do you need?"

"I need to know if it's meat or fish."

"My job is to keep the President safe. I work for the U.S. Government. The White House Staff works for the President. It's their job to keep him happy."

"Oh, come on!" Libby tapped her pencil. "When all you guys go bowling after a hard day protecting the President, someone must let it slip that he liked the foie de veau better than the fra diavolo."

"Listen, I don't care which he likes. So long as what he eats doesn't kill him."

"I assure you nothing he eats here is going to kill him."

"No, I'm the one who can assure you of that. My men have been watching the place since Monday." He opened a folder. "We have the names of the meat man, the fish man, the bakery . . ."

"Are you telling me that you had someone out there spying on Charlie Ryan?"

He looked at his list. "I don't see any Charlie Ryan."

"Well, there you are! So much for Birnbaum of the Secret Service. Charlie Ryan is my fish man."

"No, he's not. Your fish man is Mazzelli."

"Mazzelli? Are you crazy? I've been doing business with Charlie since the day I opened. Mazzelli is a two-bit . . ."

"We found that a number of your suppliers had been changed in the past few months."

"What do you mean *you* found? How?"

"Tax forms. We checked the sales tax exemptions and . . ."

"My God! What a bunch of yentas!" She hesitated. "Who have you got for flowers?"

"Horton-Ness."

It was worse than she thought. He knew it wasn't Flowers by Sophie before she knew it wasn't Flowers by Sophie. There was no telling what else he had found out. "If you don't mind," she said, getting up, "I'll check this with Sonny."

"I think you should hear what I have to say first."

"Birnbaum . . ."

"I have to talk to you."

"Please don't talk to me. You don't talk to me and I won't talk to you. You're a real killer when you talk."

"Me?"

"You should quit the Secret Service. You should become ambassador to Russia. All you'd have to do is buy a ticket for the opening night of the Bolshoi. Go to Russia, Birnbaum, and talk to the party officials. By intermission, they will all be dead."

"Sonny wanted a kickback on everything. Your old suppliers refused. He got rid of them."

Libby sat back. It was intermission at the Bolshoi. She swallowed hard. "You're wrong. I told him to get rid of them," she said defensively. "Do you have any idea what that bitch Sophie was charging for begonias?"

"I thought you ought to know."

"Don't be stupid, Birnbaum." Libby picked up her papers and began shuffling them. "Do you really think someone could change all my suppliers without my knowing it? Do you really think I wasn't aware that Sonny was padding the bills?"

He looked down at his notes. "I need permission for my men to advance the room."

"I'd hate to tell you how many times I've sent fish back to Charlie Ryan!"

"We need half an hour today to check the premises. Then after you close tonight, we'll sweep the room. Make certain it's clean. No explosives. No electronics. Next we bring in a communications line. The bomb dogs. And that's about it."

Libby nodded. "You know, I started out in this business with Sonny. He was the only one I could trust." She got up.

He held onto her arm. "We're not finished yet."

"Birnbaum, doesn't this ride ever stop?"

He let go. "I'm not the police. What you do about Sonny is your business. Same as what you do about the dishwasher."

"What about the dishwasher?"

"We don't want him here tomorrow. He's an illegal alien."

"Oh, my God. I can't fire Alfero."

"Why not?"

"I just promoted him! I can't do it." Libby looked up as she heard the front door open. "But I know who can."

Steven walked in carrying his suit on a hanger. He stared at Birnbaum. "Table 51. Birnbaum."

"Darling!" Libby said with forced gaiety. "Have you seen Fay's column?"

Birnbaum stood up and shook hands with Steven. "You've got quite a memory for faces."

"Faces, insults, injuries." He turned to Libby. "Would you mind telling me what's going on? It looks like there's a convention in front of the building."

She waved the morning paper. "I really must congratulate the kitchen." Libby got up. "Oh, Steven, that reminds me. Would you please fire Alfero?" She started walking away.

"Mother!"

Libby stopped. "And be sure to go over the reservations book with Special Agent Birnbaum."

"I'm meeting the fire inspector in a few minutes," Birnbaum said.

"He needs twelve tables for lunch tomorrow. No one in and no one out. And there's something about communication lines and dogs! Oh, yes! Bomb dogs." She smiled. "Now I really must tell the cooks how happy I am."

Steven blocked her path. "Not before you tell me what's going on."

Libby nodded. She rolled up the newspaper and held it in front of her as though it were a microphone. She pinched her nose. "Good evening, Mr. and Mrs. America and all the ships at sea. Thursday. Lunch. Libby's. The President of the United States."

Steven's mouth dropped open. He looked at Birnbaum, then at Libby. "The President?"

Libby's eyes filled with tears. "Yes, darling. Isn't it wonderful? The father of your country."

o

Bud didn't want to share his excitement with Tessa. He expressed indifference to Fay's column. Showering and dressing quickly, he paused only long enough to make a doctor's appointment for Tessa before leaving to meet with one of his suppliers. Bud walked downtown from his loft to the live chicken market on Broome Street.

Roselli's was filled with old Chinese and Italian women straight from the pages of an old travel guide. Although there were no chickens in sight, the cackling and the smell were everywhere. Feathers covered the floor. The walls. Even the ceiling.

"What's wrong?" Roselli shouted. "I send you my best. The same chickens I send my mama, she rest in peace."

Bud stepped around the women with their shopping bags. He nodded toward the back. "Okay?"

"What? You think I hide the good ones? Go. Go look. You see what crap I have left for them." Then Roselli turned and smiled at his customers. "Next?"

Bud walked along the wooden slats caked with droppings into a room filled with crates of frightened, screaming chickens. Two fat women sat on stools, plucking feathers while blood dripped from their plastic aprons. The executioner was a wiry old man with one eye closed to avoid smoke from the cigarette in the corner of his mouth. Depending upon the customer's preference, he slit the chicken's throat or chopped off its head. The chicken had no say in the matter.

Bud reached into the sack for a handful of feed. He stepped close to the cages, as close as he dared put his face, and whispered, "Here, chick-chick. Here, chick-chick." He threw the feed as though tossing coins into a very deep wishing well. Stupid birds, he thought. More concerned about lunch than about the old man with cigarette smoke curling up the side of his face. Not so with the birds who hung out at Libby's. They wouldn't have taken their eyes off the old man for a minute. No matter what you fed them. Not until Truffle Pot Pie. Bud's moment had come. He had triumphed over indifference. It was time to give back.

He unlatched the cage and grabbed a chicken by the neck. "Here," Bud said to the old man. "Kill it."

While the chicken gurgled and flapped its wings, the old man nodded. He brought his hand down like the blade of an ax. The chicken struggled. Bud shook his head no and mimed a very slow slit across the throat.

The chicken screeched as its blood spurted onto the floor. The old man handed the dying bird to one of the fat women. She grabbed it by the throat and while it was still kicking, pushed it into a pail of hot water to make it easier to pluck the feathers. Bud didn't wait. He walked out front.

Roselli looked up. "So you satisfied?"

Bud took out a twenty-dollar bill. "Give the change to the old man."

Roselli called after him. "Why?"

"You always tip the shaman."

○

The kitchen was well into the adolescent phase of its daily life cycle. Stockpots bubbled broth impatient to mature into sauce. Frypans sizzled with sweaty onions losing the opacity of innocence. The prep men washed heads of radicchio and pulled stems from wild mushrooms. Liang and Gan, at the cold station, cut frozen beef into paper-thin slices for carpaccio, and ground up walnuts for the spaghetti squash. Louie, muttering to himself, waited for the fire inspector to get out of his way.

Fire Prevention Inspector Sidney Green wore no uniform, held no rank, was not a member of a fire-fighting team, and had never even owned a pair of red suspenders. He was an inspector. Humorless, pedantic, an idolater of the fire code, he had no doubt been an inspector in kindergarten.

"Sidney, shame on you!" Libby shouted as she came into the kitchen. "They are dying like flies at Trader Vic's! Table after table is ablaze with flaming pu-pu platters and you stand here staring up at my sprinklers?''

F.P.I.S. Green pointed to Birnbaum who stood behind her. "He wants to see it work."

"No, he doesn't."

"I have to see it work," Birnbaum said simply.

Libby shook her head. "Jesus Christ. The tooth fairy never even had a fighting chance with you."

"I need to know that it works."

F.P.I.S. Green sighed. "Do you need to *know* that it works or do you need to *see* that it works?"

"I cannot know that it works unless I see that it works."

F.P.I.S. Green narrowed his eyes in admiration. "Very good. An excellent argument, albeit one that presumes we agree on a definition of what is knowledge."

"I'll save you a lot of time," Birnbaum yelled. "We don't agree. Second, I don't want to agree. I just want to see the fucking sprinklers work!"

"No sprinkle now!" Louie shouted, quickly transferring Truffle Pot Pie cases from a baking sheet onto a rack.

"Now. I want to see them work right now!"

"You make these ruined!" Louie shouted. "You want sprinkle to work or me?"

"Good morning! Health Department! Hiya, Libby!" Senior Inspector Irving Dubinsky came in the back. "Fire Prevention Inspector Green! What are you doing here?"

"Senior Inspector Dubinsky! What a pleasure."

"Listen, Sidney, we must do lunch!"

o

It had been a disastrous night for Cal. He pretended he was asleep while Libby dressed, waiting for her to leave before heading back to his hotel.

He had never expected her to say no. Not that it was an out and out no. It was a studio no. A non-answer. As though the question had never been asked. A typically Pacific Coast response designed to save face in Southeast Asia and in Beverly Hills where face was all they had.

He knew he had hurt Libby. He saw the pain in her eyes and

felt the desperation as she held tight instead of laughing with him about Rikki. Janos was right. Cal didn't need six million dollars. He wanted it. But Cal wanted Libby even more. He picked up the phone and dialed his agent in LA. "Smitty?"

"Where the hell have you been? I left four messages."

"Why? What happened?"

"Nothing happened. I wanted to find out if you were all right."

"Nothing happened?"

"Not yet."

"I was at Libby's."

"What's wrong with the suite? Goddamn it, I told them . . ."

"There's nothing wrong with the suite."

"You have a view?"

"Yes."

"You're on a high floor?"

"Yes."

"So everything's all right?"

"Everything's all right," Cal said.

"Then what is it?"

"Everything is terrible."

"Of course everything is terrible," Smitty said. "This is a terrible time. Terrible things are happening to you."

"I need a picture."

"I know you do."

"I put all my money into *Hearsay Evidence.*"

"I know."

"I need a picture."

"I got you a picture."

"You got me *The Desert Song.*"

"I got you a picture."

"Smitty, I am lying here naked in the middle of October and I am sweating."

"You told me you wanted a picture. I got you a picture."

"Smitty, the sweat is all over me like liquid neon."

"They're ready to start anytime you are. You don't have to pack. Nothing. All you have to do is get into the limo. I'll meet you at the airport. I'll take you to Morocco. Trust me. You'll make enough money on this picture to comfortably declare bank-ruptcy."

"No stupid jokes, Smitty."

"You asked me to get you a picture."

"I know."

"I got you a picture."

"You got me a joke."

"I got you a picture."

"I don't want to do it."

"What do you want to do? You want a guest shot on 'Dy-nasty'?"

"Smitty, I can't stop sweating."

"How do you feel?"

"I feel like a failure."

"Listen to me. You are not a failure. Everybody goes through what you're going through. The difference is when you get through going through whatever you're going through, you wind up as Cal Dennis. I'm a fifty-three-year-old fat fallen Lutheran. I have two children somewhere in Seattle who are on drugs and have arrest records with more entries than my bank account. I have no talent. I have no education. I have no sex appeal. The only fucking I get is when I make a bad deal. However, I do not regard myself as a failure. But don't get me wrong. That doesn't mean I'm secure enough to keep company with failures. If I am talking to a failure, please hang up." There was a long silence. "I need you, Cock of the West, to make my sun rise. If you are not strong, I am nothing. And I will not be nothing."

"I hate you, Smitty."

"You can tell me all about it in Morocco."

o

Senior Inspector Irving Dubinsky shook his finger in Birnbaum's face. "One roach means instant failure! One mouse, dead or alive, and it's a $175 fine." He started to laugh. "I only wish I had a deal like that with my landlord!"

Like Romulus and Remus, Sidney and Irving were carving up the empire for themselves. They explained it all to Birnbaum.

"While I'm checking the fire extinguishers in the dining room, and the exit doors, . . ." Sidney began.

". . . I'll take my temperatures," Irving continued. "The water in the dishwasher has to be 170 degrees. The cold food has to be 45 degrees or less. And the hot food has to be 140 degrees or more." Irving smiled. "With the exception of roast beef. Because some people like it rare, we let them get away with 120."

"I hate rare roast beef," Sidney said. "Irving, you feel like deli? You want to go to the Carnegie for lunch?"

"What's the matter? You don't like the Stage any more?"

"I like it. But they know me better at the Carnegie. I walk in, I'm a person."

Irving shook his head and muttered to Birnbaum, "He's such an old lady." Then, getting back to work, "I also check the mixers and the slicers to make sure they don't have filthy little pieces of food encrusted anywhere."

Sidney rolled his eyes. "How would you like to go to lunch with this guy?"

Birnbaum was serious. "I expect you to check the stove for gas leaks, the wiring on the air conditioning, and the safeties around the fuel oil."

Meanwhile, Irving got down on his knees and opened the cabinets. "Good morning, roaches," he said, turning on his flashlight.

"No roaches here!" Louie shouted.

"Do you see any roaches?" Irving asked Birnbaum.

"I don't have to see them to know there must be roaches."

Sidney was on a ladder, checking the nozzles on the ceiling. "The roaches he doesn't have to see. The sprinkler he does."

"It's not so unusual," Irving said. "Every good restaurant has its own sanitation consultant. I come in once a year and I ask to see the records. I look around. Thirty percent have no roaches and no mice. They have no flies. But if I find one, I'm back in three months. If it's still dirty, it costs them $275 and they go onto the 'rat list' in the *Times*. The third time I catch them, I close them down." Irving slammed shut the last of the drawers. "You know how I check for rats?"

"Yeah," Sidney answered from the ladder. "You follow my brother-in-law."

Irving took a pencil from his pocket and waved it in front of Birnbaum's face. "Droppings. You find a dropping and you test it with a pencil. If the dropping is hard, it could be from a long time ago. Maybe they didn't clean up enough. But if it's soft," he said triumphantly, "it's fresh! Then I know I got them!"

"No soft rat shit here!" Louie shouted angrily. Suddenly he began to giggle. "Except Sonny." He translated promptly for the rest of the staff.

Sonny was in the dry storage room. Without taking his eyes from Libby, he sat down on the floor. He pulled a cellophane wrapper from his pocket and waved it in her face. "What the hell? I'm glad you found out."

Libby watched in horror. "Oh, God. Oh, my God."

"I've been averaging three, four hundred a week. Produce. Dry goods. Fish. It's hard to make deals with the meat men. I tried but they're such fucking prima donnas. I couldn't take a chance with them anyway." He smiled. "I had to get you good meat."

"I would have given you the money." She kneeled down next to him. "I would have sent you to a clinic."

"A clinic? What the hell for? I'm no dopehead. I don't have a drug problem. I got the same thing everybody's got. I got a people problem. Listen, some asshole decides to pull your tooth, you want a little something for the pain. That's all. It's not my fault everybody's a dentist."

"Let me help you."

"What's all this help-me shit? Don't you understand? I've been stealing from you."

"It's not your fault, Sonny. It's the drugs."

"The hell it is. I didn't steal from you to support a habit. I stole from you because I wanted to steal from you. Then I had to look for a way to spend the money. And let me tell you, it wasn't as easy to spend as it was to steal. I thought about the ponies. Fancy French furniture. I even thought about mutual funds." He began to laugh. "The goddamn money just kept piling up. I was really getting worried. The pressure was terrible."

Libby sat down on the floor next to him. "We've been friends for years. I don't care."

"Bullshit. You do care."

"Bullshit," she said softly. "I do care."

After a long silence, Sonny asked, "So, who's the VIP?"

"The President."

He nodded approvingly. "I guess you've arrived."

Libby nodded slowly. "Yeah. Right on my ass."

Sonny reached over and took her hand. "I'm glad you know the truth."

"You're glad?" she shouted. The room became still, bursting with negative sound. The sound in a mine shaft after the canary stops singing. Libby pulled her hand back as she whispered, "What the hell is it with people today? They hate you, they tell you they hate you. They steal from you, they tell you they steal from you." She stood up. "It's people like you who give lying and cheating a bad name. You think the truth is supposed to make you feel better?" She grabbed Sonny by the arm. "Didn't you ever read the Bible? Don't you know what God was trying to protect Adam and Eve from? What the hell do you think was growing on that goddamn tree?" Libby screamed loud enough to banish the demons inside her. "Truth! That's what was growing on that goddamn tree!" She pushed back her bangs and took a deep breath, speaking quickly, afraid she might not finish all she wanted to say before bursting into tears. "And just in case you don't believe me, only a few minutes ago I was speaking to someone very high up in the truth business. He confirmed exactly what I've known for years. Everybody lies!" Libby cleared her throat. "Why the hell else would the United States Government have a Secret Service?" Libby reached behind her and opened the door. There seemed to be no air. Not enough air. She began to cough.

Alfero stepped out of the linen room where he had been counting napkins. "Señora? Are you sick?"

Libby was hyperventilating. She held up her hand. "Oh, no. Not you!" She felt Alfero's hands balancing her. "For God's sake, not you!"

"I take you inside." Alfero brought her into the dining room. Libby gasped. Secret Service agents had moved the banquettes away from the walls. They had taken apart the ceiling fixtures. Tables and chairs lay upside down in the aisles. God knows how many thick-necked linebackers were rummaging through her restaurant as carelessly as they had rummaged through her life. And there were dogs barking.

The moment Birnbaum saw her, he knew something was wrong. "Libby?"

"Señora?"

She pushed Alfero away and went back into the kitchen. But Sidney had just turned on the sprinklers. She looked up, opening her palms to the fine white spray of sodium bicarbonate that fell from the ceiling. It was as though she had stepped into another dimension. Libby stood in the center of the kitchen, watching the powder cover her. Birnbaum rushed her toward the linen room. Once inside, he put his arms around her.

Libby began to cry. "You're right. I haven't told you everything."

"That is not exactly a late-breaking bulletin."

"It's a lot worse than you think."

He smiled and gave her his handkerchief. "If it's any consolation, there are very few things that are worse than I think they are."

"Trust me, Birnbaum. I wouldn't steer you wrong."

He nodded. "Overheard on the *Titanic.*"

But Libby had gone the *Titanic* one better. Torn apart and rapidly sinking, she still managed to stay afloat. Astonishingly, she had been saved by the iceberg. The moment Birnbaum took her in his arms, she felt a rush of emotion. It didn't matter which emotion. It could have been despair or fear or lust. It was the affirmation of life that was important. The sudden realization that there was life before death.

Libby blew her nose. "Oh, Birnbaum. You can't imagine what's going on."

"Yes, I can."

"You don't know how many problems I have."

"Yes, I do."

"No, you don't!"

He put his arms around her. "Well, let's say I know one of them."

She leaned against his shoulder. "Which one?"

Birnbaum brushed the powder from her cheek. His hand lingered. "Me."

o

The staff had gathered for the morning meeting as though it was a memorial service. No one spoke above a whisper. Maxie the waiter even offered Ursula a chair. The bartenders took seats instead of standing. Alfero, in the first row, sat bolt upright, determined to do honor to his new uniform. For the first time, not only Bud but all the cooks attended the meeting.

Steven raced through his notes without any interruptions. He read Fay's comments on Truffle Pot Pie and even the waiters applauded politely. The catalyst for this unusual behavior was the sight of Birnbaum in the seat usually occupied by Libby.

Steven looked up from his papers. "In case someone here just arrived from Mars and hasn't heard the rumor, the rumor is true. The President is coming to lunch."

There were cheers, some whistles and an immediate exchange of cash among the waiters. They had already made book on it. Simon, holding a fistful of cash, stood up. "Okay! Okay! Next. Whose table?"

"We're not going by tables," Steven said. "There are a number of switches we have to make."

"Who?" Simon waved the cash impatiently. "Who gets his table?"

"I have been advised that the team handling the President cannot work any other tables."

Simon looked around the room. "Could you die? Who is it?"

"George."

"I picked George!"

"Me, too!"

"Oh, shit."

"I told you I should have played George."

George, the only waiter to bet on himself, winked at Alfero. Alfero thought his heart would burst. It was his first day as a busboy and already he had been selected to serve El Presidente. What a country!

Steven rapped his knuckles loudly. "All right, can we please get back to business? I'd like this over with as quickly as possible."

"That's what Maxie's wife says!"

Steven slammed his fist onto the table. Birnbaum turned quickly, a second away from reaching for his gun. It wasn't that Steven had startled him, it was that Birnbaum had been trained to react to violence. He had a precognition for violence the way ballet dancers have elevation. Inexplicable talents. Imperative for success.

Finally, the room was still. Steven, unaware that his lack of control rather than his authority had silenced them, cleared his throat. "We have with us this morning Special Agent Birnbaum of the Secret Service. I want you to give him your full attention."

Simon passed Maxie a note. It read, "12–2 Norm gets George's tables. $10 min."

"If we lived in a dictatorship," Birnbaum began, "it would be relatively easy to ensure the President's security. But living in a free, open democracy makes our job a hell of a lot harder." Birnbaum reached out and grabbed the note from Maxie. He put it in his pocket. "However, even in a democracy, there are things we cannot do. One of the things I cannot do is let this restaurant become another Dallas. Another Ambassador Hotel. Another Washington Hilton. My job is to die rather than let that happen." He paused. "The problem is that I don't want to die. So I need your help. Here is what you have to do to keep me alive." Birnbaum paused. Purely for effect. "Don't tell anyone that the President will be here tomorrow." Birnbaum knew that was impossible. But it was part of the routine. "Should there be an incident of any kind tomorrow, should there be any disturbance, whether successful or unsuccessful, we know that you are the only people without security clearance who have foreknowledge of the President's visit." He tugged at his belt, a move contrived to expose his Smith & Wesson. "I am authorized to advise you that each and every one of you will be detained indefinitely for investigation. All civil rights, in such an event, will be terminated immediately. In short, ladies and gentlemen, you will wish you had been caught smuggling opium out of Istanbul." He paused. "Is that clear?" Then he walked around the table and went to each person in the room. "Is that clear?"

"Yes."

"Is that clear?"

"Yes."

Louie poked Bud and whispered, "What he say, boss?"

Steven asked Alfero to remain after the others had left. He motioned for him to sit down.

Alfero's mind was racing. He had thought of the most wonderful plan. He was going to steal the plates and silverware that the President used and bring them home for his children. He wanted his sons to realize that in America anything was possible. One day you were no one, and the next day . . .

Steven sat down opposite Alfero. "I have something serious to talk to you about."

Alfero smiled. "You don't have to worry. I swear I do not tell Dolores about the President."

The phone rang. Steven picked it up and said, "Libby's." Without any expression, he motioned for Alfero to pass him the reservations book. Something caught Alfero's eye as he glanced at the open page. Alfero stretched across the table and began reading upside down. By force of habit, Steven asked, "How many?" Then he put a hand to his forehead. He interrupted with, "I'm sorry. Tomorrow is fully booked. No. I'm sorry. Please call again."

Alfero pointed to a name on the reservations list. "Señor Ensesa?"

Steven nodded. "Who is he?"

Alfero could not believe that on the very day he was going to serve the President of the United States, José Ensesa would be in the same room! "He is the richest man in South America!" Alfero said. "My father, for many years, took the garbage for the Ensesa family. Every year, at fiesta, they send new shoes for my brothers and sisters. For new beginnings, they say." He smiled and lifted his leg to show Steven that he was wearing a pair of new shoes. "Dolores and Tía buy me these. For new beginnings."

Jesus Christ, Steven thought, blaming it all on Libby. If she hadn't made him fire Chickie. If she hadn't made Alfero a busboy. But as usual, he was left with all her garbage. He was no better than Alfero's father.

Alfero stared at the reservations book, his eyes devouring

the call-back number Ensesa had left. He could call Ensesa and tell him he was now a busboy. 599-2654. All he needed was a quarter. 599-2654.

"Alfero, the Secret Service found out that you are an illegal alien. They don't want you on the premises when the President is here. Furthermore, I have a responsibility to the restaurant. I cannot continue to employ an illegal alien." That should do it, Steven thought. "You are fired. I want you out of here immediately."

Alfero's face still had the remnants of a smile. Steven had spoken so quickly that Alfero's battered emotional circuitry hadn't time to respond fully. "I have no green card," Alfero said. "But I am an American!"

"That is a lie," Steven said matter-of-factly.

"Señor Steven, I beg you. I love America. I work hard. Please do not fire me."

Steven reached for Alfero and grabbed him by the wrist. "Don't blame me," he said softly. Suddenly, Steven wanted to kiss Alfero. He wanted to put his hands between Alfero's legs. "It's not my fault. It's my mother's."

"Please, you let me speak to the Señora. She will understand."

"The Señora told me to fire you. She told me she wanted you out of here immediately. She told me to report you to the Immigration and Naturalization Service."

Alfero's eyes became watery. "But why? Why does she say such things?"

Steven let go of his wrist. "She is a no-good bitch. You cannot trust her. I hate what she is doing to you."

Tessa was counting coat checks as Steven walked over. He smiled uncomfortably. "Listen . . ."

Tessa rolled her eyes. "Don't worry. I won't shoot the President."

"I'm not worried. But the big bad Secret Service doesn't want you here tomorrow."

"What do you mean they don't want me here tomorrow?"

"That's what they said." Steven shrugged. "Blame not the messenger."

"I don't understand."

"It's nothing to get upset about. They found out you were arrested at some protest rallies. They suggested you take a personal day and just not come in tomorrow."

"The hell I will!"

Steven didn't want Tessa to get her nose out of joint. He didn't need any further strain on his relationship with Bud. "You won't lose any pay."

"You think I care about the money?"

"Listen, I really want to help. I'll do whatever you want to ease your upset."

Tessa smiled. "Good. I want you to tell the Fascist pigs that since, according to them, we live in a democracy, you are not prepared to discriminate against me because I chose to exercise my constitutionally guaranteed right of peaceful assembly."

"How about I treat you to a shampoo and set instead? What the hell," he smiled, peeling off bills from his money clip. "Have a facial. The works." He held out a hundred dollars.

Tessa took the money and tore it up. "You think you can buy and sell everyone, don't you?"

"Obviously not."

She took hold of his arm. "Are you going to fight for me?"

"I'm sorry. I left my charger home."

Tessa let go of him. "You faggot. Bud was right. You don't have any balls." She picked up the pile of numbered coat checks and threw them into the air. "I'm not coming in tomorrow or any other day. I quit!"

Alfero was in a hurry to leave. Beneath his street clothes, he still wore his busboy uniform. They could take away the job but, like Pelé, they would have to retire the uniform with him.

There was another reason Alfero was in a hurry. He had stolen all the truffles. Fortunately, the jars were small. He stuffed them into his underwear, inside his shirt, and in his pockets. Alfero knew he was stealing something they would miss. He heard Tessa shout, "I quit!" and stopped. He watched with awe as she threw the coat checks into the air.

"You call this a democracy?" Tessa screamed, grabbing her books. "If I'm not good enough to be here tomorrow, then neither is the President!"

Alfero was astonished. He would never have taken her for an illegal. Walking away quickly, he let himself out the front door. But instead of feeling relief at not having been caught, he was overwhelmed by despair. He looked up at the canopy. He touched the black lacquered panels. Only a few hours ago, Dolores posed with him in front of the door. Carlos had taken pictures that would be proof of his disgrace.

Alfero stood in the sunlight wondering what he would tell Dolores. How could he face his sons? He realized for the first time how much the new shoes hurt his feet.

○

It was one o'clock and every table was filled. Cal stood behind Steven at the reservations desk and stared into the room. He wanted to apologize for what he had said the day before. But Steven never accepted apologies. Harsh words were like bad weather to him—they came and went as part of his environment. It hurt Cal that Steven was so willing to accept pain. The only thing he could do was put a hand on Steven's shoulder as though nothing had happened. "Hey kiddo, how do I get to Janos without taking the scenic route?"

Steven nodded toward Burt Reynolds and Michael Caine. "For starters, avoid Mount Rushmore."

"Jesus," Cal said. "Don't they look great? Who's at the next table?"

"Sigourney and Chris are back from London. The reviews were terrific."

"I don't need that."

Steven glanced down the other aisle. "Wait a minute. This one is a piece of cake. Zubin and Beverly Sills."

"He looks terrific, too, doesn't he? Where is Libby?"

Steven sighed deeply. "When last sighted, she was off the coast of Andre." He leaned forward. "No. She's surfaced at Carly Simon."

Cal watched Libby as she listened in that special way of hers that made people feel there was no one else on earth. Libby used listening the way a lion tamer used a whip. Except last night. Cal didn't think she'd heard a thing he said.

Steven nudged him. "All you have to worry about in that aisle is Helen Gurley Brown."

"I wish." Cal squinted. "Who's with her?"

"George Hamilton."

"Shit." Cal shook his head. "That guy just doesn't show any wear. He must have a picture in his attic."

"Take the low road. You can slip by Helen's table."

"The hell I can. She's a friend." Cal raised his eyebrows. "Cut off at the pass by Helen Gurley Brown."

Steven turned around. "What's going on with you?"

Instinctively, Cal smiled. He started knocking himself on the head. "Vell, I tell you, Doctor, it hoits ven I hit myself."

"I hate to see you like this."

Cal put his hand on Steven's shoulder and again stared into the room. "Movie stars to the right of me, movie stars to the left of me."

"Come on. Stop stalling. Into the valley of glitz."

"A coward dies many times . . ."

"Yours is not to reason why . . ."

Cal leaned toward Steven and softly sang the opening lines of the march from *The Desert Song, "Over the ground, There comes a sound, It is the drum drum drum of hoofbeats in the sand."*

"Hey, Red Shadow?"

"Yeah?"

"Why don't you take your own advice?"

"Such as?"

"Stop hitting yourself on the head."

Hots had his usual plate of Bumble Bee tuna. Dr. Loren Sawyer had ordered pheasant on rye. They both watched ex-hostage Wanda Fogelman concentrate single-mindedly on her pork chops in beer batter with home-fried yams and creamed onion purée.

"Is it good, Wanda?" Hots asked, raising his voice as though speaking to a dog.

Wanda smiled and nodded. Her mouth was full. She glanced momentarily at Loren and then refocused on her plate.

"I'm handling Wanda's contract with William Morris," Hots said, watching as she picked up a pork chop and broke it in two.

"I'm doing it for free." Hots shrugged. "The kid's been through a lot."

Loren leaned forward as Wanda's tongue circled her lips, licking off a smudge of creamed onion. "Maybe she'd like a free examination."

"I'll ask her."

Loren kept his eyes on the room as he reached slowly into his pocket. "I'll give her a Pap test, check for any growths in her colon, and make certain there's no cellular trauma to her mammaries."

Hots put his hand under the table and took the small plastic envelopes filled with cocaine. "Loren, you're a real patriot." Hots picked up his phone. While dialing, he asked, "How many extras did you give me?"

"Two was all I could spare," Loren said.

"Why? Colombia fell into the ocean?"

"Take a little bit from your clients. It wouldn't be the first time."

Hots raised his eyebrows and spoke into the receiver. "Mama? I could only get two extra. Ma, it's enough to get you through the weekend. I love you, too."

Loren couldn't take his eyes from Wanda. "I'm serious. If there's anything I can do to help. An examination . . ."

Hots raised his voice. "Wanda, as part of your contract, you need a medical." He dipped the edge of his napkin into the water goblet and handed it to Wanda, pointing to the gravy stain on her blouse. "I've arranged for you to see Dr. Sawyer." Then Hots turned to Loren and rolled his eyes. "While you're at it, maybe you can do a charisma implant."

Loren winked at Wanda. She smiled and waved a pork chop bone at him. It looked as though it had been picked clean by a vulture.

Phyllis turned to Donald. "I'd give a thousand calories to know what that blonde is doing with Hots."

Donald removed a bone from his smoked trout. "Perhaps he's covering for Loren."

"Don't be ridiculous. Prince Valium's got as much class as a Lotto millionaire."

"Then let's just assume she's Loren's fuck du jour and get back to what we were talking about."

Phyllis pushed aside her salmon tartare. "I thought that's what we were talking about. You were telling me . . ."

"I don't need subtitles, Phyllis."

"You were telling me," she repeated angrily, "that it's perfectly all right for the earth to move for you and my best friend's son, but that I'm not allowed to hop onto the Richter Scale with her ex-husband."

"It loses something in the translation."

"Do you think Cal is avoiding me? Why the hell would he rush over to Helen? Do you think he's really going to do the play?" Phyllis lit a cigarette. "Oh God, I need a leading man."

"Don't we all, dearie."

"Cal would be perfect if I could get him to do it."

Donald nodded. "I've thought that many times myself. But you've got as much chance getting him into your play as I have getting him into my bed."

"In that case, there's only one thing to do." Phyllis shrugged. "I'll get him into *my* bed."

Donald took her cigarette and stubbed it out. "Shut up, Phyllis, and eat your lunch. Think of all the starving people on Broadway."

Richard L. Horton was the advance man for the White House Staff. He was very short, very thin, and very smart. It was his job to know exactly what the President wanted, then listen to the Secret Service say it couldn't be done, and then make certain it was. The perfect job for a very short man.

Birnbaum and Anders watched as Horton took the last breadstick for himself and said, "I'd like some more breadsticks."

Anders looked at Birnbaum. Birnbaum nodded. He put out his hand and stopped a waiter in the aisle. "More breadsticks, please."

As soon as the waiter left, Horton reached into his jacket and took out two envelopes. Each contained a single-spaced, twelve-page memo from the White House Staff concerning their requirements for the President from the time Air Force One landed at Newark (0850) to the time it took off less than seven hours later (1540).

Birnbaum shook his head. "Dick, this doesn't make any sense."

"Please don't call me Dick. It sounds like you're calling me *a* dick and I don't like it." Horton took the last pat of butter and put it on his plate. "I'll need more butter, too."

Anders leaned over to Birnbaum and pointed to three items on the first page. The two men nodded. "What the hell's going on here?" Anders asked Horton. "Why all the layering?"

Birnbaum kept turning pages. "Why the big window in his schedule? How come you guys don't want anyone to know the President is having lunch here?"

Horton used his butter knife as a pointer. "I am directly responsible to the Chief of Staff and he is responsible to the President. I'd appreciate it if you did not use that tone when you speak to me."

Birnbaum reached across the table and put his hand around Horton's hand, squeezing hard until Horton dropped the butter knife. "And I'd appreciate it if you'd kiss my ass. Listen, you short shit, this is not Harvard Yard and I'm not here to park the car. In case you forgot, when the shooting starts, I'm the one who doesn't duck. Whether you know it or not, and whether you like it or not, you are responsible to *me.*"

"The reason for the President coming here tomorrow is none of your business," Horton said flatly. "It is my decision that you do not need to know why he is coming in order to protect him. Furthermore, the fact that you are willing to take a bullet in the head is no more surprising to me than the fact there are millions of people out there who voluntarily listen to Elvis Presley or eat Velveeta cheese. This great nation of ours is filled with idiots."

For the moment, it wasn't at all clear to Birnbaum why he should be willing to die for a President who had a Richard L. Horton on his staff. Men like Richard L. Horton were the precise reason Birnbaum had never wanted to be on the White House detail. He didn't want to see the warts. He didn't want anything to challenge his memory of those boots reversed in the saddle.

The closest Birnbaum had ever been to the President was the night he drew piss patrol outside the men's room at the Waldorf.

"Before we begin," Horton said, "I'd like something else understood. In the event there is an incident, or in the event the President is terminated, it is our intention to proceed without alerting the media."

"That's impossible," Anders said. "You've got your own press car doing a body watch."

Horton nodded. "We'll take care of them. The decision is a news blackout until after three P.M."

"Until the market closes," Birnbaum said.

"The economy doesn't need a jolt right now." Horton explained. "The market lost eleven billion dollars after Dallas."

Birnbaum looked at Horton, wondering whether it was possible for the human ear to differentiate between lower case and uppercase letters. "Well, dick, what do you think will happen to the market if I get killed?"

Horton smiled. "I'll have the networks interrupt every fucking soap opera and announce it myself."

"Breadsticks!" the waiter announced.

As Horton reached for them, Birnbaum leaned forward, pretending it was an accident as he knocked the basket out of the waiter's hand. The breadsticks, like mute fireworks, sprayed into the air and fell to the floor.

Cal slid onto the banquette. Janos was on the phone. He looked up, winked, and then turned quickly back to the receiver. "One six!" He smiled at Cal. "I'm bidding against the Met! On a Picasso!"

"They don't stand a chance."

"One seven!" Janos slapped a hand against his forehead. "The schmucks are bidding against me even though I told them I'm going to give them my entire collection."

"Why would they do that?"

"Why? Because they know people don't pay to get into the Museum of Cheap Paintings. With art, a bargain is no bargain." He shouted into the receiver. "Enough. I have no more time for this. I have to eat lunch. Tell them two million and get it over with!"

Cal had to smile. Two million for Picasso. Six million for him. He glanced across the room. Libby was still with Carly Simon. But suddenly she looked up as though knowing exactly where he was. Thank God for sunglasses. He pretended not to have seen her.

Janos was flush with victory. He had won the Picasso. "And what about the gonif from the Louvre?" he shouted into the phone. "Can you see his face?"

A waiter was standing in the aisle. Cal couldn't see Libby's face. He watched Carly start to laugh and imagined Libby pushing back her bangs, opening her eyes wide and spreading her fingers as she spoke.

"I want a shot of Rikki looking at the painting," Janos said into the receiver. "Call her in the limo." He looked at Cal. "She wanted some exercise so she went for a ride in the park." Then, into the phone. "Give her something to say. Picasso is her favorite artist. Whatever. Just be sure to get her tits in the shot." He slammed the receiver down.

"I have to talk to you," Cal said.

"You know, boychik, they all think she's such a sexpot. But when I found her, she was nothing. Worse than nothing. She was dead. A corpse. Like Dr. Frankenstein, I brought her back to life. I taught her how to be a woman. I taught her how to dress. I taught her how to undress. I taught her what to do to me. I taught her what to do to herself." Janos leaned close. "I taught her more ways to climax than a symphony by Tchaikovsky."

"And all this time I thought you were nothing but a dirty old man."

Janos laughed. "That's what they all think. Let them think. I know the truth." He put a hand to his heart and spoke softly, as though quoting the Psalms. "I taught her the poetry of a finger up the ass."

It wasn't the vulgarity that upset Cal. Janos was simply being Janos. Cal had heard men say far worse things about their wives on movie sets. In airplanes. Even at their funerals. Cal was upset because he had decided to tell Janos he had changed his mind about the deal. He was going to say it had nothing to do with Rikki. He had finally read the script and it wasn't for him. That way, no one would be hurt.

"So, boychik, what is it we have to talk about? You getting nervous? You need a little advice from the maestro?"

But then Cal caught sight of Libby again. She was looking at him as though his being Cal Dennis and her being Libby Dennis was strictly an accident. Normally, she would have blown him a kiss and he would have winked at her. They would have shared a smile. But all they did was stare like strangers. Suddenly, just saying no to Janos wasn't enough.

"I'm looking for the right way to put this." Cal slid into the role of Cal Dennis, All-American Boy. He averted his eyes, shifting his body to indicate modesty. "We both know that Rikki's going to get a big kick out of sucking my cock and I want the moment to be as perfect for her as possible."

Janos appeared to have stopped breathing. He spoke without any trace of emotion. "You pull down her pants. You unzip your fly. You go in. You go out. And then you go to the bank."

"The hell I do!" Cal protested. "What do you take me for? This isn't some hide-the-salami deal between two strangers. If you're paying me six million dollars to lay your wife, I'm damn well going to do it right!"

"I don't want your cock in her mouth."

"But Janos, you and I are like family!"

"But nothing. I have to kiss her afterwards."

"Jesus. You're so sensitive! I never thought you were so sensitive."

"What do you think? Only people with blond hair and blue eyes are sensitive?"

"Janos, I'm only thinking about Rikki. You and I know what we're getting out of this deal. But what's in it for her?"

"Who cares what's in it for her? This is *my* deal. Not hers."

Cal smiled. "But Rikki is the fuckee."

"Of course she's the fuckee. She's always the fuckee. I created her to be the fuckee!" Janos's face had begun to flush. He was breathing faster.

Cal sat back and shrugged. "I just thought as long as I was at it, why not let Rikki have some fun." He grabbed Janos by the arm. "What about her nipples? I could bite them very gently. Some women like that."

"Forget it."

"I'm only asking for Rikki's sake." Cal nudged him with his elbow. "Come on. What does she like you to do to her?"

"Who cares?"

"Janos, does she like you to undress her?"

Janos stared out into the room. "No."

"I get it. She likes to surprise you! Naked under the covers?"

"No."

"Well, then does she like to watch you get undressed?"

Across the aisle, Margaret Truman Daniel was being seated. "She likes to pull down my pants."

"Son of a bitch!" Cal said, patting Janos on the arm. "Now we're getting somewhere. You really know how to tease the hell out of her, don't you? Then what?"

"She gets undressed."

"All right, I don't want to mess this part up. Does she like you to touch her while she gets undressed?"

"How can I touch her if she's standing on a chair!"

"On a chair?" Cal cleared his throat to prevent himself from laughing. "She's standing on a chair?"

Janos whispered angrily, "Why the hell are you asking all these questions?"

"You never heard of *An Actor Prepares?* Janos, where should I be when she's on the chair?"

Janos shook his finger angrily in Cal's face. "I don't want you sitting on my toilet!"

Cal started to laugh. "That's where you are? You sit on the toilet while she gets undressed?" He held up a hand in self-defense. "Okay. Okay. How about if I walk around the chair? I brush my shoulder against her thighs. Put a hand on her ankle. Then slowly, fingertip by fingertip, I walk my hand up her leg. Inside her thigh. Then one finger at a time . . ." Cal paused, asking matter-of-factly, "What do you think? You think that would please her?"

Janos banged his fist on the table. "Who cares? I didn't hire you to please her! I hired you to fuck her. The deal is: You fuck her, you please me!"

It was time for a drum roll. All Cal had to do was raise the pie and aim. "You know," Cal said calmly, "I have an even better deal. *You* fuck her. And then you go and fuck yourself!"

Libby couldn't take her eyes from Cal. If only he had smiled at *her* instead of smiling at Janos. She needed that Cal Dennis smile, however perfect it was, to reassure her, however imperfect she was. Instead, he had turned back to Janos. Laughing. Whispering. She knew they were working out the details. The time. The place. And however often she reminded herself that only a fool would walk away from a six-million-dollar deal, she wanted to see Cal run as fast as he could. She wanted him to hop the first available camel and carry her off into the desert sunset.

But the desert sunset would have to wait. There were no liver dumplings in the celery broth.

Diane von Furstenberg tried to stop Libby. "Please, darling. It doesn't matter."

But Libby snatched the bowl and headed toward the kitchen carrying the plate as though it held the head of John the Baptist. She passed the busboys in the service area and shouted, "Check the pitchers! I want ice in the water!" Pushing open the door, Libby shifted sensors from the chic buzz of the dining room to the harsh clatter of the kitchen. The rattle of silverware. The crash of china being stacked. The nervous sizzle-spit of the grill. And the shouting.

"Pots! Pots!" Cham repeated angrily, waiting for the porter to remove the dirty saucepans.

"Fire the chops!" Ursula yelled.

Norm stood in the middle of the room. "Where the fuck are my veggies?"

Libby grabbed hold of Stu and showed him the bowl. "What do you call this?"

"Oh, shit!"

"Fire one duck thighs!"

Libby tapped a finger on Ursula's shoulder. "You're not checking plates."

"Fire one lobster hash!" She looked at Libby impatiently. "If they don't stop, I don't check. I don't have eyes in the back of my head."

"Then you better get a pair up your ass," Libby said. Ursula put a hand to her mouth, laughing loudly. Libby shouted to the waiters, "Pick it up, boys. You're too slow."

"His wife wishes!"

"Ready on the chops for 52!"

"What about my bluefish?"

"Ready on the livers!"

"Fuck your bluefish!"

"Fuck your chops!"

"He no wait!" Liang shrieked at Libby while putting dumplings in a fresh bowl of broth. "He rush rush rush!"

"Rush you!" Stu said.

"Fuck you!"

"Ordering one swordfish naked!"

"Extra sauce on the crabmeat!"

"I no give extra sauce!"

Libby took the plate from Liang. "I do!"

"Pick up two TPP's!" Bud shouted. He slapped his palm on the counter impatiently as Al took the plates. "Come on! Come on! Before they're old enough for social security!" Bud walked around the chef's table to Libby. "We're in trouble."

Libby shook her head. "I'm closed. No more trouble today."

"Alfero stole all the truffles."

"He did what?" Libby began to laugh. "Good for Alfero."

"I borrowed enough from Caravelle and Grenouille to get started but the delivery hasn't arrived yet. I've only got six pies left."

Maxie the waiter burst into the kitchen and shouted, "You're not going to believe this! Burt's thinking about doing a play!" He handed Ursula the dupe from his order pad. "But Michael wants them to do a movie together."

"Ordering Table 22!" Ursula shouted. "One pâté! One crab!"

"What play?" George asked.

"What play! Phyllis Elgin's play!"

George shook his head as he picked up two orders of chicken livers in raspberry vinegar. "I was afraid of that. Burt's totally wrong for the part. Wrong! Wrong! Wrong!"

Bud put his hands on Libby's shoulders, pleading with her to understand. "I'm running out of truffles!"

She shrugged. "Welcome to the club."

Abner Waxman, as lean as Cassius, pale and balding, stood up as Mary Borden approached the table. "And how is the world's greatest agent today?" he asked, not expecting an answer from her. "Kiss kiss," he said, without bothering to lean over.

"Christ, you're not in one of your moods, are you?"

Abner nodded. "I spent all yesterday listening to *Bachianas Brasileiras* and eating nothing but lobster Newburg. Captain Depresso."

"You'll get fat," Mary warned.

"Step on a crack, break your mother's back."

"Can you take me to the theater tonight?" Mary asked. "It's an opening. One of my clients. I have to go."

"The theater is for illiterates," Abner said. "It's for people who can't read. That's how it all started, didn't it?"

Abner Waxman was a brilliant editor with a penchant for first novelists. Editing virgins was the only part of the business he enjoyed. As far as Abner was concerned, it was all downhill after the first book. But his first-novel fetish was costing the house a fortune. Which is why when Mary offered to bring him best-selling author Tully Ireland, she knew he would do anything in return. Even publish John Sessions's book, one of the few first novels he truly hated. Still, it was the quintessential Mary Borden deal: In the end, everyone got what they really wanted. Tully got more money, Abner got out of the red, John got published, and Mary got rid of John.

"I spoke to Junior yesterday about *Before Dawn*," Mary said. "I gave him the 'Good Germans versus Bad Germans' routine and said it was perfect for Cal Dennis."

"What did Cal Dennis ever do to you?"

Al, the waiter, nodded politely. "Are you ready to order?"

Abner leaned over to Mary. "Who's paying for lunch?"

"You are."

Abner smiled at Al. "Then I'd better cancel the '34 Petrus." His face brightened. "You know what I'm in the mood for? Lobster Newburg!"

Mary was impatient. She took both menus and handed them to Al. "I'll pay. Two chicken paillards. No veggies. Salad with lemon."

Abner waited for Al to leave. "I hate what you did."

"It's for your own good. You want to look like the Michelin Man?"

"I'm talking about *Before Dawn.* It's too early to send it out. I know you want everything tied up as quickly as possible for personal reasons, but it's too distracting for him. Why should he waste time on the rewrite? I can't compete with an offer from Junior and Cal Dennis."

"Don't worry. I'll see that John does whatever you want."

"Not with a movie option from Junior under his arm. You're giving him the gold medal before the torch is lit."

"John is very serious. He's dying to have you edit him. This is his first novel."

"It reads like his *third* first novel."

Mary ignored Abner's remark. "Besides, he's not about to screw around with a forty-thousand-dollar advance."

"Forty? I offered you twenty!"

"Forty and an author tour."

"How about his own rocket ship? We could launch him into space and you'd never have to see him again."

"You'll make it all back on Tully. I've read the new manuscript."

"How about *my* reading the new manuscript?"

Mary shook her head no. "I want to tell him that you didn't have to read it. You're willing to take it sight unseen."

"That about sums up publishing in America."

"Trust me, Abner. It will sell his usual million copies. I've leaked it to the clubs. You're safe."

"You went through all of that?"

"I want you to edit John's book."

"At your service, madam." He smiled. "I majored in Advanced Rumpelstiltskin. I've turned crap into gold before."

"You damn well better do something." She smiled for the first time. "He dedicated that piece of crap to me."

"Say no more. I shall do battle against the dreaded third-person singular. Armed with my faithful blue pencil, I shall vanquish all errant commas and rampant sentimentality." He reached for Mary's hand and held it tight. "However, there is still one huge loose end. I understand why you're giving me Tully for John. But who the hell are you giving Putnam as compensation for stealing Tully away? Now that has got to be one hell of a deal."

Andre picked up his glass and swirled the Château Lafite '70 wondering what the inmates at the Pritikin Center were having for lunch. After Junior backed out of the deal, Andre postponed his reservation again. He had been granted a reprieve. Andre was almost glad Junior had passed. He couldn't imagine spending the rest of his life on tofu.

Still, he knew something had to be done. It was increasingly difficult to breathe. He sat up half the night with palpitations worrying about his clogged arteries, his nicotine-stained lungs, and his nearly petrified liver. It had taken three Courvoisiers from room service before he calmed down enough to think about something more cheerful—imminent poverty.

Andre had one more day before his check to the Grandma Moses Foundation bounced. By drawing it on an Italian bank, he had been able to stall for a few weeks. But the bank notified him that the check had been submitted for collection and gave him only until the close of business Thursday before telexing the Foundation. He had thirty-six hours left in which to lay off the property.

"To miracles," Andre said, clinking glasses with Broadway composer David Gene.

"Is this stuff any good?" David asked, holding up his glass.

"Don't Chernobyl me, David. I've seen your cellar."

"Smart ass."

"Smart enough to invite you to lunch."

"You invited?" David asked. "Listen, I don't want to have a scene when the check comes. Please. I invited."

"David, if you recall, I was the one who told you last night that we ought to concept at lunch."

"Whatever. As long as I pay."

"If you can find a check, you can pay."

"What is that supposed to mean?"

"It means that I don't get a check. They send a bill."

"Like the IRS?"

"David, is this what we came to lunch to talk about? The bill? You want a house account, I'll make it part of the deal."

"What deal?"

Andre sloshed the wine from cheek to cheek, swallowed hard, and breathed in through his mouth.

"What deal?" David repeated.

"David, I'm not here to talk deals. I'm here to talk dreams. Do you remember what you said before dinner last night?"

"I said I was hungry and when the hell was C.Z. going to serve?"

"You said that *Sunday in the Park with George* should have been called *Sunday in the Park with Sondheim.*"

"Don't get me started again."

Andre reached over and put his hand on David's. "That's the whole point, dear friend. You got started and couldn't stop. They called dinner and you didn't move. You and I sat there at the piano well into the Lady Curzon soup. You said, and I shall never forget this, David, you said that if you were writing a musical about an artist, and 'artist-to-artist' was the precise phrase you used, you said you'd make damn well sure to have a song you could hum!"

David nodded. "What the hell is Lady Curzon soup anyway?"

Andre raised his glass. "A toast, David."

"It's that good?"

"I'm toasting your next Tony award for best musical of the year."

David stared at him. "In that event, keep talking."

"Open your hand, David." Andre pretended to pour something from his hand into David's palm.

"What is that?"

"My dream. My dream for Anna Mary Robertson Moses. Play it on your piano, David."

David looked at his open palm. "Grandma Moses?" he whispered.

"A musical about a woman trying to recapture her youth

armed only with a paintbrush and a canvas. Not some pointillist punk making dots. I am talking songs you can hum.''

David continued staring at his hand. "You want me to write a big Broadway musical about some little old lady with one foot in the grave and the other in a tube of burnt sienna?''

Andre was breathing heavily. "I have it all, David. All the merchandising rights. Coasters. Posters. Toasters. You name it. I'm willing to give you part of the action.''

David began to flex his fingers, as though suddenly hearing a melody. He looked at Andre. "Maybe it's not such a crazy idea.''

"It *is* a crazy idea, David. That's the reason it's going to work. It's totally crazy.'' Andre stopped to gulp some air. "That's why if we're very careful, if we guard zealously against losing any of our insanity, we're going to come up with the most important musical of the eighties.''

David moved his fingers as though playing a brand new song. He glanced up at Andre. "I get a cut on the T-shirts?''

"You get everything you want.''

David, his eyes ablaze, leaned toward Andre. He tapped his forefinger on the table. "And I pay for lunch?''

Andre raised his glass. Breathlessly, he said, "To 'Grandma!' ''

J held up two fingers. She needed a double if she was going to hear Bumps Whitney retell the story of how she single-handedly fought to get Bergdorf's landmarked. Bumps had been given her nickname by David Eisenhower when he was a tot and she was entering the postpubescent winter of her flat-chested discontent.

"I don't see why we can't have those cute blue circle things they have in London telling you that Disraeli lived here,'' Bumps said, noting in her alligator Filofax that she was having lunch with J. "I think putting all your appointments down in advance is like peeking at the end of a mystery novel. It spoils all the fun. Don't you think? I mean, I think a diary is a diary. Not a pre-diary. Dear Diary, today I am going to feel sad. Why do you think it is, J darling, that people misuse things whenever they can? At every turn.''

"Disraeli didn't live here.''

"What time, J darling?" Bumps asked, poising her thirty-nine-cent Bic pen.

"Do you want me to look at my watch?"

"No. I don't want you to do that. I just thought you might know what time—I don't mean what time it is, I mean what time was our reservation for lunch?"

"Twelve-thirty."

"Oh, I like twelve-thirty so much better than one. Trust you. One o'clock runs the risk of getting a used table." Bumps jotted down twelve-thirty in her diary. "J darling, if you really think about it, and I do when I get depressed, what about all those times we stayed at hotels and slept in beds that other people had slept in? Taken actual baths in tubs that other people had used? It makes my skin crawl to think of all the dangerous things we did while growing up. It's a wonder we made it. Don't you think?"

J leaned forward as the waiter put her double margarita on the table. She took a sip immediately and then raised her glass. "I think it's time we toasted the women of Belgium who make all that wonderful lace."

Bumps shook her head and raised her Riesling. "Oh, God. I feel so guilty. I've never even thought about those wonderful women. What would we do without them? J darling, you are a saint. The Bernadette of Southampton."

"Well, I suppose we could have those little blue circle things. The first condo. Halston lived here. Original site of the Stork Club. Certainly there's enough to commemorate."

"Oh, J darling, would you espouse my cause? One nod from you and I'm virtually assured an entire season of fund-raisers on my very own." Bumps put a hand to her bumps. "Think of it. Dorothy Kilgallen's house. Gloria and Leopold. Gloria and Sidney. Gloria and Wyatt. Nelson and Happy." She began to giggle. "And then Un-Happy."

"Who's unhappy?" Libby asked, sitting down.

"Holy Hermès!" Bumps glanced around quickly, hoping someone would notice that Libby was sitting next to her. "Libby darling, you know those little round blue things . . ."

Libby caught Cal's eye. Those little round blue things of his were watching her. She turned away. "What are you guys up to?"

Bumps was all excited. "Those little round blue things that tell you who lived and who died . . ."

Libby pointed to her heart. "Libby Dennis once lived here."

Bumps's face lit up. "Did anyone famous die here?"

"Mrs. Pagano." Libby emptied the water from J's goblet into the wine bucket. She poured herself some Riesling and raised the glass.

"Who?"

"To my darling, Mrs. Pagano," Libby said, breaking her own first commandment about not drinking on the job. "Once upon a time, before Perrier or glasnost, this used to be a restaurant called Pagano's Villa Capri."

"Oh, God!" Bumps gasped. "You mean this was once an *ethnic* restaurant?"

J rolled her eyes. "Don't mind her. She thinks Côte Basque is an ethnic restaurant."

"I worked double shifts at the Villa Capri when I was first pregnant with Steven. After I couldn't hide it any longer, Mrs. Pagano let me work as cashier, then expediter, then steward. She gave me a job and a place to stay."

J held up her hand. "If this is another landmark story, I need a refill."

"Everything was going wonderfully. The Paganos were like grandparents to Steven and me. Until Mrs. Pagano died."

Bumps took a sip of wine. "This is better than *Upstairs, Downstairs*."

"The Villa Capri closed. I didn't know what I was going to do. Mr. Pagano wanted to sell."

"And you bought it for a song," Bumps said, leaning forward. "Oh, God! I just love real estate stories with happy endings. Wait until Ivana and Donald hear this!"

Libby was lost in thought. "I got the staff together. We all chipped in to buy what we needed to make Mr. Pagano's favorite meal. Then I invited him to dinner. I didn't tell him it was going to be at his own restaurant."

J took a deep breath. She was getting edgy. "Is this going to be touching?"

Libby sipped the wine. "The dining room looked just as it

had the night before Mrs. Pagano died. All the waiters and busboys were at their stations. Mr. Pagano's eyes filled with tears."

"That's enough for me," J said, signaling Maxie for another round.

"And as always, there was a single white rose at Mrs. Pagano's table."

Bumps picked up her menu. "Come to think of it, I'm starving."

Rikki Lee could not believe her ears. "Cal said no? Just like that, Johnny? He said no?"

Janos nodded. He flipped the pages in *High Life,* staring at her nude photos. He couldn't understand it. Janos banged his fist on the magazine.

Rikki leaned close and whispered, "Maybe he's a faygeleh."

Janos looked up. "Now that's using your tuchis!"

"Which is my tuchis again, Johnny?"

He tapped his temple with one finger.

"Johnny, how much money do we have in *The Last Cowboy?*"

"Nothing! Nobody wanted the script. It's been hanging around for years. Barry gave me a seven-day exclusive."

"For how much?"

"For nothing! He should be paying me." Janos banged his fist on the table. "Nobody, but nobody, would want that turkey!"

"When is the week up?"

Janos looked at his watch. "It's up."

"So who cares? We didn't lose any money."

"That's not the point! It's not the money." Janos watched as Cal sat down at Junior's table. "It's the deal. I lost the deal!"

"What are you going to do, Johnny?"

"I'm going to get back into the game." Janos motioned Stu the waiter to his table.

Rikki leaned close and kissed his ear excitedly. "Get him, Johnny. I want you to get him."

"Yes, sir?" Stu asked.

Janos pointed across the room at Mary Borden. "Who is she having lunch with?"

Stu leaned over and spoke quietly. "Abner Waxman. A big deal editor. I see him here with a lot of agents."

"What are they talking about?"

"Some book about Germans."

Then Janos pointed to Cal and Junior. "What is the name of the manuscript on that table?"

Stu winked. He took a pitcher of ice water from the service station and walked briskly to Junior's table. Without a word, he refilled the glasses and came back to Janos. "You're not going to believe this! It's the same book. *Before Dawn.*"

"I want to know what they're saying."

"Hold on. For that I better find Maxie. It's his table."

As Stu hurried away, Rikki bent her fork. "Is this going to take long, Johnny? You said you were going to screw him. How long is it going to take?"

"I don't like that tone in your voice."

Rikki poked him angrily. "I don't like being made a fool of."

"What are you talking about? He wasn't trying to make a fool out of *you*. You're not worth a fart in the breeze as far as he's concerned. He was trying to make a fool out of *me!* You, you're nothing. Nobody gives a shit about you!"

Rikki leaned forward and looked into his eyes. "Johnny," she whispered cautiously, "you're not just saying that to make me feel good, are you?"

"You dumb broad. You think I really give a damn how you feel?"

Rikki smiled. She nuzzled against his shoulder. "Oh, Johnny. You always know just the right thing to say."

Cal knew that Libby was watching him. She kept looking over as though he were on a train and she were on the platform. He wanted to tell her that he wasn't going anywhere. He had torn up his ticket. But it was too big a ticket to tear up for nothing but pride. Cal couldn't tell Libby about it until he had another deal. He turned to Junior. "So. How's your lunch life?"

"You know, before Senior took over the studio, when the other kids asked me what my father did for a living, I used to tell them he did lunch. My poor mother couldn't afford anything but red caviar because the son of a bitch spent every penny we had on lunch. He even got his mail at the Polo Lounge."

Cal began to laugh. "My poor mother couldn't afford mayonnaise."

"Jesus. What the hell were you? Puerto Rican?"

"I had an aunt who was very rich. She always had Hellmann's mayonnaise and Heinz ketchup on the dining room table. And she only sent Hallmark cards."

Junior smiled. "It's funny what you remember."

"The things you wanted and couldn't have."

"Nobody remembers the things you got." Junior laughed. "Except for the clap I got from our Mexican maid when I was fifteen."

"You were fucking around at fifteen?"

"Are you kidding? By fifteen, I was an old man already. The life span of a Hollywood brat is different from the rest of the world. We were all little King Tuts, groomed to inherit the dynasty, intermarry, and take our percentages of the gross into the afterlife." Junior glanced over at the empty table reserved for his father. "The son of a bitch still does lunch. What the hell. At his age, what other pleasure lasts for an hour?"

Cal smiled, wishing Junior would get to the point. He hated reminiscing with people he hardly knew. But, according to The Official Rules of Lunch, you sat down as strangers, became best friends over drinks, lovers over the entrée, and made the deal before dessert.

Junior was still becoming a best friend. "You must have been very young when you married Libby."

Cal was a dry forest waiting for a match. "My family couldn't afford a Mexican maid." The moment he said it, Cal hated himself. After giving up six million dollars to prove his love for Libby, how could he have said something that stupid? The only way to regain his self-respect was to strip himself bare. "We were both virgins on our wedding night."

"Come on."

"I was twenty."

"I don't believe it! Cal Dennis a virgin at twenty? And you still made something of yourself? That's incredible!"

"We were in the chorus of *Camelot*. It didn't seem that life could get very much better. We were married at the Actor's Church after the matinee. That night, still in costume, we hopped into a cab. The farthest the driver would take us was the George Washington Bridge. We walked across and spent our wedding night at the Riviera Motel in Fort Lee, New Jersey." Cal couldn't resist looking over at Libby, hoping she would glance up at him and read his mind. "She was a Lady-in-Waiting. I was a Knight of the Round Table." He smiled, thinking Libby was still as beautiful as she was then. If only she would turn around, he knew she'd see that in his eyes. "I gave the guy at the desk a couple of bucks and he got us a bottle of Lancers and a bag of M&M's. Our wedding dinner. We had this really crummy room, but it had a color television set. It was the first time we had ever seen color television." Cal forced himself to look directly into Junior's eyes. "We never made love on our wedding night. We were too afraid. We watched TV until we fell asleep. We woke up in the morning still in costume, the test pattern flickering. We started to laugh. The wedding night was over. We were safe. We couldn't ruin it. So we ripped off our clothes and fucked our brains out." Cal had never told anyone the story.

"I have a book," Junior said. "Good Germans versus Bad Germans. It was made for you."

According to Libby's inner clock, she had been sitting at the table with Birnbaum, Anders, and Horton for two or three thousand years. It had to be at least that long for Libby to have worked her way through a second glass of wine.

She knew that Birnbaum was staring at her and she was afraid to look at him. As afraid as she was to glance across the room at Cal. There was no telling what either of them were thinking. God knows what was in their eyes, let alone their heads. Best not to look. Best not to ask. She pretended to be studying the seating chart while Horton and Anders babbled on.

"While the President is in the southeast corner . . ."

"Service staff will enter and exit along the west aisle . . ."

"Only the code group will access the men's room . . ."

"What west aisle?" Libby asked as she filled her glass. "There was no west aisle at the Villa Capri," she said, stopping all conversation.

"I beg your pardon?" Anders said.

"After Mrs. Pagano died, I reopened this place. You should have seen me. No wonder I wear pink all the time. Every night I put on a black dress just like Mrs. Pagano wore. And every night, after we closed, I ate dinner with Mr. Pagano. Just as she had." Libby began to laugh. "I was a twenty-two-year-old Sicilian widow." Suddenly she realized they were all staring at her. Unsmiling. "All right." Libby leaned across the table and looked straight into Birnbaum's eyes. "Enough is enough!" she shouted. "I want the truth! Meat or fish?"

Ashanti followed Steven down the aisle as though the million-dollar cover girl was a small child on the way to the bathroom in the middle of the night. Her eyes were barely half open, her hair was a flurry of tangles, and the necklace she should have been wearing was clutched in her hand. She had rushed from bed into a waiting limo. She was terrified of missing lunch.

As Ashanti approached, Hots and Loren got up. But she stood frozen in the aisle. She stared at the bread plate filled with crumbs and the water glass stained with lipstick. Ashanti's voice was husky from lack of sleep. She growled, "Who's been sitting in my chair?"

"Wanda Fogelman," Hots said. "She's in the ladies, washing some cherry relish off her blouse."

Ashanti sat down next to Loren. "And what brings you to a room without a bed?" He took her hand, immediately checking her pulse. She smiled at Steven. "He's been my M.D. for years. Miltown and Dexamil."

As soon as Steven left, Loren pressed the skin under Ashanti's eyes and then pushed aside her hair to look at her cheeks and ears. "I just want to check the fascia." He shook his head. "You people are like hothouse flowers. One sleepless night and you fall apart."

Ashanti grabbed hold of Hots. "Darling, how fast can you draw up a prenuptial agreement?"

"For who?"

"For Dagwood and Blondie! I told you! For me and Bill!"

Loren shrugged his shoulders. "Pulse is all right. Somewhere between dead and alive." He got up. "I better see what happened to Wanda."

Hots waited for Loren to leave. "Let me tell you something. You don't love Bill."

Ashanti rolled her eyes. "Oh, please. I just want your basic pre-nup, not a palm reading."

"How basic?"

"Basic Black, darling. Utter simplicity." Ashanti took a bite of Loren's leftover sandwich. "I'm going to be the grand finale in his spring collection. I walk out wearing a wedding dress and I want a priest waiting at the end of the runway. Applause. Applause. I do. I do. And it's done. Happily ever after. When we split up, I get the farm in Connecticut, a limo until the day I die, and you figure out how much I need to grow old gracefully without having to make an exercise tape."

"What if Stephanie wants the farm?"

"Fuck her. I'm giving her half the business and the apartment in Paris. What more does she want? Hotsy Totsy darling, I have been standing on my head all night encouraging Mr. Wonderful's spermatozoa to fertilize what must be, by now, my thousand-year-old egg."

"Did he ask you to marry him?"

"Of course he didn't ask me to marry him! How could he ask me to marry him until he knows what I want when we split up?"

"You expect me to believe you love Bill Perry?"

"I want to get married. I don't care to who. I want to make a public commitment to heterosexuality."

"Why the hell would you do a stupid thing like that?" he asked. "It's like registering at Fortunoff's."

Ashanti dug her fingernails into Hots's arm and gasped. Her eyes widened and then narrowed as she stared across the room.

"What is it?" Hots asked.

"It's the Ghost of Lunch Past." She couldn't take her eyes from the couple Steven was seating. It was Moina and Fay. Arm in arm. Laughing.

o

"A grasshopper?" Victor the bartender looked up at Stu. "Are you kidding?"

Stu raised his eyebrows. "Two yet. For Fay Fox and the Bride of Frankenstein."

Norm had been waiting at the bar. "Jack Daniel's straight?" he reminded Victor. "Stoli rocks?"

"What the hell goes into a grasshopper?" Victor asked, reaching for the green crème de menthe.

"A boy grasshopper," Stu said, putting napkins on his tray.

"Why don't you just give me my JD and Stoli?" Norm asked.

Victor reached for the white crème de cacao. "You see Liza?" he asked. "Isn't she something?"

It didn't do Norm any good to complain. Because Stu tipped out ten percent to the bar, he got quicker service. Bigger drinks. His customers got the third round free. All of which resulted in bigger tips from which he paid his bar dues.

Moina held tight to Fay's hand. "I bet you don't remember the first time we had these."

Fay picked up her drink. "Newport."

"That sleazy little bar."

Fay smiled. "You were in a white sailor suit. You had your hair cut real short. And you were wearin' those Montecatini pearls I always wanted." Fay's recollection was keen. It should have been. That scene opened her biography of Moina.

Moina nodded. "I was on every cover that season. *Vogue* had Avedon do me in black and white. Very smart of them. No one could do faces like Avedon. That tinny Victrola of his going for hours. Garland and Astaire was all he would play." She waved her hand. "They wanted Eisenstaedt. But he was an ambulance chaser. Too serious for my face. He had no respect for contempt."

"I have missed you, darlin'," Fay said, raising her glass.

"Nothing like you're going to miss me."

"I can't drink to that," Fay said.

"Stop fussing. I shall leave you my Montecatini pearls."

"You'd be fine if you just had the goddamn operation. I know it."

Moina put a finger to Fay's lips. "Promise me something."

Fay's eyes filled with tears. "Bitch."

Moina held tight to Fay's hand. "Promise not to look at me when I'm dead."

"Sweetie, you're already dead."

Moina started to laugh. "Well, then it didn't hurt a bit." She leaned close to Fay. "How would you feel if I wanted to kiss you right now?"

"I think I'd feel pretty damn good. All things considered."

Moina kissed her gently on the lips. "Is everyone looking at us?"

"Nobody in this room cares about a couple of old dykes. Actually, I think they're lookin' at the grasshoppers."

Moina put her hand atop Fay's drink. Slowly, without losing eye contact, she lowered her middle finger into the green liquid and rubbed the inside of the glass.

Fay whispered, "Slut." She took Moina's hand. "What the hell am I goin' to do without you?" Fay was actually going to do fine on the royalties from her book. Unwittingly, Moina had given her the ending she needed to dig her heels into the best-seller list. Not that she wasn't going to miss Moina once she was dead. But there would be a lot less wear and tear not having her around when the book was published.

Without waiting to be invited, Hots sat down. "Would you mind telling me what's going on here?"

Moina sipped her drink slowly. "Harold, I have decided how I wish to die."

He rolled his eyes and muttered, "Let's hope it's fast."

"I want peonies, a string quartet, and Vivaldi." She turned quickly. "What did you say?"

"Aside from heartburn, you're giving me one hell of a conflict of interest."

Moina was angry. "What are you talking about?"

Hots looked across the room at Ashanti. "Little Miss Pickaninny has shifted gears. She just x'ed out her prenuptial agreement with Bill Perry. She's decided it would be more profitable to sue you for palimony."

Fay sat back and laughed. Perhaps the last chapter hadn't been written yet.

o

Rikki was bored. She picked up *The Last Cowboy* and turned to page one. A moment later she stopped reading. "Johnny, what's this about?"

"It's about a princess with a beautiful ass. The most beautiful ass in the kingdom."

Rikki flipped through the pages and slammed the script shut. "I don't want to do *The Last Cowboy!*"

Janos looked across the room at Cal. "That's not our problem. *The Last Cowboy* doesn't want to do you."

Rikki punched Janos in the arm with every word. "You said you were going to get back at him!"

Mary Borden walked over to the table and sat down. "Rikki, I love your earrings." Without giving her a chance to reply, Mary waved the note Janos had sent to her. "You haven't even read *Before Dawn.*"

"I once bought a Gutenberg Bible. I didn't read that either."

"But there's nothing in it for Rikki," Mary said.

"There was nothing in the Gutenberg. They still took my money."

Mary smiled. "Taking money is my specialty."

Janos snapped his fingers. Rikki, like Pavlov's accountant, reached into her purse for the checkbook and handed it to him. "A year's option for fifteen," he said. "Second year for ten, two percent of net, and if you twist my arm, whoever wrote the cockamamie book can do the first draft of the screenplay before I throw him off and hire Bo Goldman."

Mary was angry. She hated having to deal with people like Janos. Not that she expected everyone to be a David Brown. "Don't be ridiculous," Mary said. "I'm not at all sure I'd consider an option. And if I did, it certainly wouldn't be for fifteen."

"How much did Junior offer?" he asked.

"Nothing yet."

"He's over there. Ask him."

"What do you expect me to do? Hold an auction in the aisle?"

"Good idea!" Janos waved Stu over as he scribbled a note. "Give this to him."

"I won't be bulldozed," Mary said.

"The offer you have is zero. I am offering fifteen."

"Fifteen is not enough."

"Fifteen is more than zero. Are you going to walk away from fifteen?"

Mary glared at him. "Yes! Janos, what do you want?"

He smiled. "I want only what I'm entitled to. Everything."

Junior came to the table. "Hi," he said, holding the note. "I don't understand this."

Mary smiled at Junior. "Janos wants to option the book."

Junior was astonished. "Why? There's no part in it for Rikki."

"He just offered me fifteen and he wants to close the deal."

"Are you kidding? You know I'll give you more than fifteen."

"When?" Janos asked. He tore a check from the book and held it out to Mary.

Junior laughed. "Excuse me, Janos, but this book is not the usual soft porn you buy for Rikki."

"Of course not! You think I pay fifteen thousand dollars for that dreck?"

Rikki sneered at Junior and held proudly to Janos's arm. "You think he's dumb?"

Junior glanced back at his table. Cal had left. He was sitting with Senior and Liza. Damn. It was his own fault. Senior had warned him that even if your mother was dying in the screening room next door, you never left a star alone.

Janos waved the check in Mary's face. "You can go back to your publisher and tell him you have a movie option. You can go to the book clubs and tell them this book, whatever its name is . . ."

"Before Dawn," Mary said.

"Whatever, has been optioned as a major motion picture. You can tell the paperback houses . . ."

"I know how to conduct business," Mary said.

"Or, you can tell the author, whatever his name is, that you turned down my option. You can tell him you pissed away the thirty thousand I was going to give him for a first draft screenplay. And you should also tell him that you turned down his chance to have a piña colada by the pool at the Beverly Hills Hotel."

Junior leaned over and kissed Mary on the cheek. "A few days. Once I pitch it to the studio we'll make a big announcement."

"Why wait?" Janos asked. "All you have to do is offer her more. Offer her sixteen. Go ahead. I swear to you. You write out a check for sixteen, it's yours." Janos sat back and folded his arms. "Junior, you spend sixteen at Bijan in one morning, just on your underwear." Janos waited. "Surely you believe in this wonderful book as much as you believe in your underwear?" Janos leaned forward and whispered, "Steal it from me!"

Mary pushed away the table and stood up. "Sorry, Janos. You are not the seller. I am. And I'm not ready to sell. When I am, I'll let you know. And it won't be for fifteen or sixteen. I'm telling you right now I wouldn't take a penny less than fifty for an option."

Janos stopped smiling. He held up the check for Mary to see. It had been made out for fifty thousand dollars. "Deal!"

The indieprods sat bolt upright, each hidden behind a menu. After a long silence, the female said, "I hope she doesn't order barbecued foie gras with grilled radicchio. You see what that costs?"

The male, with a large silver hoop in his ear, said, "Times four, yet."

The female leaned around her menu. "Don't be stupid, Raggedy Andy. Only if she orders something under ten bucks, do you order what she does, thereby complimenting Meryl on her fine taste. If she orders above ten . . ."

He put down his menu. "I'll order the grilled goat cheese on radicchio, thereby bonding with her in a shared love for red lettuce?"

"Don't you dare! This is supposed to be a power lunch. You can't exude power if you eat lettuce."

The male stared angrily at her. "Oh, yeah? What if I order bull's balls on lettuce?"

"Irving Thalberg did not eat lettuce."

"I bet he did! I bet he loved lettuce and I bet Norma Shearer made it for him all the time." He put a hand to his chest and spoke in a mock falsetto. "Irving, darling, shall I throw another head of lettuce on the grill for you?"

"Irving Thalberg could afford to eat Jell-O and Animal Crackers if he wanted. But we can't. We have to order tough. Raw. No sprigs of parsley. No relish. And for God's sake, if you ever want to see your name on the screen at a Loew's Sixplex, no dessert!"

The male rolled his eyes. "Hello, Hollywood! Goodbye, crème brulée!"

The female kicked him under the table as Libby approached. "Guess what?"

Libby shrugged. "They found a Japanese soldier in the play department at William Morris."

The male tugged at her hand. "Be serious. Think actress. Initials M.S. Has costarred with Redford, Nicholson, and Hoffman." He beat his fists in the air. "Is absolutely dying to do our picture. Loves the script. Will be here tomorrow!"

Libby sat down. "Tomorrow?"

"It's just like you said!" the female squealed. "Tomorrow the lunch!"

Libby liked the indieprods. They were so crazy about the movie business. A throwback to the days when people who made movies really loved them. "Tomorrow?" she repeated.

"You've just got to have a table for us," the male said.

Libby needed a moment to think. "What bank did you rob to finance this caper?"

The female smiled. "First National Mother."

"Well, then," Libby said, "this calls for a bottle of bubbly on the house." She grabbed hold of Stu. "A bottle of our best Perrier!"

The male looked worried. "You do have a table for us?"

"But not just any table," the female pleaded.

The indieprods glanced nervously at each other. "Our whole lives depend on it," they said.

Libby stared at them. Her eyes filled with tears. "Don't be

ridiculous! How can your whole life depend upon someone coming to lunch tomorrow?''

Stu was in the back. On the phone. He had just dialed Fay's number. "It's me, Miss Fox," he whispered. "I've got two biggies for you. Table 83's expecting Meryl Streep tomorrow. And Mr. Vatsl just beat out Singer Junior on *Before Dawn,* from what I hear, a very hot new book.''

Junior stood at the urinal in the men's room. He didn't bother to unzip his pants. He didn't have to pee. He just needed a place to stand.

There was no sense going back to his table. By now the news that Janos had optioned the book would be all over the restaurant. He'd never even get Cal back to finish lunch. No doubt Senior was regaling Cal with his plans for Liza in *Dorothy— The Woman.* Junior knew the pitch so well he could do it himself. Fade in on a clip of Judy singing "Over the Rainbow." Match dissolve to Liza singing at Auntie Em's funeral. Jesus. Someone came in to pee.

Junior unzipped his pants and took hold of his penis. The man stood in front of the other urinal. He unzipped and nodded at Junior. Not that they knew one another or that he was trying to pick Junior up. It was simply a nod of acknowledgment. Congratulations on being successful enough to pee at one of New York's most chic pissoirs. If the men ever got to know one another, they probably could have traded names of the same brokerage firms, tailors, limo services, and wines. They might even have slept with the same women.

The man was peeing loudly. With great force. Junior stared at the wall in front of him, ashamed that he wasn't making any noise. The guy must think he was a fag. Men who peed side by side could trust one another. Like men who fought side by side. The few moments during which two men peed together was as bonding as years of prep school. But one man not peeing was an even more deafening silence than one hand clapping.

Junior continued staring at the wall. The man shook his penis as though he were Gorbachev and his penis were Malcolm Forbes. "You know," Junior began, hoping to recoup his image, "ever since they sold *The New Yorker,* nothing has been the same."

The man washed his hands meticulously. As he dried them, he turned to Junior and said, "If you want to know what's killing the economy, it's everybody going private."

The man left. Junior stood there holding his penis, wondering why he'd always felt uncomfortable calling his penis his cock. Senior called it his thing. Well, calling it his penis was at least better than calling it his thing. And who knows, perhaps someday Junior would have a son and his son would call his penis his cock and then the economy would be strong again.

Without saying a word, Libby slid onto the banquette next to Phyllis. She reached for Phyllis's water goblet and emptied it into Donald's water goblet. Then she poured half of Phyllis's wine into the empty goblet and drank it in one gulp.

Donald and Phyllis were astonished. They had never seen Libby drink at lunch.

Libby reached for Donald's plate. He had eaten only half his trout, almost none of the candied orange rice, and hadn't touched the freshly grated horseradish. She took Phyllis's knife and fork. With great concentration, Libby cut a small piece of trout and ate it. "I'll never forget the night you slipped and fell outside the Villa Capri. You were on your way to a preview of *Funny Girl.* Your date carried you inside. You were going to sue the owners for every penny they had." She pushed the plate away.

Donald looked at Phyllis and shrugged his shoulders.

"We hadn't seen each other since Washington," Libby said. She reached for Phyllis's salmon tartare and put it in front of her. Without looking up, she began to eat. "You promised to bring everyone back after the show. I hadn't seen any of the kids in years."

Phyllis looked at Donald and shrugged her shoulders.

"I waited until midnight," Libby said, pouring herself half of Donald's wine. "I was heartbroken when you didn't show up. But just as I got into bed, I heard singing in the street. You brought the entire chorus with you. When I opened the door, they all shouted, 'Hello, gorgeous!' "

Phyllis took the glass from Libby's hand. "Hello, gorgeous?" she said, trying to rouse her.

"You'll never know what I went through to convince Mr. Pagano to have an after-theater menu. He let me keep the place open until 2 A.M."

"The hell he did!" Phyllis added. "*I* kept it open until 2 A.M."

"The hell you did!" Libby grabbed her glass back. "I was the one who brought the gypsies north. I promised they could eat now and pay later. I brought actors and writers! And writers begat directors and directors begat producers and producers . . ."

"And good friend Phyllis," Phyllis said, "begat actors and writers who could also write checks."

"After Mr. Pagano died, Cal offered me money to buy the Villa Capri." Libby smiled to herself. "But I couldn't let him do that. Fortunately, good friend Phyllis was already on her second millionaire." Libby had finished her wine. She turned to Phyllis. "You know something else? Cal and I are not getting married."

"Oh, darling."

"Not ever!" Libby said. "I will most likely never have sex again. Not to mention love."

Phyllis groaned. "For God's sake, don't mention love."

Libby shrugged. "I hear it's sweeping the country. Even my chef is in love." She saw the horror in Phyllis's eyes. "Oh, not with me! With the checkroom girl!"

Phyllis reached out for Donald. He took her hand.

"Well," Libby said, getting up, "I don't want you to think this hasn't been wonderful, but I've got to go back to work."

There was a long silence after Libby left. Without moving, Phyllis said flatly, "I suppose this is what they mean by nuclear winter."

George, the waiter, stopped at the table. "Mrs. Elgin, is anything wrong?"

Phyllis handed him the salmon tartare. "Take this back into the kitchen, George. Give it to the chef. Please quote me exactly. Tell him it made me sick to my stomach. Tell him I said it tasted like something he found in the checkroom." George nodded and left. Phyllis stubbed out her cigarette very slowly. "It was the best of lunches, it was the worst of lunches . . ."

Stu brought Rikki a plate of French fried potatoes and a Cherry Coke. It was her favorite meal. But she did little more than pick at it as she stared at Cal laughing with Liza Minnelli. "It doesn't look to me like we got back at him, Johnny."

"I stopped the deal, didn't I?"

"Yes."

"So we got back at him."

"But Johnny, what are you going to do with that dumb book? You heard what they said. They said there was nothing in it for me. You paid fifty thousand bucks for a dumb book with nothing in it for me."

"Who said I paid fifty? All I did was write a check for fifty."

"They said it was a book about Germans, Johnny. Why would anybody write a whole book about Germans?"

"I gave her a check. It means nothing until I sign a contract. But first they have to send me a deal memo. And who says I have to like the deal memo they send me. Never mind until the lawyers kvetch out a contract. By the time I get through with the deal memo, they'll be begging me to take back my check. And you know what? I'm such a nice guy, I'll take it back. So, it will have cost me nothing to stop Cal from making a deal with Junior."

Rikki nodded. "Just like the toilet paper from the Pierre. It's always free for you to wipe your ass, isn't it?" Janos laughed but Rikki couldn't take her eyes from Liza. "I wish I was her, Johnny."

"What are you talking about? She's got her mother's figure."

"She's got excitement, Johnny. Look at Cal's face. Look at how he's listening to her. You never listen to me that way."

"What the hell do you say worth listening to?"

"She's bigger than life, Johnny. It's as though all hell broke loose inside her. She's beautiful."

"So now you're an expert on beauty?"

"No, Johnny. I'm an expert on hell."

Libby sat down next to Horton. She handed him the reservations book. Anders looked up from making notes on his schedule and nodded. He had already seen the book, checking for security risks. Horton was more elitist. He was looking for people whose presence might offend or embarrass the President. Libby still didn't know what Birnbaum was looking for. Or why he had the nerve to think he was going to find it in her eyes.

Horton poised a well-manicured finger and began to check the names for Thursday. Libby watched his finger move across the page, half-expecting it to scrawl MENE MENE TEKEL UPHARSIN. Every few names, he stopped to compare his list against her list as though she were being graded. There was no way to tell from his face whether she would pass or fail. "You get a lot of the same people every day."

"Always have," she said. "It's my job to make people feel at home. Nurse them through their disappointments. Celebrate their victories." She pushed away the glass of wine. "Not too shabby for a Thursday."

He looked up. "José Ensesa? The South American sisal king?"

"Why not?"

"Fay Fox?"

"Fay's one of my regulars."

Horton shook his head. "I'm afraid we don't consider her a consociate."

"What the hell does that mean?"

Birnbaum smiled. "If he were Judge Roy Bean, she'd hang."

"Fay's a friend!"

Birnbaum put up his hands. "Don't tell *me*. Tell him."

But Libby wanted to tell Birnbaum. "She's here practically every day and she pays her rent on time." The gall of the man. Where did he come off to think she could possibly be attracted to him? And with Cal in the room, too! Just across the aisle.

Horton leaned close. "The point is we haven't even cleared our familiars in the press. This lunch is to be a nonmedia event."

"Fay stays." Why was Cal so far away? He was right there a moment ago. Why had he moved? He couldn't have seen her in Birnbaum's arms.

"I don't see Mr. Dennis's name on the list," Horton said.

Libby stared at Birnbaum. Cut to Rick's Place. Ilsa/Libby hesitates. Rick/Birnbaum stares at her. Major Strasser/Horton smiles enigmatically.

"I love my husband," she says. "I always will."

Ilsa turns away. She can't bear the look in Rick's eyes. But she knows that whatever she had with Rick, it didn't amount to a hill of beans. After lunch and dinner and lunch, he would be gone and she would be safe.

The hell she would. Libby would never be safe again.

o

Donald's office was in the Empire State Building. Not just because it was an old money address, but because Donald's father had negotiated a ninety-nine-year lease on an entire floor for himself and his heirs. Donald's father needn't have bothered. Donald was the end of the line. Which was exactly where he felt he was while staring at Phyllis.

"You know why these things keep happening to us?" he asked, brushing a speck from the von Knobelsdorff library table. "We're too damn nice, that's why."

Phyllis flicked her cigarette ash onto a Savonnerie carpet that once belonged to Frederick the Great. "Nice guys finish last."

Donald opened a bureau originally made for the Palazzo Balbi-Durazzo. He took out a can of Diet Pepsi. "Exactly."

"We've got to toughen up, Donald."

He filled two etched Jacobite goblets with soda. "It's us or them."

"We expect too much of people."

"We expect too much because we give too much."

Phyllis sipped the Pepsi and then covered her eyes. "The checkroom girl! Oh, Donald!"

He sat down on the Corradini chair. "We've got to stop feeling sorry for ourselves, Phyllis." He took a deep breath and drank his soda in a single gulp. "I should have given Steven the money months ago. He'd be out of my hair by now and I wouldn't be in this predicament."

"Nor I."

Donald leaned forward. His voice was tight. "What does that mean?"

Phyllis got up from the Queen Hortense chaise. "It means that if you had given him the money, he would have left Libby's and taken Bud with him before Hatcheck Hattie made her move."

"So now it's all my fault?"

"Donald, this is not the time to turn on one another. However, it might save a few bruises in the future if you accepted your role as an aging queen whose main attraction was his money."

Donald sat frozen in the Corradini. Unable to speak. Abandoned in outer space. Cut loose from the mother ship without any support systems. Eternally alone.

"I, for one, have learned my lesson," Phyllis said. "I'm going to stop fucking around with mindless young studs and find someone experienced enough to appreciate me."

Donald moistened his lips and cleared his throat. "And just what the hell makes you so certain your fatal charm is between your legs and not in your wallet?"

"My check stubs," she snarled. "I don't know anyone named Cash!"

Donald moved in for the kill. "I suppose you think I haven't paid anyone off for you?"

"You didn't pay Bud," she screamed, hurling the diet Pepsi at the Balmoral tapestry. Suddenly, her mood brightened. "But then that would explain it all, wouldn't it?" She smiled at Donald. "You paid him off!"

Donald smiled back. "Yes. Of course, I did," he lied.

"My darling!"

"My love!"

The phone rang. It was Donald's private line. They turned to one another like two trapped rats. He picked up the phone. "Yes? Hello, Steven." Donald put his hand over the mouthpiece and whispered, "He's calling from the lobby." Phyllis gasped. She put on her shoes and picked up the Jacobite goblet.

"No, Steven. This isn't a very good time for me."

She rubbed her cigarette ashes into the carpet and took a can of room spray from the cabinet to remove the scent of smoke.

"But it's always urgent," Donald said.

Phyllis washed her ashtray in the wet bar.

"You're such a Nellie. Yes. If you must." Donald hung up and pressed the intercom for Bruce. "I'm expecting Mr. Dennis momentarily. Show him into the sauna. He likes it between 195 and 200. Then we'll have tea in the music room. And Bruce, I do not want him to know that Mrs. Elgin was here."

Phyllis laughed as she picked up her handbag. "What a switch! Hiding your wife from your lover." She glanced around for telltale clues. "Sometimes I think we should have told him I know about the two of you." She touched his cheek lightly. "If you want to keep the little wretch, give him the money. It's all right with me."

Donald kissed her. "Do you mind going out the back?"

"I've been thrown out of worse places."

"What are you going to do?"

"Something terribly expensive. What about you?"

"I'm going to dump him."

Phyllis squeezed his hand. "He's not very strong, darling. Be gentle."

Donald watched as she walked to the door. "When you say expensive, do you mean costly or daring?"

She turned to him and smiled. "Last one in bed is a rotten egg."

Donald stared out the window. He was fifty years old and lonelier than he had been as a child. All the years that one normally spent building relationships had been spent destroying them. Now he was about to destroy Steven.

There was a knock on the door. "Yes?"

Donald's secretary, Bruce, came in. "Mr. Dennis doesn't want a sauna. He wants to see you in here."

"Even better."

"Is there anything else?"

Donald nodded. "Yes. Before he comes in, take off your clothes."

o

Phyllis rushed through the lobby of the Empire State Building. Elliot, the chauffeur, snapped to attention the moment he saw her. He nodded and opened the door to the Rolls-Royce Silver Shadow sedan. Phyllis held onto his arm as she prepared to step inside. She hesitated and then let go quickly. No, not Elliot, she thought. He wasn't nearly expensive enough.

As Phyllis sat back on the buttery beige leather, the flashing light on the phone caught her eye. She pressed PLAY. The message was from Cal.

"George the waiter thinks your new play is all wrong for Burt. Why don't you get back to me within ten or twenty seconds and let's talk about it. But don't tell Libby. I want it to be a surprise. Oh, yeah, friend to friend, there's one thing you better know before we begin. I'm very expensive."

Phyllis sat back and began to cry. Thank you, God.

Donald opened the door and said casually, "I do hope it's nothing serious."

"I'm at the end of my rope, Donny." Steven waited for him to close and lock the door. Then he threw his arms around Donald. "You've got to help me."

Donald looked into his eyes. He knew it would be the last time he would see anything in them but hate. "Poor bear. I'll get you a drink and you can tell us all about it."

Steven accepted Donald's "us" as the royal "we" and followed him to the bar. "I've got such knots in my stomach. It's so bad there are times I can't even breathe." And then Steven saw Bruce lying naked on the Queen Hortense chaise. "Oh, no," he groaned.

"Isn't he butch?" Donald asked. "I thought he'd cheer you up. You sounded like hell."

Bruce smiled at Steven. "Mr. Dennis."

"That's not what I came here for!" Steven shouted. "I don't want Bruce."

"Of course you do. Look at him. Bruce is hung better than the Castelli Gallery."

"You know why I'm here," Steven said softly. "You know what I want."

Donald turned angrily. "What the hell ever happened to what *I* want? Who elected me Father Christmas? What about the knots in *my* stomach? The times *I* can't breathe. Do you think I can make it all disappear by writing a check to myself?"

Steven's voice was tight. "Please, Donny. You're the only one who can help me."

Donald sat behind the desk. "I know." He unlocked the top drawer, feeling Steven's eyes riveted to his every motion. Donald took out his checkbook. He opened it. He reached for a pen. And then he hesitated. "But first, I want you to do something for me."

"What?"

Donald pointed to Bruce.

"Please don't put me through this," Steven whispered.

Donald closed the checkbook. "I want to watch you fuck Bruce."

Steven's eyes filled with tears. He stared at Donald in disbelief.

"Don't be an ingrate, Steven. There's nothing I hate more than an ingrate."

Bruce walked over to Steven. "Let me help you with your clothes, Mr. Dennis."

Steven pushed forward against Bruce, knocking him off balance. Then he walked slowly backwards to the door. "I did love you, Donald. Maybe not as much as you thought I should, but as much as I was able."

Donald pushed a button on his desk, unlocking the door. "If it's any consolation, I wouldn't have given you the money even if you had fucked Bruce. You're not enough of a man, Steven. Not for my love or my money."

Steven felt the tears run down his cheek. "I can prove to you, Donald, just how much of a man I am."

Donald sighed. "Oh, dear. You're not going to try to kill yourself again?"

"No." Steven wiped the tears from his face. "I'm going to try to kill *you.*"

Instinctively, Donald reached inside the drawer for his gun.

"You're right about one thing, Donny. My fucking Bruce wouldn't have proved anything. There's only one person really worth fucking. The one person you can't." Steven took a deep breath and screamed at the top of his voice, "Phyllis!" He struggled to be heard above his own hysterical sobbing. "I'm going to fuck Phyllis!" Steven flung the door open and ran out.

Donald stood up. He held the gun in his hand, pointing it after Steven. He had never felt his heart beat as rapidly. Bruce sat wide-eyed and naked on the floor. "Put your balls away," Donald said. "I'm going home."

o

Cal walked through the Fifty-sixth Street entrance to Trump Tower. He was pleased by the double-take of recognition from the concierge behind the reception desk. "Good day, sir."

"Mrs. Elgin?"

"Thank you, Mr. Dennis." He dialed Phyllis's penthouse, glancing up at Cal while waiting for her to answer. "Lovely day, isn't it?" Then he raised his eyebrows. "Mr. Dennis is here. Thank you." The concierge hung up the phone and stepped from behind the desk. "If you'll follow me, Mr. Dennis," he said leading the way.

"Thank you," Cal said.

The concierge then nodded to the elevator operator and said, "Mr. Dennis to see Mrs. Elgin."

"Mr. Dennis," the elevator operator said. He nodded to the concierge. The concierge nodded to Cal. Cal nodded back. The operator pressed the button for the sixty-seventh floor. The door closed. "Lovely day, isn't it?"

Phyllis waited in the open doorway as Cal stepped off the elevator. She wore gray silk pajamas and a very serious look. "I have a '61 Margaux breathing in the kitchen." She smiled. "Breathing very heavily."

Cal knew he was in trouble. "Nice jammies," he said. Phyllis turned and walked along a foyer lined with erotic Japanese woodblock prints of men and women with grotesquely enlarged genitalia in the midst of grotesquely enlarged sex. "Lovely day, isn't it?" he said to himself.

The kitchen was black tile. Black appliances. A black marble counter on which the Margaux was breathing. Phyllis poured some wine into a Baccarat glass, swirled it around and, without once taking her eyes from Cal, tasted it. "Needs more air," she said.

"I know just how it feels."

"Have you ever been to Château Margaux?"

"Are you kidding?" Cal asked. "I haven't even been to Coca-Cola."

Phyllis poured the wine into her black Cuisinart, careful to stop before she reached the sediment. "Contessa Labarde taught me this trick." She locked the bowl in place and, dramatically poising her finger, pressed down on the lever. "Pulse. Pulse. Pulse." Phyllis took off the cover, put her finger into the wine and licked it. "Yum." She reached for a crystal decanter. "They say in Médoc that if you can see the river and feel pebbles under your feet, you can make good wine."

"What do they say if you feel like you're standing on hot coals?"

"They say get the glasses and follow me."

"I figured they might."

The late afternoon sun streamed in through floor-to-ceiling windows that wrapped around the living room like a myopic mural. The tops of Manhattan's tallest skyscrapers were startlingly close, out of perspective against a cloudless, colorless sky.

Cal followed Phyllis to the window. She leaned against a pillar, framed by a view down Fifth Avenue to the Empire State Building. Opening her arms dramatically, Phyllis said with crystal clear ambiguity, "All this can be yours."

The sun hit her at a perfect angle. It was a pose she must have struck often, he thought, admiring how professionally Phyllis had found her key light. He smiled. "Where do I sign?"

"I have a wonderful little office right above the Drury Lane Theatre in London."

"London?"

Phyllis clinked glasses quickly and sipped the wine. "I've got it all figured out. You'll open *Kingdom of God* in the West End just before Christmas and play it through June. A week or two at our place in the Caymans and off you go to Broadway with the new play."

"London?" he repeated.

She kissed him on the cheek. "Don't worry, darling. You'll pick up the language in no time."

"I didn't say I wanted to go to London. I said Broadway."

"Sweetie, you get to Broadway the same way you get to Carnegie Hall."

"Christ, Phyllis, this is me you're talking to! You think I don't know that a nice big fat American movie star will get you off the hook in London and on the boards in New York? And unless everyone and his brother knows that I'm locked into the movie version, the studios won't put up the money to produce the play in the first place. You and I are old army buddies, Phyllis. Lunch is over for today. If we're going to fuck one another, let's do it out in the open."

Phyllis stared at Cal. She shrugged her shoulders, threw her arms up in the air, and walked into the bedroom. The door slammed behind her.

"Phyllis?" Cal walked to the door. Not a sound. "Phyllis! I want to do a play in New York so that I can be near Libby." He knocked on the door. "It makes no sense for me to go three thousand miles in the other direction."

From behind the closed door, Phyllis said, "You could Concorde back and forth every weekend. No jet lag. It's only three hours to London."

"Phyllis, I love Libby. I don't want any more long distance relationships. I want to marry her."

"May The Force be with you."

Cal knocked on the door again. "Phyllis, can I come in?"

"I thought you'd never ask."

He hesitated and then opened the door. Phyllis was lying on the bed. Quite naked.

Donald rushed through the lobby, not stopping to acknowledge any of the concierges. The elevator man smiled and stood aside. "Mr. Elgin."

Donald said nothing. All he could think about was the gun in his pocket.

"Lovely day, isn't it?" the operator said, pressing the button for the sixty-seventh floor.

Donald had never fired the gun. Never even taken it out of the office. In all the years he had the gun, Donald never considered himself capable of actually using it. He kept it in his desk to discourage hustlers from becoming too greedy or too uncooperative. But it was always empty. It was only a threat. Until Steven Dennis threatened him back.

The elevator operator turned around. He was smiling. "Mr. Dennis is upstairs."

Donald's hand reached for the trigger.

Cal stood in the doorway to Phyllis's bedroom. He couldn't believe his eyes. "What the hell are you doing?"

"Following instructions. You said, 'If we're going to fuck one another, let's do it out in the open'."

"Jesus."

"Surely you've had women throw themselves at you before, pleading to be ravaged between your famous loins."

"Phyllis, put your clothes on."

"I'm in the mood for loins."

"Goddamn it, you're ruining the one chance I have to stay in New York. Don't do this to me! I need you, Phyllis."

She stretched her arms toward Cal. "And I need you, my darling." Phyllis suddenly gasped and covered her mouth as though in pain.

"What is it? Phyllis?" Cal heard a loud noise from behind him. Then Phyllis screamed. He tried to turn around. But he couldn't move. He felt very cold. He fell to the floor.

o

There were a lot of empty seats on the boat, but Alfero wanted to stand. It hurt more when he stood. He had been walking for hours, hoping the pain from his new shoes would help him forget his despair. Alfero didn't know where to go when he left Libby's, but he knew he couldn't go home. He couldn't tell Dolores and the niños that he had been fired on the first day of his new job. He couldn't tell them that he was out of the tips business no sooner than he had gotten into it.

Most of the other passengers were inside seeking protection from the wind and the spray as waves crashed against the hull. Alfero stared at the Manhattan skyline. Like the wall of a great fortress, it protected the island. There seemed to be no entrance. No way in.

It didn't make sense to Alfero. America was a country where

everyone was equal. Where the son of a garbage man could rise to the top and clear away the dirty dishes of the President.

What could he tell Dolores? She had let him do it to her last night but now she would never let him do it to her again. She would make him wait even longer than after the baby died. This was a bigger death. It was his job. They had taken away his future. He wasn't good enough to be a busboy. He was no longer a man.

Suddenly, Alfero remembered Tessa screaming at Steven, "If I'm not good enough to be here tomorrow, then neither is the President." He wondered whether she was right.

The boat docked at the landing. Children ran to the front of the deck, excited but still holding hands as instructed by their teacher. Alfero stayed close to them. His feet hurt so much that he limped all the way from the pier, hurrying to keep up with the children and hear about Mr. Bartholdi.

Near the entrance to the pedestal, he saw the bronze plaque engraved with words he had heard before. The words he had come to see.

Give me your tired . . .

Alfero was tired. His feet were killing him.

. . . your poor . . .

Alfero was poor. The ferry had cost $3.25. All he had left was a dime and a subway token.

. . . your huddled masses yearning to breathe free . . .

Alfero looked up at the face of the Statue of Liberty. He began to cry. Tessa was right. If he wasn't good enough to be there tomorrow, then neither was the President.

o

Lunch was over. Libby lay back in the tub, imagining herself far away from the restaurant downstairs. In some distant place where there were no clocks. On a mountain top. The Swiss Alps. A very exclusive clinic for the terminally sentimental. A place where people suffered from broken promises and lost letters. Where they died from dreams that never came true. Barbara Stanwyck had once died in just such a clinic. Beautifully dressed. Libby scooped up a handful of soap bubbles and made a fist. Some of the bubbles escaped between her fingers.

There was a knock at the door. "Cal?"

No answer.

"Who is it?"

The door opened slowly. "Libby?"

"Go away!" Libby reached for her towel. "Don't you dare!" The door kept opening. "One more step and I'll . . ."

"Don't be afraid."

It took Libby a moment to recognize the man standing in her bathroom. "What are you doing here?" She gasped as he took off his aviator glasses.

"Why didn't you answer my letters?"

Letters? Libby couldn't believe it. He had written to her! "You're not supposed to be here until tomorrow."

"There is no tomorrow." He took her towel, inhaled it for a moment, and then sat down on the edge of the tub. "I wrote dozens of letters." He raised his eyebrows. "I should have known they'd be intercepted."

"By whom?"

"Who do you think?" The President of the United States reached into the water and pulled the plug. "Birnbaum."

Libby felt a chill on her shoulders. "Why are you here? What do you want?"

"I want my son."

Libby covered her breasts as the water slid away. "I don't know what you're talking about." She was exposed. Cold. Libby put a hand to her mouth as she heard herself scream. But it wasn't a scream. It was the phone. She picked it up.

"Libby, this is Birnbaum."

The President was gone. The bubbles were back.

"Birnbaum?"

"I have a car waiting," he said. "How fast can you get downstairs?"

Her eyes clouded with tears. "I told you yesterday. No more chow mein!"

"Libby, get dressed. Cal's been shot."

o

Libby stared through the car window as they arrived at Roosevelt Hospital. The Fifty-ninth Street entrance was swarming with reporters. "That looks like more than a flesh wound crowd."

"Trust me."

"Are you crazy?" She turned to him. "I don't know why people think they're doing you a favor when they say 'It's nothing serious' until you get to the hospital and then they tell you he was eaten by an alligator." Libby smiled nervously and put a hand on Birnbaum's arm.

"No alligators," he said, putting his hand over hers. He expected her to take her hand away. She didn't. "It's only a flesh wound."

"Listen, Birnbaum, you're not just trying to make things easy for me, are you?"

He smiled. "Would I do a thing like that?" The driver took them around to the Emergency entrance.

Libby hesitated. "Wait. I'm such a mess. My eyes are swollen. My nose is all red. God knows what I'm wearing. They're going to take one look and wheel me into intensive care."

"You look fine to me," he said, opening the car door and getting out. Libby was wearing a pink wool jumpsuit and an orange fox vest.

"What do you know?"

Birnbaum reached for her hand. "You look great. I wish you were rushing to my side."

She brushed his hand away and got out by herself. "Don't be dumb."

Not that some women wouldn't have found Birnbaum attractive. Some women were threatened by men with style. Some women preferred men who hummed along with the music, couldn't read a French menu, and whose hands were too large to do their collar buttons. Libby felt sorry for the elitist Mrs. Birnbaum. It must have been sheer hell until he took off his Timex watch and his Sears suit and hopped into bed.

Birnbaum led the way. He knew exactly where to go. He had been to the hospital on Monday checking things out for the President. "We can take this one," he said, ringing for a Staff Only elevator.

Libby stared straight ahead. The door opened. She couldn't move. "I'm frightened."

"He's all right!"

Libby was afraid Birnbaum was going to put his arms around her again. Even worse, she wished he would. Instead, he led her into the elevator. The doors closed. She stared at the No Smoking sign. "Do you smoke?"

"No."

"Good. It's a filthy habit." She paused. "I used to. Years ago."

"Years ago doesn't count."

"The hell it doesn't!" she shouted. "I know people who stopped smoking years ago and they still get sick. It all catches up with you. Everything catches up with you. Oh, Birnbaum. I'm so terrified that all those lousy cigarettes are going to catch up with me!"

"It's okay," Birnbaum said. "Cal is fine. It's only a flesh wound."

Libby made a fist and raised her hand as though it were an SOS. "Whose flesh, Birnbaum?" She stared at him, then slowly closed her eyes as he reached out, took her in his arms, and kissed her.

The moment the elevator doors opened, Libby broke away from Birnbaum and ran down the corridor.

Finding Cal's room was as daunting as Scarlett searching through the wounded in Atlanta. Libby glanced anxiously into each room, afraid she might actually find him. Or find what was left of him. She was afraid she might be too late. But she didn't know whether it was too late for him or too late for her.

Libby stood frozen in the doorway of Room 824. Two enormous bouquets of balloons were tied to the headboard. Cal, barechested and laughing, sat up in bed. His right arm was in a sling. A barber was trimming his hair while a pretty young woman gave him a manicure. A dozen vases were filled with roses. Extra phones had been brought in and they were all in use. Cal's lawyer Arny. Barry from the agency. Jerry the press agent. In the corner, Cal's manager, Freddy, dictated notes into a tape recorder as though the tape recorder were deaf. The noise was earsplitting.

"Babe!" Cal shouted, flashing his baby blues. He raised his hand to wave at her and winced at the pain from his bandaged shoulder.

"You're not dead!" Libby blurted out.

"I will be if Sweeney Todd cuts my hair any shorter," Cal said. "Can you believe that today of all days Leslie is on a shoot with DeNiro?"

Libby put her hands on her hips. "No! I can't believe it."

"That's what *I* said! And DeNiro is definitely not a hair person!" Cal rocked back and shouted, "Ouch!" He pulled his hand back from the manicurist. "Honey, it's the nail you cut, not the finger!"

Libby stood in the doorway, tapping her foot. "So I hear you got shot."

Jerry, the press agent, rushed over to Cal. "I've got the *Enquirer* on the phone. What do I tell them?"

Barry shouted from across the room. "Oy vay! The *Enquirer* knows? They know?"

"Everybody seems to know." Libby took the towel from the barber and pointed him toward the door.

Freddy slapped his head. "How much do they know?"

"Everything!"

"Everybody seems to know everything." Libby ankled the manicurist away from the bed. "Later."

"How much of the cover do I get?" Cal shouted across the room.

"An eighth," Jerry shouted back. "But for an interview, you could get the big cover shot and a two-page spread."

"Visiting hours are over," Libby announced. "You may feed the animal again at eight P.M." She went from Arny to Jerry to Barry to Freddy. She hung up their phones and greeted them each with a goodbye.

Jerry nodded. "Maybe I should go down and talk to the *Enquirer.*"

"Is there any place to eat around here?" Freddy asked.

"Dynamite outfit," Barry said, kissing Libby. "Very retail."

Arny the lawyer scooped up all of his papers. "He changed

his will. You get everything. That means you get nothing. You'd get more if he cut you out and you contested. Don't tell him I told you."

Once they were alone, Libby walked slowly to the bed. She took Cal's hand, held it tight, then leaned over and kissed each finger. "Would you believe that I was a young, beautiful woman just a few minutes ago?" She sniffed back the tears. "I aged a hundred years on my way over here. Look at me. I went from Brooke Shields to Brooke Astor just going crosstown. For God's sake! What happened?"

Cal put a hand to her face. "Oy vay. I thought you knew."

"Don't say oy vay. You only say oy vay when you've been around Barry too long."

"Once in a while I can say oy vay. It's a very New York thing to say."

"Cal, all I know is that you were shot at Trump Tower." She smiled. "I feel so guilty. You must have been buying something ridiculously expensive for me."

"I wasn't buying."

"Well, then what were you doing?"

"I was selling." Cal cleared his throat. "Donald shot me."

"Donald who?"

"Donald!"

Libby stood up. "Listen, the only Donalds I know are Phyllis and Donald and Donald Duck." She stared at Cal. There was a long silence. "Oy vay."

Cal nodded yes.

Libby crumpled into a chair. "Why would he do such a thing? Did he go crazy? I can't believe it! Oh, my God. Does Phyllis know?"

Cal stopped Libby from picking up the phone.

"But I have to talk to her. She must be going through hell. I don't understand any of this." She reached for the phone again. "Is Donald in jail?"

Cal grabbed hold of her. "I went to see Phyllis about her new play. I had spoken to Mike. He was willing to direct." Cal paused. "For some bizarre reason, Donald thought I was fooling around with Phyllis."

"Are you kidding?" She laughed nervously. "You are kidding?"

"I swear I never touched Phyllis. Nothing was further from my mind."

"Then what gave Donald the idea?"

Cal hesitated. He started to smile but shook his head, trying to make sense of it. He took a deep breath and suddenly burst into laughter. "Maybe it was because Phyllis was on the bed naked." Cal winced. He pointed to his bandaged shoulder. "It only hurts when I laugh."

Libby stared at him in disbelief. "I don't know. Maybe it's me. It just doesn't strike me funny."

Cal breathed a loud sigh as he regained control. "All right. Here's what happened. I'm in the living room with Phyllis. In the middle of the conversation, she goes into the bedroom and closes the door. I stand there like a dummy, shouting to her. Finally, I knock. She tells me to come in."

Libby watched suspiciously as a smile crept back onto Cal's face. "I guess this must be the funny part."

"I open the door. All the lights are dim. I see Phyllis lying there like Venus on the half-shell. Donald rushes in, thinks God-knows-what is going on and the son of a bitch shoots me!" Cal started to laugh again.

Libby shook her head. "You're absolutely right." She stood up angrily. "That is hilarious. My best friend's husband thinks you're having an affair with her and he tries to kill you." She paused, unable to stop herself from smiling. "I'm not smiling at that."

"Then what?"

Libby pretended to cough. "Venus on the half-shell." She tried to stifle a giggle. "It must be the way you tell it." She doubled over with laughter. "Oh, poor Donald. I feel so sorry for him."

Cal was barely able to catch his breath. "To hell with him! I turn down a six-million-dollar tumble with Rikki and I still wind up on the front page of the *Enquirer!*"

Libby stopped laughing. "You what?"

"I still wind up on the front page . . ."

"No. The other part."

He wiped the tears from his eyes. "The reason I went to see Phyllis was because I told Janos no."

"You told Janos no?"

"I told him I didn't believe in his Big Bang Theory."

"You gave up the six million?"

Cal nodded yes and they burst into laughter again. Finally, Libby reached for a tissue and blew her nose. "You gave up six million dollars," she said softly.

He leaned over and kissed her. "Six million dollars."

Libby rubbed her cheek against his. "Six million dollars."

Cal put his hand to her hair. "Six million dollars."

She nuzzled her chin in his palm. "You know how much chopped liver I have to sell to make six million dollars?"

Cal pulled back. "So now I'm chopped liver?"

Libby stared at Cal, realizing she had never loved him more than at that moment. "The hell you are." She nestled close on the bed. "You know, I really think that's one of the nicest things anyone's ever done for me."

"You've really got one hell of an ego."

She ignored him. "And I didn't even bring you any flowers."

Cal was defensive. "What do you mean *one* of the nicest things?"

"Or even a box of candy."

"It occurred to me you might think I did it for you. You really get my goat sometimes!"

She looked up at him lovingly. "Do I?"

"Yes!" he said, melting. "You do."

Libby began to purr. "How often?"

"Not often enough."

She laid her head on Cal's chest. "When do you get out of this joint?"

"In the morning."

"Well, what am I supposed to do tonight?" she asked.

"Same thing I'm going to do."

Libby smiled. "You can't. Your arm's in a sling."

"How are we going to get through this crisis?"

She kissed Cal. "God, I wish I knew."

"If only I had something to look forward to."

"No!" she said, putting her fingers to his lips. "Don't ask me again, Cal. Let me ask you."

"Sure. Go ahead." He waited. "Well, when are you going to ask me?"

"Tomorrow. After lunch."

"And what if you don't?"

She shrugged. "Then I owe you six million."

"Come on, babe. What do you think is going to happen tomorrow?"

"Oh, Cal. Don't you read the papers? Haven't you heard the news? Everyone's been talking about it. Tomorrow, after lunch, all the angels will fly down from heaven. The grass will turn green. The flowers will burst into bloom and all the birds will sing." Libby kissed him gently and whispered, *"I know that sounds a bit bizarre, but in Camelot . . ."*

". . . in Camelot," Cal sang sadly.

". . . that's how conditions are." Libby held him tight as she kissed his nose and his eyes and his chin. But all the kisses in the world couldn't get Birnbaum out of her mind.

As Libby walked down the corridor after leaving Cal, she half expected to find Birnbaum waiting for her. The devil come to collect his due. But his due wasn't due yet. She had to tough it out for one more day. After lunch tomorrow she would be rid of him.

She glanced into the waiting room to be sure he wasn't there and saw Steven. He got up anxiously. "Cal's all right," Libby said. "There's nothing to worry about." She reached out for him. As always, Steven pulled away.

"Why won't he press charges?"

Libby forced a smile. "It was only a flesh wound."

"She jests at scars . . ."

"He'll be out in the morning," she said flatly.

"Barely enough time to have Libby of Lourdes embroidered on your undies."

She tried changing the subject. "I'm worried about Donald."

Steven shot his arms into the air. "Forget Lourdes! Go directly to Nazareth. If you pass Go, collect two hundred hosannas."

"God knows, I'll never forgive him, but I'm still worried."

"This just in! Phyllis Elgin has arranged bail for Deadeye Don."

"Bail? Why bail? Cal didn't press charges."

"There was a shooting, ma'am. One human being tried to kill another human being with a weapon even more deadly than a table next to the service area." He grabbed hold of Libby. "Why won't he press charges?"

"Because they're friends," she said. "Life is not an eye for an eye."

"He has to press charges!"

"No!"

Steven was nearly out of breath. "You've got to make him do it. I'm the one Donald was trying to kill."

Libby thought Steven had gone over the edge. She was afraid he had slipped into paranoia the way a coin slips into the crevice of an overstuffed sofa. "Donald would never try to hurt you."

"Jerry and Barry and Freddy and all the people whose names end in Y think they can keep it a secret from Mr. Macho. It's not exactly the greatest press in the world. Faggot Son Fucks Banker."

Libby felt ill. She held onto the wall.

"I want my father to defend me. I want him to fight for me."

"You and Donald?" She felt dizzy. "For how long?"

"Only since I asked him for money."

Libby put a hand to her mouth. The only thing worse than having sex with Donald was having money with Donald.

"I know," Steven sighed. "It's tacky beyond belief. You can imagine how desperate I must have been."

"Does Phyllis know?"

"Everybody knows. By this time, they're writing folk songs at Régine's. Everybody knows except for dear old dad."

"I didn't know."

"Well, of course you didn't know. You're the one I needed the money to get away from. You're the last one I wanted to find out."

Steven always had a little extra hurt saved up for her. But this time he had outdone himself. "Where were you planning to go?"

"Not far. Chez Marie is up for sale. Only two blocks away."

Libby didn't want to cry. She didn't want to give him the satisfaction. But that would have been unfair. He deserved to see her cry. After all, he had won.

o

Birnbaum came back upstairs looking for Libby. He saw Dr. Derek come out of Cal's room. "Everything okay?"

The young Irish doctor was making a notation in the file. "It will be if you people leave me alone." He looked up. "Do you think the President knows all the trouble he's causing?"

"The President isn't causing trouble. I am." Birnbaum glanced toward Cal's room. "I need Mr. Dennis out by eight in the morning so that we can seal off this floor."

"You're a real pain in the posterior, Special Agent Birnbaum. I've been tripping over your people all day. What the hell is going to happen here tomorrow?"

Birnbaum smiled. "How about letting me handle that?"

"And how about you letting me handle my patient?" Dr. Derek pointed to one of the sheets in his file. "I certainly hope you protect the President better than you take hemo profiles."

"What do you mean?" Birnbaum looked at the page. It was a list, according to blood type, of everyone who worked at Libby's. Standard information in the event live donors were required. "What's the problem?"

"The problem is the very first name on this list. Steven Dennis. Look at that. You've got him as O-negative. That can't be right."

"Why not?"

The doctor pulled back the file. "Because if he was O-negative, then Cal Dennis couldn't be his father. Their blood types are incompatible. Any first-year medical student could tell you that."

o

Birnbaum pushed past a line of ticket buyers in the lobby of Radio City Music Hall. He flashed his badge and told the guard he wanted to see the manager.

"You one of the guys from the sixteenth precinct?"

"Treasury Department."

The manager, who was even younger than the guard, came out chewing nervously on a wad of gum. "So now I got to hire from Treasury, too? You going to give me a discount on my taxes?"

"I don't want a job."

The manager squinted. "Don't tell me you're a narc?"

"I want to see Mr. Goldberg. His office said I'd find him here."

The manager nodded. "They all bring their lawyers. Like they were going to court instead of Radio City." He knocked three times on the glass door. "I'll tell you this. Billy is clean. And the Hall is clean. Always has been." Two muscular men who looked as though they had been squeezed into their sharkskin suits opened the door.

As Birnbaum walked into the Grand Foyer, the first thing he saw was the graceful staircase sweeping down from the mezzanine. His eyes clouded over with childhood memories. The giant mural rising to a gold-leaf ceiling. The gleaming Art Deco balustrades and railings. The carpeting as lush as a remembrance by Proust.

Hots was walking back and forth in front of the enormous candy counter. He shouted into his cellular phone, "Christie, darling. Let me be the judge!"

Music wafted in from the auditorium as Billy Joel began rehearsing "Pressure." Birnbaum approached Hots. "Mr. Goldberg . . ."

Hots put his hand over the receiver and waved Birnbaum aside. "I only accept summonses on Simchas Torah."

Birnbaum held out his ID. "I have to speak to you."

Hots continued his phone conversation. "Jesus, Christie, what do you mean how do I know?" He began pacing again. "There are thirty people in the whole world and twenty-nine of them are yentas. Huey is coming in his maroon-sequined jacket, and Whoopi is still sorting through the latest shipment from

Goodwill. Wear the green, darling. It's stunning. You can't go wrong. Green is the color of Kermit and money." He motioned for Birnbaum to get out of his way.

"I want to talk to you about Libby Dennis."

Hots stopped pacing. He nodded that he was winding up the phone conversation. "I'll say a brocho, sweetie. I love you." He disconnected the call, then quickly dialed another number. "One second, please." Then, angrily into the receiver, "Who the fuck has the keys to the candy counter? And fast!" Hots motioned Birnbaum over to the staircase. They sat down. "You want a candy bar?" he asked.

"Thanks."

"They'll be down in a minute."

"That's okay."

"You know what you want or you need time to browse?"

"I know what I want," Birnbaum said.

Hots leaned back and stared up at the cylindrical chandeliers. He took a deep breath. "So. You find a fly in your soup or something?"

"Something."

"Fuck you."

Birnbaum sat back. He spoke softly. "I hate it when people say that to me. It's as though they were really saying that nothing I had ever done in my life mattered and that I was totally unimportant."

"You're absolutely right. But it's easier just to say Fuck You."

"What makes you think you have all that power?"

Hots smiled. "I have the key to the candy counter."

Birnbaum grabbed Hots by the collar. "But I have the key to your ass."

"Hands off, T-Man, or else I'll make you poster boy at the Centers for Disease Control." Hots shut his eyes until Birnbaum let go of him. "You want to talk to me, I strongly suggest we engage in safe talk."

"Who is Steven Dennis's father?"

"You call that safe?"

A huge woman in a bright red flowered dress stomped her way across the foyer as though walking through a field of mud. In one hand she held a large circular ring filled with dozens of keys that jangled with each step. "You want candy?" she asked.

Hots got up and walked quickly to the counter. "I want a Baby Ruth bar." He looked back at Birnbaum.

"Does she have Milk Duds?"

"I got 'em," the woman said. "One Baby Ruth. One Milk Duds." She unlocked the glass door, took out the candy, and slammed them on top of the counter. "You name 'em, I got 'em."

"Put them on my tab." Hots took the candy while the woman locked the counter and trudged back across the lobby.

"Want some?" Hots asked, ripping the paper on his Baby Ruth.

"No. You?" Birnbaum held out the box.

"No." Hots bit into the candy bar and shook his head. "Those fucking Swiss. What the hell do they know about chocolate?"

Birnbaum nodded. "Can you believe what they charge for these things today? A buck."

"A buck and a half at my movie. But I've got a candy store a block away. I buy whatever I want for fifty cents before I go in."

Birnbaum chewed on a Milk Dud. "You and I both understand that client confidentiality is second to national security."

"I don't know what you're talking about."

"I'm sure you realize that members of the President's immediate family must be protected around the clock. We're not as worried about them getting killed as we are their being kidnaped and held hostage. You can understand what a terrible position that would put the President in. God forbid he should have to surrender Cleveland in order to get Steven back."

Hots pointed toward the auditorium. "You ever listen, really listen, to Billy's lyrics? That song, 'Pressure,' it gets to me every time."

"I know you've been a good friend to Mrs. Dennis. But we've still got one hell of a file on you. To save time, we know who you bought and who bought you. We know all about the drugs. The boys in Albany can get you on so many counts of tax evasion they could make you head of the IRS. In other words, if we were putting up crucifixes on the West Side Highway, you'd go first, Mr. Goldberg."

"Hots. My friends call me Hots."

"Now here's the good news. I promise that Mrs. Dennis will never know the truth came from you. Not because I like you, Mr. Goldberg . . ."

"I hate being called Mr. Goldberg! It makes me feel like a goddamn old man. My father was Mr. Goldberg."

"She won't know you told me, Hots, because I don't want her to know that I know. Not yet anyway."

"I can't go to jail. It would kill my mother."

"I didn't say jail."

"Why the hell are you asking me, Birnbaum? You already know."

"I want to hear somebody say it."

"What good would it do anybody to find out? Leave it alone. Nobody knows."

"You know."

Hots crumpled the candy wrapper and threw it down the stairs. "So now *you* know. So what?"

Birnbaum stood up. "Shh!" He put his box of Milk Duds into his pocket. "Loose lips sink ships."

o

Although the meeting at Headquarters was scheduled for seven-thirty P.M., Birnbaum went into the Briefing Room just before seven. He carried a file that had TOP SECRET stamped in red on a cardboard cover.

If Secret Service Headquarters was the most secure place in the City of New York, the Briefing Room was the most secure place at Secret Service Headquarters. It was a square, white, windowless area with four bare walls. There was no desk, no place to put down papers or hang up a coat. The floor was not carpeted. All corners were visible. There were six rows of white folding chairs. Electrical outlets were on eye level. Locked. There was no switch to turn the lights off because the lights were never turned off. There was no thermostat in the room. Temperature and access were controlled by a computer behind a glass panel on the back wall. The computer projected film footage, schematics, and kept the room under surveillance around the clock.

The only thing the computer couldn't do was read Birnbaum's mind. He sat down and stared at the file in his lap. TOP SECRET. Even if the computer could read his mind, it hadn't been programmed for irony.

As head of the New York field office, the largest in the nation, Birnbaum felt entitled to have major problems. But this time he had a problem more appropriate for the Chief Rabbi of Judea. Or, at the very least, Solomon himself.

He entered his access code on the remote control and waved the unit toward the computer. The lights dimmed automatically as he coded in the instructions for a schematic of Fifty-fifth between Fifth and Sixth Avenues. He signaled for enlargements until, like God pushing aside the clouds, he had a clear view of the parcel of land that was Libby's.

Birnbaum had to make a decision. Tell or don't tell. It was very simple, like most difficult decisions. Once he realized that he had no choice at all, his genes took over for his brain. He began to consider the question of why he had no choice. At which point, the problem of the problem became more intriguing than the problem of the solution. It was pure Talmudic torture and he loved every minute of it.

Even before the door opened, the projector shut off and the lights came up full. Anders stood in the doorway, holding his file marked TOP SECRET. "I want to see you. I've got the FDA on my ass."

"Too bad. You should have gotten a butterfly or a nice big heart."

"They're only willing to approve the food if they prepare it in advance, seal it in metal containers, and put it under guard. Or if they purchase the ingredients, post a guard, watch the cook . . ."

"Tell them to go fuck themselves."

"I did. But they haven't approved that yet either."

"So what do you want to do?"

"I want the FDA there. Anything happens, I blame them. My men will be stationed in the kitchen. We can check for atomic dust. All that crap. But I want one of your men as a taster."

"That went out with the Middle Ages. And why one of *my* men?"

"Because I'm not losing a White House agent. That's what regional offices are for."

While Birnbaum stared at Anders, the room began filling up. The men knew that a seven-thirty meeting meant everyone in place by seven-thirty. If you arrived precisely at seven-thirty for a seven-thirty meeting, you were late. By seven twenty-five, everyone was there.

To someone walking in off the street, presuming someone could walk in off the street, the occupants of the room appeared to be attending a management seminar for successful young entrepreneurs. A supposition not entirely off the mark. Each agent was the CEO for his own business: himself. Each agent was his own corporation under contract to the government. With a top pay scale, before sliding into a desk job, of $36,000 per annum, each corporation had only one client: the President of the United States.

The Secret Service didn't offer the rough and tumble camaraderie found in patrol cars or locker rooms or fighter squadrons. There was no common enemy, no war to be won, nothing but battle after battle after battle. Agents were not trained to protect themselves or their colleagues. Their unique moment of truth was not the split-second during which they had to decide whether to kill or be killed. It was the split-second during which they had to decide to be killed.

Anders took out his remote, entered the access code, and dialed up the West Side Heliport schematic. "Pads, please."

Each agent's pad was a single three-by-five card on which he was expected to note all pertinent information. On one side only. It was a technique held over from Anders's days at the FBI.

As the lights dimmed, and Anders focused the schematic, Birnbaum glanced from face to face wondering which of his rookies to appoint court taster. He wondered which of Anders's men would eventually be assigned to Steven, to defend and protect, even to die to save the little shit from being taken hostage.

Conaway reported to Anders on his meeting with Assistant Chief DeVito, head of Manhattan South. "We decided not to pull a Yellow Alert since we were mobilizing under 1,500 men. The

Blue Alert goes into effect two hours prior to arrival. DeVito's still catching crap from the yo-yo who heads the Bureau of Traffic Operations because we want to go uptown on Second Avenue. They're afraid of confusing New York's finest because we're traveling uptown on a downtown street."

Anders had already switched to a schematic covering Second Avenue up to Fifty-fifth Street. "This is not a course in abnormal psychology," Anders said. "I am not interested in reaction or motivation. My concern is results. Did we get the choppers?"

"Two choppers with videocams for roof sweeps."

"Plus ours," Anders said, pointing to Moran. "I don't want any blank screens in the video van." To Conaway. "Sharpshooters?"

"Usual UN sites. Six counterassault teams will cover the block between Fifth and Sixth." Conaway smiled. "DeVito will give us as many shooters as we want. They don't come out of overtime."

"I am not interested in the fiscal problems of the City of New York."

As Conaway continued, Birnbaum winked at him. Conaway was too good a man to be the taster. "After assessing, I decided it would not be necessary to seal all manholes since the motorcade route has not been released."

"Trashcans . . ."

"Trashcans and mailboxes will be removed on the block between Fifth and Sixth and all manhole covers and sewers will be secured on that block."

"How many mounted units did you get?" Birnbaum asked.

"Two at the UN and I ordered six for the block."

"Good," Birnbaum said. "There's still nothing better than a man on a horse."

Davis raised his hand and stood up. "I drove the route four times today. We checked for construction sites, had a run on tenants in all buildings on the route, and I foresee no problems. We should be able to go from A to B in well under three minutes."

"How much under?"

"We're talking a route approximately one mile. At thirty miles per hour, that's two minutes."

Davis was one of Anders's men. But he was too much of a pro to wind up babysitting Steven at leather bars or Turkish baths.

Anders raised his remote and dialed in the schematic of Libby's. "I want our security screen in place two hours prior."

"I've scheduled a briefing at ten o'clock," Birnbaum said.

"Thank you. But I'll handle that briefing myself."

Miller stood up as though addressing his stockholders. "We disassembled tables and chairs for irregularities. Floors, walls, and ceilings are clean. No listening devices, detonators, etc. The AV crew did a search before the electronics people came in. Outlets, phones, lights, etc., were all negative."

Anders looked at his file. "I'll assign shift leaders in the morning." He turned to Birnbaum. "I want Technical Security sweeping for bombs at ten. The sniffer dogs at eleven. No one allowed in after twelve-thirty. No one allowed in or out from twelve-thirty until the man leaves."

"That may be a little difficult," Birnbaum said.

"I don't care. Make sure we can read all phones as soon as the place opens."

"Ambulances, fire trucks, and the White House Medical Unit will be out front from eleven on."

"Okay!" Anders shouted. "I want all entry and exit points covered two hours before arrival. Once the Explosive Ordnance people give the all-clear, we have a frozen zone. Birnbaum, how many men at the door?"

"Four."

"Back door?"

"Four."

"Upstairs?"

"Two on each floor."

"Roof?"

"Two SWAT teams."

"Adjoining?"

"Countersniper teams."

Birnbaum added, "We already have emergency generators hooked up in the event of a power failure."

Anders stared at him. "I know that."

Well, I know something you don't, Birnbaum thought. I

know something you'd give your left ball to find out. Birnbaum
put a hand to his forehead. First things first. A taster. Livingstone
was the only one without kids. But he had just bought his girl a
sexy nightgown and Livingstone was planning to go home for the
fuck of his life.

Anders wound up by discussing the dress code: suits, ties,
blazers. No guns up their sleeves. That was okay in crowds but
not in close contact. Flack vests were to be worn. "You'll get
your pins tomorrow," he said. "As always, gentlemen, it is what
we *don't do* that counts."

Those words had a special meaning for Birnbaum. He
couldn't begin to remember how many times he had used that
same phrase. "It's what we *don't do* that counts." As in, "it's what
we *don't tell* that counts." Certainly, Steven could only be an
embarrassment to the White House—under the best of conditions. If no one had found out after all these years, what was the
point of telling them now?

Once the room emptied out, Birnbaum went over to Anders. "Why the hell are we going through all this?"

"Because the President wants to have lunch at Libby's."

"But why?"

"Who gives a shit?"

"I do! It's too dangerous! Things can happen. All kinds of
unexpected things."

"You sound just like J. Edgar."

"I don't care! Anders, you'll just have to trust me. There are
too many risks." Birnbaum began to pace. "Listen, it's simple.
You've got this window built into his schedule. No one knows
where he's going. There's no press coverage. We can cancel the
whole thing."

"Are you crazy?"

"Anders, you don't know protection like I do. You know
the White House. Protocol. Limo One. You know the presidential insignia on the doors, and the flags on the fenders. In a city
like this, things can happen."

"There is no car in America safer than the presidential limousine." Anders spoke softly, as if to a child. "It is bulletproof. It
is bombproof. It is a masterpiece of engineering. Do you want
him to leave the UN in a Honda?"

"I'm not talking cars!" Birnbaum shouted. "I'm talking about protecting the President. I know it's not safe for him! I don't want anything to happen just because you like riding the point seat in that car!"

Anders finally understood Birnbaum. "So that's it."

"What's it?"

"Burnout." Anders put his hand on Birnbaum's shoulder. "You're in the midst of a divorce. It happens to all of us. You'll be okay."

Birnbaum looked up. Anders was right. He would be okay. Hots would never tell anyone. And as long as Libby didn't know that he knew, he could keep her secret.

Anders patted Birnbaum on the back. "Go home and get yourself a good night's sleep."

"Thanks."

Anders walked to the door. He turned back and smiled. "Oh, yeah. I almost forgot. Who's the taster?"

"Me."

○

Libby stood in Birnbaum's lobby, an enormous bouquet of balloons in one hand, two large shopping bags in the other. The doorman rang Birnbaum on the intercom. "Your delivery is here."

"I didn't order anything."

The doorman looked at Libby. She whispered, "Tell him it's from the Lotus Inn."

"It's from the Lotus Inn," the doorman said.

Birnbaum's voice was impatient. "I didn't order anything from the Lotus Inn!"

"Don't be dumb, Birnbaum!" Libby shouted into the intercom. "It's a surprise!"

There was a long pause. "Is that you?"

Libby glanced at the doorman. She didn't know whether it was or not.

"Hot stuff coming through," she said, handing Birnbaum the balloons. Libby walked into his apartment, careful to avoid the piles of rubble that had once been walls. "Where did the kitchen used to be?" she asked.

"Somewhere over here." He smiled at the balloons and led her around a hole in the floor.

"Birnbaum, do you have any holes in the ceiling?"

"No."

"Then let go of the balloons and take these shopping bags. My fingers are killing me."

They both watched the balloons rise and bounce once against the ceiling before accepting their limitation. Birnbaum took the shopping bags. "You really went to the Lotus Inn?"

Libby rubbed her hands. "You want a lot of chitchat or you want to eat?"

He put the shopping bags on top of the counter. "I'm just surprised."

Libby unpacked the take-out containers. "Life is full of surprises."

He pushed aside a dropcloth to make more room on the counter. Glasses shattered as they hit the floor. "So that's where they were."

"How about some champagne?"

"I don't have any."

She reached into a shopping bag and lifted out a bottle of Dom Pérignon as though it were a white rabbit.

"You really are something." He tried opening the bottle but couldn't get his fingernail under the foil. "I was just sitting here watching a rerun of my favorite 'Lassie' show when the bell rang. It's the one where Lassie finds the little calf that was bitten by a rattlesnake."

Libby grabbed the bottle from him. "Birnbaum, stop yapping and put the cake in the fridge. You do have a fridge?"

He opened the box. The cake had an inscription in pink frosting. "Good Luck Estelle?"

"It was the only party cake they had left. And don't think it was easy to get. Estelle had just made it for herself." She held tight to the cork and began twisting the bottle.

"Looks like you thought of everything," he said unwrapping two glasses.

"Not everything. I forgot a table and chairs."

Birnbaum put stools on either side of the counter. *"Voilà!"*

Libby poured the champagne. Suddenly she gasped. "What is wrong with me?" She reached into a bag and took out two party hats and streamers.

Birnbaum put on a hat and opened the streamers. "Great." He raised his glass. "Okay. I give up."

Libby threw some confetti in the air. "It's my engagement party." She put on her hat. "Cal and I are going to get married again."

He tapped his glass against hers. Without taking their eyes from one another, they sipped the champagne. Then Birnbaum, forcing a smile, threw a streamer at her. "Congratulations."

She threw a streamer at him. "Thanks."

Birnbaum nodded. "This is some terrific party." Libby shrugged her shoulders. "Well, I guess we might as well dig in. No sense letting all that MSG get cold."

Like distant relatives at a family gathering neither wished to attend, they stared at each other.

"You okay?" he asked.

"Sure."

They sat down on opposite sides of the counter. A curtain of balloon strings hung between them.

"Birnbaum, I lied. I'm not okay." She pulled the balloons down to hide her face.

"You look okay."

"The hell I do! If I were okay, do you think I'd be sitting here in my coat!"

"Your coat?" He pointed to her orange fox vest. "I didn't think that was a coat."

"Actually, it's a vest."

"That's what I thought."

"But it's also a coat."

"Let me hang it up for you."

"Thanks." Libby fluffed her hair as he walked to the closet. "So, how's the old chow mein look to you?"

"You want the truth?"

"We'll never get anywhere if we don't tell each other the truth, Birnbaum. I, for one, would still be sitting in my coat."

"Okay," he said, closing the closet door. "I don't like the way it looks. It looks different."

"That's just what I was thinking."

"Why don't we dump it?" he asked.

"Good riddance to bad chow mein."

He began to laugh. "How about we start from scratch?"

"I have a better idea. Let's start from itch. I feel like cooking."

Birnbaum threw the containers into a large metal trash basket. "I warn you. I'm all out of caviar."

Libby took a sip of champagne. "Well, there must be something." She opened the refrigerator door and stood there in astonishment. The shelves were crammed with freshly cooked food. Turkey. Ham. Meat loaf. Butter, cream, milk and eggs. Fresh vegetables in the crisper. A bowl filled with fruit. Four cheeses. Three juices. Unopened packages of smoked meat. Jars of stuffed olives, fancy relishes, and imported marmalade. "What the hell is going on here?"

"Don't ask me. The cleaning lady does all the shopping."

Libby turned quickly. Her mouth open, she pointed to the piles of rubble separated by paths of newspapers. "You have a cleaning lady?"

"You think the papers get there by themselves? Of course I have a cleaning lady. She comes in twice a week. She dusts the rocks and changes the papers. I'd be lost without her."

Libby began to laugh. "And she still has time to shop?"

"She does my laundry, makes the bed, puts the cap on the toothpaste and she's finished. Every Tuesday and Thursday she goes to the market and buys a complete refrigerator full of food. We have an unspoken agreement between us. She takes home the Tuesday food on Thursday and the Thursday food on the following Tuesday." He smiled. "Everybody needs perks." He shrugged. "Besides, you never know who's going to drop in."

Libby put out her hand, wanting to touch him. Instead, she reached for the champagne.

They clinked glasses, and then stared at each other, wondering what they were celebrating.

"How'd you like to help Mommy make dinner?"

"Sure."

Libby opened the refrigerator. "You think the cleaning lady would mind if we used some eggs?"

"Don't be ridiculous. They're *my* eggs." He shrugged. "I can always tell her they broke."

"Tell her you broke a couple of apples, too." She took out butter, cream, and a slab of cheddar. "How about putting the other bottle of champagne in the fridge."

"You drink a lot of this stuff?"

"Everybody needs perks." She laughed. "You know, Cal and I . . ." She stopped. "I'm sorry." Libby turned away. "The champagne was for Cal. I was going to surprise him at the hospital. Cake. Hats. It was going to be such a wonderful party."

"What happened?"

"I don't know. I didn't feel very festive and I was afraid Cal would see through me."

"But I wouldn't?"

She smiled. "You don't matter, Birnbaum. You're going to walk out of my life after lunch tomorrow."

"So it doesn't matter whether I see through you or not."

"Don't read me my rights, Birnbaum."

"What do you think? I'm some kind of hardship case. You think I'm so desperate I'll let anybody in?"

"Oh, shit. I thought you were the one frog who didn't give a damn about being a prince."

"You really think I'm flattered because you came here?"

"Are you?"

"What are you crazy? Of course, I am!"

"It has nothing to do with my feelings about Cal. I just needed to be out of it for a while."

He raised his arms. *"Mi casa es su casa."*

"You know why I like it here, Birnbaum? It's like being stranded in a transit lounge. There's only a few hours left before your plane leaves for the North Pole and my plane leaves for the South Pole."

"We can still write."

"You know what I mean? You meet a perfect stranger and pour your heart out."

Birnbaum shook his head. "Do me a favor. Don't pour your heart out. I'm not perfect."

"What's wrong with a little truth if it makes the time pass?"

"North Pole. South Pole."

"Birnbaum, what if I told you I was scared to death?"

Birnbaum put his hands on Libby's shoulders. He forced her to look up at him. "Don't tell me."

Libby leaned close and spoke softly. "I want to make my omelette."

He smiled. "Did I tell you I hated eggs?"

"No."

"I hate eggs."

"Not my eggs." She handed him an apple. "Can you peel this?"

"Did Columbus find India?"

Libby heated butter and sugar in a pan. "I need the apple cored, quartered and sliced paper thin."

"You expect me to cut my fingers to shreds? Listen, how about if I shoot it instead?"

Libby took Birnbaum's hand and curled his fingers toward his palm. They stared at one another. "This is the way . . ." She stopped speaking and put a hand to her forehead.

"Headache?"

"Worse. Déjà vu."

"I don't want to know. Don't tell me," he said nervously.

Libby took hold of Birnbaum's hand. "He said he was afraid of cutting his fingers. Just the way you did."

"Welcome aboard Flight Zero to Disaster."

"I showed him how to curl his fingers under at the second joint."

Birnbaum couldn't resist. He held up his hand. "Like this?"

"He put his arms around me."

"Like this?"

She gasped as Birnbaum circled her waist. "I gasped."

"And then?"

"I couldn't believe it. I was cooking my Apple Pie Omelette for a senator."

"What else do you remember?"

"I leaned back against him."

As Libby leaned back against Birnbaum, he whispered into her ear. "You have the right to remain silent."

"Suddenly he was kissing me on the back of the neck."

Birnbaum kissed her on the back of the neck. "You have the right to a lawyer during questioning."

"I don't remember how we got into the bedroom." Libby followed Birnbaum as he led her into the bedroom. She hesitated. "Did I tell you I was scared to death?"

"Anything you say can, and will, be used against you." He leaned close and kissed her.

"Birnbaum, I need someone to save me."

He kissed her again. "Saving is my business."

"But you're the one I need protection from."

Birnbaum smiled. "There is no protection from me. I'm about as high up in the protection racket as you can get." He dimmed the light. His hand reached for the zipper on her jump suit. "I am authorized by law to protect the President of the United States."

As he pulled the zipper all the way down, Libby asked, "The Vice President, too?"

Birnbaum put his hands on her bare shoulders, nudging the jump suit to fall to her ankles. "And the immediate families of the President and Vice President."

Libby began unbuttoning his shirt. "Who else?"

"The President-elect and the Vice President-elect."

She slipped the shirt back over his shoulders. "And?"

Birnbaum unhooked her bra, barely touching her skin. He leaned toward her, stopping the instant he felt her nipples against his chest. "A former President and his wife during his lifetime."

Libby opened his belt buckle and reached for the zipper. "Who else?"

"The widow of a former President until her death or remarriage." Birnbaum's trousers dropped to the floor.

"Anybody else?" Libby stepped out of her jump suit. She wore pink lace panties.

Birnbaum kicked aside his trousers and faced her in his Sears Perma-Prest briefs. He smiled. "Major presidential and vice presidential candidates."

"Is that it?"

"No." Like a nervous safecracker, he rubbed the tips of each thumb against his forefingers just before taking hold of her pink lace panties. He knelt and then slowly lowered them. Birnbaum pressed his cheek against Libby's thigh. As he stood up, his eyes followed her body from toe to head. His voice was thick. "All visiting heads of foreign states or foreign governments."

Libby stared into his eyes as she pulled down his shorts. She stepped back and put a finger on his lips. Very slowly, she traced an imaginary line down his lips and chin, onto his chest, pausing to circle his navel, then along the dark strands leading to his pubic hair. "So this is the body that stops the bullet."

From the moment Libby and Birnbaum got into bed, they inhaled and tasted each other like two hungry animals savoring the kill. Neither knew for certain who was the predator and who was the prey. They exchanged roles cautiously, effortlessly, then willingly as they became one another's secret dream and worst fear come true. Holding tight, they bit and licked each other, pausing to kiss only when the temptation to speak became too strong.

No words. They sighed, moaned softly, rolled back and forth, first one on top and then the other. And then, suddenly, they lay still, silent flesh on silent flesh, barely breathing until dangerous thoughts passed safely by.

They could not believe they were in bed together. Yet, holding tight to their disbelief, could not imagine themselves apart. Yin had discovered Yang. Black, White. Day, Night. And once discovered, each became more separate. Distant. Then closer. Almost redundantly, Birnbaum eased himself inside her. He groaned, his sound deep, a sonar growl that produced an image on her face, her expression defining his size and strength. It was as though he had seen himself for the first time.

Libby had anticipated no less than death. Her breasts disappeared within the grasp of his fingers, her stomach flattened against his, their legs, entwined, became a single limb. She felt vindicated, conquered, incandescent. He thrust forward and forward and forward, unwilling to move back from her. Libby cried out. He gasped. She murmured. They hummed. Still afraid to speak, they listened for something to happen. Something as deafening as a sigh. They listened so hard that they missed the sounds of their own pleasure. They fell asleep in each other's arms.

NAN AND IVAN LYONS

Libby woke in the middle of the night to find him staring at her. "Birnbaum," she whispered.

"Yes?"

"What the hell was that we did?"

He smiled. "Beats me."

Libby put a finger to his mouth and circled his lips. "I was sure you'd have a name for it."

Birnbaum nodded. "It's called cheating."

She sat up. "Oh, shit. Can't you do anything like a normal person? You're supposed to feel great."

"I never cheated on my wife before."

Libby tucked the sheet under her arms. "They're right! God really does move in mysterious ways. I knew he was going to get me. He had to. He always does. But I never figured he'd get me this way."

"Which way?"

Libby closed her eyes and screamed, "The Birnbaum way!"

He held her face tenderly in his hands. "I can't tell you that I love you."

"God two. Libby zero."

"Did you think I would?"

"Birnbaum," she said, taking his hands away, "I honestly don't know if I expected you to tell me that you loved me. But I was hoping you might stop somewhere short of regret."

"Regret? I never said regret."

"I know. You wouldn't have missed me for the world. But you still feel guilty. Which you also wouldn't have missed for the world. By the way, did you know that Theda Bara was Jewish?"

"Listen, what happened here is not the same as what my wife did."

"Of course not."

"We were still living together when she slept with another man."

Libby nodded. "And now you're not living together and you didn't sleep with another man."

He was adamant. "This is a different kind of cheating!"

Libby put a hand to her forehead. "Birnbaum, it's not your fault. It's all my fault. I set you up. I knew what was going to happen when I came here. You didn't stand a chance."

"What the hell are you talking about? You want to think that, go right ahead. But don't expect me to fall for a line like that. I wanted you from the moment I saw you."

"You did?"

"You didn't put anything over on me. I was out to get you. I wanted you. And I got you!"

Libby looked up and smiled. "Do everybody a favor, Birnbaum. Forgive yourself. I don't mean anything to you." She put a hand to his face and slowly brought him close. "Give me a kiss, Birnbaum. One really good kiss. I'll prove it to you." She closed her eyes. "Be honest with yourself. You're not thinking of me."

It was the sweetest kiss of Libby's life. Mouths open, exchanging breath and tongues, they kissed a very loving kiss, a kiss that deserved thousands of votive candles. It was the Sistine Chapel of kisses.

After a moment, breathless, Birnbaum whispered, "I'm sorry. I couldn't help it. I thought of you."

"Son of a bitch."

"I kept telling myself it was empty and meaningless."

"You got a real way with words."

"I want to kiss you again." He took her in his arms and nearly squeezed the breath out of her. His lips pressed tight against her teeth. He pulled back as though to rescue himself. "It's only physical."

"You're a regular Browning."

He drew her close again. "It's not as though I loved you."

"Let me *not* count the ways."

"I loved her."

"Love is like money," Libby said. "It doesn't buy happiness."

"What the hell does it buy?"

"Time. Love buys you time to get over your mistakes. Time to realize how stupid you've been and to kiss and make up. If all you want is happy, you can be happy without love and without money. Most of the world is."

"Except you."

"You can't go by me, Birnbaum. Nobody's going to give you odds on the life of Libby Dennis. What are the chances that my pipsqueak senator would become President?"

He laughed. "You really think he was a pipsqueak?"

"No. He was really very cute."

"Cute?"

"Preppy. His clothes didn't wrinkle. He wore garters to hold up his socks. He put on a tie for breakfast."

"Were you in love with him?"

"Birnbaum, if it's any consolation, I put him through the same garbage you just put me through. Cal and I had separated. He'd gone off to LA for his first picture. I'd never slept with anyone else."

"You were a virgin when you married Cal?"

"It was a long time ago, Birnbaum. It was an age when virgins still roamed the face of the earth."

"He really put on a tie for breakfast?"

"Well, it wasn't just any breakfast. I made my Apple Pie Omelette."

Birnbaum pointed toward the kitchen. "That omelette?"

"Same one."

He laughed. "Did he like it?"

"Oh, Birnbaum! Did he like it? What was he wearing? Why don't you ask me what he was like in bed?"

"I was getting to that."

Libby reached over and turned on the light. They both squinted from the glare. Somehow, Birnbaum looked younger. His hair was tousled, his eyes open wide in anticipation. "You're asking me to tell you what he was like in bed?"

"He's the President. Anybody would be curious."

She wondered what he must be thinking of her. She had to look a hundred years old. Her makeup smudged, eyes red, hair all tangled and knotted. Those creases on her neck. Why hadn't she let Loren get rid of them? "This hardly seems like the time or the place."

Birnbaum reached over and turned off the light. "There is no time. There is no place."

Libby stared up at the ceiling as though speaking to a cosmic inquisitor. "What do you want to know?"

"I want to know everything."

She felt a hand on her shoulder. At first, she thought he was encouraging her. But the hand pulled her back as though the verdict had already been delivered. He pulled the sheet away from her. She felt unbearably naked. Libby put out her hand to touch his chest. "He didn't have hair on his chest."

Pause. "Oh."

"And his nipples were enormous."

"Go on."

Libby thought it must be some sort of occupational neurosis. Perhaps just a bad case of hero worship. She reached for Birnbaum's face in the dark, her finger outlining his lips. "I remember that lower lip of his. Such a strong line. A little fleshy but I liked it." Birnbaum moved her hand aside. He began tracing the line of his lower lip.

"Oh, yes," she said nervously. "He was an outsie."

Birnbaum moved his hand to his stomach. He was breathing hard.

"And come to think of it, I never heard him breathe. No panting. No sweat."

Birnbaum rolled onto his side and then hovered above Libby. "How did he make love to you?" He was expectant. Erect. "How?" he asked.

"Oh, it was wonderful," she whispered, shutting her eyes tight. Libby was afraid to admit she didn't remember anything. "I'll never forget the moment. He kissed my neck, I kissed his ear."

Birnbaum kissed her neck. He waited. "Go ahead. Kiss my ear."

Libby was titillated by the prospect of creating her own *post facto* fantasy of how the President had made love to her. Like a dime-novel sex slave, Birnbaum did exactly what she told him to do. "Then, oh, yes, I'll never forget this, he leaned over and whispered . . ." Libby stopped herself as she suddenly realized what was happening. "Oh, my God."

"Oh, my God," Birnbaum whispered.

"It's not me you want!" she gasped.

Birnbaum was confused. "What? Who said that? You or him?"

"Me! Me! Me! I'm saying it! And I'm saying it now. It's not me you want. It's him!"

Birnbaum knew he'd been caught in the act.

"You son of a bitch," she said, pulling away. Libby wrapped the blanket around her and sat up on the edge of the bed. "It wasn't me, it was him!"

"Listen, lady . . ."

"Lady? Libby to Lady. Ashes to ashes."

"Don't you understand?" he shouted. "I'm supposed to die for him. I've been programmed to spread out and make myself as big a target as possible. Don't you think I'd be curious?"

"Damn you, Birnbaum. I feel like the team whore."

"You want to talk whores," he said, covering himself with the sheet. "I didn't even vote for him."

"You must have put your wife through some hell, Birnbaum."

He smiled. "I didn't put her through anything. I never asked her anything."

"Didn't you want to know why she did it?"

"No. She did it! That's all that mattered."

"I don't understand you, Birnbaum."

"It's very simple. I was a real jerk. I believed in my marriage."

"But not in your wife."

He took a chunk of plaster and hurled it against the wall, not saying a word until it fell to the floor. "I haven't touched a thing since the day she left."

"Why not?"

Birnbaum sat down next to Libby. "I want her back."

"Does she want to come back?"

"Yes."

"But you won't let her."

"I can't stand knowing she was unfaithful."

"You're a real company man, Birnbaum."

"The best there is."

"You really believe in the presidency."

"Yes, I do."

"But not in the President," she said. "You didn't even vote for him. Just like you didn't vote for your wife." Libby reached over and touched his cheek. "I'll tell you something, Birnbaum. I'm glad I'm not divorced from you."

There was a long silence and then he asked, "What the hell happens now?"

"Well, for starters, I'd fire the cleaning lady and call in the National Guard."

He sighed deeply. "They want to transfer me to the LA office."

"Thank God."

Birnbaum shrugged. "My wife hates LA."

"If she loves you, she'll go."

"I guess."

"It's a good way to find out."

"That's what I'm afraid of."

"Don't be afraid. Tell her."

"I'd never tell her about you."

"Of course you wouldn't tell her about me. It's not important to blab every little thing to the person you love. Telling Cal the truth wouldn't have solved anything then. Or now. You know, Birnbaum, I don't think I'm going to tell him about tonight either."

"Strangers on a plane."

She hugged Birnbaum. "North Pole."

"South Pole," he said, kissing her for a very long time. As Birnbaum held her in his arms he began to laugh. "Is he really an outsie?"

"Yes. And there aren't too many of them around."

"Maybe that's why he's President!"

They lay back on the bed. "No. I think it's because of the way he held his coffee cup. I'd often think about the way he held that cup as the months dragged on. Not that I didn't think about Cal, too."

The room had suddenly become very still. Or perhaps it disappeared entirely. Libby spoke without Libby speaking. There was a pause in eternity, a blinding flash defenseless against itself, powerless against logic, blinded by its own incandescence. Libby held her greatest fear, Special Agent Birnbaum, in her arms.

"The day I found out I was pregnant, I hired a divorce lawyer. Even if the baby were Cal's, I wanted him to finish the picture without a wife or kid to worry about. That was the way we had separated and I wanted to keep my end of the bargain."

She traced Birnbaum's eyebrows with her finger. "I called the senator. Not that I had any intention of telling him I was pregnant. But I did want to see him again. I wanted to see him hold that coffee cup. Unimportant things suddenly became important because of the way he did them. I wanted to memorize all the mannerisms I knew were reproducing themselves inside me. We made a date for lunch. The old Willard Hotel. I took the train to Washington but I never left Union Station. I just sat on a bench and waited for the next train back."

Libby covered Birnbaum gently with the blanket. "I didn't want an abortion. There was always the chance it might have been Cal's baby. Besides, I could never give Cal up entirely. I loved him too much. And I never took any money from Cal. Not a penny. I raised Steven on my own. But I thought it would be good for him to have a father. I owed him that." Tears fell from the corners of her eyes. "I think I did okay for Steven in the father department. I think he would have chosen Cal over some dumb old President, don't you?"

Libby waited for Birnbaum to say something. To comfort her. Reassure her that by trusting him, she had done the right thing. She would have nothing to fear.

Instead, she saw fury in his eyes.

Birnbaum hardly moved his lips as he whispered, "Why did you have to tell me?"

THURSDAY

"HE'S NOT HERE YET," STU SHOUTED AS HE RUSHED into the kitchen.

Ursula snatched the dupe before Stu had finished tearing it from his order pad. She looked at it, and took a deep breath. "Ordering one shrimp pâté. One crabmeat cocktail." Then, checking the other dupes, she yelled, "Fire the duck breast for 33!"

Louie slammed a frying pan on the stove. "You no order duck breast for 33! You order chicken liver!"

"Duck breast!" Ursula screamed.

Louie opened his mouth as though his teeth were a deadly weapon. "Chicken liver!"

Norm turned to Special Agent Mitchell. "Didn't she say duck breast?"

Steely-eyed, one hand pressed to the minispeaker in his ear, Fred Mitchell was not about to be distracted by whether Ursula had said duck breast or not. Mitchell was senior man in the kitchen. He had five other agents posted around the room, near the grill, the cold station, the dishwasher, and two at the doors. His men wore round red pins with a horizontal white stripe. The two inspectors from the FDA, who stood on either side of the chef's table, wore small white pins.

"Well, I heard her say duck breast," Norm snarled.

"You hear only tips!" Louie shouted. "I cook good. You get tip." Louie poked Special Agent Thompson who was stationed near the grill. Instinctively, Thompson reached for his gun and then pulled back. "You tell President when he come. No fair. Customer like food, customer tip *me*. No him."

"Where the hell is my bluefish?"

"Fuck your bluefish. What about my chops?"

"Fuck your chops."

Bud pulled Louie back to the stove. "The bluefish, Louie."

"Yes, boss. I got nice one here."

"Hands off." Bud took the plate away from him. "That's mine."

"You eat bluefish, boss?"

"It's for the President."

Louie leaned close to Bud and whispered. "Boss, you know what President order? I change my bet. We make big money."

"Louie, the bluefish!" Bud walked up and down the aisle, checking his cooks. He pressed a finger on the chops as Ho took them from the grill. Then he crossed to the cold table, watching Liang cut a slice of shrimp and walnut pâté. Bud glanced up at Special Agent Keller, who was also watching Liang.

"You hungry?" Bud asked.

Keller shook his head no.

"Liang, more mayonnaise," Bud shouted. He opened the reach-in fridge. "Save me your best oysters for the President."

Liang nodded, translated for Gan, and then whispered to Bud, "You know President order oyster?"

Bud shook his head. "Forget about the goddamn pool! That's for the waiters!"

Liang nodded and smiled. He repeated his question. "You know President order oyster?"

"No," Bud shouted. "I don't know President order oyster. I just want the best of everything for him."

Keller looked at Mitchell. Mitchell nodded and motioned to Bud. "I don't want anything put aside for him. Whatever the President orders, he gets the same as anybody else. No special portions."

Bud showed him the bluefish. "But I hand-picked the best."

"No special portions."

"What do you think? I'm trying to kill him?"

"Please use up those portions now or we'll have to throw them out."

"What good would it do me to kill him? You think I want the President of the United States to die eating my lunch? That's not exactly a rave review."

Al pushed open the door. "Still not here," he reported.

Ursula reached for his dupe. "Ordering one smoked tuna," she shouted. "One salmon tartare." She turned to Al. "I never figured Julie Andrews for smoked tuna."

"You know what I never figured? How come she wasn't in the movie of *My Fair Lady?*"

Stu groaned loudly. "How long you been working here? Did they give Mary Martin *The Sound of Music?* Don't you know how the studios work? Christ! And you call yourself a waiter?"

Shelly rushed in. "He's not here! I want to change my bet to steak tartare."

"Oh, shit," Stu complained.

"He's not here yet. I can still change!"

"Fuck you!"

"Fire one jalapeño pasta," Ursula shouted. "Extra sauce. *Al dente.* Customer wants it split four ways. One plate very light."

Bud banged his fist on the chef's table. "Fuck the customer!" He looked over at Special Agent Mitchell. "No special portions!"

"You're dragging my veggies!"

"Why the hell so much mayonnaise on here?"

Bud leaned across the table. "Which one of you assholes took that pasta order?"

The waiters closed ranks. The line cooks turned from the stoves to face the enemy. The Special Agents glanced at one another, tensing as they waited for the next move. The only sounds were the sizzling of the grill and the hiss of sauté pans.

The door swung open wide. George, who had been anointed the President's waiter, strode into the kitchen as though he were MacArthur reviewing the troops. "Should be any minute now," he announced briskly before turning to leave.

"Hey!" Louie shouted, holding two truffles in front of his eyes. "You tell President order this. Very famous dish."

"Oh, my God!" Ursula squealed. "Did I order a gravlax and a curried oysters? Table 61?"

"Boss, what you pick? I pick Truffle Pot Pie."

"I didn't bet, Louie."

"Boss, you serious?"

Maxie was out of breath as he came into the kitchen. "He's not here yet and Calvin Klein has a headache."

Stu picked up his shrimp pâté and a crabmeat cocktail. "Don't worry. His head doesn't hurt like real people's."

"Wait a minute," Maxie said. "I want to change my bet to swordfish."

"Fuck you," Stu said, hurrying out the door.

Maxie pointed to the chef's table. "Where the hell is my gravlax and curried oysters?"

"Fuck you!" Ursula screamed. "Fuck you fuck you fuck you fuck you!"

Louie began to giggle. "Oh, boy, boss. We in big trouble now. I never hear wide woman speak curses."

"Shut up, you little yellow shit!" Ursula jumped off her stool. She made a full turn, a goldfish in a leaky bowl. "What are you bastards staring at?" she screamed. "I forget one gravlax and one curried oysters and you all gang up on me?"

Norm shook his head. "Let's not forget the duck breast." He turned back to Special Agent Mitchell. "You notice how forgetful she's getting?"

Ursula picked up her stool and banged it on the floor. "I didn't forget the duck breast!"

"You no say duck breast! You say chicken liver!" Louie slammed down the plate.

Ursula took the livers and threw them to the floor. "Duck! Duck! Duck!"

"Quack! Quack! Quack!"

"Cheep! Cheep! Cheep!"

"Oink! Oink! Oink!"

Bud banged a pot lid on the table. "Shut up, you morons! Get the hell back to work. This isn't a zoo. This is lunch!"

"Today very important," Louie shouted. "You give correct order, big lady. Today important because of President!"

"The hell it is!" Bud snapped. "Today is important because of *me*. The President is coming to eat *my* food. This is *my* lunch!"

At the other end of the restaurant, Special Agents Meehan and Conaway were seated at the bar. Taylor and Roth stood at the door. Taylor, wearing a red pin with a horizontal white stripe, had a clipboard against which to check names as people arrived. Roth, wearing a rectangular orange pin and holding a metal detector, checked the people. He was on the bomb squad.

Libby, who felt like the bomb, was working the front door. She hadn't worked the front door in years. But it was her responsibility to be there to welcome the President. Casting by Kafka. Libby Dennis, well-known restaurant roach, awoke one morning to find she had turned into Josephine K, the quintessential eighties victim. The unanswered question was no longer that old chestnut, what did I do? Or even the somewhat more provocative, do they know? It was, instead, the very trendy, will he tell?

Will Birnbaum tell?

Maxie rushed up to the bar. "I need two aspirin for Calvin Klein's headache," he shouted. "And two for mine." He turned to Libby. "I put all my money on the tartare but now I'm not so sure. I have a terrible feeling he's going to order the swordfish."

Libby put a hand to her stomach. "Me too."

"You think he's going to order the swordfish?"

"No. I have a terrible feeling."

Maxie turned back to the bar. "A Perrier for Calvin and a seltzer for me."

Victor, the bartender, shook his head. "I'm out of aspirin."

"How could you be out of aspirin?"

"I could be out of aspirin because I'm not running Mount Sinai."

Paul, the second bartender, said, "The only pills we got is somebody's birth control pills."

"Let me see." Maxie leaned across the bar. "Do they look like aspirin?"

Libby reached over and took the pills. "Ask Sonny for aspirin. He always . . ."

"Sonny?"

Libby nodded. "Right, I forgot." Sonny had been the first casualty in The War Against Birnbaum. She pointed a finger defensively at Maxie. "Sonny didn't cheat me. He cheated himself."

Maxie shrugged. "As long as he didn't cheat me."

"It's always worse on the person who does the cheating." Libby turned to Meehan as though he had been part of the conversation. "You know I'm right about that."

Meehan didn't answer.

"Never mind! What the hell do you know anyway?" Libby shouted. "I can't imagine why Birnbaum left you in charge."

As though that were the only thing she couldn't imagine. The last time Libby had seen Birnbaum was the middle of the night. He was sitting up in bed, staring into space. He didn't say a word while she got dressed. He didn't say goodbye as she leaned over to kiss him. He didn't call when she got home. He didn't call in the morning. He hadn't even shown up with the other men. Where the hell was he?

Al rushed to the bar. "Two white wines. One red. One Perrier, hold the pickles. So? Where's the President?"

Meehan leaned forward, cupping a hand over what looked like a hearing aid in his ear.

"Is that him?" Al asked.

Meehan picked up his transmitter and said, "Affirmative. Please copy."

Victor stopped pouring. "Oh, my God! It's the President!"

"He's here!" Paul said.

Meehan cupped his ear again as he listened to the reply.

Libby glanced anxiously in the mirror. Pink silk suit. Peach satin blouse. Strands of antique Bohemian garnets. She sniffed her wrists, suddenly afraid she was wearing too much perfume. She reached in front of Meehan for a twist of lime. She saw him glance across the bar and nod at Conaway. "Who is it?" She rubbed the peel onto her wrists, hoping to neutralize the perfume. Conaway turned to the door and nodded at Taylor. "Is it the President?" Taylor nodded at Roth. "Is it Birnbaum?"

Roth put one hand on the door.

"Oh, my God!" Libby held out her arms. "Now I smell like a goddamn gin and tonic! Meehan, is it Birnbaum or is it the President?"

Meehan said, "It's Meryl Streep."

Libby began to laugh. She opened her arms and shouted, "Circle the wagons, men! It's Meryl Streep!"

The door pushed open, nearly knocking Libby off her feet. Sam Cohn, Meryl's agent, peeked inside. "Who the hell are you expecting? Springsteen?"

"Not unless he can sing 'Hail to the Chief'!"

Meryl stood in the doorway. "Hi?"

"Hold your fire!" Libby said. "She's a star!"

"Is the President really here?" Sam said.

Meryl smiled. *The* President?"

"Excuse me." Roth held up the magnetometer. "May I see your purse, ma'am?"

Meryl smiled and put a hand to her forehead. "Oh, my God. Do you know how much junk I have in here?"

Libby embraced Meryl as Roth took the purse. "That's what you get for carrying your Oscars around."

Meryl kissed her. "I'm so sorry about Cal."

"He's fine." Libby said. "He'll be here in a few minutes." She led the way into the dining room, aware of the noise for the first time. Like a nervous coloratura, the pitch was too high. Libby glanced around the room, her eyes fixed on the agents who were supposed to blend in with the lunch crowd. They were as unobtrusive as graffiti on the Taj Mahal.

The male indieprod, with an earring that once belonged to the Duchess of Windsor, stood up. "Oh, God!" he muttered. "It's her. It's her."

"Watch it, Sparky!" the female indieprod whispered. She wore a Bond Street suit. "It's testosterone time. Be strong. Be macho."

"Stop playing Cecily B. DeMille!"

"And for God's sake, don't say anything stupid!"

As Meryl came close, the male smiled and held out his hand.

"I had a farm in Africa," he said, mimicking her Isak Dinesen accent, "at the foot of the Ngong Hills."

Meryl began to laugh. "You, too?"

Libby angled the table. "Now listen up," she said. "I gave you the best seats in the house. I expect you to order expensive." Libby turned to leave. "One more thing . . ."

Meryl and Sam and the indieprods all leaned forward and said in unison, "The laughs are on the house!"

Libby smiled. That was the perfect title for her memoirs. She'd have plenty of time to write them. Once she disappeared. To become a bag lady. What a tearjerker. Required reading with every blue rinse. If only Shirley MacLaine wouldn't go off into some other life, she'd be dynamite in the role. The real problem was who would they get to play Birnbaum now that Boris Karloff was dead?

Steven was waiting for Libby at the bar. They had been dodging each other for hours. Like tango dancers, they had side-stepped words, translating their emotions into furtive glances and silent sighs. But it was impossible to avoid each other any longer.

"I called you last night," he said.

"Last night?"

"I waited for you at the hospital. I kept calling."

"Really? I was here."

"You weren't here."

"I went upstairs for a few Z's. I guess I must have conked out. You can ask Cal."

"I don't have to ask him."

Libby was puzzled. She pushed back her bangs. What was he trying to tell her? Something was different about Steven. Something had replaced the contempt she usually saw in his eyes. Or had something replaced the love in hers? It hurt Libby to look at Steven. He barely resembled the son she remembered. And by the time lunch was over, he was likely to have changed again.

"Where were you last night?" he asked. "I thought we might have a drink."

"Aha! The old poison drink trick!" She smiled and put her hand out to brush a wisp of hair from his forehead. He didn't pull back. Something *was* different. Libby held her hand to his cheek. She knew what it was. He needed her. "Steven, it's not your fault Cal was shot."

His eyes filled with tears.

At the other end of the bar, Meehan suddenly leaned forward. He nodded as he spoke into the transmitter. "Affirmative. Please copy."

Libby grabbed hold of him. "Listen, you son of a bitch, I want some answers and I want them now! Where the hell is Birnbaum? And don't tell me he already left for Los Angeles because I don't believe it!"

Meehan gently moved her aside. He nodded to Conaway. Conaway nodded to Taylor. Taylor put a hand to the receiver in his ear and said, "Goldberg. Harold Goldberg."

"Harold who?" Libby asked. "I don't know any . . . Hots!" She turned to Meehan, shaking her fist. "Now you're in for it!"

Hots opened the front door. His face was drawn. Suddenly, the beeper went off. Before Hots knew it, he was staring into Roth's Smith & Wesson. "It's under my left arm."

Taylor reached in for the gun while Roth outlined Hots with the magnetometer and then gave him a quick pat search.

As soon as he was finished, Libby threw her arms around Hots. "I have to talk to you."

"It can wait. First I have to talk to you."

"Excuse me," Taylor said to Hots. "May I have your permit, please?"

"What the hell are you doing with a gun?" Libby asked.

"You think I'm going to step into a taxi unarmed? Let me tell you, if Bernie Goetz shot a cab driver, they'd have given him the key to the city."

"Hots, please. Let's sit down."

He shook his head. "Not at my table. It must have more bugs than a Chinese restaurant."

Libby had never seen Hots as worried. "I'm the one who's supposed to be upset."

"You will be."

Taylor gave Hots a receipt. "We have to keep the weapon until you leave."

"A lot you know about lunch if you think a gun is dangerous. You should have everybody check their mouths at the door." Hots led Libby to a corner of the vestibule. He took a deep breath and whispered, "I told Birnbaum about Steven."

Libby put a hand to her heart. "You what?"

"I couldn't help it! He had me by the gazongas. He was going to put me away for years. Sweetheart, do you think I was about to let Steve Rubell visit *me* in prison?"

"When did you tell him?"

"Yesterday. I called you last night but you didn't answer. I've been in court all morning."

"What time yesterday?"

"How do I know? What am I? Big Ben? It was late afternoon."

Libby pulled away from Hots. She gasped. "Son of a bitch!"

"It's all right. Call me anything you want. I deserve it. I feel so bad I won't even bill you for the time I spent with him."

"The son of a bitch already knew!"

"What are you talking about?"

Libby was talking about the look on Birnbaum's face when he said, "Why did you have to tell me?" She finally understood what he meant. He didn't want her to know that he knew. Libby began to cry. "If only I hadn't told him."

"You did what?"

"I told him after you did." She saw Hots stiffen. Pull back. Ice.

"How could you do that to me? I thought I could trust you! Don't you have any respect for lawyer-client confidentiality?"

"Shut up," she whispered. "You told first."

Hots put his arms around her. "What did he threaten you with?"

She shrugged. "Nothing."

"What do you mean nothing? He must have done something to make you talk."

Libby nodded. "He listened." She saw the look of disbelief on Hots's face. "He's an incredible listener."

Hots stared at her. "Should you live long enough to experience midlife crisis, do not make a career shift into espionage."

She tried smiling. "If only I had kept my mouth shut everything would have been all right."

"Stop blaming yourself. That's what friends are for. Besides, I told him first."

"But I forced his hand. He wasn't going to say anything as long as I didn't know he knew. Don't you see?"

"All I see is that he's going to tell."

She began to cry. "I thought I could trust him."

Hots put his arms around her. "Are you crazy? You don't understand who we're dealing with. Bubeleh, this is a man who loves Milk Duds!"

As she wiped the tears away, an enormous smile blossomed on Libby's face. The *National Geographic* could have done an entire issue on the flowering of that one smile. Suddenly, she knew exactly who she was dealing with. "But this is also a man who loves chicken chow mein!"

o

The white limousine edged over into the right-hand lane as it approached Fifth Avenue and Fifty-fifth Street. The uniformed chauffeur leaned forward to see what was going on at the corner. Police barricades. Mounted police. Police with walkie-talkies. He narrowed his eyes and looked into the rearview mirror at his passenger. *"¿Qué el fuck?"*

"Yo no sé." The man in the back seat wore a thick dark handlebar moustache under a white Panama hat with a broad yellow silk band. A three-piece vanilla linen suit. A white silk tie and a bright yellow silk shirt.

The chauffeur ignored the traffic cop's hand signal to move on. Instead, he pulled over toward the barricade, muttering, *"¡Fuck usted!"*

"¡Cállate!"

A police officer came over to the driver's side. "I'm sorry. The block is closed to traffic."

The chauffeur glanced nervously into the rearview mirror. *"El señor tiene una reserva."*

"¿Dónde?" asked the officer.

"Libby's."

"Gracias." The officer motioned to Special Agent Keller.

The passenger smoothed his moustache. *"Dice nada. Hace nada."*

Keller, who wore a round yellow pin in his lapel, knocked politely on the passenger window.

The man in the back seat moaned, *"¡Madre de Dios!"* Frantically, he began pressing buttons on the panel to find the right one. After turning on the air conditioner, the television, the stereo, and the weather report, he found the button that opened the window. *"Buenos días,"* he shouted above the music.

"Buenos días." Keller leaned his head inside to see who and what was in the car. "For security reasons," he said loudly, trying to be heard above the noise, "we must confirm all reservations."

The man in the white suit nodded. *"Me llamo José Ensesa."*

"Thank you, Señor Ensesa. I'm sorry for the delay." Keller pulled his head out of the car. He checked the list and then turned on his walkie-talkie. "Fifth Avenue to Barfly. Ensesa. White limo. Party of one. Do you copy?" Keller glanced back through the open window and smiled. "It'll just take a minute."

As he waited, the passenger looked nervously out the window. He saw dozens of angry demonstrators. They marched in a circle, wheeling baby carriages and carrying signs. SCREW SAFE SEX. MAKE BABIES, NOT CONDOMS. LET MY PENIS GO!

The man in the back seat gasped. Leading the demonstration, carrying a bouquet of helium-inflated condoms, was Tessa. He wanted to call out to her. Alfero wanted to tell her what he was going to do.

Keller responded, "Affirmative", into the walkie-talkie and then turned to Ensesa. "May I see your ID?"

"¿Qué?"

The chauffeur translated. *"Identificación."*

Alfero, in one grand gesture, pointed to the limo.

Keller smiled. *"Cartas, por favor."* After approving the phoney ID, he motioned the limo to proceed up the block. Barricades lined both sides of the street. Uniformed police were stationed every twenty feet. People who lived or had business on the block were allowed access only after showing identification and being checked through the FBI's computer for prior arrests or suspicion of instability. The large Command Van in the middle of the street spewed thick black cables into the restaurant. A fire truck, a city ambulance, and a military ambulance were parked just past the entrance.

A police officer waved the limo across the street. "Pull over, please," he said. "No vehicles in front of the restaurant."

The chauffeur got out, walked around the back of the car, and opened the door for his passenger. Alfero stepped from the limo looking like a Bacardi ad. Hesitating momentarily, he cleared his throat and moistened his lips. The passenger and the chauffeur stared at one another. Alfero knew he might never see Miguel again. *"Gracias,"* he whispered. Then, waving his hand at the policeman, he shouted, *"¡Vamos!"*

As they approached the door, Alfero thought of Dolores and the niños standing there only the day before.

"Señor?"

Alfero waved a hand in front of his face. Chasing flies. It was the response he remembered as a child when anyone spoke to El Patrón.

"Are you carrying any weapons, señor?"

Alfero waved his hand as though the man were a fly. *"¡Está loco?"*

"Just one minute, sir." Roth brought the magnetometer in close.

Nervously, Alfero glanced at the mirror over the bar. Even if he got through security, as his nephew Carlos had promised, he was terrified that he would be recognized. The moustache, the wig, the borrowed clothes wouldn't fool anyone.

"Señor Ensesa!" Libby smiled as she held out her hand. She was sure Ensesa would see right through her. It was all an act. Libby wasn't happy to see him. There was only one person she wanted to see. *"¡Bienvenido!"*

Alfero was afraid to breathe. He hadn't expected Libby to greet him at the door, no less offer him her hand. No woman had ever done that in his entire life. He stared at the hand, too soft and too pink to be real. For that one moment, he allowed himself to believe he was El Patrón. He took her hand and bowed, closing his eyes as he kissed it. The scent of lime filled his nostrils. He would have done anything if only he could feel her tits.

"Welcome to Libby's," she said nervously. Wealthy men like

Ensesa could sniff out phonies as easily as they avoided taxes. "I'm sorry for the inconvenience. Everyone's on pins and needles until the President arrives."

"He is not here?"

She brought Ensesa to the reservations desk. "Not to worry. Any moment now." Any moment now the earth would stop, the skies would darken, and the air would no longer support human life.

"Señor Ensesa!" Steven nodded briskly and extended his arm toward the dining room. "Mr. Pérez should be here shortly."

"Mr. Pérez?"

"I'm sure it's the traffic," Libby said. She leaned close. "Don't order dessert," she whispered. "I've got something special put aside for you."

Alfero couldn't believe it. She was practically begging him to do it to her! Yet all he could think about was this Pérez. Who was Pérez? Pérez would know that he was not Ensesa.

Once Alfero was seated, Steven asked, "Would you like an apéritif?"

He waved his hand. "No. I want something to drink."

"Of course. What would you like?"

"Champagne. One bottle of the best South American champagne. And do not open it before you get to the table."

Steven hesitated. "I'm afraid we don't have any South American champagne. I have French . . ."

Another wave of the hand. "No! Then I have rum and Coke." Alfero leaned forward and tapped his index finger on the table. "Classic Coke!"

Steven nodded. "The perfect choice."

Pérez. Pérez. Pérez. Carlos had called Ensesa. He said he was the maître d' and that there had been a fire at Libby's. Ensesa must have called Pérez. But what if he hadn't? What if Pérez showed up?

Thursday was Jessica Stanford's favorite day of the week. No starving tigers, no trendy diseases, no earthquake victims. It was her day for charity to begin at home. The masseuse appeared at seven, the stylist at eight, the interior decorator at nine. The exterior decorator arrived at ten with a rack of clothes borrowed from the city's most expensive boutiques. J's wardrobe moved in and out of her dressing room as though it were Filene's basement. She couldn't risk being seen in the same outfit twice. Especially not at lunch.

Every dress was tagged—where it had been worn and who was there. Nothing but the most personal of items survived three tags. Fortunately, there was someone in Grosse Pointe who, through J's attorney, bought—sight unseen—all of J's clothes at fifty percent off. There were but two unbreakable conditions: each dress had to be tagged for the vicarious pleasure of Ms. Grosse Pointe; and neither woman could ever know the identity of the other. J loved it. It was so Dickensian. How many sleepless nights had flown by as she forged provenances for clothes that were never worn.

The phone call from college chum Harriet Moss, restaurant critic for *The Wall Street Journal,* was frantic enough that J couldn't possibly say no. Harriet had nearly burst the stitches in her intestinal bypass after reading the rave about Truffle Pot Pie. She had been trashing the kitchen at Libby's for years—not because she didn't like the food, but strictly as a career tactic. She believed the best way for a food critic to stay on top was to take pot shots at a sacred chow.

Harriet's problem was that she had to get into Libby's, order Truffle Pot Pie, and hate it before it was reviewed by her arch rival, Mimi Sheraton. But there wasn't a reservation to be had. How could J refuse? It simply meant canceling her lunch with Estée Lauder. Or was it Germaine Monteil? One of those women.

However, no one anticipated a police barricade on Fifth Avenue. J's chauffeur thought fast and gave Harriet's name as Adrien Arpel as per the original reservation.

Harriet, who refused to wear glasses, was allergic to makeup, and had trouble finding dresses to fit, squinted her piggy little eyes and looked out the window. "This is worse than the opening of Le Bernardin. Did you have his grilled monkfish? What a laugh!"

J looked worriedly at the police lining the block. "Harriet darling, do you think they found out it was you?"

Harriet ignored her. She was busy inserting new batteries into her hidden microphone. "If you really want to talk over-rated, I could tell you a few things about the phyllo crumple at The Quilted Giraffe."

"They've got guns, Harriet!"

She looked up. "Which reminds me. Did you read what I said about the half-moon ravioli at Palio? Let me tell you, that had me steamed for a week."

"Harriet, I'm frightened!"

"Relax. You get me through this and I'll let you in on a filthy little hole-in-the-wall in Spanish Harlem that does chicken like your mother never made."

J's eyes brightened. "Oh, I bet that's the place Tom Brokaw went to with the Wyeths. How soon can we go?"

Harriet looked at her watch. "Depends on how fast you can eat. After Libby's, I've got to cover some dump Bryan Miller claims has great tapas. I can x that out fast. Let's make it my last lunch of the day."

J began to laugh. "I'm afraid one lunch is my limit."

Harriet whispered into the mike hidden in her bosom. "Thursday. Libby's." She stepped out of the limo, oblivious to the police, the sharpshooters on the roofs, and the helicopter circling overhead as she spoke into her dress. "Lunch at Libby's is about as much fun as watching your stocks slide. This week's inside-trader rip-off is called Truffle Pot Pie."

"Ma'am." Roth held the door open.

"Thank you," J said nervously.

"About as classy as penny stocks," Harriet continued into the mike, "and with a comparable payoff . . ." She looked up as the magnetometer began to beep.

Libby rushed over, shaking a finger in Harriet's face. "She's not Adrien Arpel! Meehan, get ten of your best men and sur-round this woman. She doesn't know her aspic from her elbow!"

Harriet narrowed her eyes angrily. "You can forget the strong-arm tactics. They won't work. The chicken livers *were* fro-zen and I still say your cranberry mayonnaise is boring. I'll go to my grave saying that!"

Libby smiled. "What a lovely thought." Not that Harriet's reviews mattered anymore. What mattered was the review in

Birnbaum's file. He was the only one who had the power to close her down.

J reached toward Libby and the magnetometer went off again. "I have a permit," she said defensively as Taylor took her purse.

Libby kissed the air on both sides of J's cheeks. "Poor darling," Libby cooed, watching Conaway take Harriet aside for questioning. "I didn't know you were into lost causes."

While they checked Harriet against the FBI files and the National Crime Information Center, Roth withdrew the gun from J's purse. She warned him, "I don't want one scratch on that handle." He put the gun into a plastic bag. "That's carved Burmese jade. A wedding gift that's been passed down from mother to daughter for generations." J took Libby's arm. "You've certainly made Harriet feel like a million. I had no idea you were such a practical joker."

"Don't be silly. I couldn't resist teasing Mighty Mouth. The fuss is because the President is coming to lunch."

Harriet gasped. "Holy shit! The President?" She unhooked the microphone from her bra and tossed it to Roth. "To hell with Truffle Pot Pie! The President's lunch is going to put me right on page one!"

Libby sat down next to Fay. "Time out," she groaned. "If anyone asks me another question about the President, I'm going to scream."

Fay smiled and reached for her hand. "Honey, just why is the President comin' here?"

Libby opened her mouth and whispered, "Scream!"

"I've got every stringer I know tryin' to find out but, for some mysterious reason, the jungle drums they are silent. Except for all that unidentified flyin' fertilizer comin' out of Phyllis since Cal was shot."

Libby looked down at the table. "Tell me the truth. How much do they know about what happened?"

"Lucky for you, they only know what Rapunzel of Trump Tower told the police. Cal was accidentally winged by Donald. And that's all they're goin' to get from yours truly."

"How much do you know?"

Fay laughed. "If I was Nick Dunne, I'd have a book contract even before Dick Snyder said his first Fuck You of the mornin'."

"Fay . . ."

"Darlin', I'm only sayin' you got to be careful. There are lots of animals in the forest who know different parts of this little saga. And since everybody pees under the same tree, you can't get rid of one stink until a bigger one comes along." She held up a pile of pink memo slips. "I got more callbacks than the casting director of *Gone With the Wind*. Tell me what you want me to say." Fay smiled. "But, remember, I can't let my blue-haired ladies down." She dialed quickly, staring at Libby all the time. "What I really want to know is why the President is comin' here for lunch."

Libby leaned close. "That makes two of us." She slid out of the banquette deciding it was time to move to a different tree. As she headed quickly for the reservations desk, Marvin Hamlisch reached out and grabbed her arm.

"I'm really sorry," he said.

Libby kissed him on the cheek. "Could you be more specific?"

Marvin laughed. "Cal. How is he?"

"A scratch. Gunfight at the O.K. Salad Bar. He'll be here any minute," she said, glancing at the entrance. "Uh-oh."

Marvin turned quickly, squinting. "Is it the President?"

"Worse," Libby said. "It's Janos and Rikki." She patted Marvin's shoulder. "The agony and the ecstasy." By the time she reached Janos, the magnetometer was beeping loudly.

"Beep beep yourself!" Janos shouted. He opened his arms, nodding toward the left side. "My gun is in there."

Rikki stepped back. "Johnny, I'll meet you. I forgot something in the car."

"I told you, stupid, you could go to jail if you don't carry your permit!"

"Stop calling me stupid!" Rikki screamed. She reached into her purse and took out a gun. Roth and Taylor quickly pulled their weapons and adopted a firing stance as they targeted Rikki. "Don't be stupid." She rolled her eyes. "The goddamn permit's in the fourth chamber."

Janos grabbed hold of Libby. "So, I hear your good friend Phyllis is not such a good friend."

She pushed Janos's hand away as though he were holding the six million dollars. "I've been hearing lots of things, too."

"With me, everything is above board. No secrets. A deal is a deal. Nothing personal."

Libby shook her head. "You're right. Business is business. The President is going to sit at your table."

"Fine," Janos said. "After all the money I contributed . . ."

Libby began to laugh. She couldn't have planned it any better. "They want your table. Not you."

"They said that? Or you put them up to it?"

"Janos," she said, enunciating each syllable. "Business is business. Nothing personal."

"The hell it is! So where do I sit?"

Libby took his arm. "I'm afraid you're going to have to make do. Be brave, Janos. The only thing I can give you is a really good table."

"How good?"

Libby leaned close, pausing to savor the punch line. She whispered, "The best."

Janos put a hand to his stomach. "I'd rather eat my lunch in the toilet."

"They took that away, too." Still clutching Janos's arm, Libby threw her head back and filled the vestibule with laughter.

Janos turned angrily to Rikki. "If you had your permit, you stupid ass, what was the crap about forgetting something in the car?"

Rikki's eyes narrowed. "I forgot your goddamn toilet paper and I'm not going back for it either. Tell that to *your* stupid ass!" Nearly knocking Janos off his feet, she pushed ahead of him. "Libby, sorry about Cal. I want you to know I don't carry a grudge. Love your suit."

Dr. Loren Sawyer reached for Moina's hand. "You want me to stay?" he asked, as Fay headed toward the table.

"No."

"What are you going to tell her?"

Moina pulled her hand away and reached for her martini. "That's none of your business."

"I mean, I'd appreciate your keeping my name out of it." Loren held the glass down. "That drink is only for show. You promised."

"Go away," Moina whispered.

As he pulled back his chair, Fay leaned across the table to Moina. "What the hell is goin' on? I don't like wakin' up with little notes on my pillow."

Moina stared into the room. "I had to see a doctor."

Fay pointed to Loren. "You don't mean him? You're not goin' to see him?"

"Only for matters of life and death."

As Loren left, he whispered to Fay, "Go easy."

Moina's hand shook as she brought the glass to her lips. The martini dripped onto her dress. Cocaine had muddled her coordination, but not her priorities. She looked up at Fay. "How much are you being paid to write a book about me?"

Fay sat down slowly. "Who told you?"

"You hillbilly!" Moina continued dripping martini on herself. "You shouldn't have given the nurse so much money. People will do all sorts of dreadful things for next to nothing. They assume that if they were really doing something terrible, they'd be paid more. You should have checked prices with the Mafia, love of my life. You could have had me bumped off for less."

Fay sat back. "How did that quack find out?"

"The penis is mightier than the sword. One of his nooners is your Nurse Parker." Moina began to laugh. "I did have a wonderful smile, didn't I?"

Fay turned away. She shut her eyes for a moment, remembering the Moina who stuck her tongue out at King Farouk. Moina perched atop Cole Porter's piano at the Waldorf Towers. Moina, on Dali's arm, shocking the first-night crowd at the Met by showing up with only half her lips and one eye made up.

Moina stared at the stain on her dress. "I want you to be the first to know. I've decided to have the operation." Fay reached for Moina's hand. Moina pulled back, then stopped. She needed to hold Fay's hand one last time.

"Oh, darlin', I am so happy."

"Liar!"

"I wanted to write your biography because I love you."

"Thief! My life belongs to me. I own it. You may not have it!"

"Darlin', you're in no condition to talk about this now."

"Never put off until tomorrow's lunch what you can do to-day."

"I suppose Doctor Do Little gave you some of his happy dust."

"I am allowing them to cut off my tit so that I will live long enough to write my own book." Moina realized she was still holding onto Fay's hand but she couldn't let go. "Biography lends to death a new terror," she quoted, raising her glass unsteadily. The rest of her drink spilled onto the table. "Oscar Wilde."

"My book," Fay said, "is not about us. It's all about you, the wonderful things I wanted everyone to know about you."

"And my book," Moina said, pulling her hand away, "will tell all the wonderful things you never wanted them to know about you."

Senior nodded his head slowly for emphasis. "Without doubt, there is only one woman beautiful enough to play Glinda."

Esther Williams smiled at Libby. "Glinda? I thought you wanted me for the Tin Man!"

"That William Powell-Myrna Loy crap? Esther, listen to me!" Senior took her hand. *"Dorothy—The Woman!* We fade in on a clip of Judy singing 'Over the Rainbow.' Dissolve to Liza singing it at Auntie Em's funeral. Hutz klutz, who flies in but her old friend Glinda to help Dorothy save the farm from the shmendriks at the bank." He leaned close to Esther. "I'm thinking maybe the Aunt could be buried next to the dog. I mean, you couldn't do it in a Jewish cemetery, but what do they know in Kansas?"

Esther looked at Libby. "I'm thinking maybe I could use a menu."

"You don't need one," Libby said. "I have something special put aside for you."

"I'm thinking of having the liver," Senior said.

Libby shook her head. "Not in front of Esther Williams, you're not."

"It doesn't matter what I order. I don't eat it anyway!"

"Then how about not eating a very expensive fillet?" Libby reached out for a passing waiter.

Senior nodded. "Perfect. So tell me, what is the President not eating?"

Libby turned to Norm, but something caught her eye at the reservations desk. A Gothic messenger of doom. As ominous as the caped figure of Salieri, Birnbaum suddenly appeared behind Steven.

"Ouch!" Norm whispered, trying to loosen Libby's grip on his arm. "Hey, boss, that hurts!"

Libby couldn't take her eyes from Birnbaum. She let go of Norm, patted him absently and started walking up the aisle. Walking through molasses. Each step was labored, slow, thick with apprehension. Birnbaum stood behind the desk, his face frozen as he stared into the dining room.

"Hi, sailor," Libby said softly.

No response.

"Go to hell!"

Nothing.

"Birnbaum, I know you. I understand you. I've been closer to you than anyone you've ever known. We shared more than sex last night."

Still nothing.

"Don't hate me, Birnbaum, because you were unfaithful to your wife. Don't punish me because you finally found out you were human." She grabbed hold of his arm. He didn't move or shift his eyes from his prey. "Another hour or two, Birnbaum, and I'll be out of your life for good." She tightened her grip on his arm, suddenly aware that he was staring at Steven. "You son of a bitch," she whispered. "What are you doing?"

"I'm doing my job." He turned to face her. "My job is to protect the son of the President of the United States."

Junior watched Wanda cut into her grilled breast of Long Island duckling with wild tarragon and pineapple salsa. He glanced over at Senior, to make sure the old man saw that Wanda was having lunch with him. But Senior was deep in conversation with Esther. No matter. Junior had a better way to get him.

"Be right back, honey." Junior headed for the other side of the room. He stared directly at Meryl, smiling a steady smile, careful not to accelerate into an open-mouthed grin as Meryl took note and waved her fingers. Junior was determined to position himself as one of the players. He attacked their weakest link. He stood behind the male indieprod and tapped him on the shoulder.

The male jumped up and greeted him effusively. "Well, well, well! Junior! How are you?"

Without answering, Junior elbowed the male aside on the pretext of leaning across the table to kiss Meryl.

"How are you, Junior?" she asked.

"I'm fine, love. Couldn't be better now that we're going to make another picture together. How are you, Sam?" Junior was like an animal spraying his territory. He turned quickly back to Meryl as he sat down in the male indieprod's chair.

"We've been talking to Junior," the female said nervously. "He's been so supportive. Such a good friend." The indieprods were horrified. Junior had moved in as though occupying Poland.

"Everybody talks to Junior," Sam said. "But it's like praying to Allah. Nothing happens until you're dead."

The male indieprod tugged gently at the chair. Junior wouldn't budge. A busboy waited impatiently in the aisle, unable to pass. The male smiled self-consciously and flattened himself to let the busboy through. He tapped the female on the shoulder. But, not wanting to weaken her position at the table, she ignored him.

Junior took Meryl's hand. "We don't even have to go on location. I've decided we can shoot it in LA."

"He's decided?" Sam picked up the menu. "Don't put the horse before the à la carte."

The female panicked. Junior was parroting their ideas. Suddenly, she felt the male kick her ankle and step on her foot. The yutz still couldn't find a place to sit down.

o

Mary Borden sat down opposite Ed Gilbert, the editor who was going to lose millions in sales because she had taken Tully Ireland's new book away from him. Ed pretended to ignore her. He kept turning pages in a paperback edition of *Ulysses.*

Mary signaled Stu for a round of drinks. "Well, I've had a morning!" she said, staring at Ed. "I sold Moina's autobiography for a small fortune. Wait till the ladies of America find out that the woman who's been dressing them for years has also been undressing them."

Ed sighed deeply as he closed *Ulysses.* He looked at Mary and spoke to her as though they had been deep in conversation. "What pisses me is that Bennett Cerf battles the courts to publish the book and then, after fifty years, Random House has the incredible chutzpah to reissue the damn thing announcing, with pride, that they've finally gotten around to correcting the text and catching five thousand errors. Old Bennett must have had some proofreading department! Think of all those academic assholes who've been teaching a book with five thousand errors in it. You know what I say? I say, three cheers for Judy Krantz. There's a woman who puts no period before its time."

Mary stared at Ed. "Why don't you say what you want to say?"

"There are no words for what I want to say. Not even in the libretto for the *Niebelungen.* But, let me tell you this, the one and only performance of *my* passion play would make an evening at Oberammergau look like an episode of 'I Love Lucy.' "

"God, you're attractive when you're desperate."

Stu brought a Perrier for Mary, another Pernod for Ed. She raised her glass and then her eyebrow, waiting for him to offer a toast.

"May you rot in hell!" he said, clinking glasses with her.

Mary smiled. "You know, I think I might have made a mistake throwing you back."

"Fuck you."

"That's what I was thinking."

"Don't flatter yourself. I meant it in the pejorative."

She leaned close. "I think the pejorative is vastly underrated."

"I worked with Tully for fourteen years. I baby-sat that anal-retentive son of a bitch through eight crappy manuscripts that I edited into eight crappy bestsellers."

Mary took a deep breath. "It's exciting to watch you suffer. You're almost irresistible."

"Don't kid yourself. You've got the hots because you did a deal this morning. You want to pull your pants down to celebrate."

"Actually, I was thinking about pulling your pants down," she said.

"You already did."

Stu brought a phone to the table. "Which one of us was saved by the bell?" Mary smiled as she picked up the receiver.

It was Senior. "I thought my no-good son was interested in some book about Germans," he shouted.

Mary looked over at Senior as she spoke into the phone. "He was. But he lost it."

Senior was furious. "What do you mean he lost it? Lost it to who?"

"Janos. But I have a hunch Rikki isn't going to let him do anything that doesn't have a part for her. Calm down, Senior. What do you care?"

"I care because I don't want my son to lose to anybody except to me."

"Well, if it's any consolation," Mary said with an exasperated sigh, "I have a hunch Junior can get it back if he wants."

"The hell he can!" Senior slammed down the receiver. He hated doing anything definitive except standing by his decision not to make any decisions. However, where it concerned Junior, there were no lengths to which he wouldn't go. He dialed Janos. "Those were some pictures of your wife in that magazine."

"You ever see such tits?"

"I even got my own copy."

Janos smiled. He poked Rikki. "He got his own copy."

"I understand you bought some cockamamie book about Germans."

Janos smelled a deal. "Such a book! *It* bought me! I couldn't put it down. I tell you, between the two of us, I overpaid but it was very hard to get away from Junior. You got some smart little pisher."

There was a long pause. "How much you want for it?"

"You bum! I thought you were calling to congratulate me on my wife's tits, not insult me!" Janos slammed down the receiver and said to Rikki, "He'll call back in two minutes."

"What's he going to offer you, Johnny?"

"Who cares? All I want is six dollars for stopping my check."

"That's not enough," Rikki said.

"I told you I wouldn't let Junior get Cal. I told you that he'd never make that movie and that I wouldn't lose a penny." Janos sat back. "Jesus Christ! You're right! Let him pay me fifty thousand! Why shouldn't I make fifty thousand dollars on that schlemiel? Fifty. That's what I want."

"What about what I want?" Rikki asked.

Janos was stunned. "You? You're too stupid to know what you want. I'm the dealmaker!"

"Wrong, buster!" Rikki put her hand under the table and grabbed Janos by the crotch. "As of right now, I'm the dealmaker!"

Janos began to laugh. "You think you're the first person who had me by the balls?"

Rikki took her hand away. "I've got you by a lot more than that, Johnny. I'm pregnant."

"With a baby?" He smiled and hugged her. "Wait a minute. You sure it's mine?"

"I guess we'll have to wait and see if he's got a real small pecker."

Janos slapped his hand on the table and began to laugh. "So maybe I'm not such an old man after all!" He kissed Rikki. The phone lit up. Janos reached for it. "I'm going to have a baby! A son!"

Senior paused. "I'm sorry."

Janos laughed. "You're sorry?"

"A daughter maybe you have a chance. But, then again, a lot of good a daughter did Joanie Crawford. Don't talk to me about sons. About sons, I'll write a book."

"That's what you called to tell me?"

"Did I know you were pregnant when I dialed?"

Janos put his hand over the receiver. "He wants to make a deal."

Rikki said, "Tell him no deal."

"You think I should ask a hundred?" Janos whispered. "Why not? It'll pay for college already. The kid will be free."

"Hello?" Senior asked.

"Hello," Janos said.

Rikki put her hand over the receiver. "Tell him no deal and hang up."

"So where were you when I sold Polaroid?" Janos nodded and Rikki took her hand away. "Listen, I already told you. No deal. Absolutely not." Janos hung up. He smiled and rubbed Rikki's stomach. "So. I did what you wanted?"

Rikki sat back. "Not yet. I want you to buy me *Dorothy—The Woman.*" She held tight to his arm. "I want to be Judy Garland. I want to sing. I want people to stop laughing at me. I want them to cry, Johnny. I want them to be thrilled. I don't want to be your toy anymore. Now call Senior back, Mr. Dealmaker, and you get me what I want." She leaned over and kissed Janos gently on the lips. "Or else I'll kill your baby."

Alfero looked at his watch but he couldn't tell what time it was. Miguel had given him a watch with two faces. A rich man's watch. One face for New York and one for Bolivia. Not that it mattered whether he died on New York time or Bolivian time.

Alfero was not afraid to die for something in which he believed. And Carlos had promised that no matter what happened, he would take care of Dolores and the niños. Alfero was doing it for them. The niños would know that even if their father never became a busboy, he was, at least, a fighter for justice.

Esteban slid a bread tray onto Alfero's table, slapped down a crystal butter dish, and splashed water into the goblet. Alfero shook his head from side to side. "How dare you?"

A look of horror tightened the flesh on Esteban's face. No customer had ever spoken directly to him. He looked around nervously for Norm.

"You think I do not know how a table should be set?" Alfero snarled. "You do not become the richest man in South America if you are too stupid to know that the butter plate is in the wrong place, that the silverware handles do not line up, and that there is supposed to be ice in the water."

"Your drink, sir," Norm said brightly. He had seen what was happening as he approached the table. "One rum and Classic Coke."

Alfero waved the drink aside. He sat back and pointed to a fingerprint on the black service plate as though identifying the guilty man in a lineup.

Norm nodded, picked up the offending plate and gave it to Esteban. "A clean service platter right away." Norm shook his head as he straightened the silverware. "I am sorry," he whispered, "but you wouldn't believe how stupid busboys are!"

"Not all busboys!"

"I've put away a couple of Truffle Pot Pies for you and Mr. Pérez. Just in case we run low."

Alfero waved his hand. "Truffles? They are terrible! I try to eat some of them last night. Nothing helped. Ketchup, mustard, salsa, nothing!"

"Perhaps you'd like a nice piece of melon while you're waiting for Mr. Pérez?"

"Melon is for peasants!"

"How about some of the best Beluga caviar you've ever tasted?"

Alfero nodded. *"¡Si!"* He tapped his finger on the table for emphasis. "While I wait, bring me a bowl of caviar and a cup of coffee."

"I should not be drinking," Moina said, holding her martini with both hands.

Hots shook his head. "Would you like to tell me what's going on here?"

"Harold, the only thing I would like to tell you is how much I hate the Jews."

"What?"

"I wish I didn't hate the Jews," Moina said. "For a few years, I managed to convince myself I didn't. Even after being married to Edgar. But I do. And that's all there is to it! Oh, don't look at me that way. I don't mean final-solution type hate. I mean your ordinary everyday elitist prejudice. You've been to parties where someone tells you how much they hate the Swiss or the French. That sort of thing. Deep down, I feel the same way about the Jews."

Hots took her hand. "Shut up, Moina. You need your friends."

"Desperately." She smiled sadly. "That's why I had to tell you. I need you more than ever, Harold. I've decided to have the surgery."

"Thank God." He leaned over and kissed her on the cheek. "I was planning to increase my retainer. It annoyed the hell out of me that you were going to die at the old rate."

"Die? I haven't felt this good since Persepolis." She thought her glass was resting on the table. But as she let go, it fell into her lap. "The Shah's people had the best opium since Victorian England." She took the glass and turned it upside down. "God, what a dry martini."

Ashanti stopped in front of the table. "I haven't slept a wink all night."

Hots motioned her away, but Moina stopped him. "Harold, I can handle this. Alone."

As soon as Hots left, Ashanti sat down. "You put me through hell yesterday."

"Poor darling."

"Seeing you with Fay again drove me over the edge."

"And what drove you back?"

Ashanti leaned close. "Pussy," she whispered, "what am I going to do?"

"I thought you were going to sue me."

"That's just what I was afraid you thought. I never intended to sue *you.*" Ashanti put her hand on Moina's. "I was going to sue *your estate.*" She lowered her eyes. "Afterwards." Ashanti kissed Moina's hand. "Oh, pussy, I respect you so much for what you're doing. If you were in a hetero mode, it would be so easy. One breast, two breasts, no breasts, to a man you're still a woman. What do they know? But for us, making love is like looking into a mirror."

"You agree, then. I should die rather than have the surgery."

She put Moina's hand to her cheek. "I couldn't live with a distortion of myself in the mirror."

Moina smiled. "I've always been ugly. But what will it be like for you to watch yourself grow old?"

"Please! You know how paranoid I am about my old age."

Moina leaned over and kissed Ashanti goodbye. "Not to worry. I'll take care of you before I die."

"Then I won't have to sue? Oh, pussy. I knew you'd understand. Shit. Suddenly, I feel so sad."

"Later." Moina patted her hand. "You'll have plenty of time to be sad later."

"How can you be so brave?" Ashanti got up to leave, then hesitated. "You wouldn't want to do an Oprah with me, would you?" She answered her own question. "No. I told her I didn't think you would."

Hots came back to the table. "What the hell was that all about?"

"Unfinished business." Her voice was weak. "Before checking into the hospital, I want to go back to the apartment for an hour."

"But, Moina . . ."

She put a hand on his arm. There were tears in her eyes. "I know it sounds foolish, Harold. But I want to enjoy one last bath."

Libby had no place to hide. Meehan and Conaway were on either side of her. Roth and Taylor were at the door. There were agents in the dining room, in the service areas, in the kitchen. The street out front, the street out back. She sat like a prisoner. At the bar.

While the waiters shouted and picked up their orders, she stared into the mirror at the reflection of her accuser and judge. It occurred to Libby that "reflection" was the only way to describe Birnbaum since he was no longer a real person. She was surprised the other agents hadn't noticed that the "pod" version of Birnbaum barely resembled the original. Libby sighed. Was she guilty of that, too? By trusting the one person she thought she could trust, Libby had become a body snatcher.

Surprisingly, her anxiety wasn't confined to what the truth would do to Steven and Cal. She was also worried about what was going to happen to her. There had to be a name for it. The opposite of a victimless crime. A noncriminal event that produced nothing but victims. Libby smiled. It was called Life.

Maxie nudged her as he placed his drink orders. "If you ask me, Junior's doing a number on those kids. They've been telling us about their big lunch with Meryl all week and now he's taking over."

As though the children of Egypt had been slain before her eyes, Libby turned from the bar. "The hell he is!" Infused by the adrenaline previously reserved for Birnbaum, her feet barely touched the carpet as she went into enzyme alert.

Libby grabbed hold of Stu and whispered, "Play along." As she neared the table, she stretched out her arms. "Not again!" Libby grabbed hold of the male. "I don't care how many deals you've got going, you simply have to sit down." She looked at Meryl and smiled. "Child prodigies! He was here the other day with Milos and Vanessa and I couldn't keep him from hopping all over the place. Stu! Get us another chair."

As Junior turned to Libby and smiled, the female picked up immediately. "He embarrasses me wherever we go."

Libby kissed the male. "Junior's no dope. If Mr. Ants-in-His-Pants didn't have Paramount in his back pocket, Junior wouldn't be chasing him around." She patted Junior on the shoulder. "Yes, sir. We all know what you're up to."

The busboy brought out a chair and while the male caught his breath, Libby winked at Meryl. "Let me squeeze in," she said. "It's been such a long time. Tell me everything."

Sam shrugged. "It's the same old story. There's a script that's been floating around for years."

Junior was getting nervous. He had to jump back in. "And I suggested Meryl the minute I finished reading *The Last Cowboy*."

"The what?" Libby asked.

"The Last Cowboy," Meryl said. "Have you heard of it?"

Libby sat back. Yes, she had heard of it. She began to laugh, imagining Janos's face when he heard the news.

"Thank you," Phyllis said as Taylor held the door open. She said it as though Taylor held the door open every day.

"Thanks." Donald followed, looking somewhat pale. His

eyes darted around the vestibule taking note of all the security personnel. "Perhaps this wasn't such a good idea," he whispered.

"Nonsense," she growled between clenched teeth. "It's lunch as usual."

"It doesn't look very usual to me."

"Donald, you don't really think all this is because of you?"

"Ma'am?" Roth held up the magnetometer.

"Piacere," Phyllis said cheerily. She opened her purse and held it out for him. Roth reached in for the small .22 caliber pistol. "Yes, I know," Phyllis laughed, "it would barely crease the hide of a Gucci salesgirl. But it's enormously helpful Off-Broadway." As Roth took the purse, Phyllis leaned close. "Who's here, darling? Michael Jackson?"

Roth smiled. "The President is coming to lunch."

"The President!" Phyllis looked at Donald, her expression changing from surprise to annoyance. "Why didn't Libby tell me?" She shook her head, waiting impatiently as Roth checked her gun permit. "You know, Donald, sometimes I wonder what friends are for."

"Phyllis, I don't know what the hell to say to Libby."

"You don't have a thing to worry about, my darling. She's bound to be so involved with the President she won't remember her own name, much less your shitty-shitty-bang-bang." As Phyllis turned toward the dining room, Steven came back up the steps. Ignoring the disbelief in his eyes, she smiled broadly. "Good afternoon, Steven. I'm starving!"

Steven caught Donald's eye for a moment and then looked quickly at the reservations book. He wasn't ready to face Donald. He ran his finger down the page, realizing that he hadn't taken their names off the list. It had never occurred to him they would show up. Steven shook his head as he pretended to be checking the book. "Elgin? Elgin? Elgin?"

Libby couldn't stop laughing. The indieprods, like The Little Match Girl and Tiny Tim, sat close, hands clutched nervously beneath the table. Meryl and Sam looked at each other and shrugged. Junior was getting angry. No one knew why Libby was laughing.

"Do I have a last cowboy for you!" she said, drying the

corners of her eyes. "You know, sometimes I think that if I hadn't opened this restaurant, the only movies that would get made are *Rambo VII* and *Halloween 23.*" She took Meryl's hand. "There's only one person who can play that part and he'll be here any minute."

Meryl suddenly understood. "We were talking about Cal. He's perfect."

The male cleared his throat. "You see, Junior? I told you we were right about Cal."

Libby winked proudly at the male and turned toward the desk looking for Cal. She noticed that Birnbaum had his back to the room. He was facing the door. So was Steven. Libby stood up. "I must be seeing things." She left the table quickly.

Phyllis opened her arms wide as Libby approached. "Darling, look at you! Sheer pink perfection! Tell her, Donald. She never believes me. She thinks I say things just because I'm her best friend. She trusts you."

In her heart, Libby still did. Her emotions were notoriously out of sync with her brain. What Libby wanted most of all was to sit down with Phyllis and Donald and have them comfort her while she told them about all the terrible things that Phyllis and Donald had done.

"Get out!" Libby said.

Phyllis grabbed her arm. "Darling, I'm so glad you finally brought it up. I've been dying to clear the air. Let me explain. Cal . . ."

"Cal?" Libby shook her head. "You think I'm upset about Cal? He can take care of himself."

"*Voilà!*" Phyllis said. "My point precisely."

"It's what you did to Steven. I'll never forgive you for that."

"Oh, darling, don't be a crankypuss. After all these years you're not going to let a little misunderstanding come between us and lunch?" Phyllis put her arms around Libby.

Libby held tight. "God help me," she whispered, "I wasn't ready to lose you."

Phyllis rolled her eyes. "But you haven't lost me, darling. I'm right here!"

Libby stepped back. She pulled Donald's handkerchief from

his breast pocket and blew her nose. "Steven, get rid of this garbage!"

Donald turned quickly to the door. "I told you it was a mistake to come!"

"*C'est la vie,*" Phyllis said, taking his arm and pausing just long enough to grab the handkerchief back from Libby. "But you know what they say. It is better to have lunched and lost than never to have lunched at all."

Libby walked backward down the steps, and bumped into Phil Donahue's table. "I'm sorry," she said, pretending to brush a few crumbs from the cloth.

"Are you all right?" Phil asked.

"Why? You want to do a show on all right?"

He smiled. "No. I want to do a show on why the hell it costs so much to have lunch these days."

Before the Elgins left, Steven grabbed hold of Phyllis. "No one has to know what really happened."

Phyllis smiled meanly. "The check is in the mail."

"I don't want money," he said.

"In other words, this is really going to cost me."

"No," Steven said. "It's going to cost me. I've decided to be noble."

"Splendid, darling." Phyllis lit a cigarette. "What time will you be jumping?"

"Even if Cal knew the truth," Steven said, "he wouldn't press charges. He's too ashamed of me."

Phyllis blew a stream of smoke into his face and smiled. "We all are, Steven."

Donald was nearly unable to control himself. "I insist we leave."

"Shut up, Donald." Phyllis pushed him away. "Steven, tell me what you want. The suspense is killing you."

"I want you to produce the play. I want my father in New York so he can be with Libby."

Phyllis fluttered her eyelids. "I suppose next you're jetting off to feed tandoori chicken and mint chutney to the lepers."

"If you ever tell anyone about this," Steven said, "I swear I'll sing louder than Pavarotti."

Phyllis shrugged. "I'd hold up ordering the crown of thorns if I were you. No matter what you call it, it's still blackmail." She dropped her cigarette to the carpet, not bothering to put it out. She snapped angrily at Taylor. "Give me my gun!"

Donald was furious. "Don't let Steven pressure you, Phyllis. It's too demeaning."

"For whom? Is it more demeaning than everyone knowing I'm married to the Queen of Wall Street? My sweetheart," she said, patting his cheek and smiling wickedly. "If truth be told, your shooting Cal makes for great box office."

"My sweetheart," he said softly. "If truth be told, I was aiming at you."

While Libby was still reeling from her close encounter with Phyllis, Junior took her arm and headed toward the dining room.

"I can't," she protested. "The President is going to be here any minute!"

"You can see the door from my table." Junior guided Libby into a seat. Wanda, who was just finishing her salad, looked up as Junior lifted her plate, took her fork and grabbed her hand. He led her across the aisle to Fay's table. "Fay, I want you to meet Wanda." Without waiting for Fay's response, he put down the plate and fork, knowing Wanda would sit.

"I can see why you want to make a Nazi movie," Libby said as Junior came back to the table.

"Forget the Nazi movie. That was yesterday. I did a lot of stupid things yesterday. That's what I like about the picture business. You can be stupid one day and a genius the next."

"Okay, genius. The meter is running."

He leaned closer and spoke softly. "Everybody and his brother passed on that script. Now that Meryl is interested, suddenly it's got legs. But I'm the one who can make it walk. I can make it run."

"The kids stay."

"Why? Why the hell are they so important to you?"

Libby put a hand to her forehead. "I'm old-fashioned. I like happy endings. That's the trouble with the picture business today. Nobody rides off into the sunset. Boy doesn't get girl anymore."

"And everybody says it's *producer's* wives who are a pain in the neck."

"I'm not his wife."

"Ex-wife. Same thing."

"That's what I used to think. But it's not." She reached for his hand. "You still don't understand about endings."

He pulled away from her. "This is my deal."

"Not without those kids."

"This isn't a business for kids."

"It was their picture."

"It was their script. It's my picture. They'll be carded as associates for the dog work. If they have a good agent, they'll make a profit on expenses."

Libby smiled. "They've just hired the best agent in the business. Now you listen to me and you listen hard. We both know you want Cal more than you don't want those kids. They're going to come out of this as producers. I don't care what title you give yourself. And Cal's going to come out of this with six. Plus the same percentages Meryl gets. The same perks."

Junior sat back and shook his head. "What about you? What do you get out of all this?"

"Nothing. I'm just balancing the books." Libby had promised Cal six million dollars if she didn't marry him.

"You don't see Mimi Sheraton anywhere, do you?" Harriet whispered, reaching for the butter.

J moved the dish away. "It was one thing to be oral-compulsive at Vassar, but no one thought you'd make a career out of it."

"Is she here or not?"

"Don't be so paranoid, Harriet." J sipped her margarita. "It's my day to relax. Idle rich enjoys idle. No, she's not here." J smiled, adding, "But there are still some empty tables."

While J idled, Harriet shifted into reverse. Truffle Pot Pie, instead of "the latest rip-off," would be discovered as a daring culinary sleight-of-hand. Witty. Provocative. Redolent with something or other. And Libby's would be revealed as her favorite haunt, *la corrida* of the power elite, where everyone lunched in the sun and loved it. Harriet Moss tasted front page, and even if she had to tell the truth to get it, nothing was going to stop her.

It was one hell of a comment on the current state of journalism, but then again, she never pretended to be Walter Cronkite.

Harriet reached for the dish, stuck the tip of her knife into the butter and caught a sliver on the edge. She tasted it. "Lucky for them, it's real butter."

J began to laugh. "You've just never grown up. The Moss who still wants to be a Rolling Stone. I can recall you wearing sweats and jeans long before they became South Shore. Then you wrote a novel no one read and a cookbook no one used. You entered the Great American Screenplay Contest and lost. Nothing but failure after dismal failure. And then, rather than give up and marry money, you took arms against the slings and arrows of outrageous fortune. Knowing you could never be as splendid a writer as Gael Greene, you became bitter, obnoxious and filled with loathing."

Harriet shook a finger in J's face. "Before I forget, don't believe everything you hear about the meatloaf at Mortimer's."

"Oh, Harriet. How I envy you."

By the time Junior came back to his corner after Round Two, he had finessed himself in as Executive Producer. He had guaranteed not only financing, but Cal. As far as Junior was concerned, neither Cal nor the Bank of America would be crazy enough to pass on a piece of a Streep/Dennis Christmas pie. The only thing he had to figure out was how to get a copy of the screenplay. He had never read it.

Junior was heading across the aisle to pick up Wanda when he saw Ashanti at his table. "What the hell do you want?" he asked.

She was squirting lemon onto a plate of raw oysters. "I'm desperate. Bill Perry went back to his wife."

"I don't care. Fuck off."

Ashanti swallowed an oyster in a single gulp. "Junior, will you marry me?"

He sat down. "Yes."

"Would you like an oyster?"

"I hate oysters."

"One man's *merde* is another man's *poisson*." Ashanti looked at him for the first time. "Forgive me. I must remember you're too dumb to appreciate puns."

"And what must I do?"

"You must make up with Senior."

"Are you crazy?"

"I don't want you disinherited."

"I'm already disinherited."

"Then we're going to get you reinherited. I want that money."

"You think he's going to be overjoyed when he finds out I'm marrying you?"

Ashanti put down her fork. "Why don't you just call a spade a spade? I am fully aware that you are marrying out of your race. But I, for all intents and purposes, darling, am marrying out of the species. Not that I'm complaining. If man were afraid to cross frontiers, he'd never have discovered Canada."

Junior took her hand. "I don't need Senior's money."

"Don't be ridiculous. Do you know what it's going to cost me to redecorate?"

"Redecorate?"

"Surely you don't expect me to live in a house where art is defined as a painting by Elke Sommer."

He smiled. "You're incredible. Ravishing. Greedy. Heartless. Frigid. Just like my mother."

The waiter brought a phone to the table. "I have a call for you, sir."

Junior shrugged. "Must be the KKK." He picked up the receiver. "Hello?"

It was Senior. Shouting. "I wanted you to be the first to know. I just bought that cockamamie German book from Janos. It's mine! So any ideas you had about ever getting it back, you could forget. Forever!"

"Listen, you old fart, I don't give a damn about that book. I'm producing *The Last Cowboy* with Meryl Streep and Cal Dennis."

"Big deal! Just you remember one thing! I was the first producer to drop the option on that picture. Years ago!"

Junior shrugged. There was no way to get through. "I'm getting married, Pop." He pointed to Ashanti.

Senior nodded. "Does she do windows?"

"I'd like you to meet her."

"I'll meet her when I do *Porgy and Bess.*"

"You'll like her."

"I don't like you. Why should I like her?"

"Pop . . ."

"Pop! All of a sudden the weasel goes Pop."

"I'd like you to be at my wedding."

There was a pause. "I'm very busy."

"How about lunch?" Junior asked.

"Maybe that could be arranged."

"How soon can we do it?"

"I don't know. Have your people get in touch with my people."

In all the years she had been lunching at Libby's, Fay couldn't remember anyone actually ordering dessert. Certainly not anyone with a body like Wanda's.

"No thanks," Fay said as Wanda held out a plate of chocolate-covered raspberries.

"Mmm," Wanda said, closing her eyes in ecstasy.

Fay smiled. "Oh, I know just where I'm goin' to take you tonight, sweetie."

Wanda looked at Fay, then lowered her eyes as though she had been animated by Disney.

"I know a place," Fay said softly, "where they serve the best damn grasshoppers in the city." She saw a sudden look of horror on Wanda's face and began to laugh. "Honey, it's the name of a drink. I can see I've got my work cut out for me." Fay pressed the blinking button on her phone and picked up the receiver.

"Darling! This is Phyllis."

"Somehow I just knew I'd be hearin' from you. What airport you callin' from?"

"Don't be ridiculous! Donald and I are holed up at '21.' At least for the duration."

"That's real stoic. Anybody there I'd be interested in?"

"Me."

"Oh, c'mon Phyllis. I gave at the office. I love Libby too

much not to go along with the 'let-me-show-you-my-antique-gun' routine. But enough is enough.''

"That's yesterday's news," Phyllis snapped. "I'm calling to let you break the story that yours truly is bringing Cal Dennis back to Broadway. And darling, don't think that was easy!''

Fay shook her head. "I don't know how you do it, honey, but you always manage to come up spittin' diamonds.''

Libby made herself appear very busy. She walked up and down the aisles replacing used ash trays with fresh ones, dirty silverware with clean, old worries with new.

As Libby reached for an empty glass, J squeezed her hand. "Darling, this terrible business with Cal . . .''

"I'm not interested in your personal life," Harriet said. "I came here for Truffle Pot Pie.''

"Did you? What a pity. We're all out," Libby lied. "Frankly, Harriet, if I were you, I'd stay with something simple. Certainly nothing with a sauce. That way you can be sure no one spit on it.''

Special Agent Davis left his table and came over to Libby. "Excuse me, Mrs. Dennis. It's time.''

She couldn't help smiling. It was the way he said It's time. It's time to shave your head. It's time to say your prayers. It's time to put the noose around your neck. But before Libby had a chance to say anything, Harriet grabbed her by the wrist.

"Why is the President coming here? Why did he choose this dump? There's got to be a reason.''

Libby pulled her hand away, gasping as loudly as she could. "Damn you! Is nothing sacred?''

J was shocked. "Harriet! Behave yourself!''

"It's all right, J. I know when I'm licked. A crack reporter like Harriet would find out sooner or later. She might as well hear it from me." Libby put a hand on J's shoulder as though to steady herself. "I can no longer hide the truth. I was once the mistress of the President of the United States and by his seed brought forth an illegitimate offspring who knows naught of his political provenance. And that, Harriet, is why the President is coming to lunch.''

J, unable to control her laughter, sprayed a mouthful of margarita across the table. All over Harriet.

Libby walked triumphantly up the aisle. Perhaps this was an even better moment to open her book. Then, while everyone was getting paper cuts from turning the pages quickly, she'd drop in three or four hundred pages of flashbacks that would bring her to the climactic moment. The arrival of the President. The revelation of her secret. Anna Karenina on the train tracks. The lady or the express.

Libby put her hand on Birnbaum's arm. He moved his head slightly but, like a dancer, never took his eyes from the point. The point was Steven. "Birnbaum, I want to give you one last chance."

"To do what?"

"Rejoin the human race."

"Later."

"There is no later. I've run out of time."

"Listen, your problems and my problems . . ."

"Birnbaum, don't give me the King and Country speech. Please!"

He smiled. "Goddamn you."

"Everybody gets one last request."

"The hell they do. I don't owe you anything. I owe the President. I owe him my loyalty. My life."

"You don't owe him *my* life, Birnbaum."

"I have to protect him."

"I have to protect Cal."

"Cal's not in any danger."

"Don't be dumb. There are lots of ways to die." She tightened her grip on his arm. "I want to tell Cal before he finds out."

"Cal isn't going to find out anything right now. My job is to protect the President, not deliver the Six O'Clock News. I decide what happens when."

"You can't make time stand still, Birnbaum."

"Yes I can."

Libby shook her head. "Only in your apartment."

He faced her for the first time. "Last night, you scared the shit out of me. Nothing like you ever happened to me before.

Never will again." He stared at her. "I want you to leave me the hell alone."

Libby knew that she had finally run out of track. She took a deep breath. "Okay, Birnbaum. But one last thing before the President gets here."

"What?"

She spit onto her fingertips and slicked back her bright red bangs. "Tell me I'm gorgeous!"

○

Four policemen on motorcycles sped out of the UN driveway and into the "frozen zone" along First Avenue. Two Coast Guard helicopters filled with countersniper teams hovered over both sides of the street. Marine One, the President's chopper, with its communications link to the Command Van across the street from Libby's, paced nervously in the sky above the UN garage.

Special Agent Cooley, watching all three video screens in the van, spoke into the microphone on his headset. "Phase One alert. Comet rising." He leaned close to the screen that received images from Marine One. "Headstart, do you copy?"

Birnbaum's voice responded. "Affirmative. All units copy."

"Barfly copy."

"Kitchen copy."

"North roof copy."

"South roof copy."

"Sixth Avenue copy."

"Fifth Avenue copy."

"Crosstown one copy."

"Crosstown two copy."

"Crosstown three copy."

"Crosstown four copy."

"Second Avenue copy."

"First Avenue copy."

"All right, then," boomed Anders's voice. "This isn't *Starlight Express*. Let's get the fuck out of here!"

The four motorcycle cops were pure attention grabbers, the conductor tapping his baton. The next vehicle in the motorcade was the "pilot" car, a NYPD squad car filled with uniformed police.

The "point" car was a quarter of a mile behind, allowing time for the pilot car to signal if there were any signs of trouble. It was an unmarked car filled with armed Secret Service agents and high-ranking police. They scanned the streets for anything or anyone that looked suspicious. An empty window. A glint of metal. An unpredictable movement. The men in the point car operated on pure animal instinct.

The presidential limousine, the most secure vehicle in the world since FDR used Al Capone's armored car, had a standard six-digit Washington, D.C., blue-and-white license plate. It remained five lengths behind the point car and was driven by an agent from the White House detail. Anders sat in the right front seat, maintaining radio contact with the Command Van and all other vehicles in the motorcade. He was glad to get out of the UN with its goddamn extraterritorial rights and a security force that was a real pain in the ass. Once the President was in the car, Anders didn't have to share him with anyone.

The President of the United States sat on the right side of the rear seat. The Secretary of State was in the middle, and the Chief of Staff on the left. The President's personal attorney and the White House Press Secretary sat in jump seats facing him.

"Time?" the President asked, looking out of the window.

"Twelve-thirty, Mr. President," said his Press Secretary. One of the perks of being President, in addition to never having to say you're sorry, was not having to carry a wallet or a watch.

The President shook his head. "I hate empty streets."

Sherman Simon, the President's attorney, spoke softly. "I wish you'd reconsider lunch at Libby's."

"What's the matter, Sherman?" asked the President. "Aren't you hungry?"

"This is one lunch the Administration can do without."

The President raised his tinted aviator glasses. "The Administration? You're talking like an old man, Sherman. Who the hell do you think the Administration is?"

The Secretary of State, who was an old man, said, "Fuck it, Mr. President! You do what you want. To hell with the history books. As far as anyone knows today, John Foster Dulles is nothing but an airport."

Sherman leaned forward. "We've got a wide enough window in the schedule. There's still time to change your mind."

The President sat back and smiled. "Are you kidding? I've been looking forward to this for a long time."

As the motorcade headed uptown on Second Avenue, Anders heard Cooley's voice in his earphone. "Comet on Second. Please copy."

Right behind the presidential limousine was the "chase" car. Admiral John Ellis, the President's physician, rode alongside Secret Service agents holding Israeli-made Uzi submachine guns. Next in line were two staff vans filled with electronic gear and weapons. Navy Lieutenant Commander Susan Forrest carried the "red telephone." The vans were followed by additional Secret Service cars, NYPD cars, and, finally, six motorcycle cops to signify the end of the motorcade.

"Comet turning left," Cooley announced, watching the images sent by Marine One. "Full zone alert. Please copy."

"Affirmative," Birnbaum said. "Headstart copy. All units copy."

When the motorcade reached Fifth Avenue, the driver of the pilot car slowed down, allowing the other vehicles to close ranks. As the presidential limousine approached the restaurant, it veered left, drove up onto the sidewalk and was surrounded by the rest of the motorcade.

Cooley's voice. "Comet has landed."

Libby moved into place as easily as finding her mark on stage. Meehan and Conaway stood at attention. Roth slipped the magnetometer into his pocket. Taylor put down the clipboard and opened the front door. Six agents walked in, glancing at Birnbaum for confirmation that the premises were secure. Once he nodded, they formed a human corridor—three men on each side—preparing to flank the President. While waiting for him, they looked rapidly around the vestibule, focusing with such impact, point to point, that the movement of their eyes could almost be heard.

The President of the United States came through the doorway. Upon seeing Libby, he stopped. He lifted his aviator glasses and smiled. "I should be very angry with you." He took hold of her hands. "I waited at the Willard Hotel for two hours."

"I never thought you'd come."

He leaned over and kissed her on the cheek. "You should have trusted me." And then he whispered, "I'm still waiting."

"I'm still waiting," Birnbaum said into his walkie-talkie.

Libby looked up, suddenly short of breath. "Where is he?"

The President of the United States came through the doorway. Upon seeing Libby, he stopped. He lifted his aviator glasses and smiled. "I've heard a great deal about your restaurant. I've been wanting to have lunch here for years." He shook her hand and leaned close. "I apologize for all the hoopla."

Libby was stunned. He didn't know who she was. Suddenly that was even worse than the knowing half-smile of recognition she had expected.

"What hoopla? Mr. President, it's a pleasure to have you here."

Libby had seen hundreds of pictures of him. She knew exactly what he looked like. She had followed his campaign from the day he first announced himself as a candidate. She had watched his press conferences on television, seen him sign bills into law, stared in fascination as he greeted world leaders and led them into the White House. But nothing, least of all having once slept with him, prepared her for the intensity of the force field around him. He wore power the way other men wore cologne.

As he let go of her hand, she saw something in his eyes, a look she had seen many times over the years. There was someone else who looked at her just that way. "Mr. President," she said, grabbing hold of Steven, "I'd like you to meet my son."

Suddenly, the world melted into slow-motion photography. Click. Click. Click. Steven's hand reached out. Click. Click. Click. Innocently, irrevocably, forbidden flesh had touched, held tight, let go. To everyone but Libby, it was a casual moment in a disposable world. It was a moment Libby would remember forever.

"We're honored to have you here, Mr. President," Steven said.

The President turned to Libby. "Surely, this young man can't be your son?"

Libby smiled at the President. He is *your* son, she told him in utter silence. Afraid that her thoughts had been overheard, she turned quickly. "By the way," she blurted out, "Have you met Special Agent Birnbaum?"

The President shook his hand. "Head of the New York detail," he acknowledged. "You've done a terrific job."

"Thank you, Mr. President."

The President laughed. "I'm the one who should be thanking you."

"Mr. President," Anders said impatiently.

The President winked at Libby. "They want to put me in my playpen."

"May I?" she asked, pointing toward the dining room.

"You damn well better. I'm hungry."

Libby walked down the steps, the President at her side. Everyone at the front tables automatically stood up. Within a moment, the entire room was on its feet, applauding. Libby felt the corners of her eyes moisten with tears. Of all the thoughts that had crossed her mind, there was one that caught her by surprise. Libby couldn't help wondering what it would be like if she were the First Lady.

The President stopped to say hello to Meryl. Fay stood up and shook his hand. Julie Andrews and Tommy Tune. Senior and Esther Williams. Horton had a diagram of the room with a list of who sat where. He followed behind the President, alerting him whether to turn right or left or keep going.

"Right," Horton whispered. "Señor Ensesa. Bolivia. Money. Anti-drugs."

"Señor Ensesa." The President smiled and extended his hand.

Alfero broke into a cold sweat. *"Señor Presidente!"* As he leaned across the table to shake hands, he spilled his coffee into the caviar.

"I appreciate your help on that drug matter."

Alfero could hardly speak. "You need more, you let me know."

As the President walked away, he told Horton to invite Ensesa to the White House dinner for the Venezuelan ambassador.

Alfero watched with a broken heart as Juano, the busboy, stood at attention while the President took his seat.

"Well," Norm said, "we don't have to worry about Mr. Pérez anymore. He's never going to get in now." Norm handed Alfero a menu and smiled. "You might as well get on with it."

Libby stood at the desk, holding onto the reservations book as though it were the edge of a cliff. The President of the United States was at Table 42. Unbeknownst to him, his own son was taking the drink order. It was not unbeknownst to Birnbaum, however. He stared at Steven like a bird watcher on the first day of spring.

She answered the phone, "Libby's Last Chance Saloon."

"Babe?"

"Cal! Where the hell are you?"

"These fuckers won't let me through the barricade on Fifth Avenue. They say my name isn't on the reservations list!"

"Of course it isn't. Let me speak to them."

"It's no use. They say even if it was, no one can get in or out while Der Führer is there!"

"Cal, you've got to get in. I just spoke to Junior. You won't believe what he said."

"Nobody believes Junior."

"Listen to me. Meryl is here with Sam. She wants to do *The Last Cowboy!*"

"With Rikki?"

"No! Janos's option lapsed. Meryl wants to do it with *you.*"

Cal was stunned. He let out a deep groan. "Goddamn, I knew I should have read it!"

"Cal, will you shut up and cut to the chase? You've got to get here."

"How? These clowns won't let me through."

Libby clutched the phone. "Leave it to me." She slammed down the receiver and went over to Birnbaum. "I want to make a deal."

"No."

"I want you to let Cal in. I love him, Birnbaum." Her voice cracked. "You and I know he's about to get shot again and it's your finger on the trigger. There's nothing I can do to stop you." She smiled. "But he's a movie star. He can get along without me. He can't get along without this movie."

"You said you wanted to make a deal. What do I get in return?"

Libby smiled. "Nothing."

He laughed. "You're one hell of a piece of work."

Libby grabbed him by the lapel. "Birnbaum, he's America's sweetheart! Let him in!"

"No one goes in or out while the President is here," he said. "I told you that."

"It's not as though you'd be doing it for me. Meryl Streep wants to talk to him. What did she ever do to you?"

"No one in. No one out."

"Don't you ever make exceptions?"

"Never."

The entire population of Hell gathered in her stomach. "Birnbaum, I beg you, don't do this. Don't make it rain for forty days and forty nights."

Andre tapped his fingers on the table as Al poured a sip of the Puligny-Montrachet "Folâtières" '85. Smiling at Mark van Heuven across the table, Andre picked up the glass. He held it to the light, swirled the wine around and watched it coat the crystal. He sniffed suspiciously, sipped it slowly, and sloshed the chardonnay from cheek to cheek. Andre swallowed with a loud gulp. Finally, he sucked in air and tilted his head to one side. He narrowed his eyes and tapped his finger on the table. "Piss! Pure piss! Take it away!"

"Yes, Mr. Riley. I'm terribly sorry." Al handled it perfectly. Just as Andre had rehearsed it with him. "Is there something else I can bring you?"

Andre shook his head wearily. "I'll try the '84 Corton-Charlemagne."

Al nodded. "A superb choice, sir."

Andre reached for a slice of bread. "Forgive me, Mark, but I've always been a perfectionist." He buttered it evenly. "I guess that's why I'm so impressed with the level of your work at GNF."

Mark van Heuven was head of GNF's Breakfast Cereals Group. He nodded appreciatively. "Andre, just between *du* and *ich,* any schmuck can spend his life jacking off premium offers and line extensions. I'm not that kind of caballero. I don't get my kicks out of decoder rings or adding a handful of raisins to a box of kiddie kibble." He raised his very blond eyebrows. "After all, that's not why I spent four bloody years at the Technische Hoogeschool in Delft. Is it?"

Andre forced a laugh designed to set new standards for male bonding. He handed Mark a menu. "Why don't we get this out of the way so that we don't have to be interrupted?"

Mark nodded toward the President's table. "I'd love to know what he eats for breakfast."

Andre didn't care what the President ate. It was his last lunch and he had to make it count. Andre had lost the deal with PBS. He had lost the movie deal with Junior. He lost the deal for a musical. If he lost Mark, all that lay ahead was a one-way trip to the Pritikin Center. Once there, he would have to find a way to finance the rest of his life. The only cash he had left was $300 in small bills. For tips. Andre had no money to pay his hotel bill, the plan being to walk out bequeathing Leona Helmsley the fat suits for which he would have no future use.

"I can recommend the curried oysters," Andre said.

"You know, it takes three years on a cereal," Mark said. "You can't roll out any sooner than that."

"As well as the barbecued foie gras. All I need is your letter of intent." Andre leaned over toward Mark and spoke sincerely. "Foie gras for me."

Mark shook his head. "Historically, licensed character cereals have never done as well as generics like Corn Flakes or Shredded Wheat."

Andre didn't look up from the menu. "Listen, Hans Brinker, you can't kid me. You've got your finger in a three-billion-dollar dike. One share point in the cereal market is worth thirty million. Even if Cheerios has only a five share, that's a hundred and fifty mil." Andre put his menu aside. "I'd say we're talking somewhere between one and five shares. Somewhere between thirty and a hundred and fifty million. Of course, I've always been partial to the salmon tartare with sliced figs."

Mark shrugged. "What I like is that even though character cereals are usually kid-driven products, we're talking a mom-buy. Jesus. I'm a sucker for smoked fresh tuna." He smiled at Andre.

"But since you're paying, I just might join you in the foie gras." Mark took the letter of intent out of his pocket. "After all, I'm going to make you a very rich man, Andre."

Andre pretended to read the menu while Al opened the Corton-Charlemagne. But all he could see was the envelope Mark was holding. Andre broke into a cold sweat. His mouth became incredibly dry. Al poured a sip of the green-gold wine into his glass. Andre swallowed quickly, not even tasting it. His mouth was like blotting paper.

When both glasses were full, Mark smiled. "A toast." He opened the envelope and handed Andre the signed letter of intent. "To 'Grannie's Brannies'!"

Andre clinked glasses with Mark, knowing that the letter in his hand meant he could stop worrying at last. He was rich!

Mark sipped the wine and sat back. "Superb. Deep. Flowery. And yet, with a rather surprising finish."

Andre didn't hear him. Andre just stared into space. Andre was dead.

o

Cal stood near the limo at the corner of Fifty-fifth. He looked up the block toward the restaurant, waiting for a signal from Libby to come ahead. Traffic on Fifth Avenue was near a standstill. Horns honked angrily as cars jammed together fender to fender. Cal shouted at Special Agent Mason. "You do realize how dumb this is?"

"No."

"Do you really think I'm going to kill the President?"

Mason smiled. "No."

"Then what's the problem?"

"No one is allowed in or out while the President is there."

"I thought this was a democracy! Whatever happened to freedom of lunch?"

"Mr. Dennis, I know you're a big movie star . . ."

"I've got a deal waiting! If I don't get there now, I could lose it. You know how Hollywood people are. You can't trust them!" Cal smiled his million-dollar smile. He pointed to the sling around his arm. "With a clipped wing, yet! What harm could I do?"

"The basic principle of effective security is eliminating the element of surprise. If everything is planned, with no adjustments allowed, then security can be maintained. One single unexpected moment can undermine the entire effort. I'm sure it's the same in your business, sir. The director says . . ."

"Oh, shit!" As Cal walked back to the limo, he heard a woman call his name.

"Mr. Dennis! Mr. Dennis! Hi! Over here! It's me! Remember me?"

Cal looked across the street. A young blonde carrying a sign saying SCREW SAFE SEX was waving at him.

"It's me! Tessa! The coatroom?"

Cal walked over, suddenly finding himself in the midst of the protesters. "Sure!" he said. "Listen, I've got to get in there. Can you help me?"

"Are you kidding? I wouldn't set foot in that piss pot!"

Cal was furious. "You looking for a lawsuit or a smack in the mouth?"

"Oh, God! I'd kill for a good smack in the mouth!"

The driver brought Cal the car phone. "It's Mr. Smith."

Ignoring Tessa, he shouted into the receiver, "Smitty? Where the hell are you?"

"The pilot says we're still circling Kansas City. Where are you?"

"I'm on Fifth Avenue. Meryl and Sam are having lunch at Libby's. They want to talk to me about *The Last Cowboy*."

"So talk to them. But remember, don't say anything."

"Smitty, I can't get in! The Secret Service won't let me through. I'm standing here in the middle of some protest group and damn it, there's a CBS camera crew heading right toward me."

"What kind of protest group?"

Cal read the posters. "BETTER WED THAN DEAD. MAKE BABIES, NOT CONDOMS."

"Great! Join the group."

"You want me to get involved with a bunch of nuts?"

"You want to get into the restaurant?"

Cal tossed the phone back to the driver. He rushed across

the street, dodging baby carriages to find Tessa. "What did you say your name was?"

Before either of them realized what was happening, the CBS crew had started to shoot. Someone held a microphone in front of Cal. "What is it you're protesting, Mr. Dennis?"

Cal looked around uneasily, trying to translate the signs into something intelligible. He felt the heat of the lights on him. Instinctively, he looked into the camera, glanced down momentarily, then giving coast-to-coast sincere, put his arm around Tessa. "This young girl wants to make love. I don't think that's a crime. I don't think she should have to die because of it. But is the President of the United States listening?"

The protesters started to chant. "No! No! No!"

"And you know why he's not listening?" Cal shouted. "Because he's having lunch!"

o

Al, the waiter, staggered toward the bar. "Oh, my God. You're not going to believe this!"

Birnbaum turned immediately. Meehan put a hand over his gun but never took his eyes from the dining room.

"Andre Riley just dropped dead."

Conaway checked his list for Andre's table number. "One-oh-three."

"Only he didn't *drop* dead," Al continued. "He's too fat to drop. He's just sitting there like his batteries ran out."

Steven hung up the phone without finishing his conversation. "What do we do?"

Birnbaum picked up his walkie-talkie. "Medic alert. Spare to one-oh-three. Immediate."

"I think the guy he's with is dead, too," Al said. "I haven't seen him blink an eye."

They all watched from the vestibule as Special Agent Davis went over to Andre's table. It looked as though he was whispering into Andre's ear.

Libby came back into the vestibule after circling the room. She winked at Steven. "So far, so good."

He groaned. "Brace yourself. Andre is dead."

"Oh no, what a shame!" Libby shook her head. "He was counting on that deal. What the hell is he going to do now?"

"I mean, Andre is dead."

Libby pointed toward the dining room. She opened her mouth, then looked at Steven. He nodded yes. She nodded no. She pointed again.

Steven raised his eyes to the heavens. "Mother, he is somewhere out there with *Ishtar.*"

"Oh, my God!"

Birnbaum was listening to his earphone. "It appears to have been a stroke. Massive. Instantaneous. Nothing could have been done."

Libby put a hand to her forehead. "We have to get him out of there."

"No, we don't," Birnbaum said.

"What do you mean, no we don't?"

"Nobody in, nobody out," Birnbaum repeated.

"This isn't nobody!" Libby whispered angrily. "This is a dead body! In case you forgot, I run a restaurant, not a funeral home!"

"I've got men flanking him on both sides," Birnbaum said. "The table on his right is filled with our people. They'll sit close and talk to him as though nothing had happened."

"The man who makes time stand still." Libby shook her head. "Thank God it's only Harriet Moss at the next table. She'll never notice."

Al walked over to Libby. "You expect me to serve a dead man?"

"For God's sake, Al, bring him something he really liked."

Anders rushed up the steps into the vestibule. He grabbed hold of Birnbaum. "What the hell is going on here?"

Libby looked at Birnbaum. "I told you they'd find out."

"You know?" Anders asked.

"Of course I know!" Libby stopped, trying to hold back the tears. "Poor guy . . ."

"Poor guy, nothing!" Anders said. "CBS is giving him whatever he wants."

"What's CBS got to do with it?" Libby asked.

"Mrs. Dennis, I'm not blaming you. I'm asking for your

help. I don't think you want to embarrass the President any more than I do."

She pointed to Birnbaum. "He's the one! He said no one in and no one out. I pleaded with him to make an exception to the rule."

Anders looked as though steam were about to come out of his ears. Heading toward the bar, he spoke into his walkie-talkie. "This is Charger. Fifth Avenue, please copy. Immediate. Have Midtown arrest all demonstrators. Suspicion of subversion. My authorization. Exception: Cal Dennis. Immediate. Bring him to the restaurant. There is to be no incident. Velvet glove CBS. Please copy."

Libby stood close to Birnbaum, unable to hear what Anders was saying. "You see? I told you," she whispered. "You can't keep a dead man sitting in a restaurant without someone noticing. Birnbaum, you dope, sometimes you have to break the rules."

Anders motioned Birnbaum over. "Personally, I don't give a shit," Anders said softly. "But Grumpy and the other dwarfs built this window into his schedule so that lunch would be a nonevent. You knew that. Apparently, you also knew that Dennis was out there taking pot shots at the President. So the question I'm going to have to answer back in D.C. is why the head of the New York detail went AC?" His tone changed suddenly. "You dumb bastard! Sometimes you have to break the rules."

Al left the kitchen carrying three orders of Truffle Pot Pie. He walked up the aisle as ceremoniously as a Son of Sparta carrying the Olympic torch to its final destination.

Special Agent Cornwell, sitting next to the dumbfounded Mark van Heuven, smiled as he talked about his home town, Joplin, and how proud he was of his two boys and how he always wanted to go to Holland because he really liked windmills and tulips. Periodically, Special Agent Cornwell would look over at Andre and smile.

Al cleared his throat as he arrived at the table. Maxie, who was following Al, slowed down to take a quick peek at the deceased.

"Lunch!" Cornwell said. "I'm starving to death!"

Mark closed his eyes. "You're not really going to eat?"

"I am. And so are you."

"You are crazy," Mark said.

"Oh, God!" Al muttered as he put the plate in front of Andre. "I think I'm going to be sick."

Cornwell picked up his fork and broke into the crust. "Wow!" he exclaimed looking straight at Andre. "Smell that!"

Mark shook his head. "It must be me. Maybe I'm the one who died. I must have gone to Hell for not putting enough nuts in Crazy Flakes."

Harriet Moss had been watching from the next table. She leaned over to J. "Look at that! The bitch said she was out of Truffle Pot Pie. But she had enough for Andre Riley. You can bet that bastard wouldn't be caught dead eating crap like this!" Harriet pushed her plate aside. "He's not even eating it. I'm going to ask him for a taste."

"Harriet, you'll do no such thing. I'm not sitting here while you beg for table scraps."

"What really pisses me," Harriet said, "is that I have to write a rave for this rat trap."

"Oh, put a lid on it, Harriet! Everyone who comes here enjoys themselves enormously. For heaven's sake, just look at Andre. He's having the time of his life."

Cal rushed through the front door, only to be stopped by Taylor and Roth. "Babe, I made it!"

Libby reached out to him as though Taylor and Roth were quicksand. "I love you, Cal. Whatever I've done, I never wanted to hurt you."

Cal stepped back as Roth raised the magnetometer. "Not so much as a hand on me. What the hell kind of fascist tactic is this?"

Libby tried to get closer but Taylor was in the way. "I've never loved anyone but you. I have to know you believe me."

Cal looked worried. "You made that bad a deal with Junior?"

"I made a great deal. Cal, I need to know that you trust me."

"Of course I trust you. It's Junior I'm worried about. All

that guy knows are basement budgets. He's worse than his old man."

"Cal, do you love me?"

The question stopped him. "You mean, in general or right now?"

"I mean from now on. No matter what."

Cal smiled. "You got a deal!"

Libby began to laugh nervously. "Hey, movie star," she said as Roth stepped aside. "What do I have to do to get a kiss?"

He kissed her quickly, turning to check himself in the mirror. "Jesus, I look like I've been run over." Cal winced as he lifted his arm out of the sling.

"What are you doing?"

"You don't think I'm going to let them see me with this?" Cal hesitated. He took Libby's hand. "I've been thinking."

She was terrified he was going to ask her to marry him, but if he did she had decided to say yes.

"I'm not going to let Junior write off his staff on my tab. I want my own driver, my own RV . . ."

"Oh, Cal," she whispered.

He stopped short. "What is it, babe?"

Libby bit her lip to stop the tears. "Is that all you can think about? Limos and RV's?"

He was suddenly angry with her for being right. Or angry with himself for being wrong. It didn't matter which. In true Hollywood tradition, he didn't dare respond to either. "Who's in charge here?" he shouted.

Birnbaum walked slowly toward him. "I am."

"You've got one hell of a nerve not letting me in!"

"Cal, it's all right," Libby said. "It was just a misunderstanding."

"The hell it was! If he's in charge, then it's his fault."

Birnbaum nodded, never taking his eyes from Cal. "You're right. I'm in charge here."

Cal leaned close. "What's your name?"

Without skipping a beat, Birnbaum replied, "Jeanette Mac-Donald."

There was a stunned silence. Libby didn't know whether Cal was going to laugh or punch him in the mouth. She worked fast, leading Cal toward the steps. "Hurry up. They're already talking directors."

"Not without me, they're not."

Libby glanced back at Birnbaum, suddenly aware that she had never been in the same room with two of her lovers. She smiled. Not at the thought, but at the realization that the President made three.

Mary Borden looked at the menu while Ed flicked his fingernail nervously against the glass. "Are you still sweating?" she asked.

He nodded.

Mary put down the menu. "Is your shirt all sticky against your back?"

Ed leaned across the table. "There's a trickle of sweat from my armpit . . ."

"God, you know what this reminds me of? That week in Barbados when you forgot your deodorant and I forgot my Valium."

"I liked you better nervous," he said.

"I liked you better smelly."

Without taking his eyes from Mary, he put a hand just beneath his armpit and rubbed gently. He sat back. "Now, I'm the one who's nervous and you're the one who stinks."

She looked down at the menu. "Have you decided what you want?"

He continued staring at her. "I'll have your heart. On toast."

Mary smiled. "You could starve on that."

Ed leaned close. "Why the lunch? You want to explain it was nothing personal your taking Tully away?"

"It was very personal." She reached for his hand. "I had to get your attention somehow."

"By trying to destroy me?"

"You didn't return my calls."

"Such a vengeful God."

"I began thinking you didn't need me anymore."

"Funny. That's what I began thinking, too. I even switched from jockey shorts to a left-side hang."

"Why didn't you call me back?"

"I thought about it. I even discussed it with Irene."

"Irene?"

"Irene at Pocket Books."

"You discussed me with someone in paperback?"

"Actually, I discuss you as little as possible."

"Do you go out with Irene at Pocket Books?"

"I rarely go out with Irene. As a matter of fact, we hardly ever leave the apartment. We order up Tex-Mex and spend our nights rejecting as many manuscripts as we possibly can. It's wonderful what publishing has done for women. Such a healthy outlet for aggression."

A Secret Service agent appeared at the table. "Excuse me, Miss Borden. The President is ready to see you and Mr. Gilbert now."

"Thank you," Mary said. She reached across for Ed's arm. "This is your payoff for losing Tully. Don't fuck it up. I've been working on this deal for months. Two million five advance in an escrow, interest-bearing account. You become a member of the White House family. The good news is you'll get to plan the book yourself. He's basically illiterate. I handle the paperback auction." She smiled. "And you can bet your ass it won't go to Irene at Pocket Books."

After seating Cal at Meryl's table, Libby knew that she had solved only one problem. There were a thousand to go. Like Scheherazade after the first night, she had survived merely to be put to the test again. She would have to take it one night at a time.

Steven motioned her over to the reservations desk. "Well, we seemed to have solved The Big Mystery. Apparently, the reason the President is here," he said, "is to see Mary Borden and Ed Gilbert."

Libby felt her insides churn. "I guess the laughs really are on the house."

"According to United Waiters International, our peerless leader has just lunched himself into a seven-figure book contract."

Libby tried to hide her anger. Her whole life had been turned upside down because the President wanted to make a deal in her restaurant. "Well, why the hell not?" she said. "That's what people come here for, isn't it? Why should he be any different? That's what they all come to Libby's for. To make a deal." She waved a trembling finger at Steven. "And you're in big trouble, sonny boy, if you don't know that by this time!"

Steven threw up his hands and walked to the bar. "Here I thought everybody came just to see the fabulous Libby!"

The fabulous Libby turned to Birnbaum and whispered, "I must have been crazy."

Birnbaum reached out. "No," he said softly. *"I* must have been crazy." He glanced at the bar and signaled Meehan to take over. Then he led her past Taylor and around the corner into the phone room. Birnbaum stood with his back to the glass panel so that no one could see in as he pulled Libby close and kissed her. "I should never have let you go last night."

Libby put her arms around his neck and kissed him. "I wanted you to stop me."

"Stop." He held her tight. "Don't go."

"Don't let me go."

He nestled his face close and began kissing her on the neck. His mouth followed the outline of her chin. "What about Cal?"

"I don't know." She could barely catch her breath. "What about your wife?"

"I don't know."

Libby took his face in her hands. She kissed him. He kissed her. They couldn't stop.

"I want to make love to you again," he said.

She lay her head against his chest. "Don't let me go."

He kissed her. "I'll never let you go."

Norm came over to Alfero's table with a big smile on his face. He was carrying a phone. "I thought you might like to call and find out what happened to Mr. Pérez."

Alfero was terrified. He didn't know Pérez's number. *"¡Sí!"* Suddenly, he noticed the square red pin in Norm's lapel. He looked around the room. All the waiters and busboys had the same square red pin.

"Here you go," Norm said, plugging in the phone and handing Alfero the receiver. "I'll be right back."

Alfero stared at the dial. It was a push-button phone. His

head told him to push any seven numbers and pretend that he was talking to Pérez. Instead, he dialed Dolores.

"*¡Hola!*"

"I wish to speak to Mr. Pérez."

"*¿Querido?*" She began to cry. "*¡Venga a casa! ¡Por favor! ¡Querido!*"

"Why do you mean Mr. Pérez is not there?" Alfero said.

"*¡Te amo!*" she pleaded. "*¡Los niños aman tu!*"

"But Pérez was to have lunch with me!"

Someone took the phone from Dolores. Alfero could hear her screaming in the background. "*¿Está loco?*" Carlos shouted. He slammed down the receiver.

Alfero sat listening to the dial tone. "Then I will wait no longer for Pérez."

Libby walked back into the dining room as though nothing had happened. In truth, everything had happened. The President had happened. Cal had happened. And worst of all, Birnbaum had happened. She couldn't hide or protect herself any longer. It was time for Libby Dennis to face the music and dance.

Hots motioned her over to his table. "Whatever you do," he said, "don't take rat poison. I had a client once who did. Had to be hospitalized. She grew a long tail and big whiskers."

Libby smiled. "I've decided to tell Cal the truth."

"I don't think Hallmark has a card for that one."

"I have to tell Cal and I have to tell Steven."

"No, you don't! What the hell do you think lawyers are for? If people could tell the truth to one another, lawyers would go out of business."

"I want to do it myself."

"Not now, you don't!" He lowered his voice, widened his eyes and banged his fist on the table. "You're out of control!"

"No. I'm finally in control. No more lies. I have to be honest with Cal."

He shook his head. "Listen, bubeleh. The Lord High Executioner isn't going to say one word while The Mikado is still here. You've got time. You and I can work it out together. Trust me. In the entire history of mankind, no one ever got anywhere being the first to tell the truth. The truth is like a piece of cheese. You have to let it age properly."

"Hots, I'm through being a victim."

"That makes you a definite threat to the rest of us in the gulag."

She took his hand. "Look across the aisle at Andre."

"The poor schmuck is still pitching Grandma Moses?"

"No. Andre is dead."

"Well, I told him it was a stupid idea."

"Andre is dead," she repeated. *"Dead* dead."

"Sure. And I'm the Canterville Ghost."

"Look at him. He's not moving. The guy with the button in his lapel is a Secret Service agent. They won't let me take the body out. No disturbances allowed while the President is here."

Hots stared open-mouthed at Andre. "I don't even know if that's legal," he mumbled. "There must be something about equal rights for the dead."

"When you think about it, maybe it's not so terrible," Libby said, staring into Andre's face. "He's got a great table. Nice bottle of wine. Good company."

Hots grabbed Libby's hand. "Please! Don't tell me you've reserved a table for two at the morgue."

"No. But maybe being dead isn't so bad." Libby and Hots stared at one another. "At least he doesn't have to pay the check." She shrugged. "Hots, I've been paying the check for more than twenty years. I don't want to be afraid anymore."

"So what are you going to do, Mrs. Anna? Whistle a happy tune?"

"No." Libby leaned over and kissed him on the cheek. "A different tune."

Special Agent Barnes had a tap on all phones while the President was at Libby's. He had just listened in to Ensesa's call and shouted across the Command Van to the agent in charge. "Hey, Cooley, I got something here I don't like."

Libby slid in next to Janos. "Those were some flowers you sent Cal."

"It was the least I could do."

"That's true."

Janos became defensive immediately. "Don't start in with me. If he had done what I told him . . ."

"What you told him was disgusting."

"What I told him was a lot of money."

"I hate what you did, Janos."

"So maybe that's the real reason you gave me such a good table."

"I would have sat you in the toilet if I could."

"What's wrong with the toilet?"

"You always come out on top, don't you?"

"Always." He smiled. "You tell yourself you're a winner, you're a winner. Darling girl, listen to me." He took her hand. "There are little villages in Czechoslovakia where the farmers can afford wine only one day a year. All year long they look forward to that day. They think they're very lucky!"

Libby pulled her hand back. "I know a village where they can afford wine every day of the year."

He nodded. "I smell a deal."

Libby smiled. "You smell deals the way a pig smells truffles."

"It's easy. Everything is a deal. You make a deal at the store, it's shopping. You make a deal with the bank, it's high finance. You make a deal with God, it's religion. You make a deal not to make deals, it's a vacation."

"Janos, before I begin, it is necessary that you understand exactly how I feel about you."

"This has got to be some deal."

"I meant what I said about your being a pig."

He sat back. "You must really want a lot of money."

"This has to be strictly business. Our personal feelings for one another have to be kept out of it."

"I have nothing but happiness in my heart for you!"

Libby took a deep breath. "And I think you're a vulgar, offensive slob."

Janos shrugged. "A deal is a deal."

"I need four million to open Libby's in LA."

He banged his fist on the table. "Have I been telling you to do that for years?"

"You get your money back off the top. Then we split the profits fifty-fifty."

"Whose profits? Your accountant's profits or my accountant's profits? Please, I don't do business through my tuchis. Ten percent of the gross."

"Five."

"Five in LA and five in New York," he said.

"Seven in LA and nothing in New York."

"What do you mean nothing in New York?"

"You had nothing to do with New York."

"One percent of the New York gross. For good will."

Libby shook her head. "There is no good will in New York."

Janos leaned forward. "My table in LA and New York. Free. Forever."

"There is also no forever. A hundred years is as far as I'm prepared to go."

"Free?"

"Free."

"Four million," he said. "Paid back off the top. Seven percent of the LA gross. My table free in New York and LA." He smiled. "A hundred and *one* years. Take it or leave it!"

Libby held up her hands. "You win."

Janos sat back. He was suspicious. "So what are you pulling here? You selling New York?"

"No. I'm giving New York. I'm giving the restaurant to Steven."

Janos rocked his head from side to side. "That's some present."

Libby smiled as her eyes filled with tears. "When you have a son like Steven," she said softly, "nothing is too much."

Steven knew that Birnbaum had been watching him. Even though he assumed it was merely part of the trimmings, it gave him a sense of power. He smiled at the thought that he posed a threat to the President.

The phone rang. It was Phyllis. Steven glanced around nervously. "Will wonders never cease," he said into the receiver.

"Apparently not. I've spoken to Fay. She'll break the story tomorrow. I'll offer Cal a blank check to star in the play."

"Good."

"Now that Mommy and Daddy will live happily ever after in the same zip code, I want to warn you about something, Steven."

"I have no time to talk now."

"You're in a dangerous position, little man. Your prayers have been answered."

"If you don't mind . . ."

"Now it's time for *my* prayers. I'll get you, Steven. Watch the skies."

Alfero had to make his move. Not because guerrilla cunning alerted him to the moment. Simply, he had to erase the sound of Dolores's crying.

He rose from the table as soon as he saw Esteban come out of the kitchen. Alfero walked quickly to the service area, startling the young busboy. "Kid," Alfero said, "I am a very rich millionaire. I am sorry I yell at you." He tucked a five-dollar bill into Esteban's shirt pocket, pretending to fumble just long enough to remove the square red pin from the busboy's jacket. "You are a nice kid. Like my sons." Alfero paused. "Here is an extra tip." He took another five and handed it to Esteban before heading toward the men's room.

"I'm sorry, sir," Stu the waiter said. "The men's room is closed. You'll have to use the ladies' room."

Alfero was suddenly enraged. "You try to insult me?"

"No, sir. The men's room is reserved for the President."

"So, in this great country of yours, the land of the free and the home of the brave, I am not good enough to pee with the President?"

"Security, sir."

"Oh," Alfero said. "Very smart."

"You can go in," Stu said, pointing to the ladies' room. "It's only one person at a time."

"No ladies in there?"

Stu smiled. "Well, if you want one, I'll see what I can do."

Alfero pretended to laugh. He waved his hand in front of

his face for the last time. Once inside, he leaned back against the door and locked it. Alfero had never been inside a ladies' room before. It was all pink with big glass lamps. A pink marble counter. Pink tissues. Pink towels. There was even a long pink velvet bench. It was the most beautiful room he had ever seen.

As he began to take off his clothes, he thought again of Dolores. How she would love such a room.

After Mary Borden and Ed Gilbert left, the President glanced at his attorney. "You still think I should have canceled?"

Sherman smiled. "Even I can't argue with three million dollars."

"You really threw her," the Chief of Staff said. "She obviously pegged the deal at two point five."

The Secretary of State laughed. "You see the look on his face? I haven't seen that kind of panic since we threatened to cut aid to Ethiopia."

The President sat back feeling very pleased with himself. "Plus another two minimum for paperback. That makes this a five-million-dollar lunch, gentlemen. Not too shabby."

The Chief of Staff finished his bourbon and water. "I thought for a minute there you were going to lose it."

"That's because you don't know anything about making deals," said the Secretary of State. "Maybe up on the hill they're interested in saving money. But out in the real world, power is calculated on how much you spend, not how much you save."

The President smiled. "I'm afraid I have to disagree with you, Mr. Secretary. My definition of power is how much you get."

Cooley's voice was on the line. "Headstart, do you copy?"

Birnbaum was following Steven down the aisle and didn't want to draw attention to himself by taking out his transmitter.

"Will someone copy me on Ensesa?" shouted Cooley.

"Spotter One. Copy," Birnbaum heard. He looked across the room and saw Johnson speaking into his unit. "Ensesa is in the toilet."

"There's something funny going on," Cooley said. "I want you to hold him when he comes out."

"What have you got on him?" Johnson asked.

"Nothing," Cooley said. "Just my gut."

Libby closed the reservations book. Not for the symbolism of the act, but to feel the leather binding with her name inscribed in eighteen-carat gold. Libby held on to the last of Libby's—her own personal book of days, her book of revelations, her bible.

She recalled what Mr. Pagano had said after his wife died. He told her he felt like a stranger. The heart had been taken out of the Villa Capri. As Libby glanced around the room that had become Steven's Restaurant or Chez Steven or Steven D's, she felt very much like a stranger, too. She was eager to leave it all behind, brokenhearted that her departure would have so much more meaning for him than her presence. Libby understood the sweet sadness of Charles Darnay's final steps. It was a far, far better thing that she had done. . . . But Libby wasn't going to the guillotine, she was going to Los Angeles. Comes the revolution, there would be no revolution. No one would find Libby Dennis hanging headless from a traffic light on West Fifty-fifth Street. She had out-couped the coup. Not that she had any choice. No matter how much Steven hated her, she couldn't let him walk out. The risk was far too great. He might not survive.

She saw Steven head toward her. He had that look in his eyes. But suddenly it didn't matter. Libby no longer felt guilty. "You look as though you lost your best friend."

"I'm used to that. Apparently, I have yet to lose my own worst enemy. El Presidente refuses to reveal his lunch preferences to a mere maitre d'. He wants the one and only."

"What?"

"He said he came to Libby's and expects Libby to take his order."

She smiled. "Good thing he didn't go to Café Napoleon!" She took a deep breath and pushed back her bangs. She grabbed the menus from him and put them on the desk. "We don't need these." Libby cleared her throat and arched her feet. "Come on, kiddo. Mommy's going to teach you how to fly."

As they walked down the steps into the dining room, Libby glanced at Meryl's table. Cal was holding court. He didn't need her anymore. She turned to Steven. "What is the kitchen pushing today?"

"We're going to be stuck with an awful lot of bluefish."

"You want to bet?" Libby had taken care of Cal. She had taken care of Steven. And now she was about to take care of the President.

"There you are." The President held up his glass as Libby approached. "I wanted you to join us for some champagne."

She spoke quietly. "Thank you, Mr. President. But if I had a drink on every deal that was made here today . . ."

"How do you know about my deal?"

"Just between the two of us, I've got a better spy network than the CIA. Next time you need to find something out, hire a waiter."

The President laughed. "Is that the secret of your success?"

"No. The secret of my success is keeping the hell away from the Hotel Willard." Libby hadn't expected to blurt that out. She turned to Steven. "I was in that show in Washington," she added quickly. "It was such a bomb I swore I'd never go back." She turned to the President. "Did I introduce my son, Steven? Of course, I did." Libby couldn't resist looking from one to the other. "His father is Cal Dennis."

The President nodded. "Now that you mention it, I see the resemblance."

Now that he mentioned it, so did Libby. For the first time. The smile on Steven's face was pure Cal. The way he stood. Even his speech pattern. Steven's acquired characteristics had finally triumphed over his genes.

"Well," Libby said, as though coming to the end of a very long story, "I have a surprise for you." Anders looked up at Libby from the next table. "I had my chef create something special in your honor. It's called, "Red, White, and Bluefish." And, I want you to know I selected the fish myself." Anders watched her suspiciously. "It's steamed in rice paper, and served with a red pepper purée and a julienne of white turnips."

"No," said the President.

Libby was startled by the tone in his voice. "Well, then, how do you feel about chicken livers?"

"No chicken livers."

"If you like duck . . . ."

"I don't."

She couldn't understand the game he was playing. Her heart began to beat rapidly. "Okay. We have this giant truffle . . . ."

The President reached out for her hand. "I want an Apple Pie Omelette."

Libby stared at him. He held tight. And he wouldn't let go.

Alfero had stuffed Ensesa's clothes under the pink velvet bench. He was wearing the busboy uniform that he had stolen when he was fired. He put Esteban's square red pin into his lapel. Checking himself in the mirror, he peeled away the fake moustache and took off the wig. He held his breath, for a moment seeing himself as he most wanted to be. He could have been a great busboy, if they had let him.

Then, very carefully, he opened his jacket. Around his waist Miguel had folded a half-inch-thick band of sponge rubber filled with gunpowder. Two matchbooks had been glued to the ends of the band as a makeshift trigger. When pulled from his waist, it would ignite immediately. All he needed was one free hand and thirty seconds.

As soon as Libby entered the kitchen, everyone stopped talking.

"Well?" Maxie asked. "Who won?"

She smiled and sat down on a chair. "I think I did."

Stu waved the cash he had collected for the pool. "What did he order?"

Libby couldn't stop smiling. "He ordered an Apple Pie Omelette."

"A what?"

"Oh, shit!"

"Are you kidding?"

"What the hell is that?" Bud stormed around the chef's table. "Why didn't he order from the menu? You expect me to believe you couldn't sell any of my dishes to the President?"

"All bets are off," Libby said. "I'm as surprised as you are."

"When do I get my money back?"

"Boy, am I glad I didn't vote for that son of a bitch!"

"Why he order that, lady?"

She put her hand on Louie's. "He must have had it some-where before. I guess he really liked it."

"What we do now, boss?"

Libby took an apron and shouted to the cold station. "Liang! Two green apples, cored, peeled, sliced paper thin. Pour on some heavy cream."

"Wait a minute!" Bud said. "What the hell are you doing?"

Libby pushed him aside and batted her eyes. "I am making lunch for the President of the United States!"

Special Agents Davis and Conroy walked down the aisle toward the ladies' room. Agent Scott, who had been posted near the door, came toward them. "What's the deal on Ensesa?"

Davis shrugged, unbuttoning his jacket so that he could reach easily for his gun. "Cooley's got some bug up his ass. Says Ensesa made a phone call that sounded peculiar. He says detain him when he comes out."

The bathroom door opened. All three men were surprised to see a busboy come out.

"You see him go in?" Davis asked.

"No," Scott said, checking to be sure the busboy was wear-ing a pin.

"Let's go," Davis said.

Alfero nodded at the agent posted outside the kitchen and then stepped inside.

"Stop the busboy!" Scott yelled.

But by the time Robbins, on the inside of the kitchen door, grabbed hold of his arm, Alfero had already pulled the sponge rubber tube from around his waist. It ignited instantly. A sudden burst of flame. Billows of thick black smoke.

"Halloween! Halloween! Clear Comet!"

Ursula began to scream. Liang jumped over the cold station table. Louie shouted, "Boss! Fire!"

"Urgent Urgent! Do you copy?"

Libby started pushing everyone away from the smoke and toward the store room. She was trying to reach the back door. "Out! Move it, Maxie!"

"I can't see!"

"Secure the kitchen!" Davis shouted.

"*Círu tôi vói!*"
"Who's got the money?"
"Bomb squad. Copy!"
"Lady! Lady! Where she go?"
"Do you copy?"
"*Mau lên! Mau lên!*"
"Are we all clear? Before it explodes!"
"Lady? You okay?"

Within one minute, before alerting anyone else in the dining room, the White House party was evacuated.

There was no smoke in the room, only the vague sense that something had been lit. Nothing more distracting than the aroma of a cheap cigar. The swinging doors had been insulated the day before to prevent smoke escaping in the event of a kitchen fire. Even those who noticed the President's hasty departure had no reason to believe there was any danger.

Before the presidential limousine had pulled away, Birnbaum assigned Meehan to move Steven off premises into a secure location. He looked over at Meryl's table. No one was moving. They were listening intently to Cal tell a joke. They hadn't yet noticed the activity in the room. "Excuse me," Birnbaum said, interrupting Cal as he was about to reach the punch line.

"Oh, shit," Cal said. "Not you again."

"I'm sorry, but you have to leave immediately."

"The hell I do!" Cal banged his fist on the table. "First, you jokers won't let me in and now you want to throw me out!"

"Mr. Dennis . . ."

Cal stood up. "Get out of my way, you jerk. Where the hell is Libby?"

Birnbaum had never hit anyone. He had shot a couple of people but he had never used his fists. He grabbed Cal's tie and brought him close.

"What the hell are you doing?"

Birnbaum hit Cal right on the chin, knocking him to the floor. "I'm breaking the rules!"

Special Agent Davis ordered everyone in the kitchen down on their hands and knees. The smoke was too thick to see through and the air was nearly impossible to breathe. Everyone formed a human chain, feeling the floor until Libby found the corridor that led to the storage area and the back door.

Alfero's bomb had only enough gunpowder to keep the rubber burning. It never exploded. Intended to disrupt the President's lunch, la bomba had succeeded. "I am a man!" Alfero shouted. "All men are equal in America! I am as good as El Presidente!" Six agents formed a double circle as they surrounded Alfero. They had to be sure nothing happened to him before they got the names of everyone involved in the incident. Suspect, criminal, victim—it didn't matter which he was. He had information that would help protect the President next time and that was all they cared about. "I was to be a busboy!"

By the time Libby reached the alley, she looked as though she had just crawled out of a coal mine. She had lost a shoe. Her pink silk suit was torn and covered with soot. Her face and hands were black. She refused oxygen while helping those behind her to their feet. Ursula and Louie were rushed to the hospital for smoke inhalation. The rest of the staff had only cuts and bruises.

Handcuffed, crying, and calling for Dolores, Alfero was pushed into a waiting car that took him to Secret Service headquarters. Libby turned to Davis. "I know he didn't mean to hurt anyone."

Davis, who was out of breath, shrugged as they watched Alfero being driven away. "Pardon my French, ma'am, but you just can't fuck around with the President."

Libby stared at him. "You're telling me!"

Someone had radioed from the Command Van that Steven was unhurt. Cal was in one of the ambulances having his shoulder dressing changed. All Davis would tell Libby was that he had fallen and torn his stitches. She nodded, wiped her nose with her hand and asked, "What about Birnbaum?"

Libby listened as Special Agent Robbins reassured her that Birnbaum was fine. Without warning, she grabbed Robbins by the lapels and shouted, "You tell them at the White House, the next time the President wants lunch, he should order in!"

Robbins freed himself. He held Libby gently by the shoulders. "Mrs. Dennis," he shouted, trying to get through to her, "would you like a lift around the block?"

Libby nodded and began to cry. Robbins helped her into the unmarked car parked on the sidewalk. She hesitated, watching the kitchen staff, despite their protests, being led into a police bus to be fingerprinted and have their ID's checked. "I'm sorry," she whispered, looking at them.

Robbins sat down next to her and turned on the ignition. "Do you want me to take you to Mr. Dennis or Agent Birnbaum?"

Libby ignored the question as Robbins drove slowly along the sidewalk. He went up Fifty-sixth Street and onto Sixth Avenue where all traffic had been stopped and two more police buses were parked. She slid down in her seat as she saw Fay and Loren arguing with officers who refused to let them leave. "Crazy, isn't it?" Robbins looked at her. "All this just for lunch."

Libby tried to control her tears. "You know, lunch is a relatively recent phenomenon. As late as the 1820s, the midday meal was known as dinner and the evening meal was called supper."

Robbins made a right onto Fifty-fifth, heading toward the restaurant. "But then everything changed with the Industrial Revolution." She sniffed and dried her eyes. "Factory workers had no time for an elaborate 'dinner' in the middle of the day, so instead, they ate a light meal called luncheon. Their big meal was moved to the evening." She put a hand to her forehead, unable to stop crying. "And poor little supper was moved somewhere close to midnight."

"Mrs. Dennis, you want Mr. Dennis or Agent Birnbaum?"

Libby could barely speak. "I want my son."

Steven sat waiting in the Command Van. Cooley was fielding calls from all over the city. The presidential party had taken off from the West Side Heliport. The suspect was on his way downtown. The Secret Service, the Police Department, the Fire Department, the FBI, and two bomb dogs were checking the premises for further evidence linking Alfero to a possible conspiracy.

Roth unlocked the door to the van. Libby and Steven stared at one another. She opened her mouth as if to say something. She raised her arms but then thought twice about reaching out for him. Instead, she posed glamorously, rolled her eyes and lifted her shoeless foot. "Makeup by Mount Vesuvius," she announced.

They both began to laugh. Libby flopped down onto a folding chair. "I was so worried about you."

"Only the good die young." Steven glanced at Libby, then looked away, just as Cal always did. "I think you should hear this from me before you read it in tomorrow's paper."

Libby put a hand to her forehead. "Whatever it is, I don't want to hear it. I can't take any more. It's been a day, Steven."

"I blackmailed Phyllis into producing the play for Pop. I figured that if he stayed in New York for a while you two might finally get back together."

Libby put a hand to her nose and sniffed. Steven handed her a handkerchief. She blew her nose, taking as long as possible. She sat back, shook her head, and sighed, "Where is O. Henry when you need him? I just made a deal with Janos to open a Libby's in LA."

He was stunned. "You're going to LA?"

"As soon as I can," Libby giggled.

"But what are you going to do about . . ."

"Oh, that? I'm giving it to you."

A long pause. "You're giving me Libby's? After what I was going to do?"

She became serious. "Steven, you're my son. I'm your mother. You've been a little shit ever since kindergarten and I've never carried a grudge. Besides, you know me. Once I make up my mind. That's it. Libby's is yours."

"Just like that?"

She turned away. "Well, there is one catch." She took a deep breath. "There's still a lot of Libby left in Libby's."

Steven nodded. "I know. It could take years to get you out. He smiled. "And then again, I might never get rid of you completely."

"Can you live with that?"

"I can live with that."

Libby thought it was the most wonderful thing Steven had ever said to her. She was afraid to let herself cry. She might never stop.

"But," Steven said with mock melodrama, "lest you think my life will be a bed of roses, now hear this! Phyllis's final act of vengeance was to tell Bud she would back him in his own restaurant."

Libby began to laugh. "Isn't Phyllis wonderful? Oh, God, I'm really going to miss her."

Steven leaned forward. "Can I ask you something?"

"You know I have no secrets from you."

"Why aren't you upset?"

"About Bud?"

"About Pop. About his being in New York while you go to LA. How come all of a sudden you decided on LA?"

Roth opened the door. "We're still working, but you can go back in if you want."

Libby got up. "Steven, I want to go in alone."

"Why?"

"Because I'm your mother and I say so."

"But . . ."

"And because I just gave you a very expensive restaurant!"

Steven nodded and sat down. He watched as Libby straightened her skirt and tried puffing up her bangs. "Hey!" he called out.

She turned back. "What?"

"You're gorgeous."

Black cinders were still floating in the air as Libby opened the front door. There was no damage to the vestibule or the bar or, as far as she could see, to the dining room itself. There were a few overturned chairs, some food spattered onto the floor, but nothing that a good cleaning, a paint job, and, most of all, Steven couldn't handle.

Libby went behind the bar and opened the refrigerator. She took out a champagne glass. It immediately clouded with frost. She reached for a bottle of Dom Pérignon. She'd think of something to celebrate.

The foil over the cork came off easily. Next she removed the wire frame that kept the cork in place. She held the bottle in one hand, turning slightly while her other hand gripped the cork. You held the cork and turned the bottle. Champagne 101. But she had no strength left. She put the bottle down.

"Give it to me."

Libby looked up like a little girl caught raiding the cookie jar. It was Birnbaum.

"Do you have another glass?" he asked.

"I thought you couldn't drink on duty."

"I'm not on duty anymore."

"Swell." She brought out another glass.

He reached over and took the bottle from her. "I mean as in, 'Quoth the raven, not anymore!' "

"Nevermore."

"Whatever." The cork popped.

"Goddamn it, Birnbaum!" she shouted. "You don't pop the cork! You pop the cork and you let out all the bubbles at once. They've been building up for years. You're supposed to open champagne with a sigh."

He shook his head. "I'm through sighing." He filled both glasses. They overflowed onto the bar.

"Look at that! Just look at that! Who the hell taught you how to pour champagne?"

"No one."

"You're supposed to pour a little in the first glass and while it rises up you pour a little in the second. Then the first. Then the second. You keep going back and forth."

"I don't want to go back and forth anymore." He handed a glass to her. "Nevermore?"

"You're not supposed to fill it to the top like cream soda," Libby said. "You're supposed to fill it two-thirds full."

Birnbaum picked up his glass. "Are we going to toast each other or not?"

Libby raised her glass. She was terrified. "To us."

They clinked glasses. Neither of them drank. He leaned forward and kissed her. They lingered, breathing onto one another's lips. "About what happened in the phone booth . . ." he whispered.

She nodded. "About what happened in your apartment . . ."

Birnbaum smiled. "North Pole."

"South Pole."

He took out his wallet and showed it to her. The badge was gone. "No more secrets."

Libby reached for his hand. "Whose secrets? Yours or mine?"

"I just quit."

"Birnbaum . . ."

"And I called my wife."

Libby took a deep breath. "Birnbaum, I hate to interrupt your becoming a butterfly . . ."

"She wasn't there. She has this answering machine with English movie star voices. Ronald Colman. Rex Harrison. Olivier. I gave them all the same message."

Libby put a hand to her stomach. "Birnbaum, did you tell? Yes or no?"

"No."

"No? What does no mean?"

"No means no."

"Birnbaum, do you mean that you haven't told yet but you're going to tell?"

"Why would I tell? I don't work there anymore."

Libby sat back. She began to cry. Birnbaum didn't offer to comfort her and she didn't try to hide her tears. She needed to cry and he needed to see the finale. "Where's the background music?" she asked.

"You all right?"

Libby reached out toward him. Birnbaum took her hand. They held onto one another until she nodded yes. Then he let go. "I don't work here anymore either." She smiled. "I quit, too. I'm going to LA. Cal's doing a movie with Meryl Streep."

"My wife hates LA. If they had transferred me, she would never have gone. She likes New England." He shrugged. "She likes roots. She's very New Hampshire."

"Birnbaum, you're not a very good liar. What I mean is, I can't help wondering, no offense, whether you might decide at some point that you made a mistake. I mean, where would I be, Birnbaum, if you suddenly decided you had made a mistake?"

"You'd be in LA."

"What if you suddenly came to your senses."

"I already did. Nobody gets two moments of truth."

No doubt about it, he was convincing. Or was it just that she wanted so desperately to believe him? "Birnbaum, you're not going to show up in a few years and surprise me, are you?"

"No. I'm not going to surprise you." He smiled. "I'm not even going to kiss you goodbye."

Libby smiled back. "I've had my moment of truth, too. I never thought that I could marry Cal with a lie. But I was dead wrong. And, having had my moment of truth," she said, shrugging her shoulders, "I really think one moment is all I need."

"Then, this is it," he said, overfilling the glasses. Champagne fizzed onto the bar.

Libby raised her glass. "South Pole."

"North Pole."

She hesitated. "Birnbaum, this is going to be tougher than I thought."

He drank the last of his champagne and put the glass down. Then he took her in his arms.

Libby gasped. "But you said . . ."

"I lied." He kissed her. They stared at one another knowing that this was *their* moment of truth. They would never be more, or less, in love.

"Birnbaum?"

"Yes?"

"There's something I've been meaning to ask you."

"What?"

"I hate to get personal at this late date."

"Go ahead."

"I was just wondering. Do you have a first name?"

"Yes."

She nodded. "Good."

He walked toward the door.

"Birnbaum?"

He stopped without turning back. "Yes?"

"If you're ever in LA . . ."

"I won't be."

"I know. But if you are . . ."

"Yes?"

Libby smiled. "Let's have lunch."